Emma Stirling was bo~~~~~~~~~~~~~~~~~~~~~~
her husband and two y~~~~~ ~~~~~~~~, she went to live
in what was then Southern Rhodesia and Nyasaland.
She has since returned to the United Kingdom and
now lives in London. She has three daughters and a
son, and three grandchildren. She started writing
in 1974 and has had a number of romantic novels
published under a pseudonym.

A Field of Bright Poppies

Emma Stirling

HEADLINE

First published in 1990
by HEADLINE BOOK PUBLISHING PLC

First published in paperback in 1990
by HEADLINE BOOK PUBLISHING PLC

10 9 8 7 6 5 4 3 2 1

ISBN 0 7472 3465 5

Typeset in 10/12¼ pt Mallard
by Colset Private Limited, Singapore

Printed and bound in Great Britain by
Collins, Glasgow

HEADLINE BOOK PUBLISHING PLC
Headline House
79 Great Titchfield Street
London W1P 7FN

In loving memory of my parents.
Also of my husband,
who will always be sadly missed.

Chapter One

'I can't, Alice! Me mam'd kill me.'

'Your mam won't know, you daft 'ap'orth, unless you're planning on telling 'er.' Alice snorted in an unladylike way. 'And I don't think even you, Libby Gray, are that daft.'

Alice, in a red coat and hat that all but covered her blonde hair, shivered and hugged herself in an endeavour to keep warm. 'Besides,' she went on in a cajoling voice, 'it's real nice inside. Everyone's so friendly and I could murder a cup of tea, couldn't you?'

Libby gazed doubtfully at the old soot-stained church hidden away in the side street. It was neglected and sad looking, but the sounds issuing from its doorway seemed to give it a new lease of life. The early evening gloom was broken by the light streaming from its narrow windows, laying yellow patterns on the cobbled street. From inside the church hall came the tinkling of a piano, the cheerful sound of voices raised in the words of the old song.

'. . . of Lagoona, she is my Liliee and my rose . . .'

Young men in uniform hung around the entrance in twos and threes, debating the merits of this place

1

against those of a pub. Most of them were broke so the hall of St Aiden's parish church won hands down.

With sighs of resignation, the odd mutter of 'This bloody war!', stamping their cigarettes out under the heels of their heavy black boots, they climbed the steps and disappeared inside.

Libby thought what Mam would say: Set one foot inside a Protestant church and you are surely on your way to hell! The thoughts battled with her desire to be warm and in a well-lighted place, out of this wind that threatened to whip the green knitted beret away from her head and send it soaring skywards to join the wheeling, shrieking seagulls.

Surely God would understand! Surely He wouldn't mind, not on an evening like this . . . ?

Looking at Alice, she said in a small voice, 'You've been here before, then?'

'Course I 'ave. When you've bin off wi' Vince and I've bin on me own. You don't 'ave to worry, they don't pester you to join their gang or anything like that. You just join in wi' the hymns, 'ave a cup of tea and a bun and, if you want, find someone to talk to. Nothing to get your knickers in a twist about.'

The two girls stood outside the church, heads bent against the thin drizzle of rain. If you stood on the corner of the street you could see where the wide estuary of the Ribble flowed into the sea, pewter grey in the rays of the lowering sun. The beaches were deserted except for the figures of a soldier and his girl walking arm in arm along the edge of the water. The grey November day tempted few people to rush out to sample its chill air.

In the summers before the war, the small seaside town had been a hive of activity. Now St Aiden's one claim to eminence was that it boasted the finest convalescent home on the northwest coast, furthering the recovery of the men before they were sent back to the trenches.

The two girls had already walked the length of the promenade twice, had debated visiting the Bioscope opposite the pier entrance, the idea coming to nothing when Alice discovered from the posters outside the small cinema that she had already seen the picture.

Her upper lip curling, she had told Libby, 'Not worth spending sixpence on to see again. All that custard pie throwing! Fair made me sick, thinking of the ones who 'ad to clean up afterwards.'

Libby had grinned. 'When did you see it, then? I didn't know you'd seen it.'

'You don't know everything I do, Miss Smartypants. Worry that little head of yours if you did, wouldn't you? I went wi' that sailor wot introduced 'imself to us the last time we went out together, that time your Vince 'ad to work late at 'is dad's shop.' She patted the blonde hair where it waved from beneath the brim of the cloche hat. Smugly, she had added, 'Told me I was as pretty as that actress up there on the screen, so 'e did.'

Libby had laughed. 'Oh, Alice, how is it you always manage to take me out of the doldrums like you do?'

Again that smug look. 'It's a gift I 'ave, or so me old Dad used to say.'

Now, looking at the plump girl with her blonde hair and bright red gash of lipstick, Libby had to confess that Alice was pretty. No getting away from it. But Libby couldn't help but think the black stuff she had taken to plastering her eyelashes with would have earned a few censorious glances from Mam. That and the lipstick. She knew what Mam would say: 'That Alice is not really your sort, my girl. Don't know what you see in her, sure I don't.'

But Libby liked Alice's good humour and straight-forwardness and her air of never letting anything get her down. They worked together, Alice as down-stairs maid and Libby as nursemaid for Dr Ainslie and his wife, and their free afternoons nearly always fell on the same day.

While Vince had been away Alice had been a real blessing. Of course, now he was coming back she knew he would soon put a stop to her spending her free time with Alice, wanting Libby for himself. She felt warmer just thinking about the good-looking boy with whom she believed she was in love.

She thought of the first time they had met. It had been the first fine day of spring, and a man on the promenade had played 'Daisy, Daisy' on his barrel organ and two little girls holding their dresses out at the sides danced to the music. Against the prom-enade railings, soldiers in the blue and red uniforms of the walking wounded, their caps pushed back at a rakish angle, leaned and eyed the two girls flirta-tiously, making provocative remarks. Alice, with whom, before she met Vince, she went everywhere, had giggled, meeting their eyes encouragingly.

'Will you stop it?' Libby hissed. 'You're making a show of yourself.'

4

'Shut up, Libby, you're a real bloody kill-joy,' said Alice good-naturedly. 'These men need cheering up, wot they've bin through. Who wouldn't?'

Passing a shop, Alice had grabbed her arm and said, 'Hey, what about an ice cream? This looks a decent place.'

'All right. I don't mind.' It would kill another half hour or so before they had to be back at work. Through the window of the shop they could see small zinc-topped tables, chairs standing about and a counter with red and white bunting draped across the front. Once inside they chose a table near the window. As they enjoyed their ice cream sundaes, the layers of fruit topped with chopped nuts and cream, Libby had become aware of the young man watching her from behind the counter.

His hair was dark and curly, falling over his forehead in engagingly boyish fashion, his eyebrows were thick as ropes, the eyes beneath them dark and flashing.

Glancing covertly in his direction she blushed as he gave her a brilliant smile. Alice began to chat again and Libby dragged her eyes away back to her companion.

They scraped the last remnants from the tall thick glasses and left the shop. Their next free afternoon had found them again in the ice cream shop and this time the young man himself brought their order to the table, bending close to Libby to say in a soft voice, 'You have honoured us again with your presence!'

Libby had blushed and looked at Alice who pretended not to notice. 'This ice cream is delicious,' was all she could find to say. It was made from the good, old-fashioned recipe his grandfather had brought with him from Italy in the year 1880, and Vince was used to being told this.

After a pause of a few seconds, he'd said, 'My name is Vincent. Vince to my friends.'

Alice sucked noisily through her straw, her eyes appraising him. 'I'm Alice and this is Libby.'

Libby blushed again as, with a swift look towards the counter, checking that there was nobody waiting to be served, Vince had pulled out a chair and sat down beside them. Looking at Libby, he asked, 'Are you usually so shy?'

Libby shook her head, her throat suddenly drying up. Oh, he was too good-looking to be true! Not at all her sort. Not really. Still, there was something about him that attracted her.

It had been a mutual attraction and it had not taken Vince long to beg a date with her. Alice said she had never seen Libby so taken with a young man before. That had been in the spring. They had enjoyed each other's company throughout the summer months and Libby was quite bewildered by the feelings the young man raised in her.

A gust of wind, straight from the sea, whipped the hem of her coat about her calves, snatching with chill fingers at her ankles, and brought her sharply back to the present. The afternoon had started out so promising, too, if you could ignore the dark clouds gathering out at sea.

Alice had caught the eye of a couple of soldiers who stood on the pavement a few yards away, debating like the girls, on whether to go inside the church hall or not. 'They look all right,' whispered Alice, nudging Libby in the ribs with her elbow. 'Good for a laugh. And Vince is not going to know, is he?'

'You needn't be so blatant about it. And it's got nothing to do with Vince.' Seeing the delight Alice was taking from the soldiers' approving glances, Libby thought of Vince at a family gathering way up in Glasgow where a cousin was getting married. He hadn't wanted to go but his mother had insisted. 'Italian families are like that,' he'd told Libby. 'I'll be back as soon as I can, don't you worry.'

The idea of leaving Libby had not appealed to him, for his father was closing the shop for a whole week and had said they might as well make the most of it. 'Don't go making eyes at all those fellows walking around with nothing to do,' Vince had said. 'I don't want to come back and find you interested in someone else.'

Squeezing his arm, Libby had smiled and said, 'As if I would!'

'I trust you, Libby. It's not that. But with all those men about and at a loose end not knowing what to do with themselves, well, many a girl would be tempted.'

'Not me,' Libby had assured him gently. 'You're all I'll ever want, and if you don't know it by now, Vince Remede, then you never will.'

Now Alice was nudging her again, hissing from the side of her mouth, 'Look at them two eejits now, will you?'

The two soldiers had raised their caps and were bowing from the waist. The rain started in earnest,

as it can do on a sultry day on the northwest coast.
The soldiers gazed skywards at the scudding clouds,
hunched their shoulders and hurried towards the
church entrance.

A hand-printed notice pinned to the double wooden
doors stated that free tea and cakes were available to servicemen and their friends on Sunday
afternoons.

'Listen, come 'ere,' Alice took hold of Libby's arm.
'Let's let on we're meeting someone in there, if they
ask us. This rain's making my hair go all frizzy.'
Really, you'd think she were urging Libby to enter a
knocking shop instead of a perfectly respectable
church! Even if it wasn't Catholic. Thank heavens
she had left all that religious nonsense behind when
she'd left her parents' home in Liverpool to come and
work on the coast.

More than anything, the sound of the cheerful
music coming from within persuaded Libby. She told
herself folks did some queer things in wartime.
Things they wouldn't dream of doing in normal times.
Meekly, she followed Alice.

The small stage at the end of the church hall was
festooned with red, white and blue bunting. A picture
of King George V and Queen Mary looked down on
the room filled with uniformed men who spoke in
hushed voices and eyed the women who had given up
their Sunday afternoons to help 'our brave lads'.

The piano player started again and they sang
hymns, standing in rows, facing an elderly man who
stood on the stage and conducted with waving arms.
At first Libby felt shy, finding she didn't know the

words of any of the hymns. But they all joined in with such gusto that it didn't matter. Then they sang one she did know, 'Onward Christian Soldiers', and although she felt that at any minute the heavens would open and the wrath of God fall on her, she found herself enjoying it. Her voice joined in with the rest, soaring high and true above the others and Alice noticed the admiring glances many of the men threw in their direction.

'There, that wasn't so bad now, was it?' said Alice as they followed the khaki-clad men, all pushing and jostling to be served first at the long tables that threatened to collapse under the weight of the huge silver tea urn and plates of knobbly looking cakes. 'No holy saints popping out of dark corners to grab you and pull you down into the raging fires of hell for daring to set foot inside a Protestant church! It's all superstition anyway, religion. I've felt none the worse for giving it up.'

Cigarette smoke filled the air like a grey fog and most of the men had filled up on the sticky buns and strong tea and now needed more for their comfort. In threes and fours, they drifted out to sample the delights of the pubs. The rain had stopped, to be replaced by a thin mist that drifted in from the sea.

Alice gazed about her. 'Look, those two blokes we saw outside!' She nudged Libby. The two soldiers, hands in pockets, stood near eyeing them speculatively. 'So, what do two lovely girls like yourselves be doing all alone on a night like this?' the shorter of the two asked.

'Doing our best to keep out of the rain, not that

9

it's any of your business,' answered Alice tartly.

'Only asking, love,' the man replied in mock apology. 'How about taking pity on two lads far from home and showing us the sights?'

Alice pursed her lips indignantly and said, 'The nerve of some people!'

'Aye, and without nerve we wouldn't get very far,' said the man with a sly wink at his mate as he slipped an arm about Alice's waist.

'Cheek!' said Alice, fluttering her eyelashes. But still she let the arm remain.

'What say we finish here and see if we can find a pub that's opened its doors?' the man said. He grinned at Alice. 'Unless, of course, you're too young for such things?'

Alice tossed her head, exclaiming that no one had ever asked her age before and she didn't see why they should now.

'Right!' The man grinned. 'Let's get going, then.'

They left the hall and he began urging Alice in the direction of a small public house a short way along the promenade. 'God, you're a tonic for what ails you,' said Alice, pushing at him in a playful manner. Libby heard the man who had stayed with her say, 'Come on, let's catch up with them.'

Feeling slightly foolish, Libby shook her head. 'I'm sorry, I can't. I have to be ... to be back at work by –' she stole a quick look at the big clock that hung over the entrance to the pier '– by six o'clock.' A white lie, something else she would have to ask forgiveness for the next time she went to confession.

The soldier gave her a sideways look. 'Funny hours you work!'

'I'm a nursemaid. I work for a family in one of those big houses in St Anne's Place.'

But he didn't want to know. Already his attention was wandering and he was looking about him for more promising material. Someone who didn't have to be back at work by six o'clock.

'Yes, well,' he said, thrusting his hands into his pockets. 'You'd better be off then.'

Libby nodded, smiled to show there were no hard feelings and tugged at her knitted green beret, pulling it more firmly down over the silky red hair. Alice would be all right. She always was. Alice could write a book on the way to handle men. Libby wished she had only a quarter of the assurance Alice possessed where the opposite sex were concerned. A lamp-lighter walked ahead, stopping every so often to place his ladder against the crossbow of a gas lamp.

'Mucky night, love.'

The broad vowels floated back through the thickening mist, reminding Libby vividly of home and instantly she was back in the narrow alleyways, walking on the flagstones covered in green moss so slippery that you walked carefully on wet mornings.

In her mind's eye she could see the big yellow stone sink in the kitchen, breathe in the smell of the green soap Mam used for everything, including their baths. It smelled of wet eucalyptus forests. Not that she had ever seen a eucalyptus forest, wet or otherwise, but she imagined that was how they would smell.

She thought of her father, once so tall and regal,

catching the eye of many a young woman but wanting only Mam. Dad's work in the coal mines had been his downfall. His weak chest and constant bronchial setbacks had caused him to be laid-off from work more often than he liked, leaving her brother Joseph's and sister Agnes' wages the main support of the small family.

Although Libby would have liked to help, and did, sending what she could afford to her mother each month, it still took all of Mam's ingenuity to make ends meet.

She remembered her own attacks of asthma when she was a child, the weeks spent in the tiny room at the top of the stairs, the fire in the small grate. A fire of necessity, although it meant extra work and outlay for Mam. Sometimes the fumes from the burning coal in that airless room had caught at her throat and she could feel her chest tighten and her breathing become worse. It was all she could do not to call out. Even when Mam came hurrying up the narrow staircase there was little she could do to relieve her. Mam would sit on the side of the bed, tightly holding on to Libby's hands, eyes never once leaving the small pained faced and in some obscure way Libby knew that Mam would have given her very life to have taken over her child's suffering.

Women of Ellen Gray's class did not have money to pay for doctor' fees, but Dr Ainslie had known Ellen since she was a young bride on William's arm, looking as though she had wings on her feet, going into that small house on Mill Rise as happily as though it were a palace.

12

Growing up in the district, Eric Ainslie had known William since their early school days, and meeting him in the street one Sunday had been introduced to Ellen on one of her visits to William's parents.

The doctor had married a girl from Mill Rise and couldn't help but compare his Sarah to the lovely red-haired lass that William Gray had brought home. Although a midwife had been called in for Ellen's first and third child, he had kept a fatherly eye on Ellen and her growing family and had been present at Libby's delivery because it was a breech birth. There was barely ten months between Libby and the boy, Joseph.

Sympathy for the young mother, knowing her pride, made him accept her offer to do some light cleaning in his surgery a couple of times a week. That way Ellen didn't feel she was beholden to him.

One memorable night when he shook his head and sadly told Ellen he didn't hold out much hope for Libby's latest attack, Father Brady was called to administer the last rites of the Holy Mother Church. Libby had viewed it all as a diversion. She knew she wasn't going to die. She had her whole life before her, hadn't she? Lying in bed, Mam's anguished face bending over her own, Dad standing in the doorway, looking as though his whole world was falling apart, Libby whispered between hard-won breaths, 'I'm not goin' to die, Mam, so don't look so mithered.'

The priest had come, followed closely by a small sympathetic group of neighbours. They had crowded into the kitchen and made pot after pot of tea, scalding and strong, running up the stairs with cups

13

for Mam, who refused them all, shaking her head, saying they would choke her. But Libby had recovered, as she had from all her previous attacks, surprising everyone by her strength of will.

Libby remembered winters when from early November until the first primrose of spring showed in the grubby public park she would be off school. Guy Fawkes was always celebrated in the alleyways behind the rows of mean houses and after dark Libby would watch from a window, hearing the screams of delight from her classmates, see the brilliant flashes and multicoloured stars burst above the slate roofs of the houses opposite. Although poor as church mice, the odd halfpenny could always be found for fireworks, the more adventurous children supplementing the outlay by making guys from their parents' cast-off clothing. The cries of 'Penny for the guy' rang out weeks before the big event, giving the youngsters the excuse to make as much noise as they liked. It was all legitimate, wasn't it? A penny for the guy!

Joseph was her ally in those years of protracted illness. She remembered her brother's excitement, the thrill of anticipation that even she who would not be able to join in experienced, as Joseph came running upstairs, bursting into her room to spread the squibs and Catherine wheels and sparklers across her eiderdown, unrestrainedly shouting: 'See how many I've collected! Oh, Libby, it's going to be the best display in the alley this year.'

Libby had gazed wide-eyed at the vividly coloured wrappers. 'So many,' she'd breathed. 'Where'd you get the money for so many?'

Joseph had made a disparaging sound. 'Collected old Granny McGarth's bottles, didn't I?' he'd scoffed. 'Got there before the other kids. She had a good haul this time.'

Granny McGarth enjoyed her drink and would often dump the empty bottles just inside her back-yard gate, ready for the next time she tottered along to the public house. She would then hide the bottles under her shawl, their busy clinking heralding her way.

Her habits were well known and with a halfpenny return on each bottle it was a fortunate child who got there first. It wasn't considered stealing – merely 'finders keepers'.

There had come the sound of footsteps ascending the stairs; their mother's voice crying, 'Joseph! You're not bothering our Libby with those nasty, smelly things, are you? Won't do her chest any good, that it won't, breathing in all that gunpowder.'

The young conspirators had frozen, then with one swift movement Joseph'd swept the offending items on to the floor, pushing them out of sight under the bed next to the china chamber pot with its pattern of rosebuds.

Their mother's gaze had rested on the two up-turned faces, so innocent, so guileless that instinct had warned her immediately that some mischief was afoot. 'Get downstairs,' she'd said to Joseph, 'and leave your sister in peace. I've got messages for you to run.'

During those enforced spells in bed Libby had lived in a world of her own. She read everything she could get her hands on, her favourites being the red-covered books her father had won for good attendance at school: *Coral Island*, *The Young Fur Traders*, *The First Settlers In Canada*, all boys' books, but how she enjoyed them. When there was nothing to read she lay propped on her mound of pillows and allowed her imagination to soar. Such magic journeys they took, her imagination and her. To lands she could never possibly visit. Meeting people she could never hope to meet. The nearest she had come to encountering someone from those dreams had been her big, handsome Vince . . . Vince was the culmination of all those stories that had filled her head, her Prince on a white charger. He would take her away to some wonderful land where they would live happily ever after . . .

As she had entered her teens the attacks of asthma diminished and one morning she awoke, feeling strange. Something had happened during the night that terrified her. Her stomach and back were tight knots of pain, increasing and decreasing, like waves on a seashore. She shivered with cold from the unheated room. She hardly dared to move, so scared was she as she pushed back the bedclothes, whimpering at the sight they revealed.

Agnes, who was sitting on the edge of the double bed they shared, pulling on her stockings, had glanced over her shoulder and said, casually, 'Oh, that!' She shrugged, running her hands up her calf and over her thigh, smoothing the creases in the thick cotton stocking. 'That's nothin' to worry about.'

Libby broke into a moan as the pain increased, and

huddled back beneath the bedclothes. When Agnes was fully dressed, she stood with the round door handle in her hand and looked back into the fearful eyes of her sister. 'I'll tell Mam.'

Libby had been sure, as she sank back upon the pillow, that she was on her deathbed! And Agnes did not care! Would she even bother to mention it to Mam?

Her moans had brought Mam rushing upstairs, looking pale. The frown broke into a smile when Libby showed her the blood-stained sheet and nightie.

'Sorry, love, Agnes did say something but I was that busy with your dad I wasn't paying attention.' She sat on the edge of the bed and took the frightened girl in her arms, saying as simply and professionally as a nurse, 'I've been expecting that. You'll be better now, see if you aren't.'

Libby looked bewildered. 'But Mam, what is it? Am I dying . . . ?'

Mam gave a little laugh. 'Of course you're not dying, love. It's natural. I'd have been more worried if it *hadn't* happened.' Explaining as best she could the ways of a woman's body, she had said Libby must not be afraid. Mam, who was a reserved woman and not given to going into details, told her only the things she had to know. And Libby, listening to the soft voice, was content. If Mam said it was all right, then it must be so.

She had turned fourteen that year and left school. Agnes had left a year earlier and worked in the mill at the end of the street. Mam had not wanted Libby to

17

join her there, although it was the fate of most girls on leaving school in that part of Lancashire. 'All that damp,' Mam had said worriedly, 'with her chest! I'd never rest, worrying about her . . .'

So when the offer came from Dr Ainslie, it was like a gift from God. Even though it broke Ellen's heart to see this beloved younger daughter leaving home.

The Ainslies had moved the year before, going up in the scale of society, and now lived on the coast at St Aiden's, a small town filled with wealthy stockbrokers and lawyers, enjoying their retirement. Using the legacy left to him by a spinster aunt of whom he was very fond, the doctor had purchased a small practice with its own house and surgery just off the promenade and looked forward to bringing up the two youngest children, Amy and Bertie, in an environment that was clean, without the grime of Ridley and its smoking chimneys.

'Just think,' Mam had said, hugging her young daughter, 'all that fresh air, living right by the sea! No more belching smoke to bring on one of your attacks. No more dragging in the tin bath every Friday night and doing your best to wash. They do say as 'ow the doctor 'as an indoor lavvy as well as inside bathrooms. Now, isn't that enough to make you want to work there instead of staying here and working int' mill? By the crin, I wish I'd had that choice when I was your age, snatched it like a shot, so I would.'

Mam hardly ever descended to speaking in the vernacular so it had been real evidence of her excitement. The nuns frowned on it and so it was avoided. Sister Septimus would frown and warn: 'Proper

English, girls. I will not condone sloppy speech.'

Seeing Libby's stricken face, Mam had clinched her argument with: 'And you know you like Dr Ainslie and his missis. Brought you into the world, he did, said you were the prettiest baby he'd ever delivered. And all the times he's come in the middle of the night to see you when you were taken poorly!'

Miserably, Libby had said, 'But I don't want to leave home, Mam. What would I do without you and our dad and Joseph and Agnes...?' Well, she thought, not so much Agnes. She had tried, had included her sister in her prayers every night, asking God to make her feel differently towards Agnes. But Our Dear Lord on this occasion either wasn't listening or had decided that that was how things were to be. So the ill-feeling between the two sisters grew. Libby never could decide what caused Agnes to be this way. Perhaps some people just grew up feeling antagonistic to their nearest and dearest. She knew of other girls whose sisters acted in the same way. Still...

All that had happened three years ago when Libby was fourteen. Now, with the war, young people snatched what happiness they could find and when a year ago the nanny she had been assisting left to marry her soldier, Libby had been given the chance to prove herself and take charge of the children.

Amy and Bertie adored the young girl and if at times she seemed barely older than the children she cared for, there was no doubt that she took her responsibilities seriously.

On the weekends that she was free she would

catch the train to Ridley and in no time at all be home; the feeling of warm anticipation would mount as the train neared the tall chimneys and the grey, heavy-laden skies that marked the town. She could smell the smoke miles away; acrid and bitter, catching at her throat, bringing on the remembered wheezing sensation as, disobeying the printed warning above the carriage window, she leaned out to catch her first glimpse of the chimney that pinpointed Mill Rise, where her family lived.

For all that, she loved it. To Libby, nothing was more beautiful or more welcoming than this northern town where she had been born. Even though the mill chimney towered above the roofs of the tiny houses, blotting out the sunlight, and sometimes on grey winter days the daylight too, she still loved it. It was only when she went to live with the Ainslies that she had realised with something of a shock that not everyone lived like that. Even though the kitchen and the scullery of the Ainslie house were below street level, on bright summer days the sunlight poured through the large square window and it was lovely to sit at the table, feeling the warmth on your back.

The memories flooded through her mind as swift as the scenes in one of the silent pictures. Deep in reminiscence, Libby moved from one veil of mist to another, cloaked in the eerie atmosphere created by the black cast-iron serpents that wound around the lampposts. A flock of birds moved across the blazing ball of the lowering western sun. The lamplighter repeated his first greeting. 'Mucky night, I say. Better 'urry 'ome, lass. Never know what you might come across on a night like this. They never did catch that there Jack the Ripper bloke, did they? Never knew where he went after London.'

Libby's chin lifted from the collar of her coat. 'Must be hard up if he's out on a night like this,' she joked back and heard the lamplighter's delighted chuckle as she walked by. All the same, she wished he hadn't mentioned the name. It still sent shivers down people's spines even though it had happened all those years before. She threw a nervous glance over her shoulder and at the same moment bumped into the figure of a man who, phantom-like, had materialised out of the mist.

Libby gave a frightened shriek. Only the man's arms saved her from sprawling. For a moment she was stunned, too frightened to move; then with a 'Lord save us!' she gave him a hefty push and stepped backwards, grimacing as he threw his arms about a nearby lamppost, as though unable to stand without its support. Libby saw he was in uniform, the upturned collar of his greatcoat shadowing a pale face. The yellow glow from the lamplight highlighted thick dark hair.

Suddenly she was very aware of the darkness and that no one else was near. Her first thought was: He's drunk! Then, taking in the thinness of the pale face, perhaps he's ill!

She took a step nearer, wary as a cat entering a strange room, yet reluctant to pass a fellow human in need. 'Are you all right? Is there anything I can do to help?'

Her voice came thin and unsteady through the

mist. At the same moment a gust of wind tugged at the
knitted beret and sent it whirling. 'By the crin!' She
made a wild grab and heard his laughter, seeming to
mock at her offer of help. Her cheeks flushed, and her
temper rose to the surface. Tugging the retrieved hat
more firmly on to her head, she said, 'You've only got
to say no. No need to be sarky.'

As though fending off her wrath, he raised a hand,
palm outwards. 'I'm sorry.' His voice was deep, edu-
cated. 'It's just that you looked so comical, standing
there, doing battle with that – that ridiculous hat . . .
I'm sorry,' he said again. 'I haven't laughed like that
for ages. Haven't wanted to. Please forgive me.'

'I'm glad you think it's funny. Can't say I do. Mam
would have been very upset if I'd lost that beret. She
worked so hard, knitting it.'

'Oh dear, I see your point.' Lips twisted, gazing at
the bedraggled object that covered the shining red
hair, he said, 'Can one rejuvenate it, I wonder? Will
it wash and dry back again to its proper shape?'

Libby sighed. It had never been a proper shape.
Mam's fingers, once so slim and as nimble as Libby's,
were now swollen with arthritis. But because Libby
loved her she was as proud of the beret as if it had
come from the most exclusive hat shop on the Parade.

She gazed suspiciously at the man's thin face as he
continued to regard her, a thin smile on his lips. *Was*
he making fun of her?

'I took you for a small grey ghost, coming on me
from the mist like that,' he said. 'You're the same
colour as the fog, you know, in that grey coat.'

Suddenly he swayed, knuckles white as he gripped

22

the lamppost, alarming Libby so much that she took
several steps back, away from him. Then, ashamed of
her action, she said, gazing up into his face, 'Are you
sure you're all right? You don't look well.'

'As well as I'll ever be in the circumstances, sweet
maid of the mist.'

He *was* laughing at her! Chin in the air, she said,
'Have it your own way . . .' She began to walk on,
feeling the grey eyes following her. She risked one
last look over her shoulder before she turned into
St Anne's Place. He stood under the lamppost, his
back resting against it, his face deeply shadowed by
the turned up collar of the greatcoat.

Something about him, the sense of depression,
touched her heart. But before she had time to dwell
on it she had reached the gate of the house where she
was employed. Running down the area steps, she
pushed open the kitchen door and called, 'It's me,
Cook!'

The big room was clean, bright and cheerful. A
good fire burned in the black-leaded grate, the steel
hob burnished to reflect the orange flames. Above
the fireplace a tassel-fringed mantelcloth decorated
the high shelf, on which rested Cook's most treasured
possessions: two china dogs so ugly that they defied
description, and a collection of small gifts brought
back for her by the Ainslie children on their infrequent visits to Blackpool. A card from the doctor's
eldest son, Basil, from France, took pride of place,
propped against the old-fashioned square clock.

Seated around the table with its chenille cloth
over which a smaller white one was spread, her

companions in service were drinking tea and enjoying buns straight from the oven. The stout, florid-faced woman who held the position as cook to the Ainslie household, and who had been in their employ since they first arrived from their humbler beginnings in Ridley, looked up as Libby came in.

Doctor Ainslie's father had been the local MD since qualifying thirty years before and it was natural that his one and only son should follow in his footsteps. A scholarship taking the young man to higher education helped as did his ambition to move on to better things. Thus the opportunity in the practice on the coast was a Godsend.

The young girl's cheeks were flushed to a wild rose colour; her eyes sparkled from the chill wind. Even Cook, given more to dourness than compliments, couldn't help but think that this was an exceptionally lovely young woman. In a town where brunettes and the occasional blonde was the norm, Libby's hair stood out like a bonfire on a dark night, catching the light of the fire now as she came closer to its warmth, holding her hands out.

'Ah, Libby, there you are!' said Cook. She beckoned to Kathleen, seated opposite, to fetch another cup. 'You'll be wanting a cup of tea. Cold out, is it? After that fine afternoon, too.'

Kathleen, at fourteen tall and clumsy, with a mop of dark frizzy hair her cap barely concealed, rose reluctantly and reached for a white cup and saucer.

Libby agreed. 'A fog coming in from the sea,' she said, reaching for the cup of steaming tea. Kathleen stayed close to the fire, warming her backside, causing Cook to say sharply, 'Move, girl, and let dog see t' rabbit.'

Kathleen, all big cap and freckled arms, moved away with reluctance and Libby took her place, the welcome glow of the fire warm on her cheeks. Cook lifted her cup and over its rim said, 'Where's Alice, then?'

Feeling her cheeks grow even redder, Libby answered, 'She's coming. She – she met someone she knew. Said to tell you she wouldn't be late.'

'Bet it wore trousers,' giggled Kathleen, 'that friend of hers.'

'Don't be cheeky, girl,' Cook said in a starchy voice. 'As I remember, no one asked your opinion.' Libby grimaced, catching the look the Irish girl gave her as she turned her face to the fire.

In her bedroom at the top of the house with its little round window like the porthole of a ship, Libby had been asleep for some hours before Alice came in. She crept into Libby's room and whispering in a husky voice, 'Ee, but I've had a skinful,' she pushed back the covers and slid in beside Libby. 'Move over, I need to get warm.'

Libby grunted and turned her face into the pillow. 'Go to your own bed, Alice. What time is it, anyway? Cook was asking where you were. A rare old mood she was in, I can tell you, so you'd better watch out tomorrow.'

'What did you tell her? I hope you didn't mention the soldiers?'

'Of course not! What do you take me for?' She

opened one eye, peering at the old alarm clock on the bedside table. Past midnight! Flaming heck! Alice really ought to be more careful. That came of not having a mother near enough to warm her of the pitfalls of wartime and strangers in uniform who briefly touched your life and then were gone. She twisted on to her back, nose wrinkling with distaste as she caught a whiff of gin and greasy chips.

'You certainly went off in a hurry, didn't you?' said Alice, snuggling down next to her. 'Looked around and you were off as though your backside was on fire.'

'I didn't feel like spending the rest of the evening in a pub,' said Libby, adding, 'Besides, I was cold. I wanted to go home.'

'Humph! You missed a treat, young Libby. That soldier 'as all 'is back pay and you'd think the world was coming to an end the way 'e was spending it. You could've come, you'd 'ave enjoyed it.'

'You know I never feel comfortable in a public house. Anyway, I'm glad you had a good time but,' with another shove at the solid back, 'I really do think you should get away to your own bed now. It'll be mornin' before we know it and Cook'll be giving us dirty looks because we're doing nothing but yawn.'

Finally Alice dragged herself away and went to her own room. Then Libby, turning on her side once more, found that sleep eluded her. Determinedly, her eyes tightly closed, she thought of Vince.

Before they met, Vince had said, he'd been a great one for the girls. But all that had changed now. The first time he had laid eyes on Libby, with the red hair falling from beneath the round straw sailor hat, sitting at that table, the rays from the sun catching fire from her hair, he'd known he had to have her.

Although she loved him, she had to admit he puzzled her. His was a jealous and possessive nature and although Alice, being the authority on men that she was, had warned her, saying, 'I don't know that that Vince is really your sort, love,' Libby had gone her own sweet way, seeing him when she could.

Just before she fell into a dream-haunted sleep, the thin white face of the tall man in the officer's uniform took the place of Vince's. In her half sleep she frowned. He had no place in her dreams! It was Vince she was thinking of, not some toffee-nosed officer who allowed himself to become too drunk to make his way back to his billet . . .

Chapter Two

By the following morning the rain had stopped and blue skies showed intermittently between racing white clouds. Cook poured herself a cup of tea and plumped herself down on the rocking chair. She fixed Alice with a gimlet eye and, warming to her subject, exclaimed, 'And where did you get to last night, young lady? It was late when I went to bed and you weren't in, then.'

Alice caught Libby's eye and looked away. She had a headache the size of Asia this morning and her tongue felt like red flannel. She couldn't have thought up an answer if she'd wanted. Seeming not to expect one, Cook went on, 'As long as the missis don't find out I suppose there's no 'arm done, although you know she don't like you bein' out late. Now,' she took a gulp of the hot tea, 'if you don't mind, madam, you can take that tray I've prepared up to Master Basil's room before the tea gets cold.'

Alice looked at the daintily set tray with its silver and fine china. Sarah Ainslie enjoyed her new way of life, the prestige it gave her, the comings and goings and cards left on silver trays on hall tables asking her to tea. Dr Ainslie himself, though, confessed to missing the cheery gossip of his old patients.

'Master Basil's 'ome on leave then, is 'e?' Alice remarked, picking up the tray.

'Not Master Basil, but a mate of 'is. One of his fellow officers. Been wounded and was staying at that big convalescent place outside town, but when he came to pay 'is respects to the doctor and the missis heard about it, she insisted he stay here.'

Alice grunted. 'Humph, more work for yours truly, I suppose.'

'Get along, you lazy girl. Work'll never kill *you*, for sure.'

As Alice flounced out, carrying the tray, Cook turned to Libby. 'I hope you're going to keep those little scallywags out of my kitchen today. Had enough of 'em yesterday when you was out. Proper little monkeys, they're getting, especially that Bertie. Plagued the life out of me and Kathleen, wanting me to bake those biscuits he likes and then going into tantrums because I said I hadn't any currants. There's a war on, I told 'im. Can't get currants now for love nor money.'

Libby knew that in spite of Cook's pretended indignation she had a soft spot for the six-year-old Bertie. The two children had come late into the life of the Ainslies. A surprise to everyone, even to the doctor himself. They had thought their family complete with just one son. Basil, aged twenty-two, had joined up early in the war and had risen swiftly, now holding the rank of captain.

'I'm sorry they were a nuisance, Cook,' said Libby. 'Didn't Kathleen offer to take them for a walk?'

Cook grunted. 'That girl! Useless, she is. Can't think why the missis ever engaged her. Fresh out of an Irish bog, that's Kathleen. Breaks everything you give 'er, that's why I always wash the best china meself.'

Libby, used to Cook's monologue of grievances, waited until the older woman had run out of steam, and then said, quietly, 'So Kathleen didn't take them for a walk?'

'She was too busy getting the room ready for that wounded officer. 'Ere, you should see 'im, Libby. Poor sod, badly wounded in the leg, Doctor Ainslie told me. Kathleen is to put a fire in his room every day and bring down the ashes every morning.'

Alice came back through the door, hearing Cook's last remark. 'He's just going out for a walk. All huddled up in his greatcoat, limping something chronic and leaning on 'is stick.'

Cook shook her head, thinking of all the brave young men who would end up like that, walking with a stick or crutches.

Alice raised a languid hand to pat her hair. 'A Captain, 'e is. Captain James Randle. Ever so nice, and a proper gentleman. Thanked me ever so nicely for bringing up 'is tray. That's more than Master Basil ever does.'

The two girls thought about the Ainslie son and heir, a tall, gangling young man with a receding chin and a loud and boisterous laugh. He had a fondness for catching the female staff in dark passages or on the back stairs and, it was rumoured, had been responsible for the girl Kathleen had replaced leaving in disgrace.

Cook was the only member of the staff who liked him. Basil always made a fuss of her, calling her dear Cookie and dear Gibby. With Basil she lapped it up, although if any of the servants had used such terms of endearment she would have frozen them with a look.

' 'Ere, don't you go slanging Master Basil like that,' she said now. 'Off fighting for 'is King and country, 'e is, which is more than some I could mention.'

At Cook's last remark, Libby's cheeks flushed. She knew Mrs Gibson had little time for Vince, referring to him more than once as a coward. Alice saw the way Libby's face changed and pressed a reassuring hand on her arm. Young men in civvies stood out like a sore thumb in the mass of uniforms that these days crowded the streets. Anyone not wearing uniform would need to have a pretty good excuse, in Cook's opinion.

Libby took a deep breath. 'Vince has to help his father. You must know how busy they are and he's the only son . . .'

'Do 'is bit or not,' smirked Alice, 'your Vince is the best looking feller I ever saw.'

'Handsome is as handsome does,' sniffed Cook. 'Someone still ought to give 'im a white feather.'

When Libby had received a postcard from Vince, from Glasgow, a transparent silk covering the words embroidered in blue silk that spelled out the words, 'To My Dearest Girl', Cook had sniffed again and muttered, 'Gadding off to weddings when other people are risking their lives!' Handing back the card to Libby, she'd added, 'Still, they do say absence makes the heart grow fonder. Looks like 'e 'asn't forgot you even though 'e is away.' She didn't like Vince. She wished Libby would come to her senses and see him for what he was. She didn't trust the carefree young man with his dark good looks and curly black hair. Or those flashing eyes that would linger on Alice whenever he called to see Libby.

Bedroom eyes, someone had called them and Cook had to agree, although the idea shocked her. Libby, she thought, could do better than that. She wondered what Libby's mam would say about Vince. Likely she'd not met him yet.

What impression would he make on her, this rather too handsome man of Italian descent? Cook didn't trust men who were too handsome. What was wrong with good old steady English boys with their fresh faces and brushed-back hair?

Feeling that if she stayed a minute longer she'd lose her temper, Libby escaped upstairs to the nursery. Somehow she got through the rest of the day, the thought of Vince ever-present. He would be returning today and she'd promised to meet him that evening. As soon as the children were settled in bed she would be able to slip out and meet him in the small park across the way.

'The Old Contemptibles!' Dr Ainslie's voice shook with outrage. 'Bloody cheek of the man!'

They were seated in the drawing room. The furniture was of heavy mahogany, there were plaster casts on tall polished stands, ferns bursting out of a large brass urn in one corner of the bay window, large, over-stuffed chairs and a wide settee covered in dark red plush. On an oval table at the doctor's elbow stood a lamp with a brass base, its shade a mixture of red and green diamond shapes.

There was a shocked gasp from the settee where Mrs Ainslie sat, the eternal piece of knitting in her lap. Belatedly remembering her presence, her husband coughed. 'Forgive me, my dear, but the mere thought of that man makes my hackles rise. I must be forgiven for using strong language but sometimes it is necessary.'

'I presume you are talking about the Kaiser? Just to know he is related to our dear, late Queen does not bear thinking about.' Mrs Ainslie, frowning, picked up her knitting. 'But why does he call us that and what exactly does it mean, anyway?'

'Britain's contemptible little army?' James Randle's voice held wry amusement. They were sitting having their after-dinner coffee and somehow, inevitably, the conversation had got round to the war. 'We're going to have to show him how wrong he is. And from what I've seen of our boys, we've already started.'

Dr Ainslie nodded. He was a tall, thin man with a perpetually tired look. His silver hair was brushed smoothly from a side parting. A dark suit with its waistcoat boasting a fine silver watch chain stretched across his middle; the dark tie and stiff white shirt collar gave Sarah Ainslie great satisfaction as she gazed at him from across the room.

He had come a long way from the terraced house in Ridley where his patients had been working-class miners and their families. They lived now in an elegant house in a wide turning off the promenade, near enough to the sea to reap its benefits but not too near to the rowdy groups of people who frequented its length on a Saturday night.

To Sarah Ainslie, remembering the dank, beetle-infested house where she had been born, her drunken father and sickly mother, her present home was the epitome of gentility.

She was a well-built woman in her forties. She was inclined to haughtiness, her word was law and even her husband thought twice about crossing her once her mind was made up. The dark claret-coloured silk gown she had chosen to wear this evening, wanting to make an impression on their young, well-bred guest, did little to enhance her sallow complexion, even with its fashionable knee-length overskirt and the strand of cultured pearls that fell nearly to her waist. She fondly believed this gave her a touch of refinement, instead of which, as Alice confided in comical fashion as she returned from carrying the coffee tray into the drawing room, all it did was make her look like a pouter pigeon dressed up in red silk. Cook frowned at her warningly but had to smile at the description. It was so apt!

Now Dr Ainslie reached up for the box of cigars on the mantelpiece only to have a sharp look from his wife check the movement. He drew his hand back guiltily. There would be time for that later. And then only in the garden. Sarah didn't allow smoking in the house. In fact, there were a lot of things Sarah didn't allow in the house. The servants were required to speak in respectfully low voices; it was not permitted for the younger ones to entertain men in the kitchen and Alice had been chastised a number of times for scheming to get around this rule.

With a sigh the doctor turned to James, continuing the conversation. 'Aye, we'll have something to show the Germans, James me boy. Our Basil's doing that right now and with men like him and your goodself we'll soon beat the old sod.'

Mrs Ainslie frowned again; thrust the spare needle into the ball of khaki wool and glared at her husband as though she would have preferred it to have been his heart. 'If you are going to continue using that kind of language, then I shall go to my room,' she murmured through pursed lips.

As the door closed behind her James glanced at his watch. 'If you will excuse me, sir, I think I, too, will retire to my room. Got some letters to finish.'

The doctor smiled expansively. One hand reached out to the small sandalwood box with its cargo of forbidden delights. 'By all means, lad. I shall stay and smoke my cigar in peace.' He shook his head. 'A dear wife and mother, but, by God, how that woman can mither! Let her loose on old Kaiser Wilhelm and the war would be over in no time at all.'

James smiled and left the room. A typical product of his class, James Randle had been well-educated, a captain of his school cricket team, a member of the rugby team and before the war had worked in the City. His father was in the War Office. An intelligent man, he had that inborn air of assurance that breeding and the right school gives. Not good-looking in the accepted sense – his features were rather too aesthetic for that. Josie had once told him that he reminded her of one of those old saints in a Spanish painting, 'Saint Francis of Assisi or something,' making him laugh.

Should he have been surprised that a girl like Josie St Clare, the 'Darling of the Music Halls', knew about Spanish paintings and saints? But then Josie surprised him constantly, a mine of knowledge about all manner of things.

He had lost weight during his stay in hospital after being wounded in France when a German shell had burst near the dug-out where he and his men had taken shelter. He'd been more worried about his men than himself and had lost a lot of blood by the time he'd agreed to be stretchered out to the field hospital.

As he left the well-lit drawing room now, dark shadows closed about him, and he could barely see the foot of the staircase. It was Mrs Ainslie's notion of helping the war effort: only one lamp left burning on the table beside the front door. In those shadows all manner of things lurked, all kinds of horrors. Dreams of men folded over fences of barbed wire, screaming in agony some of them, the ones who weren't yet dead. Of shells lighting up the night sky, of himself leading the charge . . .

He dragged his thoughts firmly back to the present. Concentrate on getting up those bloody stairs, he told himself. His leg ached. The effort caused beads of sweat to stand out on his forehead.

'You're doing too much on that leg,' Doctor Ainslie had warned, catching him limping painfully from his walk last night. 'You should be resting it more.'

'No, really, I'm fine,' James had replied, trying to repress the feelings of humiliation and anger the wound had left. Now as he made his way along the corridor to his own room he paused, listening. The clear, sweet voice flowed like a crystal stream along the dimly lit landing. The singer had caught the exact essence of hope and pathos that the composer had surely intended.

The words – '*Speed bonny boat like a bird on the wing*' – evoked the tempestuous stretch of water over which the tiny boat skimmed, bearing a prince to sorrowful obscurity. Shivers ran down his spine, the kind of feeling he experienced whenever he viewed a wonderful painting or listened to Tchaikovsky performed by one of the world's finest orchestras.

'. . . *over the sea to Skye*.' The song ended on a high, pure note, then the voice, rather low and husky when speaking, said, 'That's it! You've had your song. Now to bed.'

'But Libby!' The child's voice rose in indignation. 'That was only a *little* song. I'm not sleepy yet.'

'Master Bertie! You promised to go to bed if I sang for you. It isn't good manners to go back on a promise.'

'Gentlemen don't do it, do they, Libby?' little Amy said.

James was abreast of the nursery doorway now, walking slowly. He listened as Amy's words ended in a howl of pain and through the open doorway James saw the boy bend to pick up a wooden building brick preparatory to throwing it after the one he had just hurled at his sister.

Libby hurriedly placed herself in front of the little girl, glowering at Bertie. 'No, gentlemen don't. And they certainly do not throw things at their sisters, either. You are a bad-tempered brat, Master Bertie, and for that you won't have an ice cream cornet when we go for our walk tomorrow.'

Through the open doorway James could see that the nursery walls were painted in a soft shade of green, with ceiling-high cupboards and several kitchen-type chairs. Beside the fire was an armchair with sagging springs. He could remember an identical one from his own nursery days. The fire was protected by a high, brass-topped wire guard. Tea had been mugs of cocoa and plates of bread and butter and the used crockery was still on the table. Libby would carry it down later.

The boy, who at Libby's warning had gone quiet, suddenly exploded. 'I want another song. I want another song!' Leaping up and down he zig-zagged in a mad dance across the floor. Libby's brows drew together in a terrible frown.

The mad dance threatened to erupt into the corridor. Libby chased after the tiny savage, endeavouring to catch him in her outspread arms, and immediately let out a cry of pain as another well-aimed toy, this time a metal soldier, flew through the air, hitting her on the chest. Her mouth opened in a gasp as a further one followed. She stumbled towards the child. He stopped his flight and turned to gaze warily up at her.

'That hurt, Bertie.' Libby drew a deep breath. 'Come on, off to bed now. We don't want your Mama coming up to see what all the noise is about, do we?'

But the boy didn't give in that easily. 'If I promise to go to bed now, can I have *two* ice cream cornets tomorrow?'

It had been the policy of Sanders, the nanny whom Libby had replaced, never to give in to black-mail – 'Do it once, young Libby, and you'll find you're doing it all the time. Especially with that Bertie. Making a stick for your own back, that's all you'll be doing.'

Bertie was a different kettle of fish to the easy-going Amy, fiercely determined on getting his own way right from the day Libby walked into their lives. He was too young to remember much of Nanny Sanders and her autocratic ways. Libby was the perfect victim for his wiles.

At first, anyway. Young and inexperienced, she had listened to Nanny Sanders and nodded and said yes, she understood. The older woman had warned, 'Miss Amy, now, you'll find is no trouble at all. Just as long as you put her hair up in rags every night and make sure she washes behind her ears, you should have no trouble. Master Bertie, now!' and she'd shaken her head. Still only in her mid-twenties, Mary Sanders had worked with children since leaving school. She had warned Libby, shaking a cautionary finger under the girl's nose, 'And don't be fooled by that young scamp's manner. You'll find out the hard way, my girl, if you once let him get the upper hand . . .'

Amy was a gentle little creature, with her soft fair hair and big blue eyes. She idolised Libby, confiding in her all her secrets, like where she kept her special collection of sea-shells and the pretty green glass necklace Libby had given her for her last birthday.

Amy laughed easily and in everything she did was such a direct contrast to her brother that sometimes, letting her imagination run wild, Libby would ponder on gipsies and changelings and then tell herself not to be daft. It didn't mean a thing. Look at our Agnes . . . !

Now her chest hurt where the metal toy had caught it. She should be firm and decisive instead of which she stood dithering like an old maid . . .

But when the small boy rushed to hug her, head tilted back, eyes wide and imploring, it would have taken a stronger will than Libby Gray's to resist him. He was a scallywag, to be sure, but the worst kind of scallywag: a lovable one.

A warm smile lit her face, transferring to it such beauty that the man standing in the shadows of the landing felt his heartbeat quicken. A heavy dull thudding began in his ears. Only Josie had ever had that effect on him. But with Josie it had been blatant desire, so sensual it took his will away. This girl stirred him differently. It was as though he wanted to reach out and enclose her in his arms, to cherish and care for her so that no one, nothing, could ever hurt her. As that little terror had just hurt her with the hurled toy . . . He heard fading murmurs of reconciliation, a soft, 'Goodnight, sleep tight, watch the bugs don't bite,' and the door of an inner room closed.

Not wanting to be embarrassed at being caught

41

eavesdropping in so childish a manner, he turned to hurry on to his room.

To his mortification, his walking stick slipped from his hand, falling with a clatter to the highly polished boards left bare by the narrow carpet runner. He cursed aloud, the clatter of its falling magnified a thousandfold in the silent corridor.

A whisper of skirts behind him, a door softly closing on children's voices and Libby was beside him, bending to retrieve his stick.

'Here, let me, sir . . .'

'No!' The refusal came out more harshly than he had intended. 'I'm not one of the children under your care. I can manage.'

But already Libby's hand was touching the stick, slim fingers curling round the polished wood as at the same moment his own hand reached down. For a breathless moment the large hand lay on hers, almost covering it from sight. Libby felt its coldness, the slight tremor, and gazing up into his eyes it took every ounce of willpower not to lift a hand and brush back the dark hair that fell over his forehead, to say, as she would say to Bertie or his sister, 'There, now, it can't be as bad as all that. Buck up, your face'd curdle the milk.'

He thought of their first encounter, in the mist of the promenade. It had been as disturbing as it was unexpected. He had just bumped into that bloody lamppost, sending daggers of fire up his injured leg, when she came into view. For a moment he'd panicked, unable to find his stick in the mist, then saw it had rolled into the gutter. Tears of self-pity had

sprung into his eyes and it was only the appearance
of the girl and her shriek of fear that had saved him
from making a complete fool of himself. In the drifting
grey mist, the large green eyes had gazed at him with
a disdain that was almost laughable and he had realised she thought him the worse for drink. It would
have been better if he had been. Perhaps a spot of
Dutch courage would have helped . . .

The whole dismal scene had brightened when, like
a little trooper, she'd sworn as the dreadful knitted
hat threatened to join the shrieking seagulls over the
heaving waves. Now, for one breathless moment, the
world stood still. It seemed to Libby that those grey
eyes would forever gaze into hers, touching her very
soul, that her flesh tingled where his hand had been.

'Daft hap'orth!' she scolded herself, relinquishing
the walking stick as he took it from her. 'You feel
sorry for this wounded soldier, that's all. Even if he is
a toffee-nosed officer there's nothing in the law that
says you can't feel sorry for him.'

'I apologise for my abruptness,' the quiet, cultured
voice murmured. 'I'm afraid I'm not always in the
best of moods. I hope I didn't disturb the children.
You appear to have had enough trouble getting them
settled.'

Libby gave a gurgle of laughter, instantly suppressed as she clapped her hand over her mouth. All
she needed now was for the missis to come up to
investigate. After the scene with that holy terror,
young Bertie, she'd had more than enough aggrava-
tion for one night.

Unprepared for his seemingly honest concern, the

kindness in the grey eyes, she was completely disarmed by that look, by the intimacy of the shadowy landing as she stood there next to James Randle. An intimacy she would have liked to deny but which nevertheless was all too real.

'I heard you singing.'

She felt his eyes on her and blushed in the confusion of feelings they evoked.

'You have a lovely voice. I wonder if the children realise how lucky they are.'

'Thank you, sir.' The blush deepened, rising to the roots of her hair. 'They say they prefer me to sing to them rather than tell them a bedtime story.'

'Can't say I blame them. Given the chance, I'm sure I would do the same.'

Below in the hall, the grandfather clock filled the house with its mellow chimes. Seven o'clock! Libby counted. Vince would be waiting.

'You are off duty now?' James enquired politely, interpreting the hasty check made of the silver fob watch pinned to the bodice of her blue gown.

'Yes, sir. I'm supposed to meet a friend.' Vince hated to be kept waiting, not even bothering to hide his bad temper at what he called her tardiness. No use trying to explain about young Bertie and his fit of tantrums. Vince would only say she should be more firm with him.

James watched as she sped along the landing to her own room.

'Give 'em a clip round the ear! Spoiled brats! I won't allow our kids to be spoiled like that, so I hope you're not counting on it, young Libby.'

'They're only babies, Vince. You can't expect anything else at their age. And it would be no use me trying to be strict with them. Their father gives them everything they want and won't hear of them being punished.'

The wind came with a rush from the sea, causing Libby to cling more tightly to Vince's arm. Always, when he spoke of the life they would share, and especially their future children, a warm glow took hold of her, as comforting as a fire on a snowy night. Somehow, this time the feeling didn't materialise. With growing irritation she listened as Vince began a tirade about her time off and how she was always late. 'Standing there like a spare part, I am, waiting for you.' He had no time for excuses. 'You're my girl and I see little enough of you as it is,' he said, quickening his steps, pulling her along unceremoniously beside him. It had been raining and muddy water from the overflowing gutters speckled her coat with dark patches as a passing hansom clattered by. Yes, definitely, Vince's irritation was beginning to rub off on her. He never walked on the outside, as a gentleman should. Why, to give young Bertie his due, even he insisted on walking nearest to the gutter when they went for their walks.

'It's to do with those old knights and being able to get to their swords to protect a lady if they meet an enemy,' the little boy had explained, to her amusement.

'And would you protect me, young Bertie?' she had asked teasingly, laughing when he had answered, after due consideration, 'I might, Libby. It would depend on how big the other fellow was.'

She glanced up now at the handsome face beside her, unable to stop herself from comparing him with the young officer, knowing she shouldn't, knowing Vince hadn't had the same advantages, hadn't been to the posh schools.

Quick sympathy replaced the irritation left by Vince's unfeeling reception to her account of the scene with Bertie and changing the subject, she said, 'Aren't you going to tell me about the wedding? Did everything go all right? And thank you for the card. It was lovely.'

He shrugged, mumbling something under his breath. 'It was all right. You know Italian weddings! Lots of music and dancing. But I wouldn't want to live in Glasgow. A grim, grey city. I'm just glad to be back here with my lovely girl.'

The idea of leaving Libby, if only for a few days, in a town full of convalescing men with time on their hands had worried him. He remembered the first time he had seen her, laughing aloud at something her friend had said. Those eyes, he'd thought. He'd never seen anything like them. What a contrast to the other girls he had taken out with their silly giggles and too bright lipstick. Chalk and cheese, he thought. He'd fantasised about Libby, imagining them alone on a moonlit beach with wild waves breaking on the shore and a band playing soft music in the background. They would stroll barefoot until they found a secluded spot . . .

'But why are we wasting time talking like this?' he demanded suddenly and pulled her into his arms, bringing his mouth down on hers in a fierce kiss.

46

Libby shuddered. 'I've missed you, Libby,' he groaned, his mouth going to her neck. 'I don't ever want to leave you again.'

Remembering Cook's words that morning in the kitchen, Libby said, 'We ought to think about it, though. There's talk of conscription being introduced next year . . .'

'Stupid lot!' His voice held scorn. 'They can conscript all they like. They won't get me. Risk my head being blown off by a Jerry shell! You must be joking.'

Before Libby could say anything, he went on, scathingly, 'I reckon it's all a vast plot, this war, put up by the rich and powerful nations of the world, to subdue the working man. Let them do their own fighting. I don't want anything to do with it.'

Making excuses as they walked, Libby told herself that he wasn't any the less worthy in her eyes because he felt this way, although she had to admit it irked.

James closed the bedroom door behind him, noting that the fire had already been lit. The room was warm, the coalscuttle full. With a sigh he seated himself at the writing desk under the bay window and turned up the green-shaded lamp.

He'd started his letter to Josie that afternoon but his leg ached too much to sit still for long and he'd abandoned it, telling himself he would finish it later. After his stay in hospital he had been given a week's leave before going to the convalescent home. During that time he had met Josie. He picked up the pen and

47

dipped it into the silver inkwell and, the image of Josie vivid in his mind, he began to write.

> The doctor makes an agreeable companion, although his good lady could be a bit of a tartar, I guess. The children are quaint. The boy, Bertie, has the looks of a small blond angel but is really quite the opposite. Amy, the girl child, is the miniature of her nurse, or tries hard to be. Whether this is a good thing I cannot say, as the nurse comes from a working-class background. She seems pleasant enough, however. Hardly more than a child herself, with the most amazing green eyes and an unusual shade of hair . . .

James frowned, his pen coming to a stop. Why was he writing all this nonsense? Josie would not be interested in such things, especially not such a detailed account of another girl. Still, in a place like this, with only his walks along the seafront to while away the time, returning the salutes of men who, like himself, were so briefly safe from the horror of the trenches, one had to keep occupied. He laid his pen on the white blotter and leaned back in the chair, turning it slightly towards the fire. His eyes stared into its heart and in his imagination the leaping flames took on a silky texture, their colour turning from orange red to the brightness of tumbled waves cascading over bare white shoulders.

Josie would be on stage now and the theatre filled with uniformed men, noisy and more than a little drunk. British reserve would be hidden beneath a brave show of jollity. Pushed to one side would be the fear of the vast German airships that flew over London, dropping bombs, causing great fear and distress. On the last raid a school in the East End had suffered a direct hit. It had been terrible, with many children killed. Still, the Old Comtemptibles would be in fine voice tonight and nothing would stop them from enjoying themselves. It was the only way, to enjoy yourself, to drink and be merry and Josie St Clare, formerly Josie Higgins, was the girl to help them, all right. James remembered when he had first seen her. He had waited until the clapping had died down, then with a small group of fellow officers, he had gone round to her dressing room, and was disappointed to find she shared it with two others. Was it really such a short time ago?

The girls had squealed as he knocked and entered, darting behind the screen which stood in one corner of the room, gazing at him coyly over the top. He'd a glimpse of shapely figures, of white undergarments liberally adorned with ribbon and lace and he had felt his cheeks redden with embarrassment. 'Sorry! I thought I heard someone call come in.'

The girls had looked at each other and giggled. Clearly, the sight of his bewilderment amused them.

Josie, who was seated before a large square mirror, turned to smile at him. 'Well, you're in, aren't you? What can we do for you, ducks?'

James felt tongue-tied, like a new boy at school suddenly confronted by the headmaster. 'I saw your show.' He swallowed. 'I enjoyed it so much I thought it would be nice to tell you so myself.'

Josie had looked at him thoughtfully, her gaze dropping to the walking stick he held in his hand. Then with a sideways glance at the other two girls, openly listening from behind the silken screen, she leaned forward across the dressing table, one hand reaching among the clutter for a jar of cold cream. 'That's nice,' she said. 'That's what we're 'ere for, to give the boys a treat while they're 'ome on leave.'

Before his fascinated gaze, she had begun to smear the cold cream across her face, keeping up a conversation all the while. James listened, not quite knowing what was expected of him. The girls had emerged from behind the screen, fully dressed, carrying their hats and gloves.

With another sideways glance towards Josie's back, they called out, 'Well, enjoy yourself!' adding, 'and knowing our Josie, I'm sure you will. Just don't do anything we wouldn't do.'

In a fit of giggles they were gone, leaving James alone with the singer. Josie took her time wiping the thick make-up from her face before beginning on her hair. She stood up and then, bending from the waist so that her hair fell in a curtain of rich, glossy red, she began to brush it with long, graceful sweeps of her arm.

James had never seen anything that bewitched him so much. The slim white arm, raised as it wielded the silver-backed hairbrush, the silk kimono so loosely belted that it fell open as she bent, revealing a long, white stretch of leg.

Catching him unawares, she said lightly, 'Like what you see, do you, ducks? Want to take me out to supper once I'm dressed?'

James had visited the dressing room on pure impulse, not thinking of the conclusion to his actions. Of course he'd like to take her out to supper, he told her. Once he was up there in that convalescent home he was sure there would be no one like Josie. Not even Fenella's dark beauty had made him feel this way. Fenella Burroughs and he had grown up together, getting into all the scrapes that children do. Fenella had grown into a lovely young woman and James knew his parents and Fenella's father had ideas about them marrying one day, thus joining the two estates.

He dismissed the thought of Fenella and recalled Josie the last time he had seen her, from his usual place in the stalls while the audience joined in the chorus of a popular song she had made her trademark.

Josie, on stage, was a sight to behold. Clad in a full-skirted gown that left her magnificent shoulders bare, she was seated on a garlanded swing that was pushed by two gallants impeccably dressed in white flannels and pale blue blazers with straw hats on their marcel-waved hair. The swing was designed to fly out over the heads of the audience, affording the fortunate ones a tantalising glimpse of white drawers and lacy petticoats.

Until his orders came to journey north to the place where he would convalesce he had visited the show nightly, going round to the dressing room as soon as the last curtain fell, taking her out to quiet suppers. Aware that his leg pained him, Josie had been content to ride with him in a hansom cab to the small restaurants he suggested, walking as little as possible. When he said he was sorry he couldn't take her dancing, she'd laughed. 'I dance on the stage every night, ducks, with matinees thrown in. By this time of night I'm glad for a sit down.'

At the beginning of what Josie called their 'grand passion' he'd been circumspect about meeting her. The first time he'd visited her flat, he'd insisted, 'I don't want anyone gossiping about you.'

Josie had laughed. 'Don't worry about me, Jimmy me boy, although I can't say I don't appreciate it. I can't remember the last person to worry about my reputation. I suppose it must 'ave bin me mother and it takes a bit of getting used to.'

She was wearing her Chinese-style kimono, thin vivid blue silk that clung to every curve of her voluptuous body. The blue suited her pale skin and glorious hair, making his pulse leap. The wine she served was heady and Josie had seemed determined to keep his glass full.

Glancing about him, he had remarked, 'You certainly seem to have made yourself comfortable here,' looking over the velvet armchairs and settee and the scatter of small embroidered cushions that littered them.

They had had a light supper and the wine had made him feel decidedly lightheaded. Josie curled up on the settee next to him, pouring yet more wine, her eyes shining, full of mischief.

'Not so fast!' he protested, laughing. 'You'll have me under the table if you're not careful. *And* I still have to get home . . .'

'Why?' Soft arms encircled his neck, full breasts pressed against him. 'Why do you 'ave to get home? I've got a perfectly comfortable bed 'ere, or so I've bin told.' She'd laughed, shaking her head so that the silky cloud of hair brushed against his face, chasing the last remnants of his doubts away. He had felt his heartbeat quicken; he could hardly get his breath. Her skin felt warm and soft, swamping his senses.

'Josie!' His voice was thick and, knowing he was about to say something she had no wish to hear, she pressed closer to him, her lips on his. Her body arched and it would have taken a stronger will than James' to refuse that which was being offered so freely.

He should, he supposed, be jealous, knowing there had been other men before him and would be others after he had gone. Josie had made no secret of that. 'Live for today, Jimmy me boy. Don't worry about tomorrow,' she said as she nestled in his arms. 'Tomorrow might not come for the likes of us. One of them bloody great German zeppelins might come over tonight and drop a bomb on us and then where'd we be? I'm not goin' to worry about what's right and what's wrong and don't you. Let's enjoy what we have together and stick two fingers up to the future.'

That week with Josie had been a wondrous, exciting time. He suspected his mother had known – shrewd woman, his mother, and although she would be the first one to agree that a young man had to sow his wild oats he knew also she would be horrified at the idea of anything more permanent.

But after the mud-filled horror of the trenches, Josie was exactly what he had needed. His thoughts, echoing Josie's, had gone no further than the moment, when he held her close in his arms . . .

Chapter Three

'Come on, Libby! We'll miss the donkey rides.'

Bertie's strident voice echoed over to where Libby was buttoning up the back of Amy's dress. The little girl caught Libby's eye and her nose wrinkled at the bossy impatience of the male sex. Libby gave one last look about the room. The fire was well banked. The clothes that had been airing on the rack had been removed until their return. 'It's such a lovely day,' she said, following the children down the stairs. 'I thought we might walk to the lighthouse.'

The lighthouse, still in use, stood by the headland to the east; a tall, white column dominating the landscape. It was a favourite walk and the children loved it. And with the weather still so mild it would be a shame not to make the most of it. Around the base of the lighthouse one could find shells that had been washed up on to the beach from countries hundreds of miles away. Even thousands of miles away, murmured Amy as she knelt, small hands sifting hopefully in the soft sand. Nearly always she would find something and hold it out on the palm of her sticky, sand-dusted hand for Libby to examine it and speculate over where it had originated. Bertie, scorning such sissy things, would throw pebbles, trying to hit one of the dozens of seagulls that flew over their heads.

Now Amy exclaimed 'Ohhh, lovely!' and began one of her dances about the room. 'But then Bertie won't get his donkey ride.'

'The man with the donkeys might not be there,' Libby pointed out. 'He often isn't, these days.'

'Serves Bertie right if he isn't. I think he was just horrible, throwing that toy at you last night.'

'Yes, he was,' Libby agreed, and lowering her voice: 'And I'll tell you one thing, Amy, strictly between you and me and the gate post, that if he tries it again I'll jolly well throw it back.'

Bertie scowled overhearing, as he was meant to, and his sister laughed, putting out her tongue and then jumping down the last few stairs to the hallway. The sunlight threw prisms of violet, red, and green, through the leaded glass panes of the vestibule door; spilt jewels scattered across the red Turkey carpet.

As they reached the hall, the study door opened and James Randle came out. 'Ah, off for a walk!' He grinned at the agitation of the small boy, jumping excitedly from one foot to the other, at the sudden, solemn demeanour of Amy, staring up at him with wide blue eyes.

'Say good morning to Captain Randle, children,' said Libby.

There was a clamour of 'Good morning, Captain Randle', followed by Amy saying, shyly, 'Mama says we must call you Uncle James. What must Libby call you?'

'Now, that's a difficult one.' He gazed down at the little girl, a smile playing about the corners of his mouth. 'What would you suggest?'

'We're detaining Captain Randle. Come on, children, off for our walk.' Libby didn't like being condescended to, even by an officer in the King's army.

'On the contrary. I have nothing in particular to do and the whole morning in which to do it. In fact, if you and the children have no objections, I would very much like to accompany you on your walk. Providing,' with a gallant little bow that had Amy giggling helplessly, 'the children wouldn't think me in the way.'

'Oh no, Uncle James. Never.' Amy's face lit up, cheeks flushing in excitement. James caught Libby's eye, and they both smiled. 'Libby says we may walk towards the lighthouse.'

'I want a ride on . . .' Bertie, incensed by being left out of the conversation, hated being ignored. Libby shushed the boy, saying firmly, ' "I wants" don't always get their wish, Bertie. Remember that. Now come on, stop dawdling.'

James watched as she pulled on her hat, standing on tiptoe in order to see in the round glass of the hall stand, before she opened the door and ushered the children out.

'Aren't you wearing your knitted creation?' He closed the door behind them.

Libby could have sworn he sounded disappointed, and wondered again if he was teasing her.

'Mrs Ainslie likes me to wear this grey felt when I'm out with the children.'

He could see why. It went with the plain grey coat

57

and cotton stockings. 'Shame,' he said 'hiding all that lovely hair! A criminal act. It shouldn't be allowed.'

He thought she looked like a little hen, ruffling its feathers, nettled at his words. 'I have to look tidy. My position demands it. Mrs Ainslie says . . .'

'Mrs Ainslie has no soul. Forgive me, that sounded most rude and ungallant to my hostess. But why that awful potty-shaped thing? A few curls escaping in the wind wouldn't make you any less a responsible nursemaid.'

Libby heard Amy gasp and begin to giggle at the word 'potty'. She gave her a reprimanding look. 'She thinks the colour of my hair is not quite – respectable,' she admitted wryly.

'At least it's natural. Does anyone else in your family have hair that colour?'

Libby nodded, pushing the children in front of her. 'My mother and my sister. My brother, too, although he hates it, and is always trying to make it darker by smothering it with grease.' Libby chuckled, recalling Joseph's frustration over Mam's patient explanation that no matter how much grease he used he'd still be a freckle-faced carrot-top and nothing was going to change that.

James decided she had a delicious laugh, soft and throaty and contagious, which brought out a hint of dimples in both cheeks.

'They used to call me Ginger at school – among other things,' she said. 'They'd stand in a ring with me in the middle and chant, "Ginger, you're barmy, you want to join the army." I'd kick their shins if I could, especially the bigger boys. One day, after I'd given one a bloody nose – a boy who really had it in for me – they left me alone.'

He laughed aloud. 'Good for you! Small but deadly, eh?'

Suddenly he looked young and amusing and interesting to be with. They both laughed together then, the warmth of mutual amusement making each look at the other with fresh interest. Libby was perturbed to feel her heart quicken its beat. She willed herself not to blush, but could feel the colour creeping into her cheeks.

'Do you know,' he said, with that engaging smile, 'the first time I saw you you made me laugh. As good as a tonic recommended by the doctor. The fog and that ridiculous knitted beret . . . ?'

'And I'd just commited the most terrible sin by going into a Protestant church with Alice for free tea and buns!'

He laughed again. 'Did you really!'

Taking each child by the hand they crossed the road to the promenade. Walking sedately along the walkway, careful to match her pace with his, for she could see it was still an effort for him to stride out, she called to the children who had run ahead to slow down. The day was bright and breezy, gulls wheeling overhead, outstretched wings dazzling white against the blue sky. Libby clung to her hat, her skirts flapping about her ankles and wisps of hair clinging to her cheeks.

On days like this she wanted to run with the children, to take off her shoes and stockings and race across the sands ridged by the outgoing tide.

James removed his uniform cap with its shiny peak and tucked it under one arm. She looked up at him from the corner of her eye and said, 'I'm sorry about yesterday, when I bumped into you . . .'

'You thought I was drunk!'

'No – well, yes, I suppose I did. At first, until I realised you were ill . . .'

'Blast it, girl, why must everyone keep rubbing it in?' His cheeks flushed angrily. 'I'm not ill. Just temporarily out of commission.'

Libby gazed at him consideringly, head on one side. 'Don't get your paddy up, as my mother would say,' she said lightly. 'It never helps, sir.'

And James laughed, not at all annoyed at being bullied back into good humour. 'Sorry! And please don't call me sir. There's really no need to, you know. I have a name.'

'Captain Randle!' she ventured on an almost provoking note.

About to say 'James' he hesitated. Attractive as Libby was, she was not someone his parents would encourage. It was different with Josie – gaiety girls were fair game and the season was always open. More so when there was a war on. And yet, somehow, James wanted to treat Libby as he would Fenella and all the other young women of his acquaintance. But he guessed, correctly, that she considered him 'quality' but even so would frown at familiarities.

They had reached the end of the promenade. The children scampered down the flight of steps that led to the beach, Bertie screaming with uncontrolled excitement. Amy followed more sedately with frequent backward glances at the two adults.

They liked each other, the little girl decided, watching Libby's face as she talked, the bloom on her cheeks that the sea breezes had heightened. She hoped Libby wasn't going to leave, like that last nanny they'd had, the one who married her soldier. Uncle James was nice, though, and if Libby had to marry someone as she supposed all girls did once they were grown up – it was, as she had heard Mama say, their 'destiny' – then Uncle James would be better than that curly haired man Libby met on her evenings off. Secretly, peering through the nursery window, Amy had seen them, Libby rushing to meet him at dusk as he waited on the other side of the street, seen the way his arms had gone round her, like a big black bear – the little girl shuddered – and how he slobbered all over her face.

Once Kathleen had been in the nursery and curious as to what was absorbing the little girl had joined her at the window.

'Ugh!' Amy turned a disgusted face towards the Irish girl. 'Fancy letting a man do that to you!'

Kathleen, one of thirteen children back home in Ireland, had seen men do more than that to girls. She said, in her simple-minded way, 'Sure now, Miss Amy, 'tis only kissing they're up to. No harm in that. A little of wot yer fancy does yer good, as the song says. And yer must admit that Vince is a handsome divil.' She twisted a lank piece of hair between finger and thumb. 'Sure, but I wouldn't be putting any objections to a man like that. Libby's a lucky girl. I'd swop places wi' 'er any time.'

Amy wished she would. She could tell that Kathleen

was more Vince's type than Libby was. She didn't know *how* she knew, but she knew. Kathleen was a big girl, with a chest that stuck out in front and a bottom that stuck out in back. She was fond of claiming that she had a voluptuous figure, something, Amy guessed, she'd read in one of those penny papers that came to the back door and about which Mama was always warning the servants. Amy much preferred Libby's figure which was neat and straight and small enough to cuddle.

She scuttled off to join Bertie in a sheltered spot near the pier and the pair of them were soon busy with buckets and spades. Thankfully, there was no sign of the donkeys and nothing more had been said about the proposed walk to the lighthouse. Libby guessed Captain Randle would have had to refuse, as it was over rocks and rough ground, and perversely, even though she was still unsure of him, she didn't want to lose his company. She spread the tartan rug she had tucked into the big hold-all and settled down to watch.

James stood leaning on his stick, his gaze resting on the children who were intent on building the sand castles that in another hour would be carried away by the incoming tide. A waste of time – like the battles poor bloody Tommy was fighting right this minute on the other side of the Channel.

A shadow passed over his face and Libby, who was watching, suggested gently, 'Why don't you sit down and rest for a moment?'

He grunted and lowered himself to the rug. Reaching for the smooth pebbles that lay half-buried in the sand, he began to skim them across the water. The silence between him and the girl was soothing. It didn't seem necessary to carry on a conversation, just for politeness' sake, like with other people. It was, James decided, watching the small glowing face under the ugly grey hat, like being in church. Like finding yourself in a presence so calming one just wanted to stay quietly by its side, not moving in case the spell broke and the ugly everyday worries of the world intruded.

'You're a friend of Master Basil's, aren't you?'

'He's a fellow officer.' Basil was still somewhere in the hell they called Flanders. James' thoughts returned to the bomb craters of France. To that march along the treeless road to the trenches, where the possibility of dying filled his mind every minute of his waking hours. All about him men had been cursing, smoke curling blue in the chill air as they drew on a last cigarette before passing it to the man behind. It had been raining on and off for days. The road they'd walked was made of wooden planks and on each side as far as the eye could see there was a swamp of shell holes filled with water. Each side of the road had been littered with dead mules in all stages of decay, some green, some black, some with eighteen-pounder shells still in the mule pack, half buried in the mud, and the smell of decay had stunk to high heaven.

There'd been no time or place to bury them and he remembered how thankful he'd been for the low clouds that kept the Hun at bay. The nights were the worst. Very lights shooting into the air would freeze men like frightened rabbits. He recalled one particular night when the enemy never once let up, the blast of the shells shattering all else into silence. Nearby a shell had exploded, deafening him. He'd flung himself to the ground, shouting at his men to do the same. Pressed into the mud, not wanting to move, he had been terrified at what he might find when it was over. When at last he had tried to move, his legs wouldn't budge, refusing to carry his weight from this hell-hole to the safety of his own lines.

Lying there, his thoughts had rambled from half-remembered scenes of his childhood, to bright poppies in tall yellow cornfields; picnics beside the river with his mother. He'd cursed the Almighty and the men, who, safe in their offices in Whitehall, sent to their deaths with the stroke of a pen thousands upon thousands of young men. The flower of England's youth, lying there on the poppy fields of another country . . .

With trembling hands, he scooped out a handful of the fine white sand, letting it trickle slowly through his fingers. His wound had been more serious than he'd first thought and had left him with a limp. When the healing proved slow, his CO had insisted that he go for a spell to the convalescent home on the coast. 'Take things easy,' the CO had advised. 'Get to know some girls . . .'

James gave himself a mental shake and turned to smile at the girl sitting next to him. He hadn't the faintest recollection of what she had been saying.

'Sorry,' he said. 'I was miles away.'

'I could see that.' Libby wrinkled her nose

teasingly. 'Wishing you were home with your family instead of stuck up here with us heathen Northerners!'

'Not at all.' He settled himself into a more comfortable position. 'What does your father do, Libby?'

She wasn't surprised at the question. Wasn't surprised at anything this man said. His sympathetic manner invited confidence. It didn't seem at all inquisitive that he should ask questions about her home life.

'There's generally only one job a man can do where I come from, and that's work in the pits.'

'Does he earn good money?'

Libby thought of the pay packet her father brought home every Friday, of the twenty-five shillings he gave Mam for rent and housekeeping. She said, 'We manage. My mother can make a good meal with the cheapest of cuts and we always eat everything she cooks. Daren't leave a scrap on our plates or we'd be for it. I have a brother and an older sister and we live in a terraced house with a kitchen and front room and two bedrooms upstairs. We pay two and six a week rent and have a backyard with a – with a . . .' She blushed, about to say lavatory.

James laughed. 'No bathroom?'

Now he *was* teasing her! She lifted her chin, instantly on the defensive. 'We wash in front of the fire, using a tin bath Mam fills with water heated on the range.'

'It can't be a very easy life, especially for your mother. A constant struggle, I should imagine.'

Libby shook her head. 'You could never understand,

65

sir. My childhood was very happy. Although we didn't have much in material things, Mam made up for it in other ways.'

James thought of his own parents, his father busy with his job in the War Office, his beautiful mother 'doing her bit for our dear boys in the trenches', organising Red Cross bazaars and soirées, her biggest problem which gown she would wear, while this girl's mother agonised over what she would feed her family for supper.

'You say you have a brother and sister,' he murmured. 'Don't they help?'

Libby's full lips firmed. 'I wouldn't trust our Agnes to look after Amy never mind me mam and dad. And last time I was home my brother was talking of joining up. He works down pit with my father – he's sixteen – but he says he'll go off and I believe him. He'd lie about his age ...' Suddenly conscious of what she was saying – and to an army officer of all people! – Libby gasped and placed one hand over her mouth, as though to stop any further confession.

He took her free hand, holding it in his own. Aware of the tingling sensation that reached right up her arm, she pulled it gently and he let it go. 'Dinna fash yourself, as my Scottish grandmother would say,' he told her lightly. 'I can assure you I won't go rushing off to the War Office with news of your brother's intentions.'

Idly he began to throw pebbles again, content to sit and listen as this girl talked of her family. The conversation of most of the girls he knew was totally of horses and what a stifling influence this 'bloody war' was having on the breeding stock in their fathers' stables. Even Josie's interests centred entirely upon having a good time.

'Are your grandparents still alive?' Libby was saying. 'Mine are dead.' Her face clouded over, the green eyes darkening. Grandma had been taken ill with a chill from which she never recovered. Grandad, it seemed, couldn't live without her and had followed not long after. It still hurt, even now, thinking about it, although there were brighter memories, too. Perhaps more bright ones than sorrowful, which was how it should be.

She went on, her thoughts miles and years away: 'My grandmother had a lovely piano, always covered in a Spanish shawl, with silk fringes that hung almost to the floor. How I envied her that shawl! She used to let my brother play the piano and we'd stand around and sing, especially at Christmas time.'

'Was your brother any good?' he smiled.

Again Libby wrinkled her nose, recalling the clumsy attempts made by Joseph to play 'Jingle Bells' and their laughter and teasing when he made such a mess of it. Good-natured laughter, though, and the teasing at Grandma's was never anything to get upset about. But Joseph persisted and before anyone realised he was performing a fairly expert rendering of the old song and also some carols. Grandma had nodded, eyes twinkling, and said smugly, 'Aye, the boy's got it in him. Takes after my mother, he does. She could play a lovely tune, she could, not only on the piano but the violin as well.'

Tears came unbidden to Libby's eyes and she bit

her lip, aware of the man watching her. 'I'm sorry. I do go on when I get talking. Mam says I'm like a wound-up gramophone and can only stop when my engine runs down. You'll have to poke me when you get tired of listening to me.'

He grimaced. 'I wouldn't dream of poking you. And I don't think I would ever get tired of listening to you. I'd have liked to have known your grandparents. They sound a grand couple.'

A scream from Amy put paid to any further discussion about grandparents or anything else and looking up quickly, Libby saw Bertie standing behind Amy, a smirk of great satisfaction on his face. It seemed as if he had just emptied a bucketful of wet sand over his sister's head.

Libby jumped to her feet. 'That was very naughty, Bertie. You deserve to be taken home and stood in a corner for the rest of the day.' Turning to Amy, she knelt and began to comfort the small weeping girl, brushing off the sand as best she could with her hands. 'Are you all right, love? It didn't get in your eyes, did it?'

Bertie turned a belligerent face towards her. 'She threw my crab in the sea!'

'It was dead, anyway,' retorted a red-faced Amy. 'Smelly old crab. I *hate* crabs.'

'All right, all right.' James rose from the blanket and brushed sand from his trousers. 'I'm sure Bertie, after apologising to Amy, is going to behave beautifully from now on. Aren't you, my man?'

Catching the glint in the captain's eyes, Bertie said, yes, he was going to behave beautifully from now on and he was sorry he'd emptied the sand over his sister, adding in a barely audible whisper under his breath that she'd deserved it, anyway.

Libby turned a smiling face towards James, releasing Amy and rising to her feet. 'Is that the way you handle your men? Gently but firmly?'

'Something like that.'

He made to move away and she felt sudden dismay at the grimace of pain that twisted his features as he stumbled on a rock. 'How thoughtless of me!' she murmured. 'You would have been more comfortable in a deckchair.'

'Bite your tongue, woman! I'm not that old or decrepit that I have to hire a deckchair.'

Libby made no answer to that. Intuition warned her that whatever answer she might give would be wrong.

Instead she gave one of her throaty chuckles, and the children forgot their differences and ran to her, clasping her about the waist, hugging her. James reached out and ruffled the boy's hair.

Bertie squirmed away, reminding her in his most demanding voice, 'Libby, you promised us ice cream.'

'She didn't!' his sister reminded him heatedly. 'After you threw that toy at her last night she said . . .'

The boy began kicking sand all over his sister's legs and the plaid rug. 'She said she'd see!'

'Hey, sir.' James' voice was fiercely commanding. 'Remember your promise! You were going to behave for the rest of the day.'

Bertie's mouth opened to make another protest, but

James gave him no chance of further argument. 'Now, apologise to Libby for your atrocious behaviour. If you had been in my command I'd have clapped you in irons by now.'

Bertie, in spite of the fierce look on Captain Randle's face, showed what his father would undoubtedly have called 'gumption'. 'The army don't put their men in irons. That's the navy.'

'Bertie!' Libby looked amused and then shocked.

'He's right, you know.' To Bertie's annoyance, James mussed his hair again. 'Maybe, Libby, for being so smart, you will allow *me* to treat Bertie and Amy to ice cream?'

They didn't wait for Libby's answer. Sand flying under their feet, Amy's bonnet dangling from its ribbons down her back, the children made a beeline for the steps leading from the beach to the promenade. James shook loose sand from the rug then helped Libby to fold it before depositing it in the hold-all.

More slowly they followed the children, James leaning heavily on his stick. Libby reminded herself that it wasn't the easiest thing to walk on sand, even at the best of times.

The children were already at the ice-cream cart, pushing their way between half a dozen other people. To Libby's dismay she saw that Vince was serving, resplendently handsome in his straw boater with its scarlet and white striped ribbon. He'd recognised the children and his eyes were eagerly scanning the promenade for a sight of Libby.

Perfect white teeth flashed in a smile, to be

replaced a moment later by a scowl at the sight of the young officer by her side.

'Four cornets, please.' James dug into his pocket and handed the coins over.

Acutely conscious of Vince's accusing stare while he deftly scooped the ice cream from the zinc basin, Libby kept her eyes lowered, making a show of tidying Amy's long curls.

She stretched out her hand for her own cornet and heard Vince say, possessively, 'Hello, Libby. Same time tonight, all right?'

She nodded without speaking, then followed James and the children as they walked away. She smiled as James stared at his ice cream as though not quite certain what to do with it.

'Never had one of these things before,' he admitted ruefully.

'What, never? You poor, deprived thing!' she laughed. 'Look, you lick it, like this.'

James felt a shiver go down his spine as the tip of her pink tongue slowly ran down the length of the ice cream. Shaken by the intensity of the feeling, he followed her to one of the enclosed shelters that faced the sea so they could enjoy their ices away from the curious gazes of the soldiers that passed. Also, she thought wryly, from the dark and glowering gaze of Vince, further along the promenade. She'd have been wise to ask if they could have walked away, so that he couldn't see them, then decided Vince would have made something of that, too, and she didn't want to give him any more room to complain.

Far out at sea, a ship moved slowly against the horizon, leaving a long dark trail of smoke in its wake. Above it sea birds whirled and dipped, sharp eyes constantly on the look-out for scraps tossed overboard.

Libby thought of the deadly grey U-boats that might be lurking there and said a silent prayer for all men aboard such ships.

James left them before they reached the house, lifting his cap and saying, 'I've got a few things to take care of, Libby, so I'll say goodbye here. Thanks for the walk. It was – different.'

Libby laughed, watching the children as they raced ahead to the corner of St Anne's Place, now that their walk was over eager to get back to their games of toy soldiers and dolls' tea-parties. 'I'll bet it was! I wonder when you last went for a walk along the beach with a nursemaid and two boisterous children?' She gazed up at him from under her eyelashes, unconscious of the image she created.

'Too long!' He gave a tiny bow, causing Amy to erupt into squeals of laughter. Then Libby watched him stroll away, back along the promenade.

Chapter Four

Vince was waiting for her when she came across the road to the small park that evening. Frowning, he made straight for her and took her arm. 'So that's the way it is? An ordinary working bloke's not good enough for you now. It has to be an officer.'

'It was nothing, Vince. Honest. The children and I were getting ready for our morning walk and happened to meet Captain Randle in the hall, also on his way out. He asked if we minded if he came with us. I think he's bored, Vince, and I could hardly say no, could I?' She smiled. 'And the children were all for it.'

'And you? From what I could see you were all for it, too.'

The jealousy in Vince's voice dismayed her, although she knew she should have expected it. 'Don't talk wet, Vince Remede. Who asked your opinion, anyway?' she snapped.

'Nevertheless you're going to get it. My opinion and anything else I fancy. I'm sorry I'm not the toffee-nosed officer type. You seem to prefer them to your own kind. Very lah-de-dah in their smart uniforms and Oxford accents.' Vince's voice changed to one of pseudo-refinement.

Libby's lips turned down at the corners. 'You're jealous!' She had never outwardly accused him of that before and now, watching his face darken, wondered if it would have been wiser to hold her tongue.

'Jealous! Of him?' He shook his head. 'Why should I be jealous of a git with a bad leg who hobbles along like an old man? Eh, you tell me that, now? Jealous!' And he laughed, leaning his back against the iron railings that ringed the tiny park and folding his arms across his chest, looking smug. 'You do talk a lot of baloney at times, young Libby.'

Still, she had to force herself to conceal the amusement in her voice. 'I should take it as a compliment, I suppose. It's nice to have someone jealous over you, even though there isn't the slightest cause to be.'

He stared down at her, his brow low and threatening. He's been drinking, she thought, smelling the fumes on his breath. It's the drink that's talking, nothing else. Vince wasn't really like that, like Cook thought. It was the times they were living in, the worry that he might have to leave his father to run the business alone. A tiny voice deep inside her asked suddenly why she thought it necessary to keep making all these excuses for him, cataloguing his virtues to herself? Was it because she didn't really, deep down, love him . . . ?

His shoulders hunched aggressively and suddenly he was pulling her into his arms, there in the shadowy park with the gas lamp making pools of yellow light on the grass, where they were hidden from the gazes of the few passers-by. He slid his hands down her back to rest on her buttocks. Even for Vince, this was going a bit far! Libby stiffened as his hands pressed her body against his. 'Don't do that, Vince. I don't like it,' she managed to breathe, feeling stifled.

She could feel his hardness, frightening her. The pressure of his hands grew, pressing her more insistently against his body. His fingers seemed to burn through her clothing.

Like a dog with a bone, he wasn't ready to let the matter between them rest. 'Why's a snotty-nosed officer wanting to go for a walk with a couple of kids and their nursemaid, anyway? No, my girl, *you* were the attraction. Not that I blame him. You're always a sight for sore eyes, although I can't see him being deprived of what *he* wants. They do say those French tarts are easy game for anyone with pips on their shoulders and I imagine *he's* no saint.'

'Don't talk rubbish. Captain Randle's not like that.' She squirmed in his grasp, feeling the need for space to breathe, to collect her thoughts. Vince wasn't being fair, saying all those things . . .

'They're all alike, *bella mia*.' Vince lowered his head and kissed her. He wanted Libby more than he'd ever wanted a woman before. His hands fumbled at the front of the coat she had slung about her shoulders before leaving the house.

'No, Vince!' His kisses were beginning to make her feel quite weak although she tried to speak calmly. What a funny person I am! she thought. Here I am, saying no and feeling his kisses making my knees turn to water, making me feel all hot and excited! She thought of old Father Brady's reaction if she should ever confess such a sin to him. And it was a sin. She had no doubts about that. Only a married woman was supposed to feel that way about a man, and then probably not all married women . . .

She was a right stubborn little creature, Vince was thinking. Resisting him far more than any of his previous girlfriends, who had been only too eager to please the good-looking young man. 'Please, Libby . . .'

'You know I can't, so you're just wasting your time asking. It's not right, Vince.'

'Not right that I should want to show you how much I love you?' He leaned back, trailing one finger down her cheek, coming to rest against the collar of her coat. Libby shrugged it off irritably.

'I should have thought it was the most natural thing in the world to want to show you that,' he went on, ignoring her shrug.

She pulled away, avoiding his hands, thinking back to the things he had said about Captain Randle. 'Well, I don't believe Captain Randle's like that. He's so nice and polite and can't wait to get back to do his bit with his men.'

Immediately she said it she knew it was a mistake. Vince's face grew dark with anger. 'That's right, rub it in! Blaming me because I have to stay and help my father with the shop instead of rushing off to join up.'

'I'm sorry, love.' She touched his cheek with her hand. 'I didn't mean it to sound like that. I know you would go if only you could.' The glow from the gas lamp gave her eyes the colour of emeralds. Angry as he was, Vince stared hungrily into her face, pale in the lamp's glow, the soft copper hair taking its sheen.

She was magic. She always had been to him. And to think another man might be desiring her . . . !

Gently he said, 'You swallow everything anyone tells you, don't you, girl? But what I've got is principles. Conscientious objections are what they call them. I'm not ashamed of them and after all it isn't my real country so why should I bother my head about the mess they've got themselves into?'

For a moment she felt as though she had been struck by a heavy blow which took her breath away. 'How can you say this is not your own country?' she demanded at last. 'You were born here. Your family have been here for years. You don't know what you're saying . . .'

'Of course I know what I'm saying.' His look was full of scorn now. 'It wasn't easy, I'll admit, but one of the blokes put me wise to it and you'd be surprised how many men are trying it on.'

He smirked as though he had done something wonderful and Libby had to close her eyes to hide the shocked expression she knew must be in them. Not all men believed in the war. She knew that. Dad, when she was home, was always on about it, saying it was a scandal, that they should be put up against a wall and shot. Although they were generally despised by the ordinary man in the street, she supposed, to be fair, everyone was entitled to their own opinion.

'Aw, Libby.' Vince's voice took on the coaxing tone she knew so well. 'Don't let's squabble. I hate it when we squabble.' He peered down into her face, shadowed in the half light. 'Don't you fancy me any more? Is that it? You've gone off me?'

'Don't be daft. You know it's not that,' she answered tenderly. Then: 'I'd better get back,' she said, suddenly brisk. 'I've left Kathleen with the children. I'm not really supposed to be out.'

'Tomorrow night, then? We'll go somewhere nice and quiet and talk, eh?'

Regretfully Libby had to shake her head. Seeing the way his mouth tightened, she added coaxingly, 'I can't just slip out when I feel like it, Vince. You know how Mrs Ainslie feels about time off. Kathleen's quite good with the children but I can't leave her too long. The missis'd go off her nut if she found out what I was up to, slipping out like this to see you.'

'Bloody hell!' Vince kicked viciously at the park railings. 'Hasn't anybody ever told that old bitch that slavery went out of fashion a long time ago? 'Bout time they did. In fact, now's as good a time as any, I reckon . . .'

Libby made a wild grab for his arm as he started across the street but he was too quick for her. Giving her a violent shove so that she fell back against the railings, he ran over the road, pushed open the garden gate and took the half dozen steps down to the kitchen door with one leap.

Libby dragged herself to her feet. One hand touched her forehead and her fingers came away warm and sticky with blood. But her main concern was with Vince and the trouble he might cause rather than with her own injuries.

Flaming hell! she thought, crossing the road at a run, grabbing at her coat as it threatened to slip from her shoulders. The fat really would be in the fire if he got hold of Mrs Ainslie. Especially in the mood he was in. Or even the doctor. Although, of the two, she'd rather it was the doctor than his missis.

Vince thundered at the back door which was soon opened. Alice peered out. A startled expression crossed her face when she saw Vince, followed a moment later by Libby.

The training instilled in her over the years was forgotten. Alice drew back, allowing Vince to enter. She had the feeling he would have stepped over her had she not moved.

'Vince!' Libby's despairing cry followed his noisy entrance. Alice's hand flew to her mouth when she saw the thin trickle of blood running down Libby's cheek.

'Libby, you're bleeding!'

Libby shook her head, waving aside her comment. 'It's all right, Alice. Just help me get Vince out of the house before the missis hears him.'

Alice looked fearfully at the enraged man. She'd have as soon tried to get rid of a charging buffalo than Vince in this mood. Seeing she could expect little help from the frightened Alice, Libby grabbed Vince by the back of his jacket, pulling as hard as she could towards the open back door, ignoring his angry blustering.

'What you doin' in my kitchen?'

Cook's intimidating presence seemed to fill the room, a match any time for the exasperated Vince. She bent to pick up a rolling pin, brandishing it threateningly. 'Get out of here, you scoundrel, or you'll be getting this over your head. I don't want the likes o' you polluting my food. What Libby sees in you I can't imagine, a nice girl like that. She could have any boy she chooses and she goes and picks you.'

She shook her head, plump cheeks shaking, while, scarlet with humiliation, Libby grabbed Vince by the arm. Suddenly all the bluster evaporated and he allowed her to push him up the area steps to the garden.

Standing on the top step, Libby said in a furious voice, 'Well, I hope you're satisfied. Could be you've cost me my job.'

'Ah, Libby, my love,' he breathed, suddenly calm again. 'Don't let's quarrel.' He made to take her in his arms and Libby felt outrage. After the way he'd behaved he thought it was so easy to forgive and forget!

'Let's kiss and make up,' he said. 'Come on, don't be a tease . . .'

'You've got a bloody nerve, Vince Remede. Kiss and make up indeed! The devil will dance with St Peter first.'

Vince clicked his tongue reprovingly. 'Now that's a terrible thing to say. Most unladylike. Come here . . .' He bent his head, trailing a long wet kiss down her cheek, murmuring under his breath as he tasted the blood on her skin.

It was Libby who first became aware of the man standing in the shadows behind them. The aroma of a good cigar mingled with the scent of late summer roses and wet grass from the park.

Libby began to struggle, acutely conscious of the pale face glimpsed through the violet dusk. Then to her relief Vince stepped back. With a last mocking laugh he was gone, whistling jauntily, hands thrust into his pockets as he vanished into the night.

'Forgive me, I had no intention of eavesdropping.' James Randle came forward, out of the shadows, and Libby heard the slight catch of breath as he saw her bloodied cheek and temple. 'You're hurt! My God, what happened?'

'It's nothing. A slight fall . . .'

'But you're bleeding! Here, let me . . .'

Before she was aware of his intentions, he produced a folded snowy white handkerchief from his top pocket. Gently, he began to dab at the blood. It wasn't as bad as it looked, he found. A slight gash above the eyebrow. He'd arrived on the scene as the young man came up the area steps, pushed from behind by Libby, and had only witnessed the way Libby had struggled to get away from his embrace.

Uncertain how to act – after all, it was nothing to do with him, a quarrel between a servant girl and her sweetheart – still he had felt a strong desire to intervene, to lift the young man by the scruff of the neck and shake him until his teeth rattled. His training got the better of him. Better not to interfere. It took every ounce of willpower not to act. He wanted to shape her life, turn it in a different direction to the one it was indubitably going in. She deserved something better than this brute who walked away so casually, leaving her bleeding. Now, dabbing at her cheek while she stood, silent and still under his ministrations, anger stirred deep inside him. Resentment that he hadn't been able to do something about it. If this had been a girl of his own class . . .

Tight-lipped, he held the corner of the handkerchief to her mouth, indicating that she spit on it, and when she did, like a child following orders, he gave a last gentle rub to the trickle of blood at the corner of her mouth and tucked the handkerchief back in his pocket.

'There,' he said, 'all better. Although it might be a good idea to get Doctor Ainslie to have a look.'

'I'll be all right, sir. Thank you. I'd better get back to the children. Kathleen's been with them long enough.'

She lifted her heavy-lidded eyes slowly, to rest on his face in a way that caught at his heart. 'Goodnight – God bless,' she murmured in a whisper. And the impression she left behind was one of sweetness and warmth. It would stay with him for the rest of the night.

James stood for a long moment, his emotions still in a turmoil. He had longed to take her in his arms, to hold her safe and tight against the world.

Libby let herself in through the scullery door, reluctant to join the rest of the staff, dreading the questions she knew would flow. In this scullery Kathleen spent long hours of her working day, terrified of the black beetles and other things that made scurrying sounds every time anyone entered. Cook would poohpooh her fears. 'Worse things in life than that for you to worry about, my girl. Things that wear trousers and would like nothing better than to get a young inexperienced girl like you, fresh from the country, into a dark corner and . . .'

Cook would pause at that moment, infuriatingly, and watch the Irish girl with narrowed eyes.

'And what, Cook?' All pretended innocence, Kathleen would wait for Cook's next words.

'Never you mind. You'll find out soon enough. Just watch out, that's all I say.'

Now Cook looked over at Libby, frowning. 'Whatever got into that boy to act like that?' she demanded. 'I don't like it, Libby. That bloke's not right in the 'ead. I don't know what your mam and dad would say if they knew you was walking out with a boy like that.'

'Please, let's forget it,' Libby pleaded. Again, within herself, she was trying to excuse Vince's behaviour. 'I'm sure he's already sorry for what he did, Cook. He's very quick tempered and lets himself get carried away at times.'

'I'd like to see 'im carried away,' muttered Mrs Gibson in a low voice. 'Aye, give 'em an 'and I would, too.' She shook her head. 'Come to no good, 'e won't. You mark my words. You don't know what you're letting yourself in for, Libby. He's brash, loud, vulgar, the lot. *I* wouldn't 'ave 'im if 'e was being given away with a pound of prawns.'

You aren't being asked to have him, thought Libby wryly. 'They do say people improve with age, Cook. Vince'll quieten down. He's still very young.'

Cook gave her a disgusted look. 'They say, too, that love is blind, lass. It'd have to be bloody deaf, dumb and decrepit where you and that bloke is concerned.'

* * *

When Dr Ainslie began talking it was difficult to stop him. They were seated at the dinner table, the decanter between them. The doctor enjoyed his port. A couple of glasses in the evening settled his stomach, assuring him of a good night.

James had refused a second glass. His fingers toyed with the slices of apple on his plate. Mrs Ainslie had left them a while ago and still the good doctor was in full flow. James found his thoughts wandering, unable in spite of himself to concentrate on his host's monologue.

'Aye, I must say that poster is very effective; that pointing finger and scowling frown. If I were a younger man it'd get me going any old time.'

He glanced across the table at his companion. James had been quiet for so long that finally, mistaking his silence for weariness, Dr Ainslie suggested, kindly, 'But I'm keeping you up, my boy. It's not often I get a chance to talk about subjects that interest me, without my wife interrupting. I'll be accused next of interfering in your convalescence and she'll be complaining to Basil about it in her next letter.' He smiled, taking any hint of censure out of the words.

James felt uncomfortable, an imposter with these good folk who went to so much trouble to see to his well-being. He hardly knew Basil and what he did know he didn't particularly like. Basil's penchant for young girls, for example; girls he could take advantage of. Barmaids were his favourite prey. But the man's parents had been so eager for him to stay with them that it would have seemed churlish to refuse. The thought of Basil and his barmaids triggered off a reaction that he was unable to ignore. Excusing himself he went up to his room. There he picked up his top coat and cap and ignoring the bloody stick without which ordinarily he could not walk more than a few paces, he left the house quietly.

His trouble was not that he was tired. Far from it. Those moments with Libby, dabbing the blood from her forehead, watching her creep down the area steps while he himself entered by the front door, stayed in his mind like one of those picture shows. Only instead of black and white this was coloured. The richness of her hair, the entrancing freckles that dusted the top of her cheeks and nose. The vision refused to go away, to leave him in peace. 'Damn it, man!' he told himself angrily. She's only a servant. Your mother's employed – and dismissed – dozens like her in your lifetime. You've seen them come and go. What's so special about this one?'

He didn't know the answer. He, who could brave the barbed-wire entanglements with only a revolver in his hand, urging on the swearing, staggering men whom he led, was disconcerted by a mere slip of a girl.

A drink, that's what he needed. And not just some of that port, excellent as it was, that Dr Ainslie dished out. In fact, quite a few drinks. To sum up, he needed to get drunk. Yes, good and drunk. That was the answer . . .

The promenade, as usual at this time of the night, was deserted. In the distance a lighted tram clanged its bell noisily, windows misted so that the throng of people inside seemed like some exotic type of fish in an aquarium. Lights blazed ahead of him, spelling out 'Palace Bar and Hotel'.

That would do. The atmosphere as he walked in was warm and friendly. Crowded as it was, nevertheless he managed to push his way through to the bar. People made way for him, the men in uniform noticing his limp, grimacing with sympathy.

He didn't want sympathy. He wanted – what did he want? Damned if he knew. Josie! The warm sensuality of Josie St Clare. If Josie were here, now, he wouldn't need to get drunk. Not on intoxicating liquor, anyway. Being with her meant a different kind of drunkenness. And it didn't leave a man with a hangover . . .

He grinned crookedly and the blonde barmaid left the florid-faced man with whom she'd been flirting and came to the end of the bar where James stood. Her smile broadened as she approached the young captain, so distinguished in his smart uniform.

'A double whisky, please.' His voice was deep, pleasant, the sort of voice that warmed the cockles of your heart, as she confided later to her friend, as well as sending shivers down your spine.

James, unaware of the flutters he was causing in the breast of the barmaid, turned, glass in hand, to survey the room. His grey eyes skimmed over the crowded scene, the haze of cigarette smoke moving sluggishly each time someone entered, the door opening and closing quickly, shutting out the night. He noted, lazily, the small groups of people; soldiers in

uniform, the thick khaki and tightly wound puttees
looking out of place amidst the once-ornate gold and
crimson decor of the old building. The girls were, like
the barmaid, over-dressed, and making the most of
their evening out: a port and lemon and a quick kiss
with its attendant groping in one of the dark shelters
along the promenade before returning to a shabby
house with a harsh-voiced mother or maybe a larger
house with an even harsher-voiced mistress. A Saturday night dream about which they fantasised all
week.

Loud laughter caught his attention and he turned
slightly to watch a group of people sitting in one
corner of the room. His attention sharpened when he
recognised one of them as being the young man who
had served him ice cream that morning on the beach;
who earlier had stood arguing with Libby in the
garden. He frowned as the dark, good-looking boy
pulled one of the girls on to his knee and gave her a
loud, smacking kiss, one hand openly fondling her
breast as he did so.

James turned away, feeling the display distasteful.
How could a girl as fastidious and unsophisticated as
Libby be attracted to a man such as this?

'Bit too much to drink, I'd say, sir.' The barmaid
was back, leaning over the counter. James turned, his
gaze inadvertently dropping to the generous display
of bosom revealed by the inviting pose. He smiled
faintly. 'I think you may be right.'

'Some can take their booze, some can't,' she went
on, an authority on the matter as well she might be.
'He's one who can't. Gets fair nasty if anyone dares

to argue with him. Come in earlier in a filthy mood but after a few drinks he perked up.'

His mouth tight and grim, James answered, 'I can see that.' His curiosity made him ask, 'Why isn't he in uniform?'

A guarded look came into the barmaid's eye. Having a bit of gossip with someone was one thing. Getting involved in someone else's life was another. 'Dunno, sir.'

'Sally!' an impatient voice called from the far end of the bar and the girl excused herself. James turned once more, elbows behind him, resting on the bar top. His eyes sought out the young man in the shiny blue suit, standing out amongst the drab khaki of the other patrons.

The girl was still on his knee, any objections she might have stifled beneath the greedy lips of the boy. Indeed, James observed, she seemed to be enjoying it.

Even as he watched, the youth stood, pulling the girl up with him, one arm possessively about her waist. He said something to the group that was with him. The men grinned, a couple making obscene remarks, at which the girl tossed her head, answering them back in kind. Together they pushed their way through the crowd of people and out through the door.

James stayed half an hour or so longer. All desire to get drunk had vanished. Endeavouring to respond politely to the barmaid's attempts at friendship, he at last bade her goodnight.

It was raining again when he stepped into the darkness of the street. Huddled in his greatcoat, he began to walk back to the Ainslies' house. Rain spattered, blinding him, making walking difficult. James cursed, wishing he'd brought his walking stick. He hated it, though: hated to think he still had to depend on it and yet knowing full well that without it his progress would be considerably hampered.

His lips twisted with irony. Vanity! That's all it was, really. Sheer vanity – Who in this Godforsaken Northern town did he want to impress?

To his vast relief there was the sound of carriage wheels and turning he waved to the vehicle to stop and climbed in. Hansom cabs still plied along the front in the summer months, but it was exceedingly fortunate to find one so late in the year.

The shops fronting the promenade were a blur of heavy rain, the street lamps misty circles of light appearing and disappearing in the darkness. The few pedestrians hurried, the strong wind threatening to hurl them from their feet.

And James Randle sat in his damp greatcoat, thinking about a girl with green eyes and an air of courage, flying in the face of reason by refusing to see the dark young man for what he was. He felt an illogical desire to warn her, then cursed himself for his solicitude.

He grimaced, telling himself he must not get involved with this Libby Gray. No matter how sorry he felt for her . . .

Chapter Five

The weather continued mild, although wet. The seaside landladies didn't want it to change, for even with a war raging on the other side of the Channel, people still wanted to get away for a break.

The few hotels along the front that had not been requisitioned by the army were full of officers on home leave from the front in their smart khaki uniforms and shining Sam Browne belts. Usually they were accompanied by young ladies.

No hotel manager would have dreamed of querying the relationship between the couples. The lads were fighting a hard war. Who would dare to frown on the way they chose to spend their few days of precious freedom?

Entertainment was badly needed. The small seaside town did not boast a theatre; you went to Liverpool or Manchester if you wanted to see a show. At first this presented quite a problem, especially with hundreds of men sent to convalesce, roaming the streets and the promenade, all seeking diversion.

So when James was approached, with other officers, to help organise local talent, he agreed, albeit grudgingly.

'What on earth do I know about concerts?' he asked with a perplexed grimace. 'I've seen enough of them, true, but as for putting one on . . .'

'We all have to take turns on the entertainment committee and it seems it is your turn now, old boy.' The major who had been elected as chairman gazed at the young man and smiled. 'You won't be asked to do anything, just help with the arrangements. I'm sure with a bit of effort, amongst all those young ladies you know, you will be able to come up with something.' He reached across his desk and straightened a pile of typed papers. 'Got to keep the lads' morale up, y'know. Important that they should be fresh to face the trenches when they leave here.'

James felt sick, just thinking about such an event.

'And,' went on Major Thompson, 'I'm relying on you, James. I won't take no for an answer, either.' His smile widened. 'Think of it as an honour.'

James thought of it as a bloody nuisance. Might as well have asked him to officiate at the local orphans' tea-party as drop something like this in his lap. He couldn't imagine Dr Ainslie or his good lady possessing any hidden talents, either.

Then the memory of a clear young voice singing to the children came to mind and his eyes gleamed. Libby! Of course! Libby would be the perfect choice.

That evening, gazing down from his bedroom window at the moon-washed garden, he saw the slim shape wandering slowly along the narrow path that led from the kitchen door to the low stone wall at the bottom of the garden. This looked out on to a piece of waste land where wild flowers had taken over, tall golden rod and blue michaelmas daisies.

The glow from the kitchen window momentarily shone on her hair, highlighting the rich copper sheen, sending his heart thudding with its remembered glory.

Quickly he made his way along the landing and down the wide staircase. He moved with a purpose, an agility he hadn't known since that bloody shell burst only yards away from him and the men he was leading.

If Kathleen and Cook were surprised to see their guest hurrying through the kitchen to the back door they managed to hide it. James caught Mrs Gibson's eye and nodded politely, hearing Kathleen's nervous giggle which she instantly tried to subdue by clapping a hand over her mouth. Feeling the necessity to say something, James smiled and murmured, 'The evening seems so mild I thought I'd take the air in the garden.'

Cook nodded. 'Yes, sir. You do that. As you say, it's a nice evening. As long as that rain don't start again. Might as well make the most of 'em, for we might not get many more.'

'My sentiments entirely.' He escaped their guarded looks by stepping out into the garden.

Suddenly, he was awkward again. In his haste to be near her, to be close to the tranquillity that she seemed to exude, he stumbled and had to steady himself with one hand on the gnarled trunk of the lilac bush growing to one side of the pathway. Even then, so engrossed in her own thoughts was she, she didn't hear him.

'Libby, I'm going to ask you a favour and I want you to think carefully before you say no.'

His words started her out of her reverie. The small garden had been so quiet, the perfect place in which to relax after a hectic hour with the children at bedtime. James had approached her unheard, his footsteps deadened by the clusters of fallen leaves on the path.

She turned from the wall where she had been leaning. In the glow of the light from the kitchen window she could see his face, the high cheekbones casting shadows beneath.

Intrigued by his words, she leaned her back against the low wall, pulling the light shawl she wore more closely about her shoulders.

'Sounds mysterious, sir! What do you want to ask me, then?'

'I've been roped in on the entertainments committee of the convalescent home. They are putting on a concert for their patients and we're looking for people to entertain. You know, jokes and conjuring tricks and dancers and people who can sing. It crossed my mind that you might like to help.'

'You mean, showing them to their seats and suchlike?'

James laughed. 'No, Libby, I don't mean showing them to their seats and suchlike. I meant to sing for them. One of those old sweet songs you sing so beautifully to the children at night.'

Libby was appalled. 'Me! Sing on the stage in front

of a lot of soldiers! Aw, Captain Randle, I'd die of embarrassment. Besides, you said you wanted people who can *sing*. I'm not – I can't sing that good.'

'Yes, you can, Libby. You have a lovely voice. You would delight the men. You're quite good enough, believe me. And why, for heaven's sake, should you be embarrassed?'

'Oh, but I would! You're pulling my leg. That's not fair. Just because you've heard me sing to the children . . .'

Without thinking he reached out, was grasping her arms, giving her a gentle shake. 'Libby, Libby! Why do you have such a poor opinion of yourself? Believe me, I have no intention of making fun of you. I'm sorry you see it that way. This is the first time they have asked me to help organise things and I did count on you not to let me down.'

He bent his head, eyes on a level with hers. His hands still holding her arms, he gave her another shake. 'You will, won't you?'

She laughed to hide her nervousness and for the same reason began to talk quickly. 'They would boo me off the stage, sir. There's a deal of difference between singing to children to help them sleep and singing to grown-up men.' As she talked, she was looking at him, noticing the length of his lashes, the way lines formed at the corners of his eyes when he smiled. Talking too much, she was, for her heart pounded at his touch and she made a grab at the slipping shawl, hoping he wouldn't see how her hand shook.

'Grown-up men need comforting, too,' he said,

moving so close she felt his breath on her cheek. 'Those poor souls have little to look forward to. Surely you wouldn't deny them the words of one of your songs to warm them on their way?'

He was making it hard to refuse. But then, she thought, he's most likely been refused very little in his life. Oh, why did he have to put her in such an insidious position? Surely he must be teasing . . . But looking into his eyes she saw he wasn't.

'Well, if you're sure,' she was weakening, as women always would where this man was concerned. 'If you really want me. But what would Mrs Ainslie say? And what if they don't like me?'

'And pigs might fly!' He used one of her own expressions, making her laugh. 'And don't you worry about Mrs Ainslie. I'll deal with that lady.'

Although it wasn't Libby's afternoon off, somehow he got around the older woman and miraculously she agreed.

'You didn't tell her what for, did you?' asked Libby, startled.

'I did not, although I was tempted. I'm very proud of my little songbird.' He thought the flush that flooded her cheeks enchanting.

'You mustn't say that, sir. I'm not your – anything.'

He regarded her steadily and in confusion she lowered her eyes, looking away. 'No, you're not, are you? Pity!' Suddenly brisk, business-like, he added, 'We have to be at the home by two-thirty tomorrow afternoon. Where do you suggest we meet?'

Grateful that he was thoughtful enough not to suggest they met in the hall or anywhere else under Mrs Ainslie's curious gaze, Libby said, with a query in her voice, 'On the corner of St Anne's Place?'

'Right. About one-thirty, then. I'll hire a cab.'

Later, Libby agonised over what she should wear. Not, she thought ruefully, staring in the wardrobe, that she had all that choice; her blue outfit with the white lace collar and cuffs, very nursery-like, very suitable in Mrs Ainslie's eyes; a couple of lighter frocks she'd help Mam make in the summer when she'd been allowed home for a whole week; her grey cloth coat and hat; and a summer dress of white muslin with lace insertions. It was longer than her other frocks, almost touching the floor, and she'd bought it at a sale in Ridley High Street with the hope that one day Vince would ask her to go to a dance with him. Held in the Pavilion on the pier most Saturday nights, these dances were very popular. But to her hidden disappointment, Vince never had. Now, holding the dress at arm's length, she thought this would be the ideal garment. As long as no one saw her going out. She hadn't even told Alice about this, wanting somehow to keep it a secret.

She arranged her hair in a softer than usual chignon, low on the nape of her neck, with thin braids woven through the heavy waves, holding them in place.

She heard the grandfather clock strike a quarter past one and she slipped her arms into the sleeves of the grey coat. Fortunately it buttoned from throat to hem so most of her dress was hidden. Outside on the landing she could hear the children arguing with Kathleen about their rest period. Otherwise the house was silent. Feeling like a conspirator in one of those Pearl White serials at the pictures, she crept out to meet James Randle. The hansom cab was waiting. The driver sat perched high up behind the cab, with the reins running over the roof of it. He could speak to his passengers through a little trapdoor above their heads. It was the first time Libby had ever ridden in one and it added to the whole unreal feeling of the afternoon. Climbing into the cab, she found, was not easy, hampered as she was by the long skirt. But James' hand was there to help her in and soon they were leaving the small town behind. Here the country was beautiful, with a serenity she was sure would never change, despite what happened in the world outside. They turned into the drive of the home. Once a stately mansion, now given over to the forces for the duration, its large grounds were dotted with the wheelchairs of the wounded.

The white-clad figures of nurses and VAD women glided across smooth lawns. The hall into which they were escorted by a matron whose craggy face belied the twinkle in her eye was already packed with men; seated on benches in rows, a cloud of cigarette smoke already rising to the ceiling, they turned as one to stare at Libby as she and James followed the matron down the aisle. Whistles were heard and soft remarks, made out of the side of the mouth, followed by laughter.

The two front rows consisted of chairs with arms and padded seats, as befitted the officers. Libby saw

James sink into one near the centre of the stage as she was led by Matron to a cluttered dressing room in a small curtained alcove.

Hanging her coat on the hook behind the door, Libby turned to meet Matron's curious eyes. 'I – I didn't know what to wear.' She looked down at her dress. 'Will this be all right?'

'My dear, perfect, just perfect.' Pretty girl, thought Matron. In that white dress, so pure and virginal looking, the men will adore her.

Standing in the wings, watching the opening numbers, Libby wondered if she would ever be able to actually step out there and sing. Her throat had closed up, her hands were damp and shaking and she was sure she was going to make an utter fool of herself. Nevertheless, when the pianist played the opening bars of her first song, catching James' eye across the footlights she stepped out and began to sing. The pianist had struck the perfect key and with the briefest of consultations had seemed to know exactly what she required.

Her voice was pure and sweet, rising and falling as naturally as a summer breeze across a buttercup-filled meadow. Every note was true, feeling in every word. The song finished, the audience clapped, stamped their feet and called for more. Matron appeared and held up one hand. 'Now, then, let's be fair,' she cajoled. 'There's plenty more waiting to entertain you. But if you're patient, I promise Miss Gray will come back later.'

Libby smiled and gave a shy curtsey, left the stage and the concert proceeded. Towards the end she

sang again and this time did an encore, singing 'Keep
the home fires burning' and 'There's a long, long trail
awinding' and the men joined in, rising to their feet
and singing along with her: 'Turn the dark clouds
inside out, till the boys come home . . .'

James was so proud, lost in the spectacle of Libby,
her arms outstretched as if to embrace the blue-clad
men with their bandages, crutches and wheelchairs.
The curtains swished closed. Jubilantly James left his
seat and made his way backstage.

'You were marvellous! I'm so proud of you! You
held those men in the palm of your hand, a real pro.'

'Do you think so? Really?' Libby sat at the dressing-
table mirror, wiping the bright red lipstick from her
mouth. She caught James' eye in the glass, hoping
against hope that he wasn't teasing her, that he
really meant what he said. And yet, she knew it must
be true. Hadn't she *felt* the wave of emotion flowing
towards her from the convalescing soldiers, warm
and sympathetic and hungry for love?

'I tell you, you were bloody marvellous.' James
glanced round at the matron, standing there smiling.
'Miss Gray seems to doubt my word, Matron.'

Matron's smile widened. 'As you say, Captain
Randle, the voice of an angel.' She left the room and,
alone with James, Libby found herself becoming
tongue-tied. She concentrated on wiping the last
traces of the lipstick away and James said teasingly,
'We'll have you singing at His Majesty's Theatre in
London before you know where you are. I know someone who appears on the stage there, Josie St Clare.'
He wondered as he spoke of Josie what she would

make of this girl if they should ever meet. An event not even worth considering, he thought wryly. The lives of these girls were worlds apart, hardly likely to touch . . .

'I'm ready, Captain Randle.' Libby's voice broke in on his thoughts and he offered her his arm, smiling.

Chapter Six

Christmas was almost upon them and still the war
dragged on. Cook took to reading the war news aloud
to anyone who would listen, remarking on its seri-
ousness. Everyone agreed it would be a long and
costly war and when, early in the new year, conscription was introduced she made a point of reading
about it aloud to Libby and watching for her
reaction.

'Your young man'll 'ave to go now, 'is father's
business or not,' she remarked, with a certain
smugness. Libby chose not to reply but went on with
darning one of Amy's stockings.

On her walks out with the children, Libby saw boys
in cloth caps and rough jackets clambering over
rubbish dumps. Unearthing rusty tin baths, buckets
with no bottoms, broken mangles, these items were
piled onto small carts and taken away for the war
effort. Nothing was wasted. There were rumours
that the iron railings of the small park in St Anne's
Place were to go, which caused a few frowns from
the more elderly residents who enjoyed the park's
solitude on sunny days to read their copies of *The
Times*. If the railings went, any rag-tag-and-bobtail

intruder would be able to stroll in, disrupting their peace.

Bertie eyed the gangs of boys with curiosity and demanded, 'What are they doing, Libby?'

Libby explained as best she could about the need for materials for the munitions factories and Bertie, his voice filled with envy, said, 'Lucky things! I wish I could help them.'

'I somehow can't see your mama agreeing to that, young man,' she smiled.

Amy sniffed, her small nose wrinkling disdainfully. '*I* wouldn't want to go rummaging in *there*,' glancing at the pile of discarded household items. 'Would you, Libby?'

Libby bent and tucked the bright red woollen scarf about the child's neck, for today the wind was chill. 'No, love, I don't think I would. But then, those boys are helping in their own way and that's something we must all do these days.'

Christmas arrived and Mrs Ainslie outdid herself in generosity and allowed Libby more than the usual one day off. It would be lovely to be home again as it had been three months since she had seen her parents.

And as soon as she arrived, she saw the change in her brother and Agnes.

In that part of Lancashire upon leaving school, the girls usually went into the mills and the boys followed their fathers and grandfathers to the pits; there was no other way to make a living. It was expected of them and should any boy or girl demur they would be regarded as 'right queer sorts'.

Joseph had been one of those who objected to his life being shaped in that way. Joseph wanted to be a musician, a confession that earned him many an old-fashioned glance from the neighbours.

Only his mother and Libby understood and sympathised with him. When he first told his parents one evening what his plans were, that he wanted to attend the music academy in town, Dad was quietly reading the paper. At his son's words, he looked up and said, as though he hadn't heard correctly, 'The music academy? What on earth for?'

Joseph sighed. 'To learn how to play a musical instrument, Dad. The piano, if I have a choice.'

'And how much is that goin' to cost, lad?'

'Three and sixpence.'

'A week?'

Joseph nodded.

'Aye, well, it's a grand idea but not for the likes of us. Three shillings and sixpence a week! Your mother could feed the lot of us on that amount.' William Gray shook his head. 'Sorry, lad, but it's out of the question.'

In the strained silence that followed, Joseph shuffled his feet, looking mutinous, and William caught his wife's eye. Unable to face the heartbreak in them he rustled the pages of his newspaper and tried to concentrate on the report from Ridley Borough Police Court about a man who had travelled on the railway from Manchester to Ridley without a ticket. He had been fined ten shillings for a ticket that cost one shilling and threepence halfpenny.

'Silly bugger!' said William to himself.

If he thought that was the end of it he didn't know his wife very well, for Ellen went out and got a cleaning job and managed, after a lot of coaxing, to get William's permission for Joseph to attend his academy.

Daniel Naylor's Music Academy in Standishgate was the best in Ridley; in fact, the only one of its kind in Ridley, for this was not a town that went in for that kind of thing. Wasn't it a little bit sissy to want to play the piano?

Mr Naylor taught violin, piano and the concertina. Joseph chose the piano and although Mam would have much preferred him to play the violin, in her opinion a very high-class instrument, she kept this to herself, glad that one child of hers had been able to fulfil his dream.

She doubted, however, that he would ever be able to make a living out of playing the piano. The only opening for such a thing that she knew was at the cinema in town, popularly known as the 'bughouse', where old Mrs Logan accompanied the picture show on an ancient upright and had been doing it since the place opened.

But stranger things had happened and she had to admit with motherly pride that Joseph was good. He was fiercely ambitious, with one aim in mind, and that was to make a name for himself in popular music.

Working with his father in the pits during the day, each evening after a good scrubbing with a liberal amount of Mam's green soap in the big tin bath by the fire, filled with kettles of boiling water from the range, Joseph would emerge, red-cheeked and shining, every last trace of coal dust removed from his skin. Clad in his one good suit, he would then set off for his music lesson.

Of necessity these had to be conducted in the evening, for all the students worked during the day and Mr Naylor was astute enough to adjust to the circumstances. Besides, hadn't he once yearned, as these lads did, for another life far removed from the drab existence of the pit head and the everlasting coal dust that turned healthy young lads into old men wheezing their lungs out in no time at all?

If Daniel Naylor could make even one per cent of these lads' dreams come true, then it was worth the long hours spent coaxing them.

And, he had to admit, that Gray lad had a talent all right . . .

On her previous visit home, Libby could see how Agnes had matured, looking, for her eighteen years, a fine full-figured young woman. Now that she was bringing in a bit of money she seemed to think she could come and go as she liked, getting home at all hours on a Saturday night and then complaining on a Sunday morning that she was too tired to get out of bed to attend Mass.

Mam had been shocked speechless. Later there had been raised voices – from Mam, who never shouted, and Agnes, answering her back. Even swear words. Dad would hold his peace and continue shaving in front of the spotted mirror that hung by a string over the sink.

Joseph would fidget and look as though he was

anywhere but where he was right now. Although he agreed with Agnes' thinking about attending Mass, he detested the way she was going about it. When *he* left home, when he went to join the other lads who were fighting this war, he would probably stop attending, too. Church was really for women and kids, not young, healthy men like himself. He only tolerated it for the music.

He directed his thoughts to the more pleasant subject of the harmony group, as it was billed on the notice boards. Supervised by the church, with Father Brady's formidable black-clothed presence standing guard, watching the young people's conduct, it was held once a month in the old hall adjoining the church.

Joseph would proudly take his seat at the ancient piano and, trying to ignore the flat notes, his fingers would run over the yellowing keys, joined by Libby, when she was home.

Egged on by the crowd, Libby would sing the songs that were enjoyed by that generation: 'After The Ball' and 'Goodbye, Dolly Grey.' Although that was really a Boer War song it was still popular with the words, 'I can no longer stay', relevant to the present situation.

Each week, it seemed, another young man was taking the King's shilling, another young man swaggering in his rough khaki, every girl's eye on him. Joseph envied their air of having done something wonderful as they arrived with a girl on their arm for a last visit before being posted.

An appreciative audience clapped and shouted for

more and Joseph would catch his sister's eye and go into one of those jazzy numbers that were now in fashion . . .

About his head, the row went on unabated, culminating in Mam saying it just wasn't worth it, upsetting herself like this. Father Brady would just have to have a talk with our Agnes. The brassy eighteen year old, with her bold eyes and hair frizzed with the aid of hot curling tongs, repeated word for word to the scandalised priest what she had said to her mother. None of her friends went to church any more and she didn't see why she should. She was no longer a child. It was the very thing they were fighting for, wasn't it? Freedom?

'Not interested in Mass,' she said, tossing that frizzed head. 'Got more important things to do.'

'What could be more important than visiting our Dear Lord once a week in His own house? Agnes Gray, do you begrudge our Lord and Saviour even that one small courtesy?' The old priest's face flushed with indignation.

Agnes jerked a sharp chin, careful not to meet Father Brady's eye. Children in that part of town had been brought up in awe of the priest and for all her outward defiance, inwardly Agnes was quaking.

As Libby sang that Christmas, Father Brady stood with his hands touching the small polished wood and silver crucifix hanging on a black cord about his neck and smiled benignly on the assembly. Joseph ran from one tune to another, without a break, never seeming to need any music, it was all there in his head.

Although Mr Naylor insisted that his pupils learned to read music, saying you could never really call yourself a musician unless you could, the black and white printed sheets turned out every week in a never-ending stream were too expensive for most of the students to buy. Once away from the music academy Joseph never bothered his head with them.

A fact noticed by the girl who had just entered and who stood by the doorway, watching and listening. Gwenda Naylor was a pretty girl with blue eyes and coal-black hair. Dressed in a delicately woven silk frock of a pale raspberry shade with a wide satin sash of pale lilac, she was a striking young girl and noticed immediately by most of the young men in the room.

She smiled at the ones she knew and nodded to Father Brady. Three times in a row she turned down offers of a partner. She didn't fancy any of them and, besides, she wanted to listen to the young man enticing such a delightfully smooth rhythm from the old piano. For the moment she was content just to stand and listen.

When he came to the end of the medley of songs, Gwenda walked over and introduced herself. 'Gwenda Naylor,' she said. 'I've seen you at my father's academy, haven't I?'

'I attend there, yes.'

She gazed at him speculatively, with not a hint of shyness. Joseph was chuffed. Quickly he rose to his feet, hand extended. 'My name's Joseph Gray.'

She smiled. 'How do you do?'

Slightly flustered, as girls weren't usually so forward, introducing themselves like that, but usually waited for the man to make the first move, Joseph took the slim white hand she held out, feeling it cool and soft to his touch. He knew he was blushing and cursed himself for the show of inmaturity. Realising her hand was still in his, he released it as though it had suddenly burned him and his flush deepened.

The girl nodded towards the piano. 'Do you enjoy playing? You are very good.'

'Your father is very good, you mean. He must have the patience of a saint trying to teach blockheads like me all those lovely pieces. Do you know Chopin? He was a Polish composer and pianist. He wrote some lovely things. I'm learning the Polonaise but your father seems to think I'm not quite ready for that yet. A bit advanced for me.'

He stopped, suddenly aware that while he had been babbling on, she had been standing with a smile on her face, listening raptly. Was it raptly or was she just being polite? 'I'm sorry,' he said. 'Talking too much.'

'Not at all. I like listening to you, Joseph Gray. But aren't you going to play anything else?'

A warm glow had gone through him at her use of his Christian name. Now, eager to please her, he sat down again on the piano stool and looked at her expectantly. 'What would you like to hear?'

'I don't know. Anything.' Her brow wrinkled thoughtfully. 'How about a song from that new show that's such a hit in London? *Chu Chin Chow*? Do you know anything from that?'

Joseph racked his brains. Did he? He couldn't let her down now, not when she'd asked so sweetly. She began to hum 'The Cobbler's Song' and God be praised he knew it. It was no good for dancing and so the group of young people, sailors and khaki-clad soldiers with a sprinkling of men still in civvies, most of them with their arm round a girl, swarmed forward to where the piano stood. Surrounding it, they swayed to the music, enjoying the impromptu concert. This was the part of the evening when Libby usually sang. But he could see where she was busy chatting to a group of her old school friends and so didn't disturb her.

Later, boldly, he beckoned to a pal of his, also from the music academy, to take over. The young man obliged, glanced at Gwenda, then catching Joseph's eye, gave him a wink.

'Would you like to dance?' Joseph's Adam's apple bobbed nervously. 'If you don't want to we can just sit and I'll get you a lemonade.'

She pursed her lips then placed one finger flat across his own. 'I'll dance with you, Joseph. I'll be glad to.' Her smile returned. 'I just thought you were never going to ask.'

The arm that he slipped about her waist as he led her to the floor was perhaps fractionally tighter than necessary and his feet seemed to be able to execute steps he didn't know he knew. Her words had given him confidence and he found himself smiling broadly, listening to her hum the tune as they danced a slow fox-trot. 'I love these,' she said dreamily. 'They're so sensuous, so – so sexy.'

Joseph gasped and paled a little. Words, one word, anyway, he had never heard before spoken out loud, had just passed the lips of this young, angelic-looking girl. He wondered how old she was. He imagined her to be about his own age, touching seventeen.

Surprising him, she said, 'You think I'm awful?'

'No, I don't. Really.'

'I wanted to shock you. You look such an upright character, I wondered if you'd faint or scream when I said what I said. Some people do.'

'Not men?'

'Even men, sometimes.' Leaning her head back she smiled at him. They were both much the same height. She reminded herself she must wear flat shoes when she came in future or otherwise he might be embarrassed if she were taller than him.

After a while, he said, 'Why did you want to shock me?'

'Don't laugh if I tell you, but it's just that I fancy you. Something chronic, I think the expression is.'

He pushed her a little away from him and frowned into her eyes. 'I'm supposed to say that. You've got it all wrong.'

Gwenda found this amusing and just a little touching. 'All right, it's your turn to say something nice to me, now.'

When he didn't, again she smiled. 'Don't tell me you can't think of anything? Even if it's only "I think your dancing's the cat's pyjamas"?'

He licked his lips and cleared his throat and was about to say something when his mate at the piano decided he'd played enough and closed the lid on the keyboard with a bang. Joseph turned and glared at him. The dancers seemed in need of a break and refreshments anyway and as one made their way to the long table over which Father Brady presided, assisted by his elderly housekeeper.

They dished out glasses of home-made lemonade, or cups of tea for those who preferred it. 'I'll have a lemonade now,' Gwenda said. Seated together on two hardwood chairs pushed back against the wall, they sipped the sweet-tasting lemonade; a cloudy white liquid in which tiny bits of lemon floated. 'Are you usually so quiet?' she asked after the silence seemed to stretch into eternity. 'You weren't quiet just now when you were telling me about Chopin.'

He shook his head, grinning. 'I don't think my parents or sisters would agree I was quiet if you asked them.'

Suddenly, without warning, he took the glass from her hand, placing it very carefully under his chair. Then, leaning forward feeling very daring, he kissed her on the cheek. He still could not believe this attractive creature would single him out to spend the evening with, or be as attracted to him as he was to her.

As they had danced, he'd become almost intoxicated by the smell and the feel of her. The kiss was a foregone conclusion, although she said they should have waited until they were outside in the dark for whatever would people say, kissing like that in full view of everyone? Especially Father Brady!

He laughed and looked pointedly up to the bunch of mistletoe that hung above where they sat. She punched him on the arm, laughing with him, although she said, pretending to be outraged, 'You cheat, you!'

He didn't mind that Libby was looking his way or that the girls she was with were talking with their eyes fixed on him. He didn't mind if the whole room talked about him. It had been *he* who kissed *her*, in front of all his mates, and not someone else. Already, he could see the smirks on some of their faces. He vowed silently that if anyone, anyone at *all*, made a suggestive remark he would take great delight in knocking his block off.

His heart was pounding heavily and he wondered how she could still look so calm and self-possessed.

'Well, after that, I suppose you'd better walk me home,' she said. 'It's a bit out of your way but I'm sure you won't mind. And it's a nice night.'

'I'll just tell my sister,' he said, rising to his feet. 'She can walk home with her friends. Most of them live down our street.'

'Your sister!' Gwenda turned her head to gaze at Libby. 'That girl with all the lovely red hair? You should have introduced us.'

'I suppose I should,' he answered feebly. 'Perhaps another time.' The truth was he didn't want to tempt fate by putting into words the fact that he was actually going to walk this girl home. Libby wouldn't say anything, he knew, but the girls she was with would!

By morning it would have got all over town and he'd have to suffer the teasing remarks of the men at work and probably his father, too. Walking a girl home was tantamount to announcing to the world that they were courting.

They left the hall and were standing outside in the small area with its railings and notice board announcing the times of Sunday Mass. It was cold but bright, a new moon slipping between the chimney pots of Ridley, the stars bright and clear in the velvet black sky. Soot, grime and coal dust were everywhere, shrouding every wall, every tiny back yard with its moss-grown flagstones covering the earth.

'Somehow, some way, I'm going to escape from all this,' said Gwenda, slipping her hand through his arm and hurrying along beside him.

'Oh, yes?' he joked. 'And where has my lady got in mind to go to?'

She pressed closer to him and said, softly, 'I'll think of something. Maybe we both will . . .'

Another leaf fell from the calendar and one morning, walking in the garden with the children, Libby saw the first snowdrops pushing their heads above the hard soil. 'Can we go for an extra *long* walk today, Libby?' asked Amy, lifting her small face to the pale rays of the sun.

'After breakfast,' promised Libby. 'Come on, then, let's go upstairs.'

As soon as they walked into the nursery, Bertie jumped on to the back of the old wooden rocking horse, a sudden favourite of his, and began to rock backwards and forwards with maddening persistence.

'Bertie, sit down and eat your boiled egg.' Libby, with her patience tried almost beyond endurance, glared at the small boy who blithely ignored her. Bertie held the reins in one hand, a tin toy trumpet in the other. The noise had been almost the last straw, this morning of all mornings.

The early morning post had brought a letter from Mam that put Libby in no mood for Bertie's nonsense.

'I've got to catch my fox first,' the little boy cried, brandishing the bugle above his head. 'Can't stop for breakfast until I've caught my fox.'

'You horrid boy! His sister shuddered. 'When I grow up I'm going to make a law that nobody is allowed to hunt foxes.'

'I shan't take any notice of it, then,' shouted Bertie. 'I shall be the best foxhunter in the whole of England.'

Libby put one hand to her aching head. 'Bertie, if you don't come to the table this instant, I shall . . . I shall . . .'

Tears caught in her throat, making her voice husky. On her feet in an instant, Amy ran to her. 'Now see what you've done! You've made Libby cry,' she shouted accusingly.

In a trice, Bertie was all contrition. Sliding from the wooden horse he ran to the table and gobbled up his boiled egg and the soldiers neatly arranged at the side of the plate.

Amy said, conciliatory, 'Don't cry, Libby. Was it the letter you got? Was it a bad letter?'

Libby forced a smile and shook her head. It wasn't fair to inflict her troubles on her small charges. 'It's stopped raining,' she said brightly. 'Shall we take that walk to the old lighthouse?'

Bertie thrust his plate with its eggcup and bits of shell to one side and stood up. 'Hooray, the lighthouse!' he yelled in an ear-splitting shriek. Libby winced. But her family troubles had no place in the

Ainslie household. The letter from home would have to be dealt with later, as soon as the children were settled in bed.

'. . . won't be able to walk to the lighthouse, though, will he?' Amy was gazing up at her, her voice rising slightly at the end of the question.

'Who, love?' Libby dragged her mind back to the promised outing.

'Uncle James. I don't think he can walk as far as the lighthouse.'

'He might be otherwise engaged this morning. He can't spend all his spare time with us, you know.'

With a sideways glance at her brother to make sure he wasn't eavesdropping, Amy tugged at Libby's sleeve. 'When I grow up, I'm going to marry Uncle James.'

'Are you, love?' Libby smiled at the child's earnest demeanour. 'That'll be nice. Then we can keep him in the family.'

Amy nodded, old in feminine wiles already. 'But I'm a little bit worried.' Head on one side, Amy considered her next words. 'Are you really going to marry that man with the black hair and loud voice? Kathleen says you are.'

Flaminenery! I'll scalp that Kathleen, thought Libby. What's she think she's doing, discussing my affairs with this child? 'A lady has to wait for a man to ask her first,' she smiled.

Amy said, gravely, 'But if he does ask, you will say no, won't you, Libby?'

Amy sounded so concerned that Libby wondered just what else Kathleen had been saying. 'You're afraid I'll go away if I marry him?' she suggested softly.

To her surprise, Amy shook her head. 'No, I know you'll stay with us forever. Kathleen says she wouldn't mind him but I think he's horrible.'

For once in her life, Libby was speechless. She was saved from thinking up an answer by Bertie shrieking, 'When are we *going*? I want to go *now*!'

Without a word Libby turned to get her coat.

James heard their voices in the hall, the children's high and excited, their nursemaid's patient but firm.

Cap in hand, he stood at the bottom of the stairs. This morning the children were dressed in identical sailor suits of navy and white, with round straw hats. The only difference was that Amy wore a skirt that reached to her knees and the boy short trousers. Libby had on her usual grey. But even that could not detract from the pleasure he took from just watching her. He thought of her standing on the lighted stage, the men joining in the popular old songs and anger suddenly stirred in him. Anger at the young brute he had last seen escorting the girl he had picked up from the Palace Bar.

He wondered if Libby knew. If she even suspected. Even with her working-class background he guessed she wasn't the kind of girl to put up with such duplicity from any man. Indeed, because of her background, she would be more firmly against falseness than many a society girl he knew.

Most of them would shrug it off, make some light remark about boys will be boys and with a defiant air go out and do the same. Since coming to know this girl he had learned something; that working girls weren't all necessarily cheap, no more than all girls of his class were ladies.

'Good morning,' he greeted them with a smile. 'And what is on the agenda this morning?'

'We're going for a long walk. Would you like to come with us, Captain Randle?' Libby answered, then flushed a bright pink, dismayed at her audacity. It was different him asking if he could go with them. Entirely wrong for her to be doing the asking.

'I'd love to say yes, but I'm afraid this morning I can't. I have to report to the officers' home to see old Blood and Thunder.' Seeing her expression, he explained, 'our term for the army doctor.'

'Blood and Thunder. Blood and Thunder!' shrilled Bertie, catching on to a new phrase. 'Do you call Papa that, too?'

Amy gave a stifled giggle and then James was saying, apologetically, 'Sorry. I forgot the boy's got all the learning instincts of a parrot.'

Amy almost collapsed with a fit of the giggles. Libby glanced at the staircase, expecting any minute to see an enraged Mrs Ainslie descending on them. She straightened Amy's straw boater, pulled up Bertie's socks, already wrinkled about his ankles.

'Time we were off. It's a long walk to the lighthouse.'

'I'll tell you what.' Captain Randle looked at the small party with an air of complicity. 'I'll walk some of the way with you. All right?'

Amy clapped her hands, jumping up and down as though he had offered her, at the very least, the moon.

As they walked Libby thought of herself, on the stage, singing to that group of faceless men. Showing off while Joseph was making his plans to leave home. A wave of guilt washed over her, that she could have been so happy while Mam was suffering.

Bertie showed sudden interest in a flock of seagulls squabbling over something at the water's edge. 'Can we go and look, Libby?'

Libby nodded, smiling. 'You *may* go and look, Bertie. But don't move from the spot. Wait for me.'

With whoops of delight the children hurried down the flight of steps to the beach, falling over each other in their haste to get to the sand first. James removed his cap and tucking it under one arm stood regarding Libby with a thoughtfulness that was disconcerting.

'I'd better go,' she murmured, edging away. 'And you don't want to be late for your appointment with old Blood and Thunder.' They both smiled at her use of the expression.

Then, as she turned to go: 'Wait!' It was a command. Libby stopped and looked back at him. 'Before you go I want you to tell me what is wrong. Something is. Is it your family?'

Or that individual you seem to set such store on, he added silently to himself. He reached out and took her hand. 'Please, Libby, maybe I can help.'

She felt strength flow from him and remembered how easy it had been to confide in this man. She made a wry grimace. 'Only if you have a way of finding a sixteen-year-old boy who has run away from home. Yes, sir, our Joseph's gone. Last week, it was. Mam didn't want to worry me so she's only just written. She hoped he would change his mind and come back.

But he hasn't. He was longing to go into the army, seeing all his older friends going. He won't come back.' She wondered about his feelings for Gwenda. They had seemed to get on so well, too.

The clasp of his hand was warm. 'It shouldn't be too difficult tracing him, Libby. I'll do my best. My father has influence in . . .' About to say the War Office, he paused. How patronising it sounded! Instead, he murmured, 'Will Mrs Ainslie let you go home for a while?'

So soon after Christmas, you must be joking! she thought. Aloud she said, 'I don't think so, sir. I haven't told Cook or any other of the staff. I don't want their sympathy.'

A feeling of exasperation overcame him at her mistaken show of courage. 'Would you like me to talk to Mrs Ainslie for you? Or the doctor?'

'The fat really would be in the fire then.' Her mouth quirked. 'She's still giving me funny looks about that afternoon I took off. I'm sure she thought there was something going on between us.' She blushed at the thought, seeing his eyebrow raised enquiringly. 'You're very kind, but I wouldn't dream of bothering you. How can my being home help, anyway? Our Joseph's gone and my returning won't bring him back.'

'Your presence would comfort your mother.'

'Libby. Libby!' She had completely forgotten the children. Pulling her hand gently from his, she said softly, 'But thank you for offering. I appreciate it. You have problems of your own. I shan't burden you with mine.'

James thought of the young soldiers he had seen on his journeys south. The trains were filled with them; laden with kit-bags and rifles, crowding the station buffet, buying pies and hot drinks, heartbreakingly young in their ill-fitting uniforms, the peaked caps emphasising the fresh, inexperienced faces, the knee-high puttees bandaging the sharp ankle bones of boys.

He knew they would meet the eyes of the recruiting sergeant unwaveringly and to his: 'How old, son?' they would answer, 'Eighteen.' And their reply would be taken as gospel and their name added to the list . . .

Libby's brother would just be another face in the crowd.

About to walk away, Libby turned once to say, 'I hope the doctor's report is favourable, sir.'

He grinned. 'So do I, Libby. So do I.'

It wasn't until she joined the children that she realised the implications of her remark. If the doctor's report were favourable, then that would mean his returning to the front. Did he really hope for that? An icy finger touched her spine, and it was only the impatient beseeching of Bertie that drove for a time the thought from her mind.

Chapter Seven

The wooden seat in the shelter was speckled with raindrops. With a thoughtfulness that touched her, Vince spread his handkerchief on it before she sat down. Still depressed by Mam's letter, she shivered, huddled in her coat. The white caps of the waves tossed long fingers of spray at the green-painted railings that edged the promenade. Immediately they were settled, Vince's arms were around her, pulling her close.

The quarrel with him had been patched up. He'd begged Libby to forgive him, saying he must have been mad to have acted the way he did. To show he meant it, he brought her a small brooch; a cluster of tiny flowers in various shades, made of coloured glass stones.

She let him kiss her now. Then, as his kisses grew more intense, she began to protest, shaking her head, whispering, 'Give over, Vince . . .'

He gave a moan, his hands suddenly urgent. 'Oh, Libby, you don't know what it does to me, being so close to you and not being able to have you. Especially with the war on . . .'

'It doesn't make any difference because there's a

war on. Right's right and wrong's wrong, no matter what.'

'Why do I bother to go out with you when you show only too plainly that you don't want me in that way?' he complained. The spell had been broken and Vince was the wronged little boy again, petulantly sulky.

Libby sighed. She wished she had more experience as a woman. Perhaps then she'd know how to deal with him. She'd only just got used to handling Bertie's tantrums, never mind Vince's.

Tentatively, she said, 'Vince . . . ?' putting one hand out to touch his cheek. He turned his head, his smile triumphant as he reached out and dragged her to him, his throat thick with the lust raging through him.

'I'm sorry you feel like that, Vince. I do love you. But don't you see, we can't . . .' She paused, unsure of herself as he gave a mocking laugh.

'I suppose living with old Ainslie and his snotty-nosed family makes you above all that,' he sneered.

'I wish you wouldn't talk like that. You know the Ainslies are not that much different from us. Mrs Ainslie was born in the same street my family live in. My father and the doctor have known each other since they were lads.'

'And what does that make you?' he taunted. 'A bloody saint?'

Wanting to get away from the subject – she knew by past experience that once he was in this mood, there was no reasoning with him – she said, 'What you said before, about being a conchie. You didn't really mean it, did you? You were joking.'

'No!' The denial came forcefully. 'I don't joke about things like that. I meant every word I said.'

The pitying look made the hot colour flame in her cheeks. 'Poor little Libby! It's so easy to fool you, isn't it? You believe everything people tell you. I've got principles and I mean to stand by 'em. There's nothing wrong with having principles. There's a lot believe as I do, that this war should never have happened.'

She glanced at his averted profile, and said, 'I got a letter today. From my mother.' She waited until he said, brusquely, 'Well?'

'It's about Joseph. He's run away to join the army. Mam's terribly upset.'

Vince snorted. 'More fool him, then. Must be soft in the head to do a thing like that.'

Hesitantly she began, 'What about this new call-up? You'll have to go now, won't you? Only men in essential work are being spared.'

It wasn't easy to accept his views, seeing that she totally disagreed with them herself. The silent argument went on inside her head, for and against until she felt quite giddy.

'Don't let's bother ourselves with that,' he murmured and before she could guess his intention she felt his hands on her shoulders, felt him pushing her hair aside and kissing her neck, making a train of kisses along the smooth, sweet skin. Anxious to make amends for their little conflict, she relaxed, softened, knowing there was no way she could resist him. She had never been able to. His hands roamed over her in increasing exploration. Leaning against him she heard his quick breathing, felt his hands move from her waist to her breasts then suddenly she was pushing him away, reality taking the place of the near ecstasy she had experienced for those few moments.

'No, Vince, no . . . !'

She drew back, her cheeks red with shame at what she had almost allowed him to do. War or no war, her childhood training could not be denied, much as she loved and desired Vince.

They sat together in silence, Vince sulking. After a while he stood up, pulling her with him. 'Come on, I'll walk you home.'

At the gate he didn't even say goodnight to her, just nodded and strode away, hands thrust in his pockets, shoulders hunched. Utterly miserable, Libby stood and watched him as he disappeared into the darkness. She'd stand up for Vince if she had to, against the world if necessary. But deep down in her heart she knew his views on the war were wrong. There were people going around, she knew, spreading views that weren't all that popular with the rest of the country. Vince had obviously come up against such a one. Soapbox orators, her father called them. She wondered what Dr Ainslie would say if he got to know. Or Captain Randle.

Libby shuddered, a chill finger of shame touching her conscience. How could you love a man and still feel that he was debasing the very thing you held most dear!

Libby wasn't getting on very well with her letter to Mam. The words she wanted wouldn't come and it was difficult to concentrate with the children bickering. She looked up, hearing voices outside on the landing. The Captain's and Dr Ainslie's.

'Ah, James, how did your medical go?'

'Bloody disappointing, sir. If you'll pardon the expression.'

She heard the doctor chuckle. 'Sounds ominous! They're not sending you back, then?'

'I have to report to the War Ministry. I have to leave tomorrow. A desk job was mentioned.' The disgust was evident in James' voice. Through the partly open door, Libby heard their footsteps, coming closer, heard the doctor say on a questioning note, 'And that didn't please you at all, I take it?'

'No, sir, it definitely did not. I've no intention of sitting around behind a desk while I've still got the ability to fight.'

The men's voices were fading. For a long moment Libby sat, hands idle in her lap, then sighed and picked up her pen. After James' words, it was doubly difficult to concentrate. Still, if it was only to London he was going, it wouldn't be too bad. Even though he might hate it, it would be safe.

While Libby pondered over his leaving, James' one wish was to be allowed to return to his men. His father wouldn't like it. His mother even less. He didn't fool himself that he was the stuff of which heroes were made, but neither was he the sort to sit behind a desk, signing bits of paper while others fought for the country he loved.

James had gone to war expecting that he would die

in battle; convinced that he must die. It was the destiny of the young men of his generation. While better men than he had been killed, seemingly at random, he had come home after an eternity of bloody fighting with a shrapnel wound and a decoration for heroism under fire.

And now it was his last night in this comfortable house belonging to the parents of Basil Ainslie. The dinner had been wonderful; the pudding a delight to the eye as well as the palate. His mother's own deeply cherished cook could not have done better.

He thought now as he regarded the paper in front of him that he mustn't forget to go down to the kitchen and thank Mrs Gibson for the wonderful dinner and, indeed, all the staff for the way they had looked after him for the time he had been with the Ainslies.

He didn't regret leaving the bleak northern land-scape for the softer climes of the south. Although people had been kind to him there were really no friends to bid a sad farewell to. Unless, of course, you counted the children and their nursemaid.

He thought of Libby as he'd seen her on the stage, slim and graceful and heartbreakingly young as she'd captured the hearts of each and every man in the audience. He knew he was going to miss her. Miss the smell of newly washed hair, of the lemon verbena she used in the rinse. And something else he could never quite put a finger on, but it would be as well remembered: a serenity that was as soothing as a nursery tea or the scent of Pears' soap at bedtime.

He ought to seek her out and say goodbye now. To thank her once again for helping with the concert.

There just wouldn't be time in the morning. Leaving his room, he walked along the corridor, trying not to tap with that damned stick. The nursery door was ajar. He saw through the crack of the door Amy in her voluminous nightgown nursing a doll on a low stool beside the fire. The tall wire guard was hung with articles of children's clothing. Amy's soft voice whispered to the yellow-haired doll with its white china face, cherry red cheeks and baby blue eyes.

Pushing wider the door, James stepped into the room.

'Uncle James!' A shout of delight from Amy. She rose and, the nightgown dragging about her feet, ran over to fling her arms about his knees. 'Are you really going away?' The wide blue eyes stared at him accusingly. 'Won't we ever see you again?'

'Yes, Amy, I'm afraid I have to go, and yes of course you'll see me again.'

'When? When?' Running to join his sister, Bertie aimed a punch with a small closed fist at James' leg. James thought he hid the grimace of pain successfully but Libby noticed it. Pulling the boy back, she said more sharply than she'd intended, 'Bertie, watch your manners! I'm sure Captain Randle doesn't enjoy being punched like that.'

James came further into the room. 'I came to say goodbye,' he said, his gaze lingering on Libby's face. 'I'm getting tomorrow's early train.'

Libby lowered her eyes, hands suddenly busy with folding the scarlet knitted jumper airing on the fireguard.

'We shall be sorry to see you go. Won't we, children?' she murmured.

131

Bertie pouted, frowning fiercely. 'People always go away,' he said. 'I don't like it.'

Surprisingly them all, including himself, James heard himself suggesting, 'Seeing it's my last night, why don't I help Libby put you to bed?'

'Oh, sir!' Libby cast an anxious look towards the partly open door. 'I don't think you should . . . !'

'Nonsense! If I can be trusted to command fighting men, then I can help put my two favourite children to bed.'

Thinking of Fenella's and his mother's plans for him, he added, teasingly, 'It'll be good practice for me when I get married and have children of my own.'

Unaccountably, Libby's heart sank at his words. By the crin, she told herself sternly, what did you think he was going to do after the war? Become a monk? Not James Randle. Got to produce an heir, he has, carry on the family name.

The children were all agog. 'Oh, yes, please, Uncle James,' Amy breathed, eyes glowing, while Bertie pretended an aloofness that didn't fool anyone. Casually, he acquiesced. 'If you like. Only you're not to kiss me goodnight.'

James laughed. 'You have my promise. No kisses.'

'I don't mind you kissing me goodnight, Uncle James,' Amy said shyly.

At last tucked up warmly in their beds they demanded their usual song. 'How about a story instead?' Libby hazarded.

'No!' both children shouted with one voice. 'A song.'

'That one about her neck being like a swan,' said Amy. 'I like that one.'

'No!' Out of sheer habit Bertie objected. 'The one about the minstrel boy. That's better.'

'Sir!' Uncle James' eye was on him again. 'Ladies are always allowed first choice. Anyway, we haven't asked Libby what she would like to sing. Don't you think it would be polite to do so?'

Libby smiled at the two little heads on the pillows. 'We'll have Bertie's song tomorrow night.'

Tomorrow, her wayward thoughts told her, James'd be many miles away and she'd be singing about a boy who 'to the wars had gone, where the fields of battle would find him'.

She turned to look at the writing pad with its unfinished letter. Would some field of battle be her brother's home now, however temporary? Would he be crossing it with bayonet fixed, tangled in barbed wire, taking shelter in a shell hole half filled with muddy water? She'd seen the pen and ink drawings in the newspapers of such things and the very idea made her blood run cold. Thank God Vince . . .

But no, her conscience cried, it's wrong to think like that. Vince *should* be there with her brother and all those other men, fighting for a better world . . .

'We're ready, Libby.'

Amy's voice brought her out of her reverie. She looked up, saw Captain Randle smiling at her, encouragingly, and giving one last pat to Amy's pillow, she seated herself on the end of the little girl's bed and began to sing. The song told the old, old story of Annie Laurie; of the promise true she had given her lover and his promise to her – 'I would lay me down, and die . . .'

None of Josie's songs moved him like this one did,
James thought, as the last note faded away. He had
been with the young lovers as Libby sang, joyful and
then suffering with them.

The children were drowsy, their eyes heavy.
Placing one finger to her lips, Libby rose and he
followed her out on to the landing. Closing the door
gently behind him, he said, softly, still under the spell
of her voice, 'My grandmother used to sing that song
to me when I was about Bertie's age. It is one of my
fondest memories. Of course,' he grinned, 'her voice
was old and a little rusty, but they said in her youth
when she sang she could wring tears from a stone.'

Somehow his hand was touching hers, her other
hand resting on his sleeve. She would never know
how it happened, or why, but it seemed that for one
long breathless moment the world stood still. For
Libby those grey eyes would forever gaze into hers,
piercing her very soul. Their paths, hers and this
man's, might divide, stray in different directions but,
like a hummingbird to its only source of sustenance,
would always return . . .

Then in those clear grey depths something moved.
She felt his body tense, the muscles beneath her hand
tighten. With an almost visible wrench, she brought
herself back to reality and took a step backwards.
Being too close to the sun was dangerous. Like playing with fire. Too late. His left arm went around her
waist, holding her still as he tilted her chin so that her
softly parted lips were just below his. His kiss was
tender: a butterfly kiss, restrained on his part,
experimental on hers, for he had to remind himself

that this wasn't Josie. This was a young, innocent girl to whom he'd been strangely drawn.

'A goodbye kiss, Libby,' he whispered. 'A thank you for the song, for being such a brick about the concert and for the times you put up with me on your walks.'

In the shadows of the landing Mrs Ainslie's lips firmed into a hard, angry line. A wave of outrage swept over her. Walking as quietly as her bulk would allow, she hurried to where her husband was spending what he hoped would be a quiet hour in his study catching up on some medical papers. She had never totally agreed with her husband's engaging Libby Gray as nursemaid to their children. She would have preferred someone with a bit more class, conveniently forgetting that Libby's father and she had been at school together, living until her marriage to Eric Ainslie in the same cobbled street. She had never cottoned on to Ellen Gray either. Gave herself airs and graces, just like her daughter.

She had been in the corridor to witness that kiss, but not James' remark after it. Now, like an enraged bull, she faced her husband. 'Hussy! To think that we've been harbouring such a person under our roof, entrusting our two little darlings to her care. I'm shattered, Eric. Shattered!'

'Now, now, my dear, I'm sure it wasn't like that at all. James Randle!' He shook his head. 'No, Sarah, I simply cannot believe it. You must have imagined . . .'

'There's nothing wrong with *my* eyes.' His wife, outraged to think he doubted her words, glared at him across the desk top.

'I tell you, I saw her kissing him. A fine thing, after all we've done for that girl, taking her in when by rights she should have been at mill wi' her sister. I never did trust her. A sly one, I allus thought. Aye, I knew we'd rue the day we engaged 'er . . .' When excited or angry, Mrs Ainslie was inclined to revert back to her roots in the mean streets of Ridley.

'Well, for one thing, it takes two to kiss and I don't hear you saying you saw James struggling.' He smiled, trying to appease. 'As for the word hussy, well, Sarah, I simply cannot agree with you there. Libby's no hussy. It was probably a – a goodbye kiss,' hitting the nail on the head without being aware of it, 'nothing to worry about, my dear. I'll – ahem . . .' He gave a little cough. 'I'll have a little word with her in the morning.'

'I know your "little words",' said Mrs Ainslie scornfully. 'Well, just see that you do or I'll be having a word wi' 'er myself and it won't be a little word. That it won't.'

The following morning Libby answered the children's questions in such an absent-minded way that finally Amy took her hand and gazing up into her eyes, said, 'What's wrong, Libby? You're not even listening to me this morning.'

The night before, unable to sleep, Libby had lain in bed filled with an emotion she hadn't known she could feel. Until last night on the landing when Captain Randle's lips had touched hers. Nothing with Vince had prepared her for that. Daft hap'orth! she told herself. He was grateful for the company you and the children had given him. He'd kissed Amy, too, hadn't he? It meant nothing.

It wasn't until Dr Ainslie summoned her to his study in the morning that she realised that wasn't entirely true. It had meant a great deal to one member of the Ainslie family.

The doctor sat behind his desk and surveyed her quietly, after indicating that she should sit. 'I hope you're not going to take what I have to say the wrong way, lass, but it has to be said.' He paused, looking down at his hands spread across the white blotter.

Libby waited, her own hands folded primly in her lap, back straight, head up, as she'd been taught by the nuns at school. When he seemed loath to continue she prompted, softly, 'Yes, Dr Ainslie? Is it something about the children?'

'No, not about the children. About Captain Randle.'

She caught her breath and he, hearing it, wondered if the accusations made by his wife had been true after all. And yet, still he couldn't bring himself to believe that this young girl, of whom he was so fond, could be so devious and not show it. As diplomatically as he knew how, he mentioned the scene witnessed by the nursery door: James' arm about her, her face raised to his as they kissed, concluding: 'So you see, my dear, I thought it only fair to hear your side of the story before judgment was made.'

The doctor, who could remember quite clearly this child's birth, the small pink bundle that even then was pretty, saw the pink flush leave her cheeks now, then return with a flood of scarlet. If she'd been the sort of girl their son squired, she'd have told him to mind his own business, probably his own *bloody* business, that it was nothing to do with him.

But she wasn't. Although his hair was white and his eyes tired he was still as understanding as ever in his brusque way. Suddenly, embarrassed by the whole wretched thing, he said, 'Well, Libby, I'm sure there must be a perfectly reasonable explanation, or,' brows raised hopefully, 'perhaps my wife *was* mistaken in what she saw?'

'No, sir. Captain Randle did kiss me.' Her voice trembled and for a heart-wrenching moment he thought she was going to burst into tears. To his relief, she lifted her head and although her eyes were brimming with tears they were tears of laughter.

It bubbled up inside her like a spring of clear water, and shaking her head, she said through giggles, 'I'm sorry, sir. It was just the look on your face ...' She took a deep breath, got herself under control. 'It was just a – a thank-you kiss, that's what he, Captain Randle, called it. He'd come for a few walks with me and the children. I think he was lonely, sir. The children adore him.'

The doctor nodded, satisfied. 'My wife, I'm afraid, jumps to hasty conclusions. I'm sorry, Libby, to have had to put you through all that.'

The last words his wife had said to him, about dismissing the hussy, he gave not a second thought to. To bid her go would break the children's hearts. Even he would miss the smiling face and light steps on the stairs, not to mention the clear sweet snatches of song he'd heard as he worked in his study. It was as good as a tonic, was Libby's voice, and always afterwards he felt soothed, calm, no matter how hectic his day. Now, as he rose to open the door for her, he saw she sat still. 'Was there something else, my dear?'

'If you have time, sir.'

He went back to his chair. 'All the time in the world for your problems, lass.'

Pulling Mam's letter from the pocket of her dress, she pushed it across the desk. 'I got this from my mother the other day. Our Joseph's run away from home to join up. Mam must be out of her mind. I wondered, if it's all right with you and Mrs Ainslie, if I could go home for a few days. I don't suppose I can do anything, but I would like to be with Mam . . .'

The plea in her eyes touched the doctor as nothing else would. 'I don't see any problems, Libby. I'll get Mrs Ainslie to have a word with you.'

Mrs Ainslie glared down her long nose, making Libby think she had asked for something unforgivable. 'A few days off!' She echoed her husband's words. Libby was allowed a free weekend every two months. Considering she had been home for Christmas and it was still only February, Mrs Ainslie was outraged.

Libby straightened her shoulders and looked her employer in the eye. 'Yes, Madam, a couple days to make sure everything at home is all right. I can go one day and be back by the evening of the next.'

Knowing full well her husband would overrule any objections she might make, Mrs Ainslie capitulated, albeit ungracefully. Really, she thought, watching as the slight figure of her nursemaid ran lightly back upstairs to the children, the way her husband treated that girl you would think she was royalty. Treating servants as equals was quite beyond her comprehension. Again, conveniently she pushed aside any thoughts of her own humble beginnings.

Chapter Eight

Exasperated by the slowness of the train, James felt he could have got out and pushed it, thus relieving some of the tension. His first thought at boarding the train at the small, busy St Aiden's station was that he would soon be seeing Josie again.

He leaned his head back against the red plush of the first-class carriage and allowed his thoughts to wander, remembering that last stolen weekend in the country, with Josie at her merriest, her most loving, taking his mind away from all thoughts of war. It had been so short a time but exactly what he needed.

That first evening at the quiet hotel, as they had entered the stuffy, old-fashioned dining room, Josie had glanced about her and said, leaning towards him, 'Aw, get this! Remind me to 'ave a bath and mend me knickers in future!'

'Josie!'

Irrepressible as ever, as they took their places at the table in the specially selected corner where the head waiter held out chairs, she gazed about the room once more and began making comments on the collection of old colonels and their wives. ' 'Ave to be their wives,' she said from behind her hand, eyes twinkling, 'couldn't be anything else, looking like that.'

'Shhh,' James warned, in spite of himself amused at her description. 'They'll hear you.'

'Not them! All deaf as door posts by the look of 'em.'

An elderly officer with a fierce white moustache at a nearby table caught her eye and raised his glass. Josie retaliated by lifting her own, brimming with the champagne James had insisted on, and smiling brilliantly.

The Colonel promptly choked on his brandy, earning a reproachful frown from his spouse.

James grimaced as the girl laughed. 'Go on, say it! I'm awful, ain't I?'

'You're wonderful, exactly what I need. But why must we waste our time talking about Colonels and their,' he lowered his voice to a stage whisper, 'stuffy wives?' He had to report to the convalescent place on Monday. Until then, he intended to exclude all thoughts of the army from his mind.

A smile touched his lips when he remembered what had followed in the comfortable bedroom with the huge four-poster bed. They had drawn the thick brocaded curtains that matched those on the windows, and the hours before the maid arrived with their morning tea would be etched on the mind of the young officer for a long time to come.

Forgotten were the nightmare scenes of tar-black smoke billowing from burning villages; the bodies that hung on the wire of the Somme. For a moment the guns were still and in that silence you could hear the song of a bird from the tattered hedgerow.

The evening before she had come on to the stage, strutting in a red and black uniform with a short tightly buttoned waistcoat. Her hair was slicked back and tucked up under a peaked cap, a narrow moustache painted on her upper lip. The waistcoat was red, the trousers that hugged her shapely legs black with a thin golden stripe down each side.

Swaggering on the stage, all very much larger than life, she positioned her white-gloved hands on her hips and sang, 'There's something about a soldier that is fine, fine, fine . . .' and the crowd went mad.

Josie knew all the tricks of the trade. She had told him all about her background, how she came from a poor, East End family where eight children shared a two-bedroomed house with their father and mother. Josie knew she had to learn quickly in order to obtain a share of the good things in life. The second of the four girls, she had watched her elder sister struggle when their mother died at the last baby's birth, trying to run the house and see to their father, and generally care for her little brothers and sisters.

Josie confessed that she was determined that she wouldn't fall into that trap. She had sung and danced before, begging in the street for pennies, and knew she had a pleasant voice.

Her looks weren't great, her hair the colour of a house mouse (as her father had once caustically remarked when she told him she was leaving home to make her own way in the world). But Josie Higgins, as she was then, had that extra something that glowed

143

under the footlights, something that couldn't be manufactured.

The hair colour could be changed with the judicious use of Egyptian henna, and as for her looks, well, she smiled at James, what man would be looking at the nose that she prayed every night the Good Lord would change into one of patrician shapeliness when they could be looking at her luscious body!

On arrival in London he found the station platform crowded with men in uniform; a mass of soldiers hurrying to board a train to some undisclosed destination or sprinting to catch one of the scarlet buses that would carry them home to their loved ones. In one corner of the platform a small knot of soldiers huddled, their voices raised in song: 'Roses are blooming in Picardy. In the hush of the silvery dew . . .' An elderly porter tried to shoo them along. 'Come on, lads. Can't hang around here, cluttering up the platform. Thought you'd all be in a hurry to get 'ome.' Although his voice was kind he was telling himself he didn't approve of the boys being drunk this early in the day.

Ignoring the drunken soldiers, who nevertheless managed to salute him as they passed, James caught a cabby as he unloaded passengers in front of the station.

Regent's Park contained huge dumps of supplies in strange shapes put up by the Air Force. All the London parks, it seemed, were being used by the forces for drilling and storage. But his own street looked the same, the square of trees and grass with its rustic seats still surrounded by railings and gates. In spite of the war, it still possessed an air of opulent luxury that James had always taken for granted.

This was the town house his father had bought when he and his wife were first married and Isobel had craved the bright lights and theatres. After James' birth she had decided Windrush was the only home she really wanted and for years the town house had remained empty. With the coming of the war and the various functions in Town that Isobel felt compelled to attend, also with David's job, it had come into its own again and now the house in Princes' Square was the home of the Randles for most of the year. On his homecomings, James missed the peace and seclusion of Windrush, but he told himself it would seem all that much more desirable when things were at last back to normal and he was home for good again.

As he paid off the cabby there was the sound of banging and around the corner came a rag-taggle group of children. The boys in front had tin cans slung round their necks with string and were led by an older boy with a tin whistle. Some carried small Union Jacks, others wore hats folded from newspapers. One carried a stick tucked under his arm, imitating an officer.

Robert, the Randle butler for as long as James could remember, opened the door to his knock, hastening out on to the top step as he saw the way James leaned on his walking stick, his breath coming fast.

'Master James! How good to see you!' He eyed the stick with apprehension but tact forbade him to mention it. 'How are you, sir?'

James raised an impatient hand, nodding to the cabby to bring his valise up the shallow flight of steps. 'I'm fine, thank you, Robert. How are my parents?'

'Not too bad, sir. All things considering.'

'That's excellent.' James looked around him, his gaze lingering on the wide staircase that led to the upper rooms. 'My mother . . . ?'

'In her sitting room, sir. I'll have Martin take your case to your room.'

The old man watched as James climbed the stairs, slowly, laboriously with the walking stick. Halfway up, when James turned to glare at him, the butler hurried to the green baize door that separated the servants' quarters from the rest of the house, calling for Martin, the footman, to carry the young master's luggage up to his room. Master James, once so agile, so spritely, the despair of his mother with his high jinks, the pride of his house as he strode out on to the green in his cricket whites, or in the school colours, carrying a rugby ball, now so disabled that he was forced to walk with the aid of a stick.

The old butler shook his head. It wasn't right; just wasn't right. He prayed for the day when they could all return to Windrush, away from this grimy, noisy London, and continue with the life they had always lived, that of gentlemen farmers. It was the end of an era. England would never be the same again, with long queues forming outside shops for the most basic of foods – potatoes and sugar and such things, and those inventions of the devil they called Zeppelins floating over the town. The old man shook his head again. Not so cocky lately, though, the bloody Hun! Now that we'd got a special bullet which set fire to the gas which propelled the monsters! The enormous fire when one was hit you could see for miles. The staff from all the houses on the square would stand out on the pavement and cheer. A wonderful feeling . . .

James found his mother in her sitting room, in the high-backed chair she favoured, her hands folded in her lap. Hands that had never done a day's work apart from rolling bandages when she and the other ladies attended their Red Cross meetings once a week in Lady Acton's house.

She sat staring into space, her lovely face grave, somehow empty. Her still-dark hair was piled high on her forehead and she wore a pale, rust-coloured gown with delicate inserts of lace in the bodice and the flowing elbow-length sleeves.

She jumped to her feet when James entered, running to clasp both his hands in hers, to hold them caressingly to her cheeks.

'My darling! I'm so glad you came.' Holding him at arm's length, she went on, 'Didn't that convalescent home look after you? You look dreadfully thin.' Her lovely eyes devoured the face of this beloved son, her only child, as though she could never get enough of him. 'We were all so worried.'

Patting her shoulder, he could smell the warmth of the perfume of roses that seemed always to surround her. 'Dearest mother o' mine, you seem to forget that I wasn't at the home, but staying at Basil Ainslie's place. You remember Basil? The boy who was reputed to pinch the servant wenches' bottoms and think it all a huge joke! It was kind of them to invite me, seeing we weren't really friends.'

Isobel nodded, her lips turning down at the corners in distaste. 'I remember him, although I must confess my recollections are vague. I recall briefly meeting his parents at one of the school plays. They had travelled all that way just to be there, and I was very impressed with his father. A doctor, isn't he?'

'Yes, and a damn fine one.'

'Well, we must be grateful for their kindness. I shall write to Mrs Ainslie, thanking her for her concern for your comfort. It must have been a vast improvement from the home with all those wounded men . . .'

Seeing the way her son's mouth tightened, she changed smoothly to: 'But now you are here, James, how long can we keep you before you move on?'

James placed an arm about her shoulders and gave them a slight squeeze. The bones beneath the silk dress seemed so fragile, so small, she reminded him of a delicate bird.

'For as short a time as possible,' he answered, going to stand by the window and gaze out on the square beneath, hands folded behind his back. 'My marching orders can't come fast enough for me.'

Alarm flickered across her face. 'But, James, as I understood from your father, you were to be stationed here in town.'

'Only until I can persuade them to see the light of day and allow me to return to my men.'

Isobel sighed. 'I intended to invite Fenella and a

few of your friends for dinner. Would you like that, dear? Or do you feel that you'd prefer to rest for a while until you get back into the swing of things?'

'Not this evening, Mother.' James turned to smile at her; the weak sunlight coming through the wide window outlined his hair, heightening the chestnut sheen. 'It's been a long day.'

'Fenella will be devastated. She so looked forward to having you back with us.'

James' mouth quirked. 'I'm sure Fenella will understand.'

He thought of the girl with the fashionable short bobbed hair, the large, knowing eyes. Of the time she had enticed him into the loft over the stables where they had lain together in the sweet-smelling hay; of the lazy snickering of the horses and their quiet movements in the stalls below. Ecstasy had almost been in his grasp when he felt a hand tug at his collar and he was jerked roughly away from Fenella's pliant young body. He'd knelt there in the hay, face crimson with a mixture of shame and outrage, gazing up into the shocked face of the head stable man. The dressing-down he'd been given, followed by the promise that the episode would go no further, certainly would not reach his parents' ears as long as he behaved himself in the future, haunted his sleep for weeks to come.

He'd never forget Fenella's laughter, mocking, shaming him into angry response, as they walked back to the house. 'James Randle, I would never have believed it of you! Allowing an old idiot like that to tell you what you must and must not do.'

149

'Better if we forget the whole thing, Fenella,' he'd mumbled, turning away. 'I shall.'

'You liked it though, didn't you?' She had peered closely into his averted face, squeezing his arm and pressing her ripening body against his. '*I* liked it. I liked that excited, shivery feeling that made my tummy go all fluttery and my heart beat like Sorcerer's hooves as he gallops across the downs.'

When James had returned from France, ignoring the envious murmurs of his friends that wasn't he the lucky one, to get a Blighty wound, he didn't think of it like that. His parents had visited him in the Army hospital that had once been a large manor house, dismayed at finding him so depressed. His mother, especially, was at her wits' end wondering how to pierce that curtain of despair with which he had surrounded himself. How could he tell her of the sights and sounds he had experienced? The stench of rotting mules mingled with the acrid smell of gunpowder from the shells that hung over the poppy fields, negating the beauty of the purple dusk.

It had been a week from James' twenty-second birthday. He remembered his last birthday, the party given by his parents in the lovely ballroom at Windrush. Windrush, their beautiful and stately home.

It dated back to the late fifteen hundreds and had been constructed by a well-known builder to the court of Queen Elizabeth. The Randle family were descended from a courtier to the Queen who had commissioned Windrush to be built on the site of a much earlier building, using, it was said, original stone for the facing.

Successive generations of Randles had dealt kindly with the house. Sympathetic additions came from famous architects, the most important being the new south-west wing with its vaulted ceiling.

James' grandfather had restored the panelled reception hall with its gallery after a fire had all but destroyed it, and panelling in several other rooms had been carefully preserved.

James always thought the house looked grander than it actually was. He had found it a comfortable and relaxing place in which to spend his childhood and always on his return from boarding school gazed at the mellow stone walls and thick trails of ivy that partially covered the front with renewed affection.

He was an only child and his mother was inclined to spoil him, worrying about the games of rugby he would play or that a cricket ball would catch him on the head or the face. His father laughed and told her to calm down; James was smart enough to see that nothing like that happened to him.

But not so smart as to avoid the German shell that exploded near the mud-filled hole where he and his men crouched as they sheltered from the guns.

'Has Fenella been to see you?' David Randle had asked. He was seated on the hardwood chair between the two beds. The bed next to James' was empty, the wounded man having been taken to the operating theatre just as David arrived.

He was on his own, his wife having had a Red Cross meeting to attend.

James answered his question 'A couple of times. She doesn't stay long. You know Fenella!' He smiled.

'Have you and Fenella decided anything yet?' The question was asked before David realised he had asked it. Annoyed with himself, he shifted his position on the chair. What in God's name did he expect James to answer?

On the question of Fenella they had always trod warily. David knew that Fenella's father would be relieved to see his only child settle down. She'd been a handful, her mother passing away when Fenella was still a little girl and her father becoming a recluse, refusing to accept his loss.

As she grew, Fenella showed little interest in the lovely old house with its Victorian gardens and parklands where shy deer roamed. Her energies were mostly taken up by her father's horses. Fenella was sixteen, the same age as James, and was constantly reminded by her old nanny that she was now a young lady and so must behave like one. She didn't seem to have taken the words to heart, thought James wryly. Being a young lady meant taking up her hair and desisting from wearing the tight riding breeches that were her favourite attire, the silk shirt, so fine that it clung to her breasts, and the silk kerchief of bright sunshiny yellow tied casually about her neck.

James was waiting for her one morning in the kitchen of her house, playing with a new puppy – it was much warmer in the kitchen than anywhere else in the old, rambling house and the Burroughs' cook always made him most welcome – when Whittle, the head gardener, entered from the yard. As head gardener he was listened to with respect, although barely tolerated by Cook.

'That young madam looks more like a gypsy every day,' he muttered, reaching for the usual mug of hot cocoa Cook had ready for him. James sniffed the rich chocolate smell appreciatively, and listened with interest to what was being said. Warming to his subject, the old man went on, querulously, 'Come to no good, that one won't. I see 'er becoming too free an' easy wi' the stable lads, an' not just her father's workmen, either, but anyone oo's young an' don't look like one o' them gargoyles on that church in Paris.'

Forgotten by Cook and the rest of the staff, James listened to the old man's words and thought of how, just that summer, the stable man had plucked him from the compliant body of his young mistress, Fenella. Thinking about it, even now, brought a flush to the boy's face.

Cook had added a sly drop of gin to her own cocoa to give her courage and said scathingly, 'Come orf it, Albert Whittle! What do you know about churches in Paris or anywhere else, you old heathen. You can 'ardly stir yerself to wheel yer barrer to the end of the orchard, never mind talking about some froggy country.'

The old gardener had grunted and tossed back the thick, dark residue at the bottom of his mug. 'Well, maybe you'll be laughing the other side of yer face when 'arm comes to 'er, then. Just don't say I didn't warn you.'

He had stood up and walked out, pausing at the

back door to eye James accusingly and say, to no one in particular, 'I'd tell Master but 'e'd only laugh at me. Thinks the sun shines out of 'er backside, does Mr Burroughs.'

'Well, just let 'im go on thinking that and everything will be orlright,' Cook had answered crisply.

'No, Father,' said James. 'We haven't decided anything yet. She doesn't want to be tied down, and with things as they are . . .' He had shrugged. 'How can *anyone* plan ahead? Fenella wants a big wedding, the works, and she realises she can't have it the way things are.'

'Your mother will be sorry to hear it. She wants grandchildren while she's still young enough to enjoy them. And, my boy,' leaning over to pat the back of his son's hand, awkwardly, slightly embarrassed as he always would be by any show of affection, '*I* want a grandson.'

His look was steady, holding James'. It said: Supposing our very worst fears are realised and you don't come through this? How would we survive, with nothing to live for . . . ?

David reached for his hat, lying by his feet on the worn linoleum, and rose heavily. 'Well, lad,' he said, 'make sure they take good care of you and don't be trying to walk on that leg until they give their permission.'

He had glanced over his shoulder at the forbidding presence of the matron, seated at the desk and watching her charges with a gimlet eye. 'I wouldn't like to have to argue with that one, looks a right dragon.'

*   *   *

That evening it was just not possible to run off from the family and catch Josie's performance, so by the time he was able to escape she had already left the theatre and gone home. She was slumped in the big easy-chair before the fire, clad in the blue kimono he knew so well. As soon as he kissed her James knew she had been drinking. A half-empty bottle of gin stood on the table next to her.

Months had passed since she'd seen him and ordinarily she would have been in raptures at his return. Although she raised plump white arms to pull his head down to hers, returning his kiss with an expertise that aroused him, tonight something was missing.

He scooped the silken-clad body into his arms and, taking her place in the big chair, lowered her to his knee. Her hair was loose and tumbled about her shoulders, smelling slightly of tobacco and greasepaint. He thought of the lemon verbena scent of that other girl, hating to compare her to the one nestling in his lap. And of course there *was* no comparison. Although roughly of the same class, Libby was all youth and freshness, as innocent as a spring day with her silky copper-bright hair, her sun-freckled skin and a mouth that always seemed set to smile, while Josie was as fragrant as a hot summer, lightning across a midnight sky . . .

Josie said suddenly, 'Got somethin' to tell you, Jimmy. Somethin' you're not goin' to like.'

He lifted her hand to his lips, kissing the knuckles. 'Oh? You've got another lover, someone you prefer to me?'

She punched him on the shoulder, then leaned back against his chest, one leg extended, her blue eyes examining the high-heeled mule dangling on the end of her toes. Their weekend together had been in late November. By January she guessed she was pregnant. Now, she was sure. 'Don't be daft! As if I could ever find anyone nicer than you. No, Jimmy, it's – well, not to beat about the bush, I'm in the club . . .'

Although these things happen to other people, James thought, somehow you never imagine them happening to you. And yet, why not? Nature had a way of taking you by the scruff of the neck when you least expected it and shaking the daylights out of you. Why shouldn't he have expected it? He looked at her now, turning her face towards him, his finger and thumb holding her chin.

'You're sure? There can be no mistake?'

'No, no mistake.' She looked at him from under her lashes, trying to gauge his reaction. 'You're cross?'

He shook his head. 'Of course not. It takes two to enter into such a bargain. No, Josie, I'm not cross, a bit shaken but not cross. I suppose I should have realised our relationship could have led to this . . .'

Her lips twisted mockingly. ' 'Ark at 'im! Relationship!' She reached up and kissed him. 'But now it 'as 'appened, wot we goin' to do about it?'

James frowned, feeling much as he had felt when confronting the strip of earth known as 'no man's land' between the trenches. It was a situation new to him, containing all sorts of unexpected traps, frightening. No, that wasn't fair. Josie had set no traps. He was as much to blame as she was. But now it had happened a solution had to be found.

'There are women, aren't there, women who for a fee will . . .' His tone was uncertain and she smiled, snuggling back down on his lap, a kitten who instead of the kick it had been expecting had been offered a saucer of cream.

'I knew you'd say that. I have a friend who knows someone, she's not cheap but she's reliable and clean, me friend says, and if I could miss a couple of performances at the theatre it would be all over in no time . . .'

James stood up so abruptly that she all but fell from his knee. His face pale, he stared at her across the width of the fireplace. 'You're not suggesting you go to one of those back-street women who conduct business in their filthy kitchens?'

Josie laughed and thrust her chin out at him. 'Wot else, me fine gentleman? It's not somethin' you ignore and it'll go away, you know.'

He pulled her close, sudden concern for her safety taking hold of him. 'I know, Josie. I wasn't thinking along those lines. What I meant was someone, some woman, to look after it when it's born. Some nice, respectable woman, with maybe a child or two of her own, who would be willing to take the poor little mite in and love it – I would be responsible for payment, you wouldn't have to worry about a thing after it was born . . .'

Suddenly her hands were pushing against his chest, fists clenched, hammering at him as though he had attacked her. 'No!'

'Why on earth not? Josie, Josie, be sensible. You can go away to the country for the birth and afterwards return to the stage as though nothing had happened.'

He saw the way her face twisted, heard her voice, on the point of hysteria, as she cried, 'And wot 'appens to my career? You don't 'ave to worry. You've got money. I'm just startin' out . . .' She tore herself away from him and threw herself on the settee. She lay there looking at him, an unfathomable expression in her eyes, until at last she said, 'Did you know they've offered me a part in that new musical comedy? A good part, too. Make me name in it, I will.'

The look he gave her made a shiver run down her spine. Her rough upbringing came to the fore and she laughed, and getting up from the settee she came over to where he stood and flung her arms about his neck. 'Oh, Jimmy, it ain't a person. Not yet it ain't. Just a blob inside me. It 'appens to better folk than me an' you an' no one thinks anythin' of it.' One finger traced his eyebrows, ending up at the corner of his mouth. 'I can't think why you're so set against it, really I can't.'

Had the war changed him so much, he wondered, that the idea of getting rid of what formerly would have been regarded as an encumbrance sickened him? What was another death in the light of so many?

He lifted his hands and gently disengaged hers from about his neck. 'I must go. As it is I only just managed to slip out without my parents noticing. I'll come back tomorrow.' Picking up his cap and his stick, he stood by the door, looking back. She eyed him from beside the settee, lips pursed in a sulk, eyes sparking defiance.

'You'll be – sensible? Won't do anything hasty?' he asked gently.

She looked down to where the tip of her satin mule traced the pattern of the carpet. A smile played about the corners of her mouth. 'I won't do anythin' 'asty, Jimmy. I promise.'

'Good.' He placed the peaked cap with its silver badge on his head, adjusting it to a slight tilt. 'Then I'll see you tomorrow. Goodnight, my dear.'

Chapter Nine

'Libby! What a surprise! What a lovely surprise.'
Ellen Gray clasped her daughter to her breast,
almost strangling her in her joy. 'Why ever didn't you
tell us you were coming? Dad could have met you.'

'There wasn't time, Mam. Dr Ainslie insisted I
come as soon as I showed him your letter about
Joseph. Have you had any word of him yet?'

At the mention of Joseph her mother's face seemed
to crumble. She turned her head away quickly,
hating Libby to see the weakness of her tears. 'Nothing, but it's early days yet. I expect he's being kept
busy.'

'And how's my girl?' Dad came from the kitchen,
beaming with delight. 'Eee, lass, but it's great to see
you. You're looking bonny. That sea air must be doing
you good.'

Mam bustled them into the warmth of the kitchen,
out of the chill, damp-smelling hallway. 'Get back to
the fire, William,' she scolded, gently.

Libby seated herself opposite her father as Mam
busied herself making tea. 'A free shift this afternoon, then?' Libby smiled at her father. It was
unusual to see him taking his ease by the fire at this

161

time of day. Mam coughed and before Libby could say more, said, 'I didn't put it in my letter because I didn't want to worry you any more, love, but your dad got laid off.' Her mouth twisted scornfully. 'Strike action, they call it.' Her expression told Libby what *she* would call it.

'Oh, Dad!' Libby stared at him with anguished eyes, noticing the lines on his face that she was sure hadn't been there before. And he was so pale! The thick thatch of hair was whiter than she remembered, the blue eyes less piercing. Clearly wanting to change the subject, Mam started talking about Agnes as she poured cups of tea and cut a crusty new loaf. Placing her own cup on the dresser beside her, she returned to the pile of ironing Libby's arrival had interrupted.

With a padded cotton holder, she picked up one of the two flat irons heating on the fire and spat on the heel, testing for heat. The blob of spit sizzled to her satisfaction and she began sliding the iron across the snowy white sheet spread across the big kitchen table. 'You knew about the man she was going out with, didn't you?' Mam said, back on the subject of Agnes. When Libby said she did, Mam went on, grimly, 'Well, seems like he's asked her to go away with him. No talk of marriage, as far as I can see.' She shook her head. 'Eee, but our Agnes has always been a trial. A real parcel of trouble since the day she began to walk. I can see it now, Mrs Moran from next door coming in to tell me that she had been into her kitchen and helped herself to the seed cake Mrs Moran had left to cool for their Sunday tea. What she didn't eat she threw down their lavatory. I didn't know where to put myself, I can tell you. But she's always been one to help herself to what she wants, never giving a thought to anyone else.'

'Now, Ellen.' William spoke in a conciliatory tone. 'Agnes is a spirited young lass. With the war on who can blame her for wanting a life of her own?'

Mam's look could have killed, thought Libby, if it had been a weapon. 'Oh, you, William Gray!' she said, banging the iron so hard on the sheet it left a faint scorch mark. 'You'd find excuses for the devil himself.'

Libby knew Mam was joking. It was rare for a Lancashire woman to express emotion in any form, so for Mam to admit this was exceptional. The strong ties of family and their love for each other didn't need words. It was all there in the warm, clean home with its smells of freshly ironed linen and mouth-watering baking.

'Can't beat a Lancashire woman for the lightness of her pastry,' was Dad's favourite comment. 'I'd stand my Ellen against the rest any old time, I would.'

A fit of coughing put paid to any more remarks from Dad. Libby caught Mam's eye, brows raised questioningly, and Mam nodded. It was all Libby needed to tell her that Dad had been ill again. She couldn't help thinking that if it hadn't been for the loss of pay, the strike would have come as a blessing. She sighed, watching the heavy iron in Mam's hand glide skilfully over the linen in which she took such pride. They might be poor, but nowhere in that street of shabby houses would you find a whiter stoned doorstep or window sill, or fresher smelling towels and sheets.

In a town of house-proud Lancashire women, Ellen Gray would call no one her superior. The kitchen overlooked a tiny yard paved with cracked flag-stones, a lean-to coal shed and an outside lavatory with a cracked wooden seat. Libby had always been wary of that seat. If you sat down carelessly it was liable to give you a nasty pinch in the wrong place.

The old-fashioned grate shone with the polishing Mam lavished on it. In front of the hearth a hand-made rug covered the stone floor. Once the colours of the rug had been bright. She remembered how Dad had worked on it all one winter when the nights were long and dark, and his look of triumph when it was finished and Mam put her arms around him, right there in front of the children, and kissed him soundly.

'Hey, hey,' he'd laughed. 'What's all this in aid of, then?'

'For being so clever,' Mam had answered smugly. 'And for giving my kitchen such a nice, warm look.' She slid her slippered foot over the coloured rags. 'Every time I pick it up to shake it, it will remind me of different things.'

The rug was made of narrow strips of cloth worked on to a piece of sacking; cottons from summer dresses of her daughters when they were small, bits of an old scarlet dressing gown, old tablecloths and even the blue and white checked cotton of the kitchen curtains dating from the first years of their marriage.

A little bit of family history was in that rug, Dad would boast.

Later Mam cooked a meal while Libby sat at the table, listening to all the gossip. Mrs Moran from next door was having trouble with her eldest boy; the policeman had been round to talk to her, scaring the living daylights out of the child and resulting in him getting a good hiding from his dad.

Libby laughed, remembering the little boys and their mischief.

'Pinched an apple from the fruit cart down the road,' explained Mam, busy at the stove. 'Wasn't much, just an apple, but the constable said it was only the beginning and if not stopped while he was young could lead to more serious things.'

While they were talking, Agnes arrived and went straight upstairs, saying she was having tea out. Mick was waiting for her. Presently she came back down the stairs to stand in the open doorway of the kitchen. As though noticing Libby for the first time, she said, 'Oh, so you're back! Those two brats got tired of you, or something? Or was it old Mother Ainslie?'

'Agnes!' There was a warning in Mam's voice. 'Is that all you can say to your sister?'

Agnes tossed her ginger head; a parody of the star in that picture the other night. She ran back upstairs. Later, without a word of farewell, she went out, closing the front door behind her with a slam that shook the house.

'Never mind, love,' William smiled appeasingly at his wife. 'Whatever that bloke of hers treats her to for supper, she won't have as good a spread as we've got now.'

Ellen pressed his hand and gave him a look of love. She made a fresh pot of tea and bade her family sit. Half-way through the meal, she turned to look at the photograph of Joseph on the mantelpiece. 'God help him!' she said. 'I wonder where he is today and what he's doing. Wouldn't he have enjoyed Libby being at home again.'

Everyone looked towards the picture and Libby said, 'Please God he'll be all right, Mam. You might hear tomorrow; letters take a long time in coming. Don't worry. We're all praying for him, you know that.'

'I wonder what keeps people going who don't believe in prayer? Who do they turn to? Them and their wars.'

Accompanying her parents to church the next morning, Libby felt as though she had never been away. But she always felt this, she reminded herself, on her infrequent returns to Ridley. Father Brady beamed a welcome and clasped William's hand warmly, tactfully avoiding all mention of Agnes. It was, thought Libby, as though her sister had never existed, as if the few good times they had shared as children had all been a dream. Not many good times, for Agnes had always been a tell-tale and loved nothing better than when she was spreading stories about other children. Including her own sister. Libby remembered the time when she and Joseph had set off for Mass on their own, Mam having gone to an earlier service. They had each been given a penny to put in the collection plate but on the way they had to pass a tobacconist that sold newspapers and magazines. The rack of luridly coloured comic cuts proved irresistible. At a halfpenny each they would still have something to put in the collection.

Libby recalled the shivery feeling of guilt as she and Joseph had smuggled the comics into the house, Libby's folded and stuffed up one leg of her knickers, Joseph's hidden under his jersey. For weeks Libby had walked with that invisible weight hanging over her head, warning Joseph not to breathe a word in front of Agnes. The thought of being found out was too awful to contemplate.

Libby drew her thoughts back to the service. The softly spoken Latin words, the hymns, today sung by young boys, gave her a feeling of well-being that lasted for the rest of the day. The satin vestments so carefully embroidered; watered silk in purple, deep green, gold. Every colour had its liturgical meaning.

There had been a Sunday when she had knelt beside Mam and instead of following the service had been humming a new song her friend had taught her. 'Daddy wouldn't buy me a bow-wow . . .'

When Mam had leaned over and whispered, 'Elizabeth Mary Gray, pay attention to the Mass,' she'd started visibly. 'Do you want to be struck dead – aye, it can happen. Our Father has an all-seeing eye, not even the fall of the smallest sparrow escapes His notice.'

Terrified, Libby had lifted her head and gazed at the baby Jesus held in His mother's arms. Lighted candles had shone golden on the blue of the Madonna's gown, creating the illusion of movement with their shifting shadows. The face of Mary, usually so serene, seemed to frown down at the little girl's irreverence.

Foolishly she'd told Agnes about the experience and so shouldn't have been surprised when she was waylaid one morning on her way to school. The crowd of children hemmed her in, pressed against the moss-covered wall.

She was used to the taunts – 'carrot top' and 'Skinny Lizzie'. In the past she had steeled herself against them. But it wasn't easy. She forced her face into lines of stony indifference. There was no way of knowing what she was thinking, except that her eyes, green as flashing emeralds, moved warily in the small flushed face as she carefully weighed up her chances of escape. A group of girls, oblivious of the taunting boys, played hopscotch on a nearby pavement, balancing precariously on one blackstockinged leg.

The boys ringed her, jeering, 'Did ya see the Blessed Virgin, then? Did She speak to ya? Ask ya wot ya wanted for Christmas?'

A burst of laughter, then one boy, knees chapped and raw-looking in the biting wind, shouted, 'If ya see 'er again, ask 'er for a new copper for me mam. Our old one's got an 'ole in it.'

More laughter.

Libby, hands pressed behind her on the rough stones of the wall, faced them defiantly. She was one of the early Christians in Rome, facing the ferocious lions; General Gordon at Khartoum preparing to confront the savage heathens.

She'd discovered long ago that if you didn't answer

back they soon tired and one by one turned away. There wasn't much fun to be gained in baiting a tight-lipped lass who said nothing and glared at a spot somewhere high above their heads. It was the only defiance Libby knew and it worked, even though inside her she wanted to scream back at them, to hurl stones in their stupid faces.

Once, her temper had got the better of her and she'd flung herself forward, instinct telling her to choose the biggest of the boys. She'd snatched at his hair, kicked his shins, curled her hands into fists and punched viciously at his face, catching him squarely on the nose so that blood began to stream. Yelling in panic, he'd broken away and run, chased by the rest of his turncoat gang!

After Mass they stood for a while in the churchyard, talking to friends and neighbours who were all pleased to see Libby looking so well. Back at the house she started dinner while Mam baked.

Every Sunday, after early Mass, Mam baked. Secretly, Libby felt that the world would come to an end if for some reason Mam couldn't bake on a Sunday. She baked for the rest of the week: meat and potato pies; a custard tart made with real eggs, not that yellow powder you got from tins. Jam tarts, filled with whatever kind of jam she could get now that food was scarce.

They would have the tarts and pie for tea that day. There were scones with plump raisins and a jam sponge sprinkled with powdered sugar.

Libby peeled potatoes and dropped them in the big black pot already simmering on top of the stove. In it mutton stew boiled and she added carrots and onions. On top of the stew floated blobs of yellow fat that, Libby remembered, would harden into a stomach-churning mess when cold.

Mam would carefully skim this off and discard it. Well, not really discard it, for Mrs Moran welcomed the gift with open arms. It did great, spread on the children's bread with generous sprinklings of pepper and salt.

'Beggars can't be choosers,' she told Ellen, 'and my conscience wouldn't rest seeing good food like that go to waste.'

Mrs Moran was a good-natured woman in her early forties. Poor as a church mouse, she was a good friend to Mam if inclined to want to stand and gossip more than Mam liked. Mr Moran enjoyed a drink and Libby recalled Friday nights when he staggered home with what remained of his pay packet in his pocket. There always followed screams from the children and sometimes Mrs Moran herself. Libby thanked God her dad wasn't like that. Sure, he would take a drink, but she could never visualise him lifting a hand to Mam. Instead, drink made him jolly and he would grab Mam by the waist and dance wildly about the small kitchen, knocking into things and causing Mam to giggle wildly, like a young girl.

When it was time to return to the Ainslies, Libby did so with a glad heart, although Agnes was still a tribulation and she wished Joseph would write, if only to set Mam's mind at rest.

Dad had voiced an opinion, when Mam was in the back yard, that Joseph was probably keeping his head down as he wouldn't want them to know where he was stationed yet, in case someone reported him for being under age.

'He'll write when he's ready,' was Dad's belief. 'Don't worry, lass. Everything'll turn out all right, you mark my words.'

Libby was to remember those words for a long time to come.

'She ain't come in, Captain. Ain't seen 'ide nor 'air of 'er since the day afore yesterday. The gov'ner's mad, I can tell you. Not like our Josie to not let 'im know if she's sick.'

James thanked the doorman and hurried from the theatre, jostled by the crowds of people intent on getting their tickets for the show. Garishly coloured posters on either side of the doors showed Josie in loose attire; smiling coquettishly over one bare shoulder, a frill of lace barely covering her full breasts; leaning back against a table, her hands supporting her while the robe parted to reveal silken-clad legs. A pose James knew so well . . .

The artist was good, but he had failed to capture the sensual promise in her eyes, the almost translucent white of her skin. Or, thought James grimly, the determination of the full red mouth when yesterday she had said, 'I won't do anything 'asty, Jimmy, I promise.'

With a sense of foreboding he pushed open the door of her apartment. At first, the room seemed to be empty. The fire was a mere glow of embers, the gas jets had not been lit. But there was enough light through the undrawn curtains to see the still form huddled beneath the covers of the bed. Striding forward, James flung his cap and his stick on the chair and bent over the figure of the girl.

'Josie!' His heartbeat quickened, thudding in a kind of panic as he saw the paper-white face. 'My God, girl, you did it, didn't you! You went and bloody did it! Don't you realise how dangerous it could have been? Those old back-street hags are no better than butchers. You could have done yourself irreparable damage, even died . . .'

Josie turned in the bed so that she was lying on her back. Her hand came up to caress his cheek. Her gown was open and he inhaled the warm, silky fragrance of her skin.

She whispered, 'So? No more problems, me boy.'

Her mimicry of what she called his upper-class accent irritated him. His mouth tightened as she went on, 'One of us 'as got to be practically minded. Dirty nappies and squalling kids ain't for me.'

James forced his anger down. One long tendril of hair lay across her breast. He twined it about his fingers, feeling its softness, and instinctively recognising the change in his emotions, Josie made a purring sound and lifted her mouth for his kiss.

Tracing the line of his jaw with one finger, she said, 'I'm sorry I wasn't honest with you, ducks, but I know I did right. Right for me, that is.' Looking at him as she saw his face tighten and with a wisdom that was inborn, she promptly changed the subject. 'Tell me about where you bin staying. We didn't have time last night. What were the people like? The only

Northerners I've met 'ave bin comics with red noses and wandering 'ands.'

James grinned. 'They're not all like that.' Glad to be thinking of something else, he began to talk of the northern seaside town that had been his home for such a short time.

'There were these children and their nursemaid. The boy was a spoiled brat but the girl quite sweet. She, I have to warn you, plans to marry me when she grows up, so you'll have to look to your laurels.' He thought of the morning Libby had confessed this to him and their laughter as they watched the children chasing a small white dog across the sands.

'Cheek!' Josie said, smiling. 'And the nursemaid? I suppose she was a fat old thing that waddled when she walked and sniped at the kids when their mother wasn't about!'

James' grin widened. 'Hardly. Very young. At times she seemed not much older that the children. And yet there was something about her – a maturity that most of the girls of her class don't have.'

'Sounds proper common,' commented Josie. 'A big house, was it? Lots of servants?'

'Enough,' he answered. 'All very respectable as befits an important doctor's abode.' Inner caution stopped him from saying more, especially about Libby. Somehow he didn't want to discuss with Josie the girl who, in his opinion, was in love with a man who wasn't worthy to lick her shoes.

Chapter Ten

March was a bad month. Rain turned to sleet, then an unexpected snowstorm caused people to mutter, 'T'bloody weather, don't know where you are wi' it these days.'

William Gray, his face blue with cold, came in from the back yard, rubbing his hands together. 'God bless us, but the frost is cruel,' he muttered. He washed his hands under the cold tap, the black coal stains running down the yellow stone sink. Rooting in the coal house, in this weather, wasn't his idea of fun. 'Not much good stuff left, love,' he said, turning to his wife. 'I'm going to have to make a visit to the yard again.'

Ellen gave the lump of dough she was kneading on the wooden table top an extra hefty thump. 'I don't like you going there, William. It worries me that you'll be caught.'

William gave a low laugh. 'Aye, there's the chance. But it's not likely. Not many folk about this weather.'

Ellen didn't argue. She'd given over arguing with her husband years ago. Quietly, she went on with her bread-making, thinking how much William would enjoy a thick chunk spread with butter and some of her home-made jam and a mug of strong tea when he returned. He'd be frozen. But if he was lucky they would soon have a good fire going again. She smiled, looking forward to a pleasant evening with her man sitting opposite her in his big chair . . .

The snow drifted in a dazzling white curtain across the fields. Beneath William's feet the ground was iron hard. Old Tom Hardcastle's field still held a couple of dozen turnips, their tops black with frost. Still, he'd seen some of the miners' wives, the one from Gibson Street and the heavily pregnant lass from down the road hacking at the ground with kitchen knives.

They'd achieved little. No one, certainly not two young lasses like that, would be able to shift those turnips. Weren't even fit for t' pigs now, never mind stew for t' kids.

A sudden flurry of snow blew in his face, for a moment blinding him. He pulled the peak of his cloth cap further down over his forehead, wound the long woollen scarf more tightly about his throat. The thin jacket offered little protection against such weather. The only concession William Gray had made to the extreme weather conditions was an extra pair of long Johns.

Our Libby had said that Dr Ainslie had offered her an overcoat donated to the poor of the parish by the relatives of one of his ex-patients. But Mrs Ainslie had objected, pointing out that the town of Ridley was not in the ex-patient's parish.

'Do it once and you'll have everyone for miles around who considers themselves badly done to begging for cast-offs. No, Eric, I won't hear of it. I confess to feeling sorry for such as Libby's family, but you really do take my meaning, don't you?'

Libby, on relating the incident which she happened to overhear while tying the strings of Amy's bonnet in the hall, added that by the sound of the doctor's 'Hurumph' once his wife had finished talking, he didn't take her meaning at all.

Mam had been visibly outraged. Not, as many wives would, by Mrs Ainslie's cavilling attitude, but by the very idea that they needed charity. 'If there's one thing I can do without, our Libby, it's fault-finding from that woman. Forgets who she was, she does. Sarah Brownlee from Mill Rise. Poor as church mice, the lot of 'em.'

So thus in wet and practically sub-zero temperatures, William trudged through the snow on his mission. He'd been off work longer than anyone expected. With the lads fighting at the Front it didn't seem right to William that able-bodied men should have no work to do. Not that he didn't agree with the strike, mind you. A union member all his working life, like the men who toiled along beside him in the pit, the idea of the workers banding together seemed the only solution if they were to get proper pay and conditions. And although Ellen said little, he knew fine what she and the others wives felt. Principles were all right in their place, but they didn't fill hungry bellies or put coal on t' fire.

Shovelling the last few pieces, even sweeping the coal dust into careful piles ready to be collected with a shovel, he'd thought of his wife and how much he hated to see her suffer. If she tried to use that dust it would probably put the fire out. Those last few days in the kitchen had been colder than he ever remembered, the smell of soot and dampness all-pervading. They had been too generous with the coal while Libby was home, basking in front of the warm blaze in a way they hadn't done for a long time. And after Libby had gone to bed and Ellen, undemonstrative as she was, had put her arms about him, he'd felt like a young lad.

Now, as he strode across the fields, the railway embankment came into sight. The stock-piles of coal looked like miniature mountains, covered in snow. Glancing about him, he chose the most promising-looking spot and got down on his hands and knees. The coal was wet and would take some time to dry out. Slag, most of it. Still, it was better than nothing. A godsend to Ellen in her struggle for survival. Against the law, definitely against the law, to take coal from the heaps piled outside the depot. But what was a man to do?

Ah, that was better . . . The shovel dug deeply into the pile of coal. Soon he'd opened a narrow channel, just big enough for him to crawl into. The coal here was only slightly damp. A few feet further and it would be dry. Christ, it was cold! But he'd have a full bucket in no time at this rate . . .

A few yards away a girl straightened up, pressing both hands to the small of her back. She was wasting her time. The ground was too hard to get the turnips. It showed the measure of her desperation that she should even have considered it, heavily pregnant as she was. She'd seen William Gray going towards the coal heaps; guessed his purpose as she noted bucket and shovel.

The woman beside her, hands rough and bleeding from digging in the rough ground, followed her gaze and muttered, 'Old William doin' somethin', any road. Not sittin' on 'is backside at 'ome like my old man. Good luck to 'im, I say . . .'

There was a faint rumbling, a cloud of black dust and the legs of William Gray, protruding from the pile of coal, vanished.

'My God, he's buried under there!' The pregnant girl grabbed the older woman's arm and together they scrambled towards the cave-in.

William heard it coming; knew he could never hope to back out in time. There was coal dust in his eyes, his mouth. He couldn't breathe. The weight of the coal on top of him was agony. Searing waves of pain seemed to crush every bone in his body. He'd never known such agony. He wished it would end. It was his last thought.

It did.

The alarming yellow envelopes were a common sight in those dark days of war. You held your breath as the familiar bicycle appeared at the end of the road, praying to God that the delivery boy would pass you by but at the same time sorry for the unfortunate recipient.

Cook had watched from behind the lace curtains in the kitchen as the boy dismounted. Propping his bike against the railings, he came whistling up the front path. Cook's first thought was: Basil! Then, by all that's holy, he's whistling! But why should he care? It was just a job to him. While to Mrs Ainslie it could mean heartbreak.

Alice opened the front door to his ring. She took the telegram between finger and thumb, warily as though it were alive and going to bite her. She saw it was addressed to Libby. Dear God, she thought, let it not be bad news of Joseph.

Libby was seated to one side of the fireplace, plaiting Amy's hair. In a fit of pique when she'd said they couldn't go for their usual walk because of the weather, Bertie had flung his scarf and gloves into the bath water. Libby had long ago discovered that ignoring these tantrums was the best way of dealing with them. Calmly, she'd fished the knitted items from the bath, wrung them out and hung them to dry over the fireguard.

Unruffled, she'd said, 'Well, Master Bertie, that puts paid to our walk anyway. It'll take an age for those things to dry. Instead, we'll have a nice fairy story. It's just the morning for fires, hot chocolate and a book of favourite stories, don't you agree?'

'No,' shouted Bertie, then looked over his shoulder guiltily, expecting to see Captain Randle's stern and forbidding face appear in the crack of the doorway, quite forgetting that he was no longer there.

'Lovely!' exclaimed Amy, clapping her hands. 'The one about Rumpelstiltskin. I like that.'

Libby had just got to the part where the ugly dwarf forces the princess to spin the straw into gold when the door was pushed open and Alice entered.

Wordlessly, she held out the yellow envelope, her eyes filled with compassion.

Libby ripped it open and read the message. She read it once. Read it twice. Then she turned a stricken face towards Alice and cried, 'Oh, Alice!'

'Libby, what is it? Dear God.' She caught Libby as she fell. 'Dr Ainslie!'

The doctor came into the room, wiping his hands on a linen towel. He froze with horror in the doorway. 'What's happened?' he cried.

Alice was on the point of hysterics. 'Oh, doctor, please help me. Quickly, quickly!'

Together they eased Libby on to the settee. The doctor loosened her clothing and raised her feet. 'Fetch the smelling salts, Alice. Hurry.'

Alice rushed away and with his arm supporting Libby's head Dr Ainslie read the telegram. 'It's not possible!' he breathed. 'It can't be.' He let the single sheet flutter to the floor as Libby groaned.

Alice returned with the smelling salts, followed by an agitated Mrs Ainslie. She snatched the small, cut-glass bottle from which Alice had already removed the silver screw top and held it to her own nose for a moment before administering it to Libby. Meanwhile Alice stooped and picked up the telegram. The doctor saw her face go white.

'There, there,' said the doctor, gently patting Libby's cheek. 'It's all right, all right.'

Libby coughed and jerked her head away from the salts. With consciousness came memory and she started to sob wildly.

The children who, up until then, had been watching

181

with unease, immediately followed her example. Freeing herself from the doctor's ministrations, Libby sat upright, her gaze fixed on the paper in Alice's hand, seemingly unaware of anything else. Then her eyes flew to Dr Ainslie's concerned face, as if trying to gain some reassurance from him. His voice was full of pain as he said, 'You'll have to go home. Straight away.'

Ignoring his wife's startled look, he went on, 'Now, lass. Get yourself to your room and pack a few things. You're to stay home as long as your mother needs you, hear? Doesn't matter how long it takes.'

Avoiding his wife's indignant glare, her: 'Really, Eric!' he bent to pat Libby's hand. 'Remember what I say. As long as she needs you.'

Dr Ainslie had been aghast at the news of William Gray's death. He felt desperately sorry for Libby's mother. Poor Ellen! Life hadn't been easy for her. It really seemed to have a grudge against the Gray family. And yet a kinder, more beautiful soul than Ellen he'd yet to meet. She came so clearly to mind, slender and upright still, her fine hair still untouched by grey. Her voice in the church as she sang like a purling stream.

Sarah, his own wife, had rapidly lost her trim figure and with it her placid disposition, blaming the birth of their son so early in their marriage for this; Basil, who had caused a few raised eyebrows and sidelong glances when he'd arrived just seven months after the wedding . . .

Later, when their fortunes had changed and he had acquired the practice at St Aiden's, the births of their other two children, just as Sarah was gaining a foothold in the town's limited society, caused her temper to become more waspish.

It had been a joy having Ellen's daughter under his roof, instilling a modicum of that gentle goodness that had nothing to do with class or school into his children.

He could never understand what his wife had against Libby. She made no bones of her dislike. Now, with Mrs Ainslie breathing fire and with dire warnings that she couldn't be expected to put up with this ceaseless journeying home for much longer, Libby was packed off to the station. Mrs Ainslie's last words were that she should return as soon as possible, never mind what the doctor had said about staying as long as she was needed.

A few days later when a knock sounded on the front door, Libby was surprised to find Gwenda Naylor standing there. Slightly hesitant, for she didn't really know Libby all that well, having been introduced only briefly one evening at the Church Hall dance, Gwenda said, 'I just had to come. I was so sorry to hear about your father.'

Libby nodded. 'Thank you.' She bit her lip. 'Won't you come in?' Mam was next door, visiting Mrs Moran, listening, thought Libby wryly, to the woman going on about the strike, so they would have the kitchen to themselves if Gwenda wanted to talk about Joseph. Fresh tears would appear in Mam's eyes each time his name was mentioned, so Libby tried not to upset her further. 'I'll make a cup of tea.'

Settled by the fire, Gwenda began without pre-amble, 'Have you heard from Joseph?'

'No.' Libby shook her head.

The two girls sipped their tea, gazing reflectively into the glowing coals of the fire. 'Men are not very good at writing letters, are they?' Gwenda said. 'He's only been gone a few months. I expect that whenever he gets to where he's going he'll write then.'

Libby gazed at Gwenda seated in the old armchair that had been Dad's. 'You like him, don't you?'

Gwenda nodded. She liked him. More than liked him, she told herself. And yet she couldn't help teasing him, he was so immature, even for sixteen. Not at all like the other boys she had known. And yet, wasn't that the very reason she *did* like him? She felt safe with him; never threatened like with some of the other lads she had been out with. And Daddy thought he had a future in the music business! So why on earth had he wanted to go and do such a silly thing as joining up before he had to? In another two years when he was old enough, the war might be over and he wouldn't have had to go at all.

So, to punish him for going against her wishes, she had continued to torment him, knowing she shouldn't, knowing that her own conscience would bother her after he was gone, but unable to help herself. Con-trary, that was what she was. Hadn't her father told her that over and over again?

Mam had become so thin you felt you could blow her off your hand. She looked like a dry twig in her black dress. Neighbours called often, recalling what a grand man was William, what a good husband and father. How he used to go out of his way to help anyone and what terrible things this strike was doing to folk.

It took Libby a while to realise that Mam's calm demeanour was misleading. She would sit for hours in Dad's chair, eyes vacant, a piece of sewing left forgotten in her lap. Her work-worn hands would slide up and down the shiny armrests. Often Libby would have to repeat herself two or three times before Mam even heard her, and then she answered in such a vague way it brought a lump to Libby's throat.

Sometimes Mam would press her cheek against the worn plush padding of the back of the chair and breathe deeply, as though the smell of William still lingered; the odour of tobacco and the bay rum he had used sometimes on his hair.

Once Mam jerked upright in her chair, head bent forward in a listening position. To Libby's alarm, she called out, as though in answer to some unheard question, 'It's in the top right-hand drawer, William. Hold on a minute, I'll be right up.'

She rose and without a glance at Libby went upstairs. Libby sat frozen, one hand to her throat. There were other incidents, with Libby becoming increasingly dismayed, when she literally had to fight Mam; that was on the evening Mam insisted she had to go home, that her mother was waiting.

Father Brady listened gravely as they met at the church door after Mass. She'd left Mam asleep in bed, Libby explained, feeling unable to cope if Mam should suddenly stand up and wander away in the middle of the service.

The old priest shook his head, her suffering mirrored in the kindly face. 'Ah, lass, we've all got our crosses to bear but yours seems harder than most. When do you have to be back at the Ainslies'?'

Libby repeated the doctor's words, adding with a worried frown, 'But, Father, how can I? I can't leave my mother while she's like this.'

Father Brady read in her eyes the conflict of loyalties battling within her. He said, his voice harsh, 'What about your sister? Cannot Agnes shoulder her share of caring for your mother?'

Libby was too shamed to tell him that Agnes had gone. Had moved out as soon as the funeral was over, taking her few possessions with her. Libby didn't think Mam had even noticed.

The old priest grieved for her. Over the years he had become an expert at reading the minds of his flock. His voice more kindly now, he said, 'I fully appreciate your dilemma, my child, and I admire your devotion to your mother. I can understand how you are in conflict over your duty to your employers and your love for your mother. But without help I do not see how you are to resolve this matter without putting your mother's well-being in jeopardy.'

He went on to say the thing that had been uppermost in his mind for days, ever since he'd last visited the house and seen Ellen Gray sitting in her husband's chair, oblivious to the life about her. 'There is a home, Elizabeth Mary, run by the Little Sisters of the Rosary, who take in such cases as your mother and care for them . . .'

He got no further. Libby gasped with something

akin to horror. 'I mean no disrespect, Father,' she said through tight lips, 'but I'll pretend I didn't hear you say that.' She straightened her shoulders, lifted her small chin.

'Now, lass, it was just a suggestion. No need to take it the wrong way.' But a suggestion that might have to be acted upon, he thought, if Ellen showed no signs of improvement. And, with a knowledge that spanned fifty years of ministering to his congregation, he could see little likelihood of that.

More than once in the days that followed, Libby was to meditate on the priest's advice. She'd heard of such homes. Terrible people were sent there. Women whose families were unable to cope, or, as some said with tightly pursed lips, who just plain couldn't be bothered. Heaven forbid it should come to that!

From Alice there came a letter, badly spelled, telling of Kathleen's struggle with the children and their constant queries echoed by their mother as to when Libby planned to return to her duties.

As though it wasn't a duty to be with her own mother just now, thought Libby bitterly! Alice added that Cook sent her love, as did she. She added, almost as an afterthought, that Vince had been at the back door asking for her.

'I really think he misses you, Libby. Last time he came, though, Cook saw him through the kitchen window and chased him before he even got down the area steps.'

Libby tried to find comfort reminiscing about the hours she and Vince had spent together. So few of them, and then mostly in the chill darkness of the

promenade shelter or in the small park. She remembered the meeting after their difference of opinion,
as she liked to think of it. How could a man have two
completely different sides to his nature? There was
the Vince who had first been attracted to her, good-
looking and pleasant, always ready for a laugh. A
man who excited her, who promised her the world.
'We might have to wait a long time, young Libby.
Ages and ages. But we'll get it someday.'

The man who had lifted her from her feet and
carried her across the rocks when high tide had
caught them unawares, laughing at the stares of the
passers-by, refusing to put her down until they were
on the corner of St Anne's Place. 'Vince!' she'd
hissed through her teeth. 'Suppose Mrs Ainslie came
along and saw us! It doesn't take much for her to be
on my back and this would give her a perfect excuse
to nag. "How unladylike!" ' she mimicked in a high-
pitched voice. ' "Libby Gray, take a hundred lines on
how *not* to behave in the street. No, better make it
two hundred." '

Vince had laughed and with a swift kiss full on her
mouth dropped her to her feet. 'Why does she dislike
you so much?' he'd asked.

Libby had wrinkled her nose. 'Now, there's a good
question! It's always been a suspicion of mine that the
doctor fussed too much over my Mam when I was a little girl and always so ill. Mam worked for him for a
time and he always treated her like a lady. I suppose
his wife must have resented it.'

'Jealousy rears its ugly head!' Vince had joked.

'That, too,' Libby had nodded.

'I can never understand why you ended up working for her, knowing she felt that way.'

'Oh, she wasn't always like that. Not at first, anyway. And the doctor's kind. He treats me like one of his own children.'

For a moment jealousy had stirred in Vince. Then he'd thought of the elderly doctor and his caring bedside manner and grinned.

Now Libby realised, there was the dark side of Vince as well; the violence ready at the drop of a hat to take over. The lashing out at anything that got in his way. She could only pray that she would see him again. With this new call-up who knew what the future held! But times for the luxury of dreaming were few. Mam was a constant worry, although there were days when Libby imagined she seemed a little better, more coherent. She took advantage of one such time to do some shopping in Ridley High Street. The market square was a short tram ride away and she would only be gone for an hour or two. Libby asked her neighbour if she would keep an eye on Mam. Mrs Moran said she would make a nice cup of tea and seeing that Mam seemed so much better they would have a good gossip. 'Don't hurry, now,' she advised the grateful girl as she filled the kettle at the sink. 'Enjoy yourself. It'll do you good to get away for a couple of hours.'

Libby thought of her words as she hopped off the tram. It was later than she'd intended, although not yet dark, even though lights were showing in the shops and the street lamps were being lit. A thin drizzle of rain had started which would soon melt the last remaining patches of snow, turning them into muddy puddles.

The house was dark and silent. A quick check upstairs showed that Mam wasn't in her room. Libby's own room was dark and empty. Mrs Moran must have taken Mam home with her. Probably busy getting her husband's tea. Throwing a woollen shawl about her shoulders, Libby crossed the back yard and went in to her neighbour's.

'I'm back, Mrs Moran. Thank you for having Mam. I'll take her off your hands now . . .'

The woman straightened from ladling stew from the big black pot on the stove. Together with half a dozen little faces gathered about the kitchen table she stared at Libby with perplexity. 'I left your mam sleeping, lass. In her bedroom. She kept dropping off, so finally I got her upstairs and tucked her in, although she was still dressed. I've not been home more'n ten minutes.'

A quick search confirmed Libby's worst fears. Mam's handbag was missing, but not her shoes or shawl. Dear God, thought Libby, she's never gone off barefooted! She couldn't forgive herself if anything happened to her mother.

Almost instinctively, Libby's steps turned towards the cemetery on the hill. Dad was there so that was Mam's favourite place. However, there was no sign of Mam, although a jar of red holly berries, freshly plucked from the hedge guarding the cemetery, had been placed on the still raw-looking mound of earth.

Frantically she searched the churchyard, peering into the church porch and, on impulse, went in, pulling the woollen shawl over her head. She dipped her finger in the tiny white china dish of holy water, crossed herself and genuflected deeply before kneeling on a shabby stool. 'Dear Lord, help me find her,' she prayed. 'Please! The rain's coming on heavy and our Mam's not wearing a coat or shoes.' She lifted her eyes to gaze beseechingly towards the Virgin in her blue robes, the soft brown hair falling about her shoulders and it seemed to the worried girl that for the second time in her short life the Virgin's features expressed an opinion. That first time, when she'd been a small child, the Mother of Jesus had frowned. Now she could have sworn the Virgin smiled. Walking quietly to the small side altar, Libby added another candle to the lighted tiers glittering there. She slipped a penny into the tin box, then kissed the bare plaster foot of the Virgin. The tiny foot was icy cold. Mam's feet would be cold, too. Libby shuddered. Raising her eyes one last time, she prayed under her breath, 'Please, dear Mother Mary, please . . .'

She found her mother at the tram stop at the end of the road. Some kind soul had insisted she share his umbrella, for without shoes or shawl she was soaked to the skin.

The large shabby handbag Libby had known since as far back as she could remember was clutched to her bosom in both blue-veined hands. She totally ignored Libby, her mouth held in a tight line, staring ahead for the first sign of lights from the tram.

Libby slipped her own shawl about her mother's shoulders. 'Come on, Mam, let's get you home. It's a miserable night and you need a good fire and dry clothing.'

Ellen Gray pushed the girl's hands away, roughly, abruptly. 'Leave me be. I'm getting the tram to Westlea.' Tears appeared in her mother's eyes. 'I have to call the cows in. My mother expects me to call the cows in.'

Somehow, she never knew how, Libby got Mam home. That night Libby did not sleep, unable to banish the memory of her mother waiting so patiently for a tram that would take her back to a place that no longer existed, that was now a huddle of rat-infested barns and the blackened ruins of the once comfortable farmhouse where Ellen had been born.

Weary with imaginings, Libby rose just before dawn and went downstairs to make a pot of tea. Mam was still asleep. She stood by the kitchen window, sipping her tea and gazing out at the still-dark morning. A few lights shone from back windows, telling of early risers; miners on early shift or perhaps a mother nursing a fretful infant.

There, in that icy kitchen, Libby had never felt so lonely. It was as though she were the only one left in the world, as though all she knew and loved had vanished forever.

She wondered if this was how the last human being on earth would feel, the day the world ended, the way the Bible warned, in flames . . .

Chapter Eleven

Listening next morning to her tearful account of the night's happenings, Father Brady frowned in dismay.

'It grieves me to say this, Elizabeth Mary, but you are going to have to admit that you cannot cope. What if you hadn't found your mother last night at the tram stop? Barefooted, without even the protection of a shawl, how long do you suppose before she caught her death of cold? Or worse! A woman, clearly disturbed, wandering the streets with night coming on. It is a situation that invites disaster.'

Libby hung her head. 'I know, Father.'

Even so, she was unwilling to acknowledge the old priest's warnings. 'Still, I couldn't bear the thought of her going away, into that place you mentioned . . .'

'The nuns are kind. And they are there all the time. How long do you suppose it will be before you feel you must go back to Dr Ainslie's, or, failing that, have to look for something nearer home? You have to live, girl. Face it, you *cannot* cope. Be sensible now and admit it, as you will have to do eventually, painful as I know it is.'

*   *   *

Her footsteps echoed hollowly as Libby followed the black-robed figure along the silent corridors and into a small side office. Sister Beatrice sat behind a desk and waved Libby to the other chair. Lively blue eyes smiled at her from behind round metal-framed glasses. 'I will just read what Father Brady had to say and then we will go through a few particulars.'

The nun busied herself with reading the letter Libby had handed her, then looked up, a frown of distress on the pretty face. 'Your mother, I see! Indeed, it is a terrible thing but you can rest assured that she will be safe with us. You, my child, are far too young to have to bear the responsibility of such a burden.'

'I don't mind, Sister.' Libby spoke hastily, the words spilling out in her nervousness. 'I would give my life for my mother. Only Father Brady said . . .'

The woman smiled. 'That would hardly help your mother, child, giving your life. And Father Brady, you will find, was right. Now,' rising to her feet, suddenly business-like, 'we will get you to sign a few papers and all will be done.'

Libby signed her name where the nun showed her, feeling as the pen moved that a knife was slowly turning in her heart. She asked herself, with abhorrence, how could she be doing this? Her own mother! Handing her over to the care of strangers at the very time she most needed her own family!

Father Brady had assured her it would only be for a little while. That in no time at all, in the care of the nuns, her mother would recover her old spirits.

Gazing about her now, at the cool, white walls, the

high ceilings and assiduously polished wooden floors, the whole smelling of beeswax and incense from the tiny nearby chapel, Libby tried to convince herself that she was doing the right, the only, thing. That Mam *would* be better off here. Why, then, did she feel such a sense of betrayal, such anguish?

She looked at the statue of the Sacred Heart but experienced no lifting of the spirit, no gladness, such as she usually felt. Eee, something was surely wrong with her! The very worst thing that could happen to her now would be to lose her faith.

The nun watched the play of emotions sweep over the young face. 'Don't worry,' she said consolingly. 'Your mother will receive the very best of care.'

Libby smiled and said yes and thank you and allowed Sister Beatrice to lead her back to the front door of the home. The nun's parting words were, 'Your mother will be fine, so stop frowning. That look would curdle the milk.'

Libby remembered Cook using that same expression in the warm cheerful kitchen at St Anne's Place. She wondered if she would ever see it again.

That night, worn out with weeping, she crept up to her bed. She felt she had touched some rock bottom of grief, that never again, even though future tragedies might be far, far greater, would she ever plumb such depths of misery.

Kneeling at the side of her bed, she prayed for the repose of the soul of her father. She asked God's protection and blessing for Mam, for Agnes and Joseph, and that she should help herself become a better person. She ended with: 'And, Holy Mother, save us all from destruction and let Joseph come home safely and Vince and Captain Randle.'

Father Brady, in his bossy but kindly way, persuaded her it would be better if she returned now to the Ainslies.

'The children will keep you busy and you won't have much time to brood,' he said. 'I will keep in touch and I'm sure Mrs Ainslie will allow you time off to come and visit your mother.'

Libby knew that what he said made sense. That if she stayed longer in that small, shabby house with its memories of Mam and Dad, of herself lying on her lonely bed upstairs, wheezing but content as long as she had her beloved books, she would just brood and make herself ill. With Dad, Joseph and Agnes gone, at this time, above all, she had to be strong. Besides, how much longer would Mrs Ainslie put up with her absence? She'd heard no more from Alice so didn't know how things were shaping at the Ainslies'. If she tarried much longer she might find she had nothing to return to. And with the meagre wage she received from Mrs Ainslie her only source of income, that was something she could not afford to risk.

Father Brady promised that if there were any news of Agnes he would inform her straight away. 'And I'll keep my eye open for the postman,' said Mrs Moran, 'just in case there's a letter from Joseph.'

Convincing herself that everything would turn out for the best, Libby caught a train back to the coast.

*   *   *

The children went into raptures upon seeing her. It was very gratifying, knowing how much she had been missed. The reception from Mrs Ainslie was less enthusiastic. She informed Libby coldly that she fully expected her to make up for lost time. 'These shenanagins have gone on long enough, my girl. I don't keep a dog and expect to bark myself.'

'Ungrateful old cow!' Alice almost spat the word as Libby related the scene. 'She can talk! It was Kathleen that took over, not her. Fat lot she does for her kids! Lady Muck! Take no notice of her, love. No soul, that's the trouble with her, old skinflint.'

There were tears in Cook's eyes as she hugged Libby, saying how sorry she was to hear Libby's grievous news. 'And, after all that, your mother ill, too?' As though unable to grasp this terrible calamity, she said, 'It don't bear thinking about.'

At the first opportunity, whispering to Alice where she was going, Libby slipped out of the back door, her coat around her shoulders. She ran almost all the way to the prom, finding to her relief the shelter where she and Vince usually met empty. She waited for as long as she dared and finally, when she was on the point of giving up, Vince appeared.

'I knew you was back,' he explained. 'A pal of mine saw you walking from the station. I heard about your dad. Sorry.'

Libby wept bitter tears on Vince's shoulder. It was the first time he'd seen her cry and he was disturbed at the way it affected him, and with the problems he had to face he wasn't ready to begin feeling sorry for anyone.

'Please, Libby, don't . . .' His arms about her, he held the slight figure to him, one hand tangled in the heavy mass of her hair. 'It's a terrible thing but you have to bear it.'

'I don't want to bear it,' Libby protested with sudden violence. 'I want things back as they were. Oh, Vince, why do things like this happen? Dad was such a good man, a kind and gentle man. He would never have harmed a soul. Why should he have to die in such a terrible way, alone and in darkness?'

Vince's arms tightened about her. Who was to answer such questions? Certainly not Vince Remede. The first thing that had entered his mind on hearing of the death of Libby's father, was, 'Silly old geezer! Throwing away his life like that. They can't have been all that desperate for coal, surely.'

Only Libby knew they were. The days she had spent at home had done more harm than if she'd politely but firmly ignored Dr Ainslie's insistence that she visit her family. Ignoring protestations that she wasn't cold, Dad had kept the fire going all day instead of only lighting it towards evening, a habit that had come about with the strike. And now he was gone. She would never see him again, never hear that beloved voice calling her his 'little girl'.

'It's not fair, not fair,' she sobbed. 'Isn't there enough death without taking Dad?'

'Nothing's fair in this world, Libby.' Vince's voice was harsh. He hadn't yet told Libby about his calling-up papers. Vince felt he had enough troubles of his own at the moment. Much as he sympathised with Libby's, his own were of paramount importance.

Reading the papers that had arrived by post that morning, all the high principles about which he'd boasted crumbled to dust. Conscientious objectors served their country or went to prison. It was as simple as that. Only a tiny majority of genuine conscientious objectors were prepared to suffer the indignity of prison, never mind the scorn of their fellow men, and Vince Remede wasn't one of them.

'Persuaded' in to the recruiting office, he realised all too well that after the most meagre training his next stop would be the trenches. Unable to keep it to himself a moment longer, his gaze fixed over her head to the stretch of beach left by the outgoing tide, where a man walked alone, his dog yapping senselessly at the hovering seagulls, he said suddenly, 'Guess what I got this mornin'? Me calling-up papers.'

Libby, who had stopped crying and was resting her cheek against his jacket, didn't answer at once.

Vince felt anger stir in him. Putting his hands on her shoulders and pushing her away from him he held her at arm's length. 'Well, thank you for your show of concern! I might have guessed you'd be pleased. Give you more time to devote to your poor wounded hero.'

Libby was too shaken to speak. How could he accuse her of such duplicity? Of course she was concerned. She loved him, didn't she? Was going to marry him! Yet, even though she told herself these things, a strange sort of anger mixed with disappointment, welled up inside her.

Unable to help herself, she said, 'Well, we did know it would happen sooner or later, didn't we?'

His big hands tightening on her shoulders, he tried to pull her towards him again. 'Any road, maybe *I'll* return the big hero and you'll be able to look after me like you've bin looking after that snotty-nosed captain.'

Libby gasped with indignation. 'You know that's not true . . .'

'No! Swanning around on the prom with 'im, letting 'im buy you ice cream, that little brat and her brother calling 'im Uncle James!'

Then seeing how her face paled he was suddenly filled with compassion. 'Try to understand, Libby. Try to forgive me when I hurt you. I don't *mean* it. I love you so much . . .'

With a wrench of tenderness she touched his cheek. He looked so vulnerable and she had never been able to stay angry with him.

A wave of tenderness made her eyes damp and she seemed to drift towards him until he was holding her close and kissing her with a desperation that both excited her and filled her with a dread that was not fear but the instinctive caution of the times. She loved him and he was her Vince and he might soon have to go away to some terrible battlefield, leaving her cold and lonely.

He grunted, a searching hand finding the silken smoothness of an inner thigh, cursing as she gave a little cry and drew back. 'Bloody 'ell, you're not going to refuse me now, are you? Now that I'm going to be one of the death and glory boys you seem to admire so much?'

His hand was again investigating the thick petticoat she wore under her skirt . . .

With a mighty push, Libby sent him flying. Perched
as he was on the narrow wooden seat it wasn't difficult. With an expression of surprise that in any other
circumstances would have had her in fits of giggles,
he landed on his backside on the tiled floor of the
shelter. Hurt amazement gave way to anger. With his
roar ringing in her ears, Libby turned and, picking up
her skirts, ran all the way back to the safety of Cook's
kitchen.

She would see him in the morning, she told herself.
He would be furious, his pride hurt more than anything else and she would have to try and explain her
rejection of him as tactfully as she knew how.

The morning brought heavy rain and winds that
swept in from the north, making the little seaside
town a bleak place. Would spring never arrive?
Impossible to take the children out and so no chance
of seeing Vince. Before a leaping coal fire she played
games with the children, Old Maid and Snap, and
toasted thick slices of bread on the end of a long fork,
kneeling on the old hearth rug, the heat from the
flames burning her cheeks. They sipped hot cocoa
and ate the warm toast, spread deliciously with farm
butter and honey, and Libby tried not to let her
thoughts stray to Vince or what her mother might be
doing at that moment.

Ellen Gray was listening to Sister Beatrice as she
explained the various duties inmates of the home
were required to perform. Although kind, the nuns

put up with no nonsense. If you were well enough to work, you worked, and Ellen Gray they considered well enough. Physically there was nothing wrong with her. Vague, perhaps, in her manner, but still strong and comparatively healthy.

Convinced that work, plus the company of other women, would help, Sister Beatrice walked with her to the stone-flagged room that served as laundry to the home. Ellen caught her breath at the thick smell of bleach, soap and soda, and clouds of steam that rose to the ceiling. Huge zinc tubs were full of linen, and women with sleeves rolled high, their heavy dresses unbuttoned at the neck, and partly protected by rubber aprons and pieces of sacking, bent over them.

Sister Beatrice led Ellen to a tub filled with newly washed sheets ready to be mangled. Sudden doubt took hold of her as she met Ellen's blank gaze. 'Mrs Gray, are you feeling unwell? Would you rather rest?'

Ellen gave a tremulous smile. Although she didn't fully comprehend what was expected of her, she recognised the bath full of coarse sheets and gazed with awe at the heavy, old-fashioned mangle with its large wooden rollers, covered with cotton pads. Bewildered by the strangeness of everything, wondering why she was standing in this steam-clouded room with these strange women gawping at her, instead of her own tiny wash-house in the yard, she murmured, 'No, I'm all right. Thank you, Sister, for asking – you're very kind . . .'

'Very well, dear. I'll come back and see how you're

doing in a little while.' Sister Beatrice spoke to a woman who was dragging heavy sheets from the boilers into a vast sink, using the dip-stick with a deftness that spoke of long practice, the twisting and throwing of the hot linen an art.

'Keep an eye on her, Cassie. Help her if you have to.'

Despite her assurances to Sister Beatrice, resentment showed in Cassie's every move as she helped Ellen fold a sheet and then watched as Ellen pushed the ends through the wooden rollers, using both hands to turn the handle. 'Don't be afraid, Lady Jane,' she taunted maliciously, ' 'ard work never killed anyone yet.'

She swivelled her eyes to where the other women had straightened from their work, enjoying the little game of mocking the newcomer. Ellen ignored her, bending almost double as she grasped the shiny handle. Sweat soon beaded her top lip and forehead and the muscles of her back and shoulders burned as though red hot needles had been thrust into them. But suddenly, miraculously, it was a joy to see the neatly folded linen piled in the bath and ready for the washing line. She'd almost finished folding her last sheet, when Cassie came over again to inspect her work, Sister Beatrice's request to keep an eye on Ellen giving her a feeling of superiority. 'My, we 'ave bin busy! Sister'll be so pleased. But don't think you've finished yet, me lady.' She jerked her thumb to where a white-haired woman lifted towels from a boiler. 'Plenty more to do afore you're finished.'

Ellen gave her a long, steady look and without a

word walked over to where the next load of laundry
waited. Still without speaking, ruining completely
Cassie's transitory triumph, she proceeded to fold
the towels lengthwise, ready for the mangle. She
found she could do it with one hand while guiding the
washing with the other. She remembered, suddenly,
wash-days of the past, incidents both funny and sad;
once when they were newly married and she had
popped off every button on William's best Sunday
shirt with careless mangling. How William had
laughed, swearing that he bet not many lassies could
do that in one fell swoop. She recalled hanging out
the washing in the stone-flagged yard, sometimes,
when it was really cold, bringing the things in frozen
as stiff as cardboard cut-outs. They had to be placed
round the fire on the backs of chairs and they began
to drip as the heat of the fire melted them.

Automatically her hands turned the rollers, her
thoughts on another day, another time. Too late the
white-haired woman cried a warning. 'Eee, lass,
watch out! Your fingers!'

Too late to free her hand from the tight-fitting
rollers. All four fingers of her right hand had gone
through before realisation hit her and she stopped
turning.

'Turn it back! Go on, turn t'handle t'other
way . . . !'

The woman's voice rose on the edge of panic.
Stupidly, Ellen stood staring down at the trapped
hand. She felt as though her feet were rooted to the
spot. Her body was paralysed, refusing to recognise
the distress signals sent out by her brain.

There was no pain, nothing. Only that dreadful shocked numbness. Dimly she was aware of a voice shouting in her ear. The words could have been in Greek for all the sense they made. Then someone was wrenching at her other hand that still held grimly to the handle, forcibly pulling it away. Almost reluctantly Ellen let it go and at the very same moment she saw bright spurts of blood staining the newly washed linen. Her hand came free, and with it came the agony. Holding her injured hand up before her face, Ellen gazed at it as would a small child given some object it had never seen before. Blood ran down her arm, warm, sticky, disappearing under the cuff of her old woollen cardigan.

I wish that daft woman would stop screaming! was her thought. It's enough to pierce a body's eardrums.

Then, as the stone floor came up to hit her, she realised with some embarrassment that it was her own voice she could hear.

Chapter Twelve

Libby made that second unhappy journey home as
though in a trance. The tall smoking chimneys
appearing as the train neared Ridley meant only
further heartbreak. Father Brady's letter had merely
said that Mam had had an accident and was in
hospital. What sort of an accident? Libby wondered.
Surely Mam hadn't been allowed to venture out on
her own, to roam the streets in her condition? Libby
tossed her head away from the thought, as a sick
person does from pain, then tried to be more sensible.
Now was the time to think of more positive things, not
let her imagination run wild.

Could anyone ever really describe it? she thought
as she let herself into the house. That empty feeling
where silence prevailed and footsteps echoed in icy
unused rooms.

Hanging her coat and beret on the wooden peg in
the hall, she saw that one of Dad's old jackets and the
cap he wore on Sundays was still hanging there. She
buried her face in the rough tweed, tears welling in
her eyes. The feel of the cloth evoked vivid memories
of her father, that tall, soldierly man who had been
such a comfort in her childhood. Always so full of

fun, teasing, playing jokes on people, never cross, not even with Agnes at her most impossible.

She remembered one fine summer's day, sitting on the front doorstep, singing 'The Last Rose of Summer'. As the last lingering '. . . or to give sigh, for sigh . . .' died away, her father murmured, dreamily, 'Eee, lass, that were great! You're like a little brown nightingale, singing there in the sun.'

Libby had laughed. 'Go on, Dad. Nightingales don't sing in the sun.'

'You know what I mean. A voice like yours, our Libby, it's a gift from the angels. The whole world should hear it.' She wondered what he would have said if she had told him about singing for the wounded troops at the convalescent home. He'd have been proud, she was sure. Then fresh tears flooded, as she realised that she could never tell him now. That was one of the worst things about death, she thought. The wish that you had told someone about a happening, realising that the chance would never come again.

The sound of the back door opening had her wiping her eyes with the backs of her hands, turning to face whoever was there.

'Eee, lass, I never knew you was 'ere.' Mrs Moran stood in the kitchen entrance. 'I never 'eard you come.'

Neat and tidy as behoved a good Lancashire housewife in her black skirt and pinny, she smiled at Libby. ' 'Ave you bin to see your mam yet? Or 'eard how she is?'

Libby shook her head. 'No. I've only just arrived. I

want to get up to the hospital as soon as I can.'

'You'll 'ave some tea first. I've just made a fresh pot. Can't make that journey all the way from t'coast and then face your mam in 'ospital without 'aving somethin' inside you.'

'I'm all right, Mrs Moran. Really . . .'

'Your mam would be vexed if I let you go off without at least a cup of tea. Come on now, lass. It'll be brewed to death in a minute.'

To save further argument, Libby went.

Hospitals had always alarmed Libby. The high beds ranged in neat rows along each side. The faces of the patients still, arms tucked so tightly under the red blankets that only their eyes moved. One old body was insisting that she couldn't breathe, that she was in a strait-jacket.Throwing the bedclothes off she glared defiantly at the young nurse who hurried over. Libby couldn't help but admire the calm voice that explained why it was better to have the bedclothes tucked in tight. 'Don't want any nasty draught coming in the side, now, do we, giving you a chill?'

'Rather 'ave a chill than be throttled to death,' complained the old lady.

'She's a right one,' said Mam, whose bed was next to the troublesome old dear. 'Always on about something, but a good laugh at times.' She gazed about her at the dreary green-painted ward with its wooden block floor and chipped enamel beds. 'Need something to laugh about in here.'

The nurse fetched a chair and Libby seated herself beside Mam's bed. She took in the transformation from the vacant-eyed wraith she'd last seen to the woman who smiled at her now. 'Oh, Mam, you don't know how good it is to see you so well again.' The nurse had assured her Mam's hand would heal in time and had given a short account of how the accident happened, adding that it really was nobody's fault, merely one of those things. 'She's a brave little soul,' she said, 'and it was a nasty shock. But we hope for a full recovery.'

'How you getting on then, Libby?' Mam turned her head on the white pillow to look at her.

'Fine, Mam.'

Not for the world would she confess to Mam Mrs Ainslie's reaction over the arrival of Father Brady's letter.

'She's barely back than she's off again. But for you, Eric, I would have considered her dismissal long ago.'

It was against Mrs Ainslie's principles giving the servants whole weekends off, infrequent as they were. But the doctor had insisted. His argument had been, how could they refuse their staff the little freedom they had when the whole world was fighting for that very freedom? 'Slavery went out decades ago, my dear. You must admit, these girls have little enough time off as it is.' Libby, standing by the door with hands folded in front of her, received a kind look from Dr Ainslie.

'I don't agree, Eric. Our staff are lucky to be working in a good Christian home. They could be doing very much worse. As for the freedom you speak

of, Libby abuses your soft-heartedness shamefully.'
The look she gave Libby wasn't so kind.

Libby smiled now at her mother, holding her hand on top of the coverlet. 'How are they treating you, Mam?'

'Well.' Only the lines on her mother's face told a different story. Libby stayed as long as they would let her. When the bell went for the close of visiting hours, she rose and bent to kiss her mother's cheek.

'I'll be in again tomorrow, Mam. Is there anything you want?'

'If you're down the market you could bring me some of those treacle toffees old Billy Hill makes. You know his stall, just inside the side entrance near the one that sells boots.'

Libby smiled. 'Yes, Mam, I know it. I'll get some this afternoon.'

Her mother's lips were faintly tinged with blue. She looked cold. 'Only if you're that way, love. Don't want to be a nuisance.'

Libby's hand lingered on hers, then tucked in the blankets, making sure nothing she could do was omitted. It was a good moment.

'Sleep tight. See you tomorrow, then. God bless.'

She heard the swish of the nurse's skirts behind her. 'Miss Gray, everyone's left but you. I must insist . . .'

Spring sunlight was warm on Libby's shoulders as she walked home, taking a shortcut through the park. The skies were a clear pale blue, the warmth of the sun like a blessing.

It was while she was making a pot of tea for her breakfast the following morning that there was a knock on the front door and opening it she came face to face with Father Brady.

'Elizabeth Mary!' The faded eyes brimmed with compassion and, she could have sworn, tears. She stared at him, the door half open until he said softly, 'Let's go inside. It's a mite cold on the doorstep.'

Hastily she drew back. 'Of course, Father. Come in.' She led the way into the kitchen. 'I've just made a pot of tea. Sit down and share it with me.'

Without waiting for his answer she bent over the table, her hands busy with cups and saucers. The paper bag of treacle toffees her mother had requested was on the table, together with a small bunch of bronze chrysanthemums in a jam jar. She'd waited until the flower stall was nearly closing and the man had let her have them cheap. Still, placed in the jar of water overnight they had perked up and looked quite presentable. 'Not too bad, are they?' She smiled, adding milk to his cup. 'Mam'll love them. She loves flowers. Couldn't hardly ever afford them, though. And the toffees – Mr Hill must have been tiddly, gave me far more than I asked for.'

Old Billy Hill made all his own sweets: the most delicious coconut candy, both pink and white, a dark, strong-tasting brown sweet, ideal for those chesty coughs, the treacle toffee that Mam loved so much and a host of other delicacies loved by three generations of local children, aye, and by their parents, too.

Old Billy had known they were for Mam. Always had a soft spot, he did, for that slim woman with the ready smile and warm manner. He had thought Libby's mother beautiful, comparing her to his own wife, that lacklustre woman who had shared his bed for the past thirty years, and, by some miracle that even he still wondered about, had produced three sons in that same bed.

Ellen Gray was like a creature from another world. He'd felt that sorry when Libby told him about her accident that he gave the lass more than twice the weight of toffees she'd asked for.

Libby lifted her head to smile at the old priest, placing the cup before him very carefully. 'A slice of toast, Father? There's plenty of bread . . .'

Father Brady shook his head. She was too lively, chattering on about toffees and flowers, sensing that this wasn't one of his usual visits when he'd come to enquire after the family, when there *was* a family to enquire after. Striving to divert her thoughts from the real purpose of his visit, that's what she was doing . . .

Foolishly or not, he'd allowed her to chatter on, accepting the cup of tea but politely refusing the toast, even though he'd been up since five-thirty, had taken early Mass and Communion and had still not broken his fast.

Forcing himself, he cut short her chatter with an abruptness that startled Libby into silence. She gazed at him with wide eyes as he rose from his chair and came round the table to where she sat. He took both her hands in his.

At one time, when she was very small, the parish priest had terrified her, with his long black habit and the little black biretta sitting on top of his silver-white head. Most of all, she was frightened by his hard, bony hands that reached down to pat her on the head or sometimes brush the hair from her eyes.

'Elizabeth Mary, you must be brave. Braver now than you have ever been. What I have to tell you breaks my heart, as surely as it will break yours, but it must be said. Our Beloved Father works in ways we do not understand, ways that sometimes makes us want to rebel, not only against life but against everything we hold dear . . .'

The soft voice, still with its trace of Irish brogue, went round and round inside her head, the words making no sense. She wriggled her fingers inside his grasp but he didn't seem to feel them. Pouring tea and chatting about toffees and flowers for the moment had put all other thoughts out of her mind. But now, she thought, his words about being brave, of breaking her heart . . .

She raised her eyes slowly and gazed at him.

'My dear, I have to tell you. There will be no toffees, not anything, for your mother. Not any more . . .'

He was lying! He had to be. Mam was waiting in the hospital, having a quiet laugh at the silly woman in the bed next to her. Why, hadn't she gone down specially to the market last night to buy the toffees Mam had asked for and the flowers? And yet, looking into the kindly eyes, she knew that priests did not lie.

Suddenly, as though all life had left her, she collapsed into the old green kitchen chair. 'Tell me.'

The two words, spoken with icy calmness that

chilled to the core the old priest's heart, echoed in the quiet kitchen, seemed to hover for a moment, then, as though bidding goodbye forever to the happy times that shabby room had once seen, died away in the silence.

Father Brady told her. A message had come from the hospital just after he'd finished early Mass. The policeman had wanted to inform Libby himself but Father Brady resolutely insisted he would see to it.

'She had a good night, Elizabeth Mary, a peaceful night, sleeping well and enjoying the early morning cup of tea so much she asked for another. The nurse went to pour it and when she got back to your mother's bed, she was gone. Her heart could take no more.'

He studied the small ashen face with concern. The child sat as if frozen. There ought to be *some* reaction. Tears, even recriminations. That happened often; against fate, against the hospital, against even our Dear Lord. That he could manage. He'd been trained in such things. This bleakness – this numbness, he couldn't.

'Elizabeth Mary?' His own eyes filled with tears and it was that which broke the spell.

Libby drew a deep breath, stood up and exclaimed calmly, 'What must I do, Father? Tell me what I must do?'

'It seems a hard and unfeeling thing to say, mavourneen, but the realities of death will help numb the pain.'

Numb the pain! Libby thought. I feel no pain. Am I, as Vince always maintains, abnormal? I must be, else why aren't I in floods of tears by now? My mother's just died and I stand, discussing with this old priest the realities of death.

'I take it your mother had an insurance policy?' he was asking now. Libby nodded, remembering the man coming every week to collect the money. Money that sometimes Mam couldn't afford but would find, come hell or high water.

'When – when will it – the funeral be, Father? I shall have to find Agnes. And I want to see Mam, just one more time . . .'

'The hospital will let you know about the funeral and also about your mother. And of course you understand I will help in any way I can. Have you or your neighbours any idea where Agnes might be?'

'No, Father. I don't even know if she's still in Ridley.'

The old priest came as close to anger as he ever allowed. The girl leaned across the table, automatically reaching for the teapot. Mam's favourite remedy for anything from headaches to heartaches. The sleeve of her cardigan caught the jam jar containing Mam's flowers and knocked it over. Water and wet flowers spilled upon the table, soaking not only the cloth but the bag of toffees, too. As Libby retrieved them from the pool of water, the white paper bag split and the toffees spilled out.

For a long moment she gazed helplessly at the mess, then the dam broke. Covering her face with both hands, she wept as she'd never wept before, until all the tears had gone and she was left pale and cold and drained in that once warm and friendly kitchen. Somehow her dreams of Vince as her Prince on the white charger were growing more remote. There was nothing left. For without Vince, gone were her hopes for the future. A fleeting memory of James Randle crept into her thoughts, his thin face laughing at something Bertie had said on the walks they had shared together. Then that, too, had gone. And where, oh where, were Agnes and Joseph?

Somehow, she never knew how but suspected Father Brady had something to do with it, Agnes turned up for the funeral. Brassy-faced as ever, she stood at the side of the open grave, grasping tightly the arm of the man she had persuaded to marry her. And not before time, Libby caught herself thinking, then castigated herself for her uncharitablness. Couldn't she think kindly of her sister even at Mam's funeral?

Agnes' choice was the big man with a mop of unruly black hair and a weathered complexion that she had gone off with. He was dressed in a shabby navy blue suit that was too tight for him, and Libby guessed he must have borrowed it from someone. Agnes was in an equally borrowed-looking outfit; they looked a right pair. Afterwards the two sisters faced each other across the damp-smelling front room, used only at weddings and funerals.

'And where have you been all this time, Agnes Gray?' Libby forced herself to speak calmly, even though inside her emotions boiled at fever pitch. 'You didn't even come and see Mam or find out how she was. What she must have felt I shudder to think.'

'Right bleeding little angel we've got here, Mick.'

Agnes' voice was full of scorn. She turned to grin at
the man she had introduced as 'my future 'usband'.
Mick Roach had mumbled something under his
breath and made himself scarce. Already Agnes'
voice was beginning to jar on his nerves and if the
two women were going to have it out together, he'd
make his way to the nearest pub.

'He's that man Dad didn't like,' observed Libby,
giving his retreating back a shrewd look. 'Are you
sure you know what you're doing, Agnes? Dad was a
fairly good judge of character, remember . . .'

'Dad can 'ardly complain now, can 'e?' Agnes
exclaimed heartlessly, 'so I'll thank you to keep your
opinions to yourself.'

Mick returned from the pub in the middle of the
funeral feast, drunk as a gypsy's fiddler, as Mrs
Moran's husband put it. After everyone had left,
Libby managed to speak to her sister alone. 'You'll be
staying here, won't you? You've got to have somewhere to live and someone in the family must stay in
case Joseph comes home . . .'

'Bugger Joseph! If you're so worried about 'im, you
stay 'ere. *I've* had enough of this place. Mick's taking
me to London. He'll soon get a job there and we'll get
a 'ome.'

Mick, it turned out, had been deferred from active
service while he'd been working on the land. If he
gave that up . . .

'Won't he be called up?' Libby said now. 'Have you
thought of that? You all alone in a strange city, and
your husband away fighting.'

Agnes shrugged and, swinging her handbag by the

handles, made for the front door where Mick was waiting outside on the pavement. 'Oh, I'll survive. I always do.'

As she turned to go, arm linked possessively in that of the burly black-haired farm worker, Libby called, 'Please write, Agnes . . .'

Agnes never even turned her head. Libby doubted very much if she'd even heard her.

Chapter Thirteen

It seemed to Libby as though she were destined to spend the rest of her life travelling backwards and forwards on this shabby, none too clean train. An early taste of purgatory, punishing her for all the small omissions of her childhood. Like spending the collection money on the comics and singing a popular song in church . . .

She wondered if Joseph, too, had been punished, but dragged her thoughts quickly back. It was too painful to think of Joseph and what might be happening to him.

Hearing the jolly voices of the men packing the corridors with kit-bags and rifles Libby thought of her mother lying in the dank, dark earth of Ridley cemetery and tears sprang to her eyes. Luckily for her the singing men were too engrossed in the miles that separated them from Tipperary and the sweetest girl they knew to do more than occasionally smile at the young girl sitting so quietly in the corner seat, or hush someone up if the wrong word was let slip.

Darkness had fully set in as she ran down the area steps in St Anne's Place. The door was opened a crack and Alice's face peered through the opening.

'Libby!' She sounded so distressed that Libby wondered what could possibly have happened while she'd been away. One of the children? Master Basil . . . ?

'Come on, let me in, Alice. It's flamin' perishing out here.'

'I daren't, Libby.'

'Daren't what?' Puzzled, Libby placed the flat of her hand against the door panel and pushed. 'Come on, stop larking about . . .'

'It's the missis' orders, Libby. You're not to be allowed back. She said you were to be sent packin'.'

Libby was too stunned to speak. Not allowed back! Behind Cook's back Alice must have been at the cooking sherry! Maybe it was a nightmare – she was still on the train, had dozed off in her corner seat and in a minute she'd wake up to find herself surrounded by carousing troops . . .

A shadow darkened the passage behind Alice and Cook's voice demanded, 'Who's that you're talking to, girl? If it's one of your young men tell 'im to get lost. And close that door, it's like somethin' those Russkies are sending in, that draught.'

Without relinquishing her hold on the door, Alice said, 'It's Libby, Cook. What shall I do?'

For a moment there was silence. Then Cook's voice, low and more subdued than Libby had ever heard it said, 'Well, you daft thing, let 'er in, then.'

'Mrs Ainslie said . . .'

'I know what Mrs bloody Ainslie said. *I* said let 'er in.'

'But, Cook, what if . . .'

'It'll be you standing out there in the cold in a minute, my girl, if you don't do as you're told.'

Alice bridled in anger. 'I *am* doin' what I was told . . .'

'And *I'm* telling you different. Now open that door and let the poor child in.'

Cook's plump figure replaced Alice's at the door and as gingerly as a mouse suspecting a trap, Libby entered.

Placing a finger to her lips, Cook settled Libby in her own chair in front of the fire. Alice kept up a constant stream of apology, begging Libby to forgive her, but Mrs Ainslie had been adamant about her instructions concerning Libby. On no account was the girl allowed to come back into the house.

Libby gritted her teeth. 'I'll talk to Dr Ainslie. He'll . . .'

Alice was shaking her head. 'He's not here, Libby. He's going to be attending a medical conference in Edinburgh for a while. Don't know when we can expect him back.'

Libby's heart sank. With Mrs Ainslie in this frame of mind, the doctor had been her only hope. Almost apologetically, Alice went on, 'Kathleen's looking after the children. She's been upgraded from the kitchen. They fretted for you at first, Libby, but they seem to be settling in now. Young uns soon forget and as the missis says, it won't be for long. Miss Amy will be at school next year and Master Bertie soon after.'

Libby folded her arms about her body, as though seeking comfort, and sat rigid, gazing into the fire. They commiserated with her about her mother.

Nobody knew what to say. Breaking the silence there came the sound of a bell, jangling tinnily from where it hung over the door.

Cook sighed. 'Her ladyship again! Alice, see what she wants else we'll 'ave 'er down 'ere and that would never do, not with Libby sitting there.'

Alice was on her feet at once, followed swiftly by Libby. 'I'd better go, Cook . . .' She smiled at the older woman. 'Give the children my love and tell them I miss them. And, of course, Kathleen.'

'She dropped in right lucky there, did that Kathleen,' Cook observed shrewdly. 'Had 'er eye on your job all the time, I shouldn't wonder.'

'Has Vince written to me?'

'No. Wouldn't lose much sleep if I never saw 'im again. You're better off without 'im, that you are.'

Sighing a deep, heavy sigh, Libby pulled her coat more closely about her shoulders. Although the news, or rather lack of it, of Vince, was disappointing, she was sure he would write.

Alice hadn't returned from upstairs so Libby asked Cook to say goodbye for her. Cook grunted and moved over to a corner of the kitchen, bending to pick up a cane basket with a leather handle.

'Here, your things, Libby. Alice packed 'em for you. It's 'er basket, too, but she says she don't want it back. I can't tell you 'ow sorry I am to see you go, but that old cow upstairs had made up her mind and nothing was goin' to change it.'

Battling to hide the flow of emotion, Libby took the basket from Cook's hand. It wasn't heavy. The pitifully few belongings it contained were, she realised, all that stood between her and destitution. She hadn't even considered her next step. Go home, she thought. What other alternative was there? Cook embraced her, patting her back as though she were a baby needing winding after a feed.

'There, now, lass, chin up. There'll be other jobs. A girl with your nice manners and way of talking.'

Releasing her and wiping her eye with the corner of her apron, Cook went on, 'Now, you got enough money for your fare 'ome?'

Libby felt sick. She hadn't. Hadn't thought she'd need money to return home . . .

Seeing the indecision in the girl's eyes, whether to lie and say, Oh yes, she was all right, thank you, or admit to being broke, Cook reached for her own purse on the high mantelpiece. Thrusting some coins into Libby's hand, she said, 'Here, take these. You can always pay me back next time you see me.'

Libby drew back. Mam had never borrowed, either money or anything else. She just couldn't allow Cook to . . .

'I don't want to hear another word, Libby Gray.' Cook was adamant. 'Maybe you'll come this way again. You can pay me back then.'

Back in the house after so short a time, Libby crept into the kitchen, like a puppy seeking warmth. Here were all the familiar things. Here was the twinkling bright fireguard, the grate with the old-fashioned oven black-leaded so lovingly every week by Mam. After a restless night she woke to feel as disconsolate as when she had retired. She longed to go back to sleep and wake up to things as they used to be. To hear her mother singing in that low, sweet voice as she stirred the porridge and put out the blue and white dishes on the white tablecloth.

But it was no use daydreaming. That wouldn't help anything. She got up and went to the window, drawing back the net curtains to peer out. The bleak greyness of the scene struck her forcibly. After the brief spell of spring that day she had visited Mam in hospital, the cold weather had returned with a vengeance.

Downstairs in the kitchen she lit a fire, put on the kettle and washed her face and hands under the running cold tap at the sink. When the kettle boiled she wet the tea leaves and placed the heavy brown pot to one side of the range to draw.

The days passed slowly. At first she had been so worried about the house that she would lie awake at nights, her thoughts going round and round like leaves in a storm. Even the small amount the colliery charged as rent was beyond her means now. At least, until she got work. In any case, she asked herself, would the company allow her to remain there, now that her parents were gone?

The long street of small houses was owned by the colliery and rented out to their workers. She knew of one or two instances where an elderly woman had been allowed to remain in the house after her husband had died. Would she be so lucky? Or would she be turned out, lock, stock and barrel, onto the street to make way for a new family?

The house had been the home of Dad's family since

coal mining began in that part of Lancashire. His grandfather and father had brought their young brides to this small house; had watched as their children grew up here. On a sadder note, coffins had stood on trestles in the front room, candlelight flickering over tear-stained faces. The walls had listened to the clink of rosary beads as the black-clad women knelt in prayer and the predecessors of Father Brady whispered soft words of comfort.

The narrow leaves of the aspidistra in its china pot that lived all year round on the broad window sill in front of the pristine net curtain would be given an extra wipe with a damp cloth, leaving them rich and glossy, and, the utmost luxury in Libby's eyes, a fire would be lit in the small black-leaded grate. That was at Christmas-time when Mam's parents were still alive. They would make the long journey from the other side of Ridley by tram, bringing presents most of which Grandma had made herself, and, as Mam would remark, spoiling the children rotten.

There would be shrieks of laughter as crackers were pulled and soft murmurs of ecstatic wonder as Mam lifted the newly iced Christmas cake from its tin on the high kitchen shelf where it had been maturing these last few weeks, well out of reach of busy little fingers.

There was the time, as a very little girl, when Libby had been so overcome by the sight of the gleaming white cake, its miniature tableau of tiny reindeer and snowman, with Father Christmas standing benevolently to one side, attended by a fat robin redbreast, that she had wet her knickers, earning a scornful poking finger from Agnes and a cuddle from Gran. 'Never mind,' Gran said. 'It was the excitement. Just the excitement.'

Now, walking aimlessly in the park, she sat on the hard wooden bench and thought, If the worst came to the worst, would I be able to sleep on this? People did. Hadn't she seen old men stretched out on these benches on her short-cut through the park on her way to school? The lower part of their bodies would be covered in sacking as they lay with one arm curled under their heads, face turned towards the seat back.

On his early morning rounds, the local bobby would stop and jab them with his truncheon, suggesting in friendly enough fashion that it was time they moved on. She would giggle at their less than friendly reply and Joseph would grab her by the arm and pull her along, muttering, 'Mam'd have a blue fit if she knew you'd listened to words like that. Come on, Carrot-top, we're going to be late for school if we hang around here any longer.'

She would turn her head one last time to gaze back at the bench with its reluctantly stirring occupant and say, in a worried little voice, 'Oh, Joseph, it's so sad! Those men have no homes to go to, no family. Don't people *care* that they live like that?'

Joseph, at twelve, ten months younger than Libby, had hefted his old brown leather satchel more comfortably across his shoulders. 'I don't suppose people know. Not enough of the right people, anyway. Perhaps one day things will be different.'

'Every dark cloud has a silver lining, Sister

Veronica says.' Libby had known that if she had a problem, she could always go to Sister Veronica. The nun had taught arithmetic and history and although Libby hadn't been partial to arithmetic she had liked history. All those Kings and Queens and their fascinating lovers. Although Sister Veronica was inclined to skip a few pages when they came to that bit.

One morning, giving Libby a sly wink before holding up her hand for permission to ask a question, Agnes had said with an air of innocence that was so false it was laughable, 'Why was Queen Elizabeth called the Virgin Queen, Sister? Was it because she didn't have any children? Our Lady's also called that but *she* had a child.'

The young sister had seemed to have difficulty in controlling the sudden fit of coughing that overcame her. When at last she could speak, she had stood up from her desk, leant across it so that the black folds of her habit fell across her rosy cheeks, and had said in a voice that the children recognised as her 'no-nonsense' one, 'She did indeed and we all know who that little child was, don't we?' Although she wasn't supposed to have likes and dislikes, the pert ginger-haired miss in the front row had sometimes caused an anger to stir in her that she thought she had left behind in the outside world. Taking a deep breath, she had added, 'Now, what I want you all to do today for your homework, is write an essay of three hundred words about the Virgin Mary and Her life with Joseph while Our Lord was still a little lad.'

A groan had gone up. They hated essays and this

one sounded as though they would all have to use their imaginations. A gift not all of them possessed. The nun had looked across the floor to Agnes, holding the girl's eyes with her own. 'Then perhaps in future a pupil will consider a question well before asking it.'

The bad weather slowly turned spring-like again and the people of Ridley, sick to death of war news and tragedies, were glad to observe all the 'firsts': the first daffodils, the first bluebells in the woods on the town's outskirts, the first swallow. And Libby got her first refusal of work.

The manager in the glass-fronted office at the mill said they weren't taking any more staff on now. 'Full quota, lass. Got more than we need, really.'

He examined the slight figure of the girl standing before him. Neatly dressed, aye, *respectably* dressed in a grey coat (only that daft beret spoiled the effect!). He somehow couldn't see her in clogs and shawl working a loom in the noisy fluff-filled air of the mill. Cut of different cloth from that brazen sister of hers, he thought. Different as chalk from cheese. But however sorry he felt for her, he couldn't help. The place was overflowing with girls. Might even have to get rid of a few at end o' month, as like as not.

Libby tried not to let her shoulders slump as she murmured a polite 'thank you' and turned to walk away. She'd been so sure she'd be welcomed with open arms. What else was there in Ridley but the mill? Service! She doubted if anyone in this town employed nursemaids for their children. So what did that leave? Office work? Shops? She'd seen white cards pasted on the windows of a few of the shops in the High Street.

Vacancy, hard-working girl required. Well, she could be as hard-working as the rest. All she needed was a chance to prove it.

The card in the boot and shoe shop drew her like a magnet. It was situated down a narrow cobbled street leading to the market place. Libby stopped outside the cluttered window. Selling shoes shouldn't be too difficult. She'd be a right muggins if she couldn't do that. Trying to see her reflection in the window, tucking in a stray curl, smoothing her coat, she pushed open the door.

The man who came forward, sensing a customer, smiled obsequiously. Frank Dibbs was in his fifties, shorter than Libby, his belly bulging under a tightly buttoned waistcoat, bald but for the fringe of lifeless dark hair speckled with grey growing low on his skull. His eyes darted to her feet, just visible beneath her ankle-length skirt. Dainty feet! Small, he guessed about a size three. Maybe a four. Not much to choose from in that size. Not in this town of hefty mill lasses . . .

Under his intent gaze Libby felt herself blushing. Forcing a steady voice, she said, 'I came about the job. The card in the window said . . .'

Something flickered in the man's eyes. 'Ah, yes, the position of sales girl. You have experience at such work?'

He saw the slight hesitation before she answered, 'Well, no, I haven't, sir. But I can learn.' Her voice was eager, slightly breathless. 'I learn very quickly.'

'Ummm . . .' Silence while he regarded her, taking in the thick chestnut hair, the creamy pale skin and the dusky rose colour the sharp wind had brought to her cheeks. And those eyes! Amazing; hopeful, eager, as though a candle had been lit behind them. The palms of his hands began to sweat. 'I was hoping to employ someone with experience – someone who didn't need teaching.'

'You won't need to teach me, sir. Just help me with the first few customers and I know I'll manage fine on my own.'

She was pretty and somehow more refined than the usual run of Ridley girls. And that slim waist was just begging for a man's arm about it!

Libby saw the expression in his eyes and knew instinctively she'd won.

'All right,' he said, his whole manner suddenly brisk. 'No harm in givin' you a try. Can you start tomorrow?'

Libby almost laughed. 'I can start now if you want.'

Mr Dibbs smirked. 'I appreciate your willingness, Miss . . . ?'

'Gray,' she provided quickly. 'Libby Gray.'

'Well, I think we should get on just fine. You can hang your coat and hat in here.'

She followed him to a small back room piled high with shiny white boxes, all, she supposed, containing shoes.

'Ladies' this side,' he explained, seeing how her eyes examined them. 'Men's boots over here. And in here . . .' He led her to another room that was obviously used as a work-shop. 'I'm a cobbler, too,' he explained. 'Busy these days, that's why I need an assistant to see to the shop.'

232

He gave her a pinny to cover her dress; a long, grey overall which went over her head and tied at the back. He insisted on tying it for her and took an inordinately long time about it, his hands at one time fumbling at the side of her waist with a remark about how tiny it was.

Disconcerted, Libby hurried back into the shop. This was no time to get all hot and flustered, just because her new boss had paid her a compliment!

He greeted the first few customers personally and then allowed Libby to attend to them. She was to place the footstool in front of the customer at a comfortable distance, and sit on the padded end while she eased their foot, with the aid of a silver shoehorn, into the shoe, the small silver-handled button-hook always within reach.

She soon found that customers dithered about, men as well as women, asked for something they had seen in the window and when, after a frantic search, she had found the size they required, decided they didn't like it after all. It was nothing, Libby discovered, for a woman to go through the whole range of stock and then, when you could barely move for the litter of shoes and boxes, to select the pair she'd first tried on.

The door would close behind her and Libby would be left amidst a jumble that seemed to take forever to put away. On such days she'd arrive home dispirited and weary. Even Bertie in his worst tantrums hadn't left her feeling so fatigued.

Still, she was able to pay the arrears of rent and give Mrs Moran back the things she'd insisted Libby take, like bread and eggs and tea. She sent a letter, addressed to Cook, containing a postal order for the amount that good woman had lent her. Already she was beginning to feel she could hold her head up again.

She received an answer from Alice. Cook said thank you and hoped Libby was keeping well. The rest of the staff asked about her. Apparently, on his return from Edinburgh, Dr Ainslie had been told by his wife that Libby had informed her she would be staying at home and not coming back to her job. A few days later she received another letter, this time from Dr Ainslie, containing four crisp black and white five-pound notes and saying how much he would miss her.

After the formal greetings, he wrote:

I wish you every success in whatever job you take, my dear. Take care of yourself and think of us sometimes. The children I know are missing you already, although Kathleen does a good job with them. Please do not worry about the house. If you wish to continue to live there, the house remains yours. I have spoken to Mr Alec Pilkington, whose family, as you know, own the mine. I have been their physician since taking up this practice in St Aiden's and Mr Pilkington has assured me that you can set your mind at rest. The rent will remain the same, he tells me, and he will be writing to you himself to acquaint you of this. So, my dear, you can rest easy. The enclosed money will tide you over until you can find new employment.

Libby remembered the Pilkingtons coming to dinner a number of times in St Anne's Place. A tall, thin man with grey hair and a rather laconic manner, Mr Pilkington did not look the sort to be generous or concerned over the fate of a young girl living alone in one of his houses . . .

Still, she thought, you can never tell people by their looks. Folding the letter and slipping it back into its envelope, Libby wondered what sort of a cock and bull story Mrs Ainslie had given her husband concerning Libby's hasty departure. Dr Ainslie had, it seemed, been too tactful to mention this. Anyway, twenty pounds would be a blessing. She swallowed the lump in her throat, thinking of his last few lines; 'Can I say again, Libby, how sorry I was to hear you had left us, but I suppose you know what is best. God bless you, child, and keep well.'

Sometimes, in the evening, Libby would sit over a newspaper and read the dispatches from the Front. It was all very disquieting. The casualty list, including the missing, presumed dead, grew longer every day, sometimes covering the whole of the page. Notices were posted outside the local newspaper offices, and Libby was there one lunch time, pushing her way through to the front of the group of white-faced women, when suddenly there was a shrill scream and a young girl, heavy with child, collapsed at her feet.

'Poor soul!' The crowd made way for the pathetically crumpled figure and one, a matronly woman in a dark serge costume and hat, knelt beside her, chaffing her hands. Although Libby would have liked to have helped, the chimes from the Market Square clock reminded her it was time she was back in the shop.

Mr Dibbs insisted on punctuality. The half hour Libby took for her dinner he considered ample. When she wasn't busy with customers, Mr Dibbs expected her to dust the shoe boxes and rearrange the window. She was surprised when he allowed her to do this but after her first tentative attempt, he'd agreed that, aye, she had a knack for displaying the shoes to their best advantage so she might as well continue. She never got a chance to relax, to just sit and re-charge her batteries for the next bloody-minded customer. And H.Dibbs and Son certainly had their share of them.

They closed for dinner from twelve till twelve-thirty, and if she had enough bread in the larder and a bit of cheese, she'd bring it along, sitting on the foot-stool and drinking water from the tap where she washed her hands. There was no way of making a pot of tea and she couldn't afford to go out for one.

Mr Dibbs, on the other hand, always went out for his dinner, sometimes to the pub across the road, but mostly to the fish and chip shop in the square. Some-times he'd bring her back the remains of his chips, all cold and greasy and soggy with vinegar in their wrap-ping of newspaper. She'd accept them politely, then dispose of them quietly in the dustbin in the cluttered back yard where she had to go to the toilet. She hated the way his eyes would follow her, knowing where she was going, and she often waited until she got home, in her haste forgetting the cracked seat and tears springing to her eyes at the vicious nip. A lump would come to her throat, as she recalled jokes from Dad, sometimes so earthy that he'd receive one of those 'William!' looks from Mam and they'd all shriek with laughter.

Her wages didn't go far and usually by Wednesday she was broke. On that particular day when it all went wrong she had not been able to bring sandwiches. There were two slices of bread left and a scraping of marge which she'd have to save for her tea that night. Unbidden, her thoughts returned to the house in St Anne's Place, to Cook's warm kitchen with its walk-in larder stacked with food. Even though others in war-time went without, the Ainslies managed very well. Her tummy rumbled just as Mr Dibbs was passing through the shop on his way to dinner. Embarrassed, for in the quiet shop the rumble must surely be heard, she lowered her head, pretending a sudden, all-absorbing interest in a cigarette burn on the carpet.

'Get your coat on, lass. I'm taking you to dinner.'

Startled, Libby looked up, catching his grin. 'I – I've got some sandwiches,' she lied, despising the thought of his pity.

'A growing lass like you can't live off sandwiches. Go on, get your coat. We'll treat ourselves to a slap-up meal in t' King's Arms.'

The King's Arms was a public house opposite the shop. It was old, with a black and white Tudor-style timbered front and a small restaurant to one side of the bar.

'Don't dawdle, lass.' It was an order. 'Get your coat.'

Well, why not? It was a miserable day and she *was*

hungry. Buttoning her coat as Mr Dibbs closed and locked the shop door, she then followed him across the road. Inside, the pub had heavy dark furniture, with a clutter of sepia photographs on the wall. Deep red wallpaper gave an illusion of warmth. It was, Libby decided, all very pleasant. A number of white-aproned waitresses bustled about, all busy serving. One took their order, nodded, then scurried away. Mr Dibbs regarded Libby across the table. 'Take your coat off. It's warm enough in here.'

In her confusion and haste when he'd asked – ordered – her to join him, Libby had forgotten to remove the long ugly pinafore before putting on her coat.

She blushed to the roots of her hair, remembering. 'I – I think I'll keep it on, Mr Dibbs.' She spoke in so low a voice he didn't hear her. His abrupt and very loud: 'Speak up, lass, you've no fear of waking the dead, tha' knows,' caused diners to look up from their meal. He guffawed loudly. 'They're all tucked up safe and sound in t' graveyard on t' corner.'

Libby's blush deepened. The church of St Stephen with its ancient burial grounds stood to one side of the Market Square, divided from the King's Arms by a narrow passageway.

Bending towards him across the table, Libby whispered, 'I can't take my coat off. I forgot to take off my pinny . . .'

'Oh, well . . .' Thankfully his attention was diverted by the arrival of the waitress with their order. Balancing the tray precariously on one hand, she placed the plates of steaming hotpot before them, said she'd be back with the tea and hurried off again.

The steaming plate right under her nose with its savoury smell of onions and meat and the slices of potato on top glazed a lovely golden brown had Libby's saliva glands working overtime.

Watching from the corner of his eye, Mr Dibbs thought, The lass is sniffing like one of those adverts for Bisto! Bet she's not had a decent meal in ages. He wasn't far from the truth. Living off bread and cheese, with the occasional pot of soup, Libby felt this was indeed heaven.

Later, when he inspected his watch and declared there was time for a drink, she shook her head, pointing out it was past their opening time. 'We should have opened the shop half an hour ago, Mr Dibbs.'

'Won't do no harm for once, lass. Customers'll allus come back.'

Libby was unyielding. 'No, really. I enjoyed the dinner, it was lovely and thank you for asking me, but if you give me the keys I'll open the shop while you have your drink.'

'Got a mind of your own, haven't you?' Grinning, he handed over the bunch of keys, then headed for the bar.

Chapter Fourteen

He was away a long time. Libby didn't mind. Trade was slack and she spent the afternoon rearranging the window display. How she wished she could afford a pair of those grey button boots! She handled them carefully, smoothing the soft suede with her fingertips, imagining herself sauntering out in a new outfit, the sweet little boots tripping along beneath an ankle-length skirt.

Beside her would be – Vince? She bit her lip, her eyes staring unseeingly at the scene outside the window. She'd never given up hoping that Vince would write. She'd written a number of letters herself but hadn't received one single reply. She wondered if he'd even got them. The post, like everything else these days, was erratic. She tried to summon up his face, those dark bold eyes, the curly hair. But it was James Randle's features that sprang vividly to mind.

She wondered how Captain Randle was getting on, if he'd managed to persuade the authorities to send him back to rejoin his men . . . Oh, well, she'd never know, so what was the use of even thinking about it?

She replaced the grey suede boots on their stand and sat down on one of the chairs. Where were all the customers? She couldn't remember the shop being so quiet since she'd started working here, three months ago now.

The heavy meal and the muted sounds of the street lulled her into a semi-doze and she came awake with a start as a hand gripped her arm and a voice exclaimed, 'I'll have no shirking on my time, that I'll not. You're paid to sell shoes, not to sleep. Tha's can sleep all you want at home.'

Dismayed by her employer's sudden arrival, Libby struggled to her feet. 'I'm sorry, Mr Dibbs. It was so quiet, I haven't had a single customer since I opened after dinner.'

The scowl was gradually disappearing from his face. She could smell the drink on his breath. In her innocence she didn't recognise the look that glowed behind those muddy eyes.

He vanished into his workroom. Desperately wishing for a customer to appear, just so she wouldn't be alone in the shop with him, Libby found a duster and began taking the shiny white boxes from their shelves, dusting the tops, anything to occupy her hands.

She was standing on the small step-ladder, reaching for the boxes on the highest shelf when she heard him come through from the workroom. 'There's a good girl,' he said, gazing upwards. 'Get 'em all nice and shipshape. Can't 'ave sloppy workers in my establishment.'

Not replying, Libby went on with her work. A moment later she felt fingers clasp about one ankle, and linger there. Outraged, she looked down, frowning. 'Mr Dibbs!'

'Oh, come on, Libby.' It was the first time he had addressed her by her first name. Usually it was just 'lass'. 'You've got ankles like a racehorse. A thoroughbred. What man could resist wanting to touch them.' He chuckled. 'Even in those awful lisle stockings. Wi' legs like yours, you should be wearing silk.'

I can barely afford lisle, she thought, never mind silk, on what you pay me. And they were the only pair she had. The rest were all cotton. Mrs Ainslie had considered lisle 'fast'.

'If you're nice to me, now, you could be wearing silk and, after all, I did buy you a nice dinner,' Mr Dibbs was saying. His face was on a level with her feet. She considered kicking him, right in the teeth, then grimaced. Flaminenery! That would be a bloomer! Better to get out of it as gracefully as she could. She began to descend, stepping carefully, her hands holding the sides of the ladder. But as she moved, so did his hands, slipping slyly upwards, past her hips, her waist, until, her feet on the linoleum-covered floor, they rested on her breasts.

There they stayed, as he held the soft shapes in his palms. Mortified beyond endurance, Libby exclaimed, tight-lipped, 'Mr Dibbs, I'd be grateful if you'd remove your hands from my person. You don't pay me enough to allow such liberties.' Her breasts hurt, he was squeezing them so hard.

'Now, Libby, be nice to me and you'll find it'll be worth it.'

She tried to wrench herself away, but although his hands released their hold on one part of her body, they slipped about her waist, pulling her roughly to him. Sliding down, they settled on her buttocks, holding her so tightly that she was unable to move. She was amazed at the strength of this middle-aged man. His lips searched for hers, claiming them in an openmouthed wet kiss that turned her stomach. She could feel a hard protuberance thrusting against her thigh and, terrified, began to fight him.

'Oh, yes,' he breathed against her mouth. 'I like a bit of a fight. Go on, lass, it excites me. Put some life into it.' His spittle dripped, covered her upper lip and chin. She thought, if he doesn't stop I shall be sick. Wonder how he'd like that, all over his nice, blue suit! Slowly he was forcing her into the back room where he could shut the door and . . .

Please God, she prayed wildly, let a customer, a whole crowd of customers, come in. As though guessing her thoughts, he gave her a hefty push, sending her sprawling into the small room. She fell on a pile of empty boxes and before she could move he was running to put the snib on the door. Now, his sly look warned her, we won't be disturbed. His fingers scrabbled at the high neck of her blouse, then when she snatched them away, fell to pulling at her skirts. No word was spoken. The only sounds were their harsh breathing and Libby's occasional whimper.

He had her pinned down now, her skirts lifted, showing the long slim legs. Intent on forcing his knees between hers, he didn't notice her outflung hands reaching for the bone-handled button-hook she could see from the corner of her eye. With an almighty effort, she managed it. Taking a firm hold even though it threatened to slip through her fingers, sweaty with terror, she brandished it in front of his eyes.

'Give over or you'll be missing an eye!'

The sharply hooked implement threatened. Gazing into Libby's eyes, Frank Dibbs knew when he'd met his match. Breathing heavily, he hurled himself to his knees, leaning away from her.

Libby scrambled to her feet, still flourishing the button-hook before his face. 'You mangy old goat!' Her breath came harshly in her throat. 'I'll have the law on you, see if I don't.'

Mr Dibbs was pushing himself to his feet, breathing so heavily he was having difficulty doing even that. Vindictively, Libby hoped he'd have a heart attack, right there before her eyes. She wouldn't lift a finger to help him, do nowt but watch . . .

At last, standing upright, he found the strength to answer. 'The law'll do nothing,' he blustered, at the same time keeping a sharp eye on that wicked-looking button-hook Libby held like a weapon. 'Your word against mine and who's goin' to take the word of a little tramp like you?'

Libby made a threatening movement towards him and in spite of how everything had gone wrong he felt his excitement renewed. What a splendid figure she made! Eyes flashing green fire, cheeks flushed scarlet, that lovely hair undone in the battle and flowing down her back clear to her waist. If only he'd bided his time . . .

But there was to be no second chance. Libby was already drawing her coat about her. Removing the

245

dingy pinny, she had thrown it at his feet. An empress tossing coins to the rabble, he couldn't help thinking.

The shop door slammed behind her and if passers-by moved swiftly aside for the wide-eyed girl with her coat draped about her shoulders like a cape, Libby was quite unaware of the stares.

'I thought what a nice, refined job it was, too,' Mrs Moran exclaimed when Libby told her she had left. 'Suited you down to the ground. Pity about that. You probably could 'ave got your shoes at 'alf price, too.'

Still fuming at Mr Dibbs' totally unforeseen attack, Libby smiled but didn't answer. She hadn't told her neighbour the reason for her leaving. She couldn't quite remember what she *had* told her but the woman seemed satisfied with her explanation.

'You all right, lass? Looking a bit peaky this morning.'

'A bit of a headache, Mrs Moran. I woke up with it this morning and it won't go away.'

'Well, just you sit there quiet like and drink your tea and you'll feel better. Headaches! I could tell you about headaches!' Mrs Moran raised her eyes heavenwards as though calling on the Almighty to witness the truth of her words. 'Suffered wi' bilious headaches ever since I can remember. Wept buckets over 'em, I did. But wi' kids under your feet, what can you do? Just grin and bear it, I reckon.'

Although she was a dear, kind soul and had been Mam's best friend, Libby wished she would take her memories and go home. She had things to think about. Mercifully, one of the children was heard screaming in the adjoining back yard. With a muttered 'That'll be our Billy, teasing Bet again. I'll make 'is lugs ring, that I will,' Mrs Moran exited through the back door in a flurry of woollen shawl and flowered cotton pinny.

Alone, Libby sat before the feeble fire and pondered her next step. Perhaps she shouldn't have been so hasty. Perhaps if she'd handled Mr Dibbs differently, been more diplomatic like – she wrinkled her nose. How can you be diplomatic when a man starts acting like that randy old bugger had? He thought all he had to do was treat her to a meal and she was his for the asking. The fire flickered, on its last legs. Libby went out into the yard to investigate the coal situation. The yard with its high, moss-covered walls, was sheltered from the wind, but even so it swooped over from next door, bringing with it the sound of squabbling children and the mouth-watering smell of frying battered fish.

Picking up the least stony bits of coal she could find she carried them indoors. She washed the coal dust from her hands in the sink, peering into the speckled mirror on its bit of string. How many times had she watched Dad shave in front of that mirror? Had giggled at the contortions as he pulled his face this way and that, saying she was glad she wasn't a man, she'd hate to have to go through that palaver every morning of her life. And Dad's reply; that he was glad she wasn't a man, too, for what would he do without his little nightingale?

The memory brought fresh tears and she sat in his chair and wept until no further tears came. Then, with a determined frown, she got up to scrub the worn linoleum in the hall. Hard work was the only therapy she knew for grief. Sometimes it helped, sometimes it didn't.

She had got the surprise of her life when, opening the front door a few days ago to an insistent knocking, she discovered a youth with an envelope from Mr Dibbs containing two days' wages. In happier circumstances she would have loved to have thrown it back into the messenger's face, instructing him to tell Mr Dibbs what he could do with his money. But she'd earned it, hadn't she? On her feet all day, she'd worked hard for it. Six o'clock every night, seven on Fridays and eight on Saturdays, with early closing on Wednesday when she'd go home and do her housework and washing.

She spread the few coins on the table top and sat looking at them. She still had some of the money Dr Ainslie had sent, although not much, for the funeral fees had been higher than she expected and the insurance policy hadn't covered it all. And she had to think of the future . . .

But it was difficult to concentrate on something as nebulous as the future when the smell of deep-fried fish was tantalising her nostrils. Grabbing her coat, she let herself out, leaving the front door on the latch behind her. She deserved a treat and she was sick to death of bread and cheese and jam.

The fish and chip shop of Mr Hobbins drew her footsteps like a pilgrim to Mecca. It was sheer heaven, entering that shop. One of her most cherished childhood memories was going from the cold cobbled street into the fish and chip shop, feeling the warmth on her cheeks, making her nose drip; the smell of vinegar and hot oil. For sixpence you could buy a newspaper-wrapped parcel containing enough for the whole family. When her granny was still alive, her visits, always timed for the dinner hour, would culminate in Mam reaching for her purse, saying, 'Libby, go to the corner chippies for sixpennyworth of cod and chips.'

'And mushy peas, Libby,' Granny would remind her. 'Fish and chips without mushy peas is like Blackpool without its tower.'

Mr and Mrs Hobbins, who owned the shop, had had a soft spot for the young girl with the large questioning eyes and the pale face. Mr Hobbins was a short man, not much taller than Libby herself, with a shiny scalp that he tried to conceal by carefully combing what remained of his hair over the top. On reaching the middle-aged crisis, he'd grown a moustache. Ignoring his wife's frowns and murmurs of 'tut tut', he felt it gave him confidence.

'Always looked poorly, that one,' Mrs Hobbins would observe, watching Libby as she waited for service in the shop, then hurried out, the newspaper-wrapped parcel clutched to her bosom like a well-loved child.

'Well, it's the asthma, isn't it?' Mr Hobbins had a brother who suffered with asthma and knew how it dragged you down. 'Won't ever be reet until she gets away from here.'

His wife had snorted. 'Fat chance o' that! How's a girl going to leave these parts? T'mill's the only place they can go to once they leave school.'

And yet Libby had got away. They watched her grow up, in Mr Hobbins' opinion, prudently concealed from his wife, into a lovely young woman, with those large green eyes and the pleasant manner.

Mrs Hobbins had once remarked that green eyes didn't seem proper in a girl of Libby's class. 'Brown or blue, now, that's all right. But green, and especially that shade of green . . .' and she'd shaken her head. 'Seems to me eyes like that should belong to the upper classes.'

Mr Hobbins had often felt like calling his wife stupid, but on this occasion he'd almost said it aloud. Instead, plunging a basket full of raw chip potatoes into the hot fat, he'd growled, 'What's class got to do wi' it? Eyes are eyes. Can't change what you've bin born with.'

Now, after all these years, nearly five, he thought with a touch of nostalgia, the girl was back. Stories concerning the circumstances of her return abounded. Once as he made up an order of cod and chips, listening to two old biddies gossiping about the girl, outrage had got the better of him and he'd sent them scurrying off with a flea in their ear. And now here she was, handing her sixpence over the counter, and it seemed to Mr Hobbins that her whole body trembled in anticipation of those crisp golden chips and thickly battered cod. Generously, he added another piece of fish and a second helping of chips.

'Keep the lass goin',' he thought. 'Looks like a square meal'd do her the world of good.'

Mrs Hobbins had passed away two years previously and since then he had found the running of the shop, with its long hours and early morning start, increasingly difficult. Various avaricious neighbours, with an eye on an extra shilling or two to help with the housekeeping, had offered the help of their daughters after school. They were gormless and as skinny as two pieces of plywood stuck together, and Mr Hobbins had looked at them in disgust and declined the offers.

Finally, his sister came over from Liverpool to live with him. Clara had never married and for years had been living as companion/drudge to a comparatively wealthy widow who had recently died. Clara was delighted with her new-found freedom and Mr Hobbins was glad of another pair of hands to help in the shop. Although, as he soon discovered, Clara had fixed ideas about what her duties would be. She couldn't, she explained, do any of the heavy work, like scrubbing floors or counters. Her back just wasn't up to it. Alec Hobbins had sighed and agreed.

Libby's eyes widened as she saw the large portion of fish and the extra helping of chips. He must have misunderstood her! She couldn't afford all this . . .

'Mr Hobbins,' she began in a hesitant voice. 'You've made a mistake. I've only got sixpence . . .'

The man's face softened as he gave the newspaper a final twist. 'That's all right, lass. On the house.'

Pushing it across the marble-topped counter his hand brushed hers. It was many a long year since he'd experienced the emotion caused by that accidental touch. His usually stooped shoulders straightened, one finger went to his upper lip, smoothing the moustache that had been a bone of contention between his wife and him. Sarah had said it made him look ridiculous. 'Mutton dressed as lamb,' she'd said, scathingly.

It was the only time in their married life he'd ever ignored her. Still, she'd pulled her weight: even with Clara helping he was finding the long hours not so much to his liking as they used to be.

And the woman who came to clean every morning lately had become so unreliable that he was seriously thinking of letting her go. Testily he picked up a damp cloth and wiped the grease from the counter top. 'That Mrs Croft,' he mumbled, catching Libby's eye. 'Spends more time gossiping wi' customers than she does cleanin'.' He shrugged. 'Must be gettin' old or summat, but I can't keep the shop as nice as I used to. A little palace it was, once. Best chippy in the whole of Ridley.'

'Why don't you have a word with her?' suggested Libby, practical as always. 'Mrs Croft, I mean.'

'Wouldn't dare.' He eyed Libby with a touch of amusement. 'You know Mrs Croft, do you? From number twenty-seven, along your way? Sooner 'ave words wi' the devil.'

'Poof!' Libby's look of disdain made him chuckle. 'Couldn't knock the skin off a rice pudding, she couldn't.'

She picked up her supper, ready for departure. 'You've got to be firm, Mr Hobbins. If she thinks you're soft, she'll try it on. You put your foot down. Show her who's the boss.'

The lass spoke sense. It was the same with Sarah.

Never did learn how to rule her, not in all their years together. With Sarah he had known little softness. As for love – well, Sarah had had no time for that nonsense. Now, this little lass was different. He'd never have suspected she'd have grown into such a little beauty. And a good worker, too, he'd be bound.

He stood, cloth in hand. For a moment, the shop was empty. The question that had been forming in his mind forced itself to his lips. 'You're not working just now, eh, Libby? Don't you want a job? It can't be easy, not wi' your Agnes and Joseph gone . . .'

Libby paused at the door, the bell clanging tinnily above her head, and looked back. 'Are you offering *me* the job, Mr Hobbins?'

Alec Hobbins swallowed hard, gazing into the earnest face, those remarkable eyes.

'Don't be offended, lass. I just thought – well, as I said, it must be difficult . . .' He turned away, concentrating on a spot of grease on the counter so that he wouldn't have to look at her, see the polite words of refusal forming there. He had to ask her to repeat it when she said she wasn't in the least offended and that if he felt she was really suitable, she'd like to work for him.

'There's still Mrs Croft,' she pointed out. 'I don't want her to think I'm robbing her of the job.'

Suddenly, he felt all man, twenty years younger than when he'd opened the shop that morning. 'You leave Mrs Croft to me, Libby. I told you I was thinking of getting shot of her, anyway. Nay, that stuff will be stone cold.' He came from behind the counter and relieved her of the parcel of fish and chips. 'You can share my supper tonight. That is,' feeling himself blushing like a schoolboy, 'if you've no objection. There's a good fire warming the back room and we can talk while we eat.' He added with a sidewise glance that Clara had gone out on a visit to friends for the evening.

And Libby, too weary, too dispirited to argue, let herself be persuaded.

She peeled potatoes and kept the shop clean. It was hard work but in a way good for her. There was no time to sit and brood over her past life or what might have been. In all those months she hadn't heard a word from Vince. It was as if she had known him in another world, as if St Anne's Place and the children and Captain Randle had existed only in her imagination. Even the war seemed to be happening to other people. Unreal, it was something you read about in the newspapers. Sometimes she wondered about Joseph. In her narrow bed at night she would pray, 'Oh, dear Lord, keep him safe, wherever he may be. Vince, too – and, of course, Captain Randle . . .'

Some weeks later, still getting no word from Vince, she wrote to his parents at their address on the promenade. She explained that she was a friend of Vince's and having had no word since the call-up, had wondered how he was getting on. A week later a reply came from his mother, telling how he'd enlisted in the RAMC and had been sent to France and as far as they knew he was fine.

Chapter Fifteen

The car moved slowly along the narrow cobbled street, followed by a cluster of small boys. Their faces held expressions of amazed curiosity. They had never actually seen a car in that part of Ridley before. This could be something to talk about for months to come.

James Randle, resplendent in uniform, peaked cap, highly polished Sam Browne belt and all, brought the car to a standstill and immediately it was covered with children, appearing as though from nowhere, clustering like ants over a log.

He barked an order and reluctantly they let go. James climbed out, his leg not nearly as stiff now. He stood by the bonnet, slapping his leather gloves against the palm of one hand, grey eyes appraising the group of eager children.

Picking on the biggest and roughest-looking lad, he felt in his pocket, produced a shilling and tossed it to the boy. 'Here, you can have this, share it amongst your mates. The condition being that you keep the other children off my car.'

'Coo!' A shilling was a small fortune. For such a sum the lad would have cheerfully guarded it with his life, day or night.

'I'm going in there.' James nodded towards the chippy. 'I shan't be long. All right?'

The boy stood to attention, aware that the eyes of every child in the small crowd were gazing at him with envy. 'Aye, sir, you can rely on me.'

For the briefest of moments, James hesitated. He must be deranged, he thought. What on earth had possessed him, coming all this way to this mill town in pursuit of a girl he hardly knew. What Libby did with her life was no concern of his. But he no more could have stayed away than the sun could have risen in the west.

Unaware of her impending visitor, Libby knelt on a folded sack, singing in a low voice as she scrubbed the cracked linoleum floor. Her sleeves were rolled up to her elbows, the top three buttons of her high-necked gown unfastened owing to the heat of this August day. Her face was flushed and her hair, tidily pinned when she left home, hung in damp question marks about her forehead and cheeks.

She wondered what Mam would say could she see her now. Would she be proud of the way her once delicate young daughter was facing up to the future or disappointed because she had not stuck with her career as nursemaid? Old Hobbins was kind enough, even if after an already over-long day he expected her to stay late in order to help clear up after they closed.

'The wife always got down to cleaning up reet after last customer left,' he told Libby, 'and it's 'ow I've kept it ever since.'

Northerners take a perverse pride in their

weather, refusing to admit it is like weather anywhere. And so, when the sun shone so warmly that
morning, something inside her compelled Libby to lift
her voice in song.

She was in the middle of: 'Oh, Mary, we crown
Thee with blossom today . . .' the last note rising
effortlessly in the stale air of the chip shop, when the
door was pushed open and a pair of highly polished
brown shoes stepped bang into the middle of the suds
she was about to wipe up.

The hymn died on her lips and sharp words took its
place. 'Hey, watch where you're stepping! We're not
open yet, anyway. Give us a chance to clean up the
shop before . . .'

She sat back on her heels, gazing up. At first she
hardly recognised him. He looked so much better,
had put on weight and wasn't so pale or drawn. The
air in the shop was electric. James stood gazing down
into those breath-taking eyes and it was as if all that
had happened since their last meeting had been as
chaff in the wind. He remembered that parting kiss
on the shadowy landing with just the tick of the
grandfather clock below in the hall for company, the
softly parted lips, as innocent as a new babe in spite
of that ruffian with whom she professed to be in love.

She passed a soapy hand to her breast, staring at
him. She spoke first, her voice trembling. 'Captain
Randle! How did you find me?'

'It wasn't difficult. I'd heard Basil Ainslie was on
home leave and thought I'd pay him a visit and extend
my respects to his parents at the same time.' Liar! a
voice inside him cried. You came this way because

you couldn't stay away. Why don't you admit it? He went on, 'I spoke to Cook and she told me of your leaving. She also told me where you were working.' His eyes softened. 'She told me about your parents. I'm so sorry, Libby.'

She was silent, still not ready to talk about it. So she moved on to a safer subject, a subject that wouldn't hurt her. 'You went all that way just to see Basil Ainslie?'

Even to his ears it sounded a highly improbable story. He grimaced. 'Well, I have this car and it seemed a good idea at the time.' Seeing the glint of laughter in her eyes, he added, 'Damn it, Libby, I also wanted to see you.'

And the truth was, he hadn't been able to get her out of his mind. She haunted his dreams by night and distracted his work by day. The desk job they had given him in Whitehall wasn't taxing enough to take his mind off her. And, somehow, even Josie had lost her charm. Josie was so busy with her new show, anyhow, that she had little time for anything else. They occasionally shared a candlelit dinner but their relationship had somehow gone platonic. His face softened, his eyes anxious. 'You've had a tough time. I wanted to see for myself how you were.'

Unable to help himself, he put out a hand and took hers, pulling her to her feet in one fluid movement. The small hand lay passively within his. With a smile he took the clean white handkerchief from his top pocket and wiped away the soap suds. 'You'll get chapped hands,' he said softly. 'Can't have that now, can we?'

She didn't attempt to withdraw her hand. Just stood there, gazing at him through the strands of hair that had fallen over her forehead.

His fingers ached to brush it aside. A wild impulse, almost impossible to resist, took hold of him. He wanted to remove the rest of the pins holding the low chignon at the back of her head, to delight in the way it would tumble over her shoulders in soft waves of bright copper. He lifted her hand to his chest, chaffing it warmly between his own palms. It was a gesture so cherishing it brought tears to Libby's eyes. He could feel the slight tremble of her body, and a trace of warmth creep into the rough little hand.

At his touch, Libby felt a surge of emotion, the kind of feeling she used to experience on Easter Sunday entering church and seeing the beautifully dressed altar, the Madonna lilies, so pure and white, their slim shapes arranged gracefully in the silver vases, the array of candles, glittering in the semi-gloom of the old church, Father Brady, radiant in his richly embroidered robes and herself and her family proud in their new Easter outfits.

Perhaps not new every year, for Dad was often off work and then they would have to sit in the back row in their ordinary Sunday clothes, enduring the scornful glances of the more fortunate of the congregation. It was considered bad luck not to wear at least one item of new clothing on Easter Sunday. 'Otherwise the crows will shit on you,' Dad used to say, making the children laugh and evoking a frown from Mam and a sharp 'William!'

Was it a sin to compare her feelings right at this

moment to those of long ago in church? Sacrilege, she shouldn't wonder. Reality returned with a wrench and lifting her head, high and proud, making the man feel as though a red-hot iron had been run clear through his guts, she said, 'Thank you, I'm coping. But it is nice to see you again. How well you look. Is your leg healed?'

Gently she gave a tug at her hand and with reluctance, stuffing the damp handkerchief into his pocket, he relinquished his grip.

'It could be worse.'

'How was Cook? And the others?'

'Cook, as far as I could see, was her usual self, and Alice, too. I saw the children briefly. They seemed happy enough. As for me, I'm bearing up but not happy. Frustrated would better describe my attitude to life at the moment. Frustrated that I'm forced to sit behind that damned desk like a man twice my age. As for my leg, well, thank you kindly, dear child, but it's healing nicely.'

They both smiled. Aware that she must be looking a sight and that his eyes had not left her face since he appeared in the shop, Libby raised her arms and tried to tuck the errant curls back into place. The movement tightened the cotton blouse across her breasts and he felt his breathing quicken, his heart turning over at the beauty of her. She was like something from one of Grimms' fairy tales; the peasant maid forced by the wicked dwarf to perform menial tasks until it was her fate to be discovered by the Prince . . .

Really, James, old man! he caught himself thinking.

Don't tell me you're putting yourself into the place of that Prince? And here he'd been, kidding himself that he'd come seeking her out for purely philanthropic reasons.

Behind them the shop door opened and a voice said, 'Hey-up, lass, not finished cleaning t'floor yet? We'll have t'customers in soon, wanting their dinners. Better get a move on.'

'I'm sorry, Mr Hobbins.'

Trying to ignore the presence of James Randle, standing so quietly to one side of the shop, Libby gave the floor one last wipe then carried the slop bucket into the back room. There she washed her face and hands under the cold water tap. She unrolled the sleeves of her blouse, buttoned the cuffs and then did up the three buttons at the high neck of her bodice. She was doing the last button up when Mr Hobbins appeared behind her. 'That young officer, Libby.' There was speculation in his eyes. 'Is he waiting for you?'

'Yes, Mr Hobbins.'

'A friend?'

'An acquaintance. I met him at Dr Ainslie's. He's been giving me news of the staff while he was this way.'

'Decent of him.' He noted the flush on her cheeks, the averted eyes, and a pang of jealousy disconcerted him.

Taking a deep breath, he said, 'I suppose he's on leave. Won't have much time to waste. Take the rest of the morning off, lass. I can manage for once and Clara will be in later.'

'If you're sure, Mr Hobbins.'

'Aye, I'm sure. Off you go, now.'

James took her by the arm and guided her from the
shop. Outside on the pavement the boy who had been
watching the car ran forward. 'It's all right, sir. I
wouldn't let nobody touch it. Just like you said.'

James smiled. 'Thanks, lad.' He tossed the lad
another sixpence and the gasps of the watching children echoed in the quiet street. 'Thanks, sir. Eee,
wait till I show me mam.'

Libby's eyes widened as they took in the car.
'That's yours?'

'Temporarily. I borrowed it.' He looked about him
at the cobblestoned street, the shining window
panes, the whitened sills. 'Do you live nearby?'

'Just around the corner. Come and have some tea.'

He grinned. 'The panacea for all that ails you!'

She laughed. 'Well, I don't know what that is, but
I'm sure a cup of tea will cure it.'

She was glad that she had cleaned the kitchen
before leaving for work that morning. The small room
gleamed with loving care. James glanced around him
appreciatively. 'Hmm, warm and cosy.'

'There'll be lace curtains twitching this day and
my name will be mud, entertaining a strange young
man beneath my roof, unchaperoned.'

James pulled out a chair from the table and sat
down. Libby filled the kettle from the tap above the
sink and put it on the fire. Luckily she had banked the
coals up before leaving for work and it was still
glowing. Poking it into a fine blaze, she soon had the
kettle singing.

'Would you like something to eat?' she asked.
'Some toast?'

'Please don't think you have to play hostess to me, Libby. I didn't come for that. A cup of tea will do fine.'

They drank the hot steaming tea in silence. Refusing her offer of another cup, James placed his cup carefully back into its saucer. 'How about a drive out somewhere? That is, if there's anything worth seeing apart from coal dumps and mill chimneys.'

Although she knew he joked, Libby was immediately on the defensive. 'The town's quite pretty on the outskirts, once you're in the country.'

He laughed at the challenge in her voice. 'There you go again, ruffling your feathers like a little old hen.' His eyes met hers. 'Show me what hold this place has for you to keep coming back to it.'

Conscious that her skirt was still damp from the soapy water, she said, ruefully, 'I'll have to change . . .'

'You do that.' He sat back in the chair, surprisingly content and at home while she ran upstairs to her room. Never once did it occur to him to compare this room with his mother's luxurious sitting room, with its satin cushions and velvet draperies and the crystal vases filled daily with fresh flowers. This room smelled faintly of soot, of damp walls and ceilings. He thought of the pit owners, the nouveau riche, who lived in large mansions on the outskirts of town, raking in the rents week after week, year after year from the hundreds of such dwellings, putting not a farthing back into the properties while they slowly rotted about the workers' heads.

The one tap dripped constantly in the ugly stone sink, an irritating plip-plopping sound. He thought of the way he had found the girl, bent over a bucket, scrubbing a greasy floor, her hands red and chapped. Somehow he had to get her out of this life. He didn't know how but he must think of a way.

Upstairs in her bedroom, Libby changed into a cotton frock made from a length of material once given to her by Mrs Moran. It was simple and plain and the green patterned motif matched the colour of her eyes. It was the first time she had worn it since Mam had died. For a moment she felt a sense of betrayal. Then thought, Mam wouldn't mind! And it *was* the first real summer's day they had had . . . She brushed her hair and hurriedly pinned it back into place.

Back downstairs James gazed at her with appreciation. 'You look,' he said, 'good enough to eat.'

Taking her arm in what he hoped was a brotherly gesture, he thanked the observant boy as he assisted her into the car. The crowd of children had dwindled but a few cheered lustily as James left the curb and drove the car along the street. Libby found herself blushing and huddled down in her seat. He turned his head briefly to say, 'What's the matter?'

Sheepishly, she replied, 'I don't know. I just think it's better if no one sees me.'

Amusement lit up the grey eyes. 'Why on earth not? What's wrong with anyone seeing you?'

'I suppose I'm just being silly.'

'No need to feel silly. Just sit up straight and enjoy the view. After all that bragging I want you to point the attraction of the place when we come to it. I might miss it otherwise.'

Again she knew he was teasing. This time she didn't rise to his bait. Just tilted her chin and gazed straight ahead. Following her directions they left the small town behind and were soon in the country. The lanes here were narrow, hedged with high hawthorn bushes. It was shadowy and dark and she felt isolated in a world all their own, wondering if he felt it, too. Sitting beside this attractive man in his immaculate uniform, so obviously out of her class, she wanted to pinch herself to make sure it wasn't all a dream.

On either side wide fields stretched, merging into a green landscape. 'My mother was country born and bred,' she murmured. 'When she first came to Ridley she missed the fields and trees so much it took her ages to settle in. But she grew used to it and she loved my father very much. You can grow used to anything in time, I suppose, and the people of Ridley were so warm and friendly.'

Without a word he stopped the car, pulling well into the side of the narrow lane. There was a field with the yellow of ripening corn. He took her hand and helped her across the stile, laughing at the way her long skirts and petticoats became tangled on the ancient grey wood.

The path they followed was shadowed by overhanging dog roses and she held her skirts away from the brambles. There were poppies, blood red and gleaming, and James caught himself thinking that the fields of Flanders must once have looked like this.

They followed the path until they came to a spot that was flattened, probably by lovers, like them looking for a place to rest. James dropped to the ground without a word, pulling her down beside him.

'Now, let's talk.'

Libby bent her head, suddenly intent on picking the tiny white daisies and joining them together in a chain. Talking brought back memories best forgotten. Yet he hadn't come all this way to sit in a field and watch her make daisy chains.

'To begin with, you can tell me why you are working as you are, scrubbing floors. Surely you can do better than that?'

'I have to live. Have to make some money. There's such things as rent and food and coal for the fire.'

'I understand. But why that particular job? Why not something more – rewarding?'

Her lips curled. Chance would be a fine thing! What, she wondered, would his reaction be if she told him about old Dibbs and the scene in the back room of the shop? A slow anger stirred in her and sounding more bitter than she intended, she said, 'You don't have to worry about such things, do you? Your life's all nice and cosy and planned for you by dear Papa . . .'

She broke off, aghast at what she had just said. It wasn't fair. He could no more alter his life than she could. Seeing the look that passed over his face, she exhaled with a sigh. 'I'm sorry, I didn't mean to sound like that. I know it's not your choice, the work you're doing. But, don't you see, it isn't easy for me, either. Not many in this world can choose the way they live.

Certainly not in this town.' She glanced up at him from beneath lowered lashes. 'Why *did* you come, anyway? I'm sure it wasn't just to see what kind of a mess I was making of my life.'

Torn by the inexplicable feeling raging inside him, he turned on her, mouth hard and bitter. 'Have you any idea of the guilt *I've* been feeling, safe over here in the bosom of my family while men are dying in their thousands on the other side of the Channel? Don't you think I wake at night reliving scenes that my men are still experiencing? Did I ever tell you about that first Christmas I spent at the Front? The bright moonlit nights that were bitingly cold, so cold that a young Scots lad in our unit swore he'd never again complain about winter nights in the Highlands? On Christmas morning we woke to snow. The men had no overcoats, just a haversack and iron rations and water enough to last for six days. To our joy we came across a French village where a few people still lived, mostly old, but they welcomed us with open arms. Nothing in their meagre stock of food was too good for us. They held a Christmas dinner in the village hall. There was plenty of the local wine and beer and I will never forget that dour Scots lad singing in his fine baritone voice "My Ain Folk". The French, of course, didn't understand the words, but they understood the sentiments and there wasn't a dry eye in the hall.'

James paused and plucked at a buttercup, mutilating the shiny yellow petals between his fingers, before he looked up again, his gaze fixed on some distant point. 'That young Scot was killed the next day.'

Libby caught her breath, one hand going to her

267

throat. 'Oh, James, I'm sorry. I had no right to say those things . . .'

'How could you know? You've had your own sorrows to bear. I really was sorry to hear about your parents. It must have been a terrible shock, coming so close together.'

He looked at her and his voice faltered as he saw the shadowed eyes, the pale cheeks, making her look more like some spirit of the underworld than the lively young woman he remembered. 'Tell me.' His voice was so soft, it brought tears to her eyes. The words came out slowly, the words that told the story of her father, and then of Mam. Somehow, once started, she couldn't stop. Tears ran down her cheeks. James put his arm about her shoulders and said helplessly, 'Please, Libby – don't upset yourself.'

She leaned against him and sobbed without restraint. It was the first time she had really cried since that calamitous day when Father Brady had broken the news of Mam . . .

James said, 'Let me help. Please! Come to London. Start a new life – put all this behind you.'

It was the right approach. For a second she was tempted. Then she drew a deep breath and sat up straight. 'What a lovely thought. If only I could.'

There was a long silence, broken only by the sound of the wind rustling all about them. Then he said: 'You're a brave girl, Libby.'

'I'm all right now. I've accepted it. Mam wasn't very happy. She's probably a lot happier in heaven with Dad.'

She took the handkerchief he offered and wiped her eyes, smiling as he said, teasingly, 'Don't you ever carry one of these things? I've never known you yet to have one when you've needed it.' Then: 'Have you had any word about your brother?'

'Nothing. Please God he is safe, but we may never know.' Absent-mindedly she picked a poppy and tucked it behind one ear and James felt a shudder go through him. With trembling fingers he took it from her and threw it away. Poppies to him would always mean death and destruction; nightmares that still plagued him. On this fresh young girl they seemed almost profane. He rose to his feet and held out his hands, helping her up. 'All right, now?' When she nodded, he said, 'I think we should go. Mr Hobbins will be wondering where you've got to. He didn't seem too pleased to see me even though he agreed to letting you have time off.'

'He's all right. Quite sweet, really.'

'Now, I'm staying at the Victoria in Market Street. If I can help in any way or you should change your mind about coming to London, promise you'll let me know.'

She nodded, the tears already drying on her cheeks. He took her hands again and looked down at her. 'I shall have to leave at midday tomorrow, but you'll find me at the hotel until then.'

At the end of her road she asked him to stop the car. 'Let me out here. There will be enough gossip as it is without adding to it.' She smiled at him. 'Thank you for taking the trouble to come and see me. God bless.'

She began to hurry away down the road. After a few yards she turned, walking backwards, and waved.

James remained for a little while, sitting and watching, and when finally he drove off he didn't go straight back to the hotel but drove into the countryside again, gently nursing the image of Libby turning to wave, like a young girl parting from her lover.

Chapter Sixteen

Before she could open her front door, Mrs Moran appeared at hers. 'Well, there, Libby! Had a nice morning?'

Seeing the curiosity in her eyes, Libby nodded briefly. 'Very nice, thank you, Mrs Moran.'

'You're a popular girl today.' Her neighbour smirked. 'While you were out you had another visitor.'

On the point of closing the door, Libby turned. 'Oh? Who was that?'

'Didn't give 'is name. Dark, good looking in a flashy kind of way. In uniform. I thought at first, catching sight of the uniform, it was your Joseph come 'ome.' She shook her head. 'But this one I never seen before. Said he'd come back.'

Almost before Mrs Moran had finished describing him, Libby knew that it was Vince. It had to be Vince. No one else she knew fitted that description.

'Did you tell him I'd gone out?'

'Aye. When he asked where, I explained about the young officer and the car. Oh, such excitement that car caused, Libby. You wouldn't believe it! The children 'ave bin talking of nothing else since you . . .'

Mrs Moran's children missed nothing. Each new happening in the street was an event to them.

She paused, giving Libby a penetrating look. 'I 'ope I didn't do wrong, love. The young man *did* say 'e was a friend of yours.'

Libby shook her head. 'Of course not, Mrs Moran.' She began to close the door. 'I must go now. I promised Mr Hobbins I would be back in time for the dinner rush.'

Quickly she changed back into her working clothes, then hurried over to the fish and chip shop. But her mind wasn't on her work and a number of times during the afternoon Mr Hobbins had to speak sharply to her. At last, clearly exasperated, he scolded her for upsetting a tray of fish cutlets on the floor.

Libby blessed the fact that she had scrubbed the linoleum only that morning, but Mr Hobbins wasn't so easily appeased.

'Libby! What's wrong wi' you, lass? You're all fingers and thumbs and anyone can see your mind's not on your work.' A thought struck him. 'That young officer didn't 'ave news of your Joseph, did 'e? Bad news?'

Libby shook her head. Kneeling, she gathered up the pieces of fish and carried them in the lap of her pinny to the back room. A good rinse under the tap and they were ready for the batter. Returning to Mr Hobbins, she said, 'I'm sorry.'

From behind them, Clara, emerging from the back room, said witheringly, 'Fat lot of good bein' sorry would 'ave been if a customer had been in the shop at the time.'

Her brother looked as though he would like to say

something but thought better of it. Something was wrong with the girl and he was sure it was that officer. Didn't do to start mixing with the upper crust. Oil and water don't mix, any more than Libby and that young bloke with the shiny Sam Browne belt and well-pressed uniform could mix. A nice girl, young Libby, he'd give you that. A refined and good church-going lass, but still it didn't bring her into the officer's category.

He tossed a panful of golden brown chips before plunging them back into the boiling fat. Libby should stay with her own kind. Absently, with the forefinger of one hand, he smoothed the moustache across his top lip, increasingly a habit of his. How much difference in age was there between him and this girl? Thirty-odd years? He grimaced. Not a lot when you said it quickly! He could do with a smart young lass about the place, not just coming in every day but permanently there. Gave the whole shop a glow. Warmed the heart to see her smiling face. Clara was well-meaning, but had become crabby in her old age, while Libby was like a ray of sunshine. Warm his lumpy cold bed, too!

A disturbing and almost forgotten warmth stirred in him. A long time since he'd experienced *that*. Of course, he'd do it properly. Marry the lass. Wouldn't dream of anything less. Not with a girl like Libby.

Libby, completely absorbed in her own thoughts, would have been shocked could she have read Mr Hobbins'. The unknown visitor – Vince? – had told Mrs Moran he'd come back later. But what if he didn't? What if, after listening to Mrs Moran's recital of Libby driving away at the side of an officer in a smart car, he decided that whatever he wanted to say to her wasn't worth hanging about for and had gone on his way? At their last meeting they hadn't been on the best of terms. And, knowing Vince's jealousy, his ridiculous possessiveness where she was concerned, she didn't really know what to expect.

Although she was thrilled at the expectation of seeing him again, of having him hold her in his arms, his lips on hers, so hard and demanding, still a part of her brain fought shy of the image. Hard as she tried to bring his dark good looks into focus, the thinner, almost ascetic face of James Randle was superimposed before it . . .

'. . . so if you'll finish peeling those potatoes, Libby, I'll have enough for the evening.'

With a start she realised Mr Hobbins was speaking to her. She must pull herself together. This was plain nonsense, acting like a lovesick school girl dreaming of her first beau.

Without a word she began on the basin of potatoes, her slim fingers using the small knife in expert manner. Banishing the thought of the two men from her consciousness, she compelled herself to think of nothing but the pile of potatoes before her.

That night, Mr Hobbins surprised her by insisting on walking her home. She argued that it was such a short walk and he must have plenty to do in the shop. But he shook his head, as stubborn as the next man when he'd made up his mind. 'Nay, lass, the air'll do me good. I feel like a walk and it's a grand evening.'

Libby submitted gracefully. She was further surprised when he took her arm and like a man half his
age chatted animatedly as they walked the short
distance. She knew the gossip that already existed
about old Hobbins and herself, spread by the few
neighbours who resented her doing Mrs Croft out of a
job, or so they thought.

Libby didn't give a damn what they thought. Walking beside her employer that fine evening, she held
her head high, her smile wide and friendly, daring
the busybodies to make something of it. Poor souls, if
they had nothing better to talk about, then why
should she deny them a treat!

Reaching her front door she turned to fit the key in
the lock, smiling over her shoulder to say goodnight.
Somehow she felt sorry for him. All he had to go back
to was that stuffy little shop smelling of boiled peas
and old grease and the vinegary Clara. Not that she
had much more. But she could come and go as she
liked and when her day's work was over she could
retire to the warm cosy kitchen with its memories of
Mam and Dad and the rest of her small family. Oh
yes, she decided, being alone had nothing to do with
being lonely. Unbidden, the thought popped into
Libby's head that the way Mr Hobbins was acting
only seemed to make him more pathetic. Especially
when he insisted on taking her hand as he bade her
goodnight, holding it clasped to his chest as though it
was something precious, something to be cherished.

'Goodnight, Libby. See you in t' morning.'

She smiled again and escaped indoors.

She unpinned her hair and brushed it until her

arms ached. Then leaving it hanging, a shining silken curtain of red gold reaching almost to her waist, she washed in cold water before changing back into the cotton dress she'd worn earlier for James. Still she imagined the smell of hot oil and fish clung to her skin and reaching up to the tiny cupboard built high into the old dresser she felt for the small bottle of lavender water that had been one of Mam's most prized possessions. The label had once read 'a souvenir of Blackpool' and the bottle was in the shape of the tower. Very little perfume remained, most having evaporated over the years, as Mam seldom used it. But the fresh flowery fragrance lingered on the musty air. She reached for a piece of sewing – a more urgent task would have been to darn the great hole in the heel of her black stockings but the romance in her soul whispered that the small piece of fine white cambric would look more refined.

She had left the front door slightly ajar, it being a fine summer evening and still not completely dark, and when Vince arrived she could, without moving, call for him to enter. Her skirts arranged just so, hands busy with needle and thread, the fire that she'd lit to ward off the chill that would come with the going down of the sun turning her unbound hair to burnished copper, she sat and waited for his knock.

The summer evening and the warmth from the fire made her drowsy and almost without knowing it she felt her hands still, her eyes grow heavy and finally close. She didn't hear the footsteps outside on the pavement or see the shadow that filled her doorway.

The man stood still, gazing down at her. She looked

so young, a child almost, so vulnerable, with her gorgeous hair spread like spun silk about her shoulders. He'd never seen it loose before, although he'd often imagined it. She was his girl and suddenly a sense of rage, of resentment that she could even *think* of going out with another man, and, to make it worse, a snotty-nosed officer, took hold of him. All right, so he hadn't warned her he was coming, thinking he would surprise her. His mouth twisted in a parody of a smile. And surprise her he had! Leaning forward, supported by his hands resting on the wooden arms of her chair, he bent his head until his mouth covered hers.

To further fuel the fires of his anger, Libby gave a little cry of alarm and instinctively raised her hands, pushing at his shoulders. Her sleep-cluttered brain didn't at first recognise the man bending over her. 'Give over . . . !'

His face, so close, was out of focus. Then slowly, as he drew back, she uttered a cry of joy and held out her arms. 'Vince!' If she'd expected answering joy she was disappointed. He scowled down at her, his eyes black pools of suspicion. 'Oh, I'm so glad to see you. I was sure you were over there with the fighting.' She peered intently into his face. 'Are you all right? You've not been wounded and sent home . . . ?'

He thought back to the mud, the stink, of Flanders, of how he thought he'd go mad if he was forced to stay like those poor bloody sods who accepted tamely the orders given by officers younger in many cases than the men themselves.

It had been so easy to charm the young Red Cross

driver and after a few hours spent with her in the only room left standing of a once-prosperous French inn, easy to persuade the bemused girl to let him hide in the back of her ambulance on her next trip to the depot. The girl had never met a man like Vince and obliged without hesitation. From the depot his natural craftiness had got him on to a hospital ship for Blighty. They would be looking for him, of course, but first things first. Libby would help him.

The military police would have no reason to think he would be hiding in a place like Ridley. He'd come to find her, taking risks, congratulating himself on getting this far without being stopped, only to discover her gadding off, enjoying herself when she should be at home worrying about him, like any decent woman with a man at the Front. Pity her neighbour, nosy old trout, had seen him, but it couldn't be helped.

Having nowhere to go, he'd walked to the end of the road and hidden in a dark alleyway where he'd spent the rest of the day and early evening watching events in the dingy street. He'd seen Libby return and had drawn further back into the shadows. A few minutes later, just as he was making up his mind to approach the house, Libby had appeared again and hurried off to the corner shop. Later, he'd witnessed Mr Hobbins escorting her home. Pausing at her front door, the old man had taken Libby's hand and held it for what had seemed an inordinately long time before she'd smiled and slipped away.

He laughed now; a harsh laugh that grated on Libby's nerves. 'No,' he said, in answer to her question. 'I'm all right. I see you're doing all right, too, with two men hanging around, sniffing your skirts. Playing it both ways, eh? One old and one young. Well, they do say variety's the spice of life.'

Libby drew back in the chair. She'd been so glad to see Vince, had thought of nothing but him since Mrs Moran had told her of his visit, and now, after so long apart, here he was accusing her of . . .

Her cheeks flamed. 'I'm not – you mustn't say those things . . .' she began, those breathtaking eyes raised huge and puzzled to his face. A chill finger of fear touched her as she read what was written there, the handsome features twisted with jealous rage.

His breath rasped in his throat, his hands rough as they fingered the high neckline of her dress. 'Everyone tells me what to do; those officers in France and now you, well, I'll not stand for it . . .' He kissed her again, viciously, his teeth scraping against her lips, clamping her lower lip until she could feel the warm saltiness of blood.

'Stop it, Vince! *Stop* it . . .' The words came out a muffled sob. Vainly she pushed at his shoulders and heard him laugh.

'I bet you don't say that to that officer bloke! Or the old geezer that you let paw you. Was it because you were expecting me back that you didn't ask him in?'

Oh, how could she have woven dreams about this man? Imagined a future as his wife! With a mighty shove she sent him flying. He stumbled over a chair and only saved himself from falling by clutching at the velveteen tablecloth, dragging it with him, knocking over the vase of wild flowers she'd earlier placed there.

Water trickled over the table, on to his uniform. He brushed it off as he straightened, rising to his full height. 'All those months of wanting you, Libby, and you shaking your head and saying no. You've only yourself to blame for denying me. I'm a man, after all, and you've been driving me mad with wanting you.'

Desperately she turned her head away, refusing to meet his eyes. 'I can't help that, Vince. You know I couldn't . . .'

Suddenly Vince lost his temper, furious with himself and humiliated at having pleaded with her. 'You bitch!' he roared. 'You're sleeping with that officer, don't try to deny it. Not above having a tumble with him while you're saying no to me, eh?' He sneered. 'And, for all I know, that old geezer that was with you tonight outside your front door.'

Libby sighed. 'Don't be silly, Vince. Doing all the things I'm accused of doing, I wouldn't have the strength to enjoy a tumble even if I wanted to.'

His face blazed with both anger and frustration. His cheeks had gone red and blotchy. 'Are you sleeping with him?'

'No. Not that it's any of your business.'

'I don't believe you.'

'I don't give a damn whether you believe me or not.' Suddenly tired of the whole thing, she stood up from Mam's rocking chair. She went to the sink and began to fill the kettle, trying to behave naturally although her heart was throbbing painfully inside her breast. Settling the kettle onto the fire, she turned and meeting his eyes, said, 'I'll make a cup of tea. You'll feel better after.'

Seeing her so calm, so composed – did she *never* lose her temper? – he decided to put the knife in. Christ, to think how much he'd panted after this girl! Him, Vince Remede, who had been stringing girls along since his early teens. He could hardly credit he'd been so patient with this one. He said, 'You can forget the tea. I didn't come all this way for a cup of tea.'

Libby's own cheeks reddened. 'What *did* you come for, then?'

'What did I come for?' he spat contemptuously. 'What do you think? To get you into bed.'

Libby sat down once again in the old rocking chair and looked up at him furiously. 'Is that all you ever wanted? To get me into bed?'

He laughed cruelly and grabbed her hair. At last she was showing a bit of spirit. He leered down at her.

How she had once loved that face. Her eyes searched for something to defend herself with. And saw the knife with which she had cut herself a thick slice of bread earlier on. She reached out to grasp it as he hauled her to her feet again. Then he smashed at her arm and she dropped the knife.

Bending down he picked up the knife and placed it on the high mantelpiece, well out of her reach. 'You won't be wanting that again,' he said.

She cringed as his fingers curled once again through her long hair. With his other hand he grabbed her about the waist and with a sharp tug drew her towards him. Unable to think clearly, she saw the wet shine of his eyes, the scarlet patches high on his cheeks. She wanted to push him away, to escape through the back door into the maze of alleyways that backed onto the row of terraced houses.

He was holding her so tight she could hardly breathe; open-mouthed wet kisses made her shudder and she began to fight him, twisting and turning in his arms.

How could she have thought she loved him! Now she saw only the violence in his dark eyes.

'Ugh, Vince, stop it. I don't like . . .'

'I know what you like and don't like.' His voice grated. The only noise in the dim room was the sound of their harsh breathing. Libby put a hand to the front of her gown where his frenzied pawing had torn the material. If she could just get upstairs, lock herself in her bedroom . . .

Her eyes darted to the door and as though reading her mind, Vince said, 'Yes, why don't we? I'd intended ending up there, anyway.'

So smug was he, so convinced that he had her where he wanted her, that he was caught napping when she made a sudden dart for the door. She was halfway up the stairs when he caught her.

She opened her mouth to scream, but even in the midst of her terror she remembered how thin the walls were; how her neighbours could hear every sound. Pride alone stopped her from crying out. She felt his hands tug at her skirt and almost without realising what she did, she turned on the narrow staircase and kicked out with one foot. The heel of her shoe caught him on the bridge of the nose. He gave a grunt and released her long enough to clap both hands to his face.

Libby took the opportunity to run the rest of the way to her room, gasping with relief as she turned to slam the door. Vince had recovered more quickly than she'd expected and was just behind her, his face dark with rage, his nose dripping blood.

He pushed the door wide with the flat of one hand. 'You little bitch!'

The words were spoken with such heat that his spittle sprayed her face. 'Time you were taught a lesson. One you won't easily forget.'

Silently, she fought him, putting up such a fierce resistance that he lost all control and caught her on the point of the chin with his fist, as he would fight a man.

Nothing mattered to Vince Remede now but venting his rage, his frustration, against this slight helpless girl. She was taking the place of the dog he would kick until its ribs caved in; the kitten whose eyes he could, without a qualm, burn out with the lighted end of a cigarette. Vince's way of getting his own back.

James Randle sat at the bar of the hotel, long fingers playing with the empty whisky glass on the counter. He had been there for so long, nursing that one drink, that the barman was beginning to cast apprehensive looks in his direction. The long ornate mirror behind the bar reflected the brooding face.

'Another whisky, sir?'

So lost in thought was James that the barman had to repeat his query.

'No, thanks.'

The barman gave his head a little shake and moved on. The captain was obviously disturbed about something. Shame, a good-looking young bloke like that; should be enjoying life, he should, not thinking about going back to the trenches. The man watched from the end of the bar until James seemed to come to a decision. He left the bar and went up to his room. A little while later, carrying his cap, the barman saw him pass through the foyer.

James stepped out into the darkening street, settled the peaked cap at an angle on his head and began to stride briskly along in the direction of the Market Square. He remembered the way he had taken earlier to Libby's house. The walk would do him good. He couldn't rid his mind of Libby on her knees, scrubbing that bloody floor. Or her tears in the poppy field when she'd leaned against him, the slight body shaking convulsively, giving vent to the grief she had buried for so long.

Damn it! He couldn't up and leave her like this. There had to be something he could do. Take her back to London with him, as he'd first suggested. Use force if necessary. Bundle her, soap suds an' all, into the car to drive until they were far away from this grey town with its careworn people and tall smoking chimneys. He should not have come in the first place. But the need to see Libby again had been insistent. Like a tongue probing an aching tooth. No use denying it. The cushy job he was doing must be making him soft in the head.

He would like nothing better than to take this girl home and introduce her to his parents, to his friends. But anything beyond the most formal relationship would have to face the barriers and injustices of the rigid social hierarchy that, although perishing in the flames of the war, was still highly evident.

The streets were quiet now, the children inside having their supper. The gas lamps cast yellow circles, illuminating only a few feet beyond their base. There were no cars. Cars did not venture into this part of town too often. At the end of the street he paused to light a cigarette, taking his time, collecting his thoughts. He wondered why his heart hammered so unsteadily.

Come on! he chided himself. You're doing the girl a favour. Showing a bit of interest in her immediate future. What's wrong with that?

He began to walk on, then, a few yards from her front door, he hesitated as a shadow passed before him. It came from the opposite side of the street and, pushing open the door of the small house, it went inside as though expected.

James drew deep on his cigarette, letting the smoke trickle slowly from his nostrils. He had recognised the figure. Had seen it half a dozen times on their walks along the promenade with the Ainslie children. Watched it from the bar of the seafront pub when Vince had made so free and easy with the trollop of a girl, in full view of everyone.

The tip of his cigarette grew bright red in the darkness. He dropped it to the pavement and grinding it under his heel, turned and retraced his steps back down the street.

Irrespective of right or wrong, Libby had made her choice. A choice with which he did not agree, but who was he to argue? Nothing he had to say now would alter that.

Chapter Seventeen

Daylight was breaking when Libby regained consciousness. For long moments she lay wondering why she was on the floor and not on her bed. She heard the banging of the knocking-up man's long pole on the windows of her neighbours: then, it seemed only moments later, the ear-deafening clatter of the girls in their clogs as they streamed down the cobbled street to start their day at the mill.

Libby tried to stand, groaned and collapsed on the bed. She ached all over. The slightest movement was agony. She managed to stagger to the old-fashioned dresser and hold herself upright by leaning both hands on its scarred top. The mirror reflected a face she had difficulty in recognising. Her eyes seemed enormous, staring at her from a chalk-white face. A dark purple bruise disfigured the point of her chin where Vince had hit her. Her bodice was ripped to the waist and through the tear she could see bruises on her breasts.

With a sob, she leaned her head against her hands and scalding tears stung her cheeks.

Never, never, had she visualised anything like this. A wave of nausea burned upwards in her throat. She leaned over the china basin on the chest of drawers, perspiration springing icily on her brow, as shock finally gripped her and she was very, very sick.

When at last the retching stopped, she crouched shivering on her bed, exhausted. Arms folded over her stomach, she rocked backwards and forwards on the bed. She had loved him so much – so much, had dreamed of him, of his strength, ached for his arms about her. She knew now she had ached for something that never existed.

By the time Mr Hobbins came knocking at her front door later that morning, concerned by her non-appearance, she had achieved a certain degree of calm, although the sudden knocking caused a quiver to run through her entire body. She could no more have crept down those stairs to the kitchen than she could have jumped over the moon.

Leaning out of the bedroom window, she could see the burly figure of her employer on the pavement below.

'Mr Hobbins!' He stepped back a couple of paces and craned his head back to gaze upwards at the partly opened window. Clearly concerned, he called, 'Libby! What's the matter? Are you ill?'

'I think I'm in for a dose of that Spanish influenza, Mr Hobbins.' No time to feel dismay at the ease with which the lie came to her lips. 'I – I thought, if you could manage, I'd spend the morning in bed. I feel awful.'

At least that wasn't a lie. She felt worse than awful. Ugly and degraded and wondering how she could ever look anyone in the eye again.

Relief showed on Mr Hobbins' face, thankful that it wasn't anything worse. 'Aye, you do that, lass. In fact, I don't want to see you back till t'morning.' Startled at his sudden fit of generosity, he added, 'Or even later, not until you're properly over it, at any road. Me and Clara'll manage just fine.'

Breathing a grateful sigh at his quiet assent, Libby closed the window and crawled back to bed. Thankfully, apart from the bruise on her chin, which she could explain away somehow – tripped on the stairs, banged it on the kitchen dresser – her face wasn't marked. No black eyes or split lips and the bruises on the upper part of her arms could be hidden by her long sleeves. She just wouldn't have to roll them up, no matter how warm the day. There were bruises everywhere on her body, ugly red and purple, making each step she took an agony. Her breasts were too sore to touch, causing her to wince as she bathed them in warm water. Inconceivable to think that Vince could have been so deliberately vicious.

Her conscience did not allow her to stay away for long and so she was back at work the next day.

Mr Hobbins fretted and fussed, shocking his sister into speechlessness when he informed her that for the next few days she would have to scrub the floors. 'Still lookin' peaky, she is,' he said, eyeing Libby with compassion. 'That 'flu takes it out of a body.'

Clara cast a vicious look in Libby's direction but held her peace.

'James will be home this weekend.' Isobel Randle smiled at the young woman who lounged before her on the brocaded settee, artlessly trailing a long scarf of scarlet chiffon from one languid hand. 'I hope you haven't arranged anything else, Fenella, for I fully intend to invite a few friends for the weekend. I know James would want you to be there.'

Isobel felt slight concern that the girl showed not the slightest interest in what she was saying. Apart from her father's horses, dancing those frantic new side-kicking numbers accompanied by loud music and driving the small car she had received for her birthday at high speeds around town, Fenella always gave the impression that everything else bored her to tears.

With the war going the way it was, Isobel wondered how Fenella still managed to escape the system that inexorably drew the young people of the present generation into its maw. Only Fenella continued her gadfly existence.

She had once declared that rolling bandages bored her to distraction and at the last Red Cross meeting had scandalised Isobel and the rest of the room by selecting a Balkan Sobranie cigarette from the silver case in her purse and, carefully fitting the black tip into the long holder, had lit the golden paper and playfully blown the smoke into the face of Lady Acton.

Lady Acton, a sharp reprimand in her voice, exclaimed, 'If you feel you have other, more important things to do, Fenella, then I suggest you go and do them and leave these good ladies to get on with their work.'

Fenella had jumped to her feet with alacrity, the

sarcasm in Lady Acton's voice completely lost on her. 'Jolly good.' With one long finger she tapped the ash from the end of her cigarette onto the carpet, then smiled at the small group of affronted women, her full mouth twisting sardonically. 'Have fun, ladies.'

'I don't know about that,' she said now, running the length of scarlet chiffon through her fingers. 'James, these days, is always so bad tempered and brusque. I swear he would rather play at silly old soldiers than be with me.'

It had been Isobel Randle's dearest wish that James and Fenella would marry, settle down and start a family. But James had become so withdrawn after returning from the trenches that she did not really know what was in his mind. She doubted if James knew himself.

'Don't *nag*,' her husband had advised. 'The boy's been through a traumatic experience. Some of our returning men, especially those suffering with shell-shock, will never fully get over it.'

Isobel had looked alarmed. 'You don't mean to say . . . ?'

David had chuckled. 'My dear, James is fine. Give him time, allow him to come to terms in his own way. The army doctors know what they are doing. Soon he'll be a new man, ready for anything.'

Which was exactly what Isobel feared. Chorus girls and such like, she thought. And where did Fenella fit into the scheme of things?

It was the accepted thing. Young men had to sow their wild oats. Stagedoor Johnnies were regarded with wry amusement and girls of the chorus with their Cockney wit and repartee made exciting companions. Old-fashioned, fastidious as she was, Isobel understood this. If some young girl had been successful in taking her son's mind off the terrible events of the war, then she could not find it in her heart to condemn either of them.

In time of war, people searched feverishly for excitement, wanting to be taken out of themselves. And who could blame them? The girls were pretty; they were lively and cared not a jot about what people thought. Some of them, the more astute, even married their suitors, earning themselves a title, wealth and a place in society, all in one fell swoop.

Last year there had been quite a scandal when the heir of the Earl of Babington, at forty-five old enough to have known better, as everyone said, married Vesta Wallace, who was barely nineteen and as witless a little creature as one could imagine.

Now Isobel said, trying not to sound critical, 'It's just an unfortunate time, that's all. James' mind is full of war and heroic deeds. Men are like that. You won't change them.' And when she continued, 'You know there's nothing his father and I would like better than to see you both happily settled down together,' some perverse devil had Fenella confessing that that was all she had ever hoped.

It seemed, that year, everyone was either getting engaged or married and Fenella was beginning to feel left out – something she couldn't abide.

She let the chiffon scarf drift to the carpet then looked pointedly at the bare finger of her left hand. Marriage to James had been a dream that had taunted her since early childhood. He had been the first boy to kiss her, the first to make her pulse leap. She pictured his handsome, sensitive face and thought of the advantages being the wife of Captain James Randle would bring.

The older woman bent and patted the slim shoulder. 'Be patient, dear, and it will all come out right. You'll see.'

Isobel was counting on that weekend in their country home in Buckinghamshire, hoping it would prompt James into discussing wedding plans.

Grateful for the fine weather, the guests seemed to prefer to spend most of the time in the garden, where beneath a giant oak tree, servants had put out wicker chairs and a table covered in a snowy white cloth on which tea was being laid. Everyone said it was going to be a glorious summer. It was as though the fighting on the other side of the Channel was happening on a different planet. The women and girls of the party wore their flimsiest frocks, voiles and chiffons in the most delicate pastel shades.

Fenella lit one of her cigarettes and, hip balanced against a stone figure of a cherub, mottled in moss-green lichen, she lazily surveyed the scene before her. She thought of last night when she and James had strolled in the garden, talking lightly about everything but what was really on their minds. They'd paused at the round lily pond and James had busied himself with lighting a cigarette. Holding it negligently between the fingers of one hand, his eyes on the reflection of the moon on the pond, he'd said, 'I suppose you know why they've invited you here this weekend, don't you?'

Fenella didn't answer, merely raised her eyes to his, a slow smile curving the full lips.

'They've been planning on this for years,' James added, sounding, she thought, vaguely apologetic. 'I trust you realise just what you are letting yourself in for?'

'Oh, James, you're so pompous!' Fenella with a graceful movement sank on to the stone bench that stood beside the pond. 'Why don't we sit and talk about it? It's such a lovely evening, it would be a pity to waste it.' She patted the seat next to her and he felt it would be churlish to ignore her invitation. 'You understand what I'm saying?' he said softly. 'I'm very fond of you, Fenella. But I'm sure you must know that.'

'This is one evening when I don't happen to have my crystal ball with me,' she answered flippantly. 'So you're just going to have to explain what you're on about.'

She thought of the young officers with whom she had been consoling herself during this man's absence. Some young and good-looking. Some, the foreign ones, of old titled European families. In their glamorous uniforms they had danced the night away, drinking champagne from her slipper, bending over her hand to kiss the knuckles with delicious languor. It was true she had been more than casually attracted to a number of these men. In fact, very attracted. One in particular, quiet, pleasant, fair with blue eyes and a slight blond moustache, was the son of a titled family from Cracow, but the little affair had ended before it became an item for public speculation. For, although titled, he was also poor and that was a category to which Fenella had no wish to belong.

'Let's stop this shilly-shallying,' James said. 'The time has come for me to settle down. I need a place that I can come home to when this bloody war is finally over, a place I can make my own. A wife. Children.'

Fenella raised thin eyebrows. 'And you want me to provide those for you?'

For a brief moment the image of a pair of emerald-green eyes and a cloud of golden-red hair framing a pale face invaded his reasoning, to be followed immediately by the scene when he saw Vince disappearing in through Libby's front door. He stared at the girl sitting beside him for so long that she began to fidget, fitting another golden cigarette into the jade holder.

She knew he was hinting at marriage; knew better than anyone that the whole weekend, with the connivance of his mother, had been as carefully staged as any West End show. Triumph bubbled up inside her. Drawing deep on the cigarette, her cheeks hollowed, she waited for him to speak.

'You have such a flair, Fenella,' he went on. 'And you know I've always admired you. Of course, it's a chancy business just now, marrying somebody like me. But if you'll take the chance I think we might find something together that will last. I'm no poet, though, so don't expect me to talk about the moon and the stars.'

His words moved her and she tried desperately to appear composed. 'Perhaps not,' she said, raising both hands to press against his chest. 'But you're doing awfully well.'

'You think we could make it work?'

She could feel his heartbeats beneath her palms. 'The old folk will be delighted.'

His mouth quirked. 'And we mustn't disappoint the old folk!'

She straightened and let her hands fall to her lap. 'Well, all right,' she said. 'We will make it the wedding of the season.'

The engagement had been announced as the small party of guests gathered in the ballroom. Champagne was drunk, toasting their future health and happiness and if the young man seemed quieter than a man in his position should have been, no one questioned it. The war took its toll on everyone. Even the newly engaged.

Now Fenella thought of marriage and what it would entail. Still, James would be away for most of the time and there was no reason why she shouldn't continue to entertain the boys. Especially those so far away from home! It was, after all, her Christian duty to do something for the war effort and what better function than seeing that some of the cares of battle were erased when they were on leave.

She wanted a big wedding and that would not be possible while the hostilities were on. Still, Isobel Randle was an enterprising woman. She would do all she could to send them off in style.

She sipped her drink and watched James approach across the smooth clipped lawns towards her. He was accompanied by an older man in civvies. A heavy-set man with a thatch of iron-grey hair and piercing blue eyes. He looked dynamic and even from where she stood Fenella could see that the suit he wore must have cost a small fortune. Of heavy Harris tweed, it looked far too warm and bulky for this weather. But, she decided with a quickening of interest, on him it looked good.

The oppressive heat didn't seem to discompose him in the least. James stooped to kiss the cheek she turned towards him, then introduced his companion as Paul Thomsson. The newcomer shook hands with Fenella, his grip firm and cool, holding her hand perhaps longer than decorum merited, murmuring how pleased he was to meet her.

'Mr Thomsson is an American. Over here for a while on business,' James went on to explain.

Fenella smiled and lowered her heavy-lidded eyes. 'Oh! And how long is "a while"?'

'As long as it takes,' said Paul Thomsson, his eyes only for her. There was a world of meaning in those words and Fenella acknowledged them by another smile but kept her own gaze lowered, not wanting the American to see the sudden interest in their dark depths.

Chapter Eighteen

Heat shimmered over the street and the children came out to play. The boys rolled their shirt-sleeves high, exposing the pale skin to the sun. They felt very daring and swaggered in front of their sisters and friends. The girls would have loved to have followed the boys' example but daren't, knowing it would be considered too flighty even at their tender age.

Libby wore her thinnest blouse and skirt and was glad that she had never needed to wear corsets. She knew this had shocked Mam but she had never remarked on it. Libby sympathised with the buxom Clara who wouldn't have dreamed of setting foot outside her bedroom without her corsets tightly laced under her dress.

One morning, Clara came into the small back yard, looking for Libby. Mr Hobbins kept spades and brooms and all the paraphernalia belonging to the shop out here. Libby had stepped outside for a few moments, feeling the need of fresh air.

Clara eyed her suspiciously. 'So here you are! I've been looking for you.'

Libby's curiosity was quickly aroused, for Clara

always did her best to avoid her. 'Don't tell me you missed me?' she murmured, solemnly.

Clara put on a false smile. 'As a matter of fact, I wanted to have a little talk with you.' Coming to stand by the shed in which her brother stored the sacks of potatoes, she said, without preamble, 'I don't think you should spend so much time with my brother. People are beginning to gossip.'

'People will always gossip if they've got nothing better to do. It's human nature,' said Libby, lifting her face to the sun and closing her eyes so that dark crimson images danced behind her eyelids.

'You needn't sound so – so smug,' Clara replied irritably, her false smile beginning to fade. 'It's just that my brother cannot possibly attend to his business properly when he wastes – when he spends so much time with you.'

'Shouldn't you be speaking to your brother about this?' Libby asked, her patience thin.

Clara's hand reached up to the high collar of her blouse and unconsciously gave it a little tug. 'Believe me, I have. But he just won't listen to reason. At his time of life he should be getting on with his business, not gadding around with a girl young enough to be his daughter.'

'It's none of my doing, Clara.'

'Of course it's your doing,' Clara snapped. 'Don't you know he's thinking of asking you to marry him? Surely you can see that's impossible.'

'You're saying your brother wants to marry me?' Libby's eyes snapped open.

'He tells me he's in love with you.' Clara's mouth

twisted with distaste. 'He's already planning on speaking to Father Brady.'

'How long have you known all this?' Libby asked, almost speechless. But, she told herself, she should have known. Should have guessed where all the consideration and solicitude Mr Hobbins was showing her lately was leading. She'd treated his attentions with teasing banter, never dreaming he was serious.

'Well, it's been three years now since my sister-in-law died. He's been waiting for you to get over your mam and dad's death,' Clara replied. 'You mean you didn't honestly know how he felt?'

'No, of course I didn't. I wish you'd told me about it sooner, so I could have discouraged him. Bloody hell!'

Clara looked more shocked than ever. 'You don't want to marry him?'

'I couldn't possibly marry him, Clara. I could never think of him that way. It would be a sin.' But, she told herself, she *did* like him and deeply regretted that she might hurt him.

'Well, I never did!' Clara could not believe she was hearing right. Although he was no longer in the first flush of youth – in fact a good way beyond it – in her opinion her brother was a catch at which any girl would jump. Especially a girl with Libby's prospects. Or, in her belief, lack of them.

Libby felt like laughing at the look on Clara's face but knew it would be cruel.

For weeks after Vince's visit she'd watched for his reappearance. The small homely kitchen that had once been a refuge had turned into a prison. She hurried between it and the shop, watchful for the slightest movement in the shadows, always alert for the sound of his step. And if he should return . . . ? What would she do? What *could* she do? Unthinkable to confess the brutality of his treatment of her. She had recalled James' words: 'If I can help in any way, promise you'll let me know . . .'

How easy he made it all sound! But then, with his background, everything would be easy. He was a dear, kind man and she had no right to inflict her troubles on him. She could not, *would* not, involve him in her problems.

A few days later, in a quiet moment between opening the shop and the first rush of customers, Mr Hobbins proposed and Libby said no as gently as she could. He seemed to take the rejection with his usual good humour, but his eyes held more than a hint of pain. Libby felt as she had when denying Amy or Bertie a treat, acting on their mother's orders.

Sadly, ironically, she understood his pain but there was little she could do about it.

When she missed her second period she knew she was in trouble. That a baby could be the result of the assault by Vince had not occurred to her. She had been insensible for part of the time during Vince's attack and in her innocence had not fully appreciated exactly what had happened, pushing the horrifying memories far back into her mind whenever they returned to haunt her.

Now, feeling the changes in her body, she wondered how she could have been such a little fool. Her breasts were tender and Mr Hobbins joked about the number of times she had to run down to the lavatory at the end of the yard. She spent sleepless nights wondering what she should do, until the dark shadows beneath her eyes caused even Clara to mutter, 'You want to go to bed a bit earlier, my girl. You're looking like an old woman.'

This remark, coming from Clara in her usual smug, tight-lipped way, brought the glimmer of a smile to Libby's face. Clara, in her inconsistent way, had never forgiven Libby for refusing her brother's proposal of marriage, even though she would have done anything to prevent it.

Libby realised all too soon that she would have to be doubly careful from now on. The smell of hot fat first thing in the morning when Mr Hobbins began to get ready for the first customers made her want to retch, resulting in another hurried trip to the yard and another joking remark from Mr Hobbins. She couldn't even risk visiting a doctor, for who was there she could trust? Now, if Dr Ainslie had been here . . . She would have trusted him with any secret. With her very life. In any case, how long could you keep the fact of pregnancy concealed? No, she would have to go away. She couldn't confess to Father Brady, who had been so kind since her parents' death. How could she face such a saintly man and admit a thing like this!

Her eyes burned for want of tears that wouldn't come. Dear God, she thought, what am I to do? Where am I to go? If only Mam were still alive – but if Mam were here she wouldn't be in the dilemma she was in.

That night she sat before her mirror and thought:

'Eee, girl, but you're going to have to pull yourself together. You look about as cheerful as a wet week in Blackpool!' She studied her reflection carefully, seeing the fall of flame-red hair, the emerald-coloured eyes, the soft mouth with its curving lips. There was, about that face, a sad air, the air of one resigned to settle for whatever fate was about to hand out.

No! she thought, with a force that surprised her. I *won't* be manipulated! It is time I took my destiny into my own hands.

Waking early the next morning she began packing the few clothes she had into the wicker basket that Alice had given her. She quickly packed everything she owned. There was no reason to leave anything behind, for she might never come back. She reached for the picture of Joseph on the mantelpiece and carried it upstairs to pack between layers of petticoats.

She left a letter for Mr Hobbins and another addressed to Father Brady, telling them she was going away but not where to, and she would be grateful if Father Brady would inform the landlord that the house was empty. She said how grateful she was to Mr Hobbins for his help, adding she would write as soon as she was settled.

Carrying the case, Libby left her room. The day had barely begun; the street was deserted, too early for the mill lasses, too late for the first shift of mine workers. She encountered no one on her way to the station. The fare to London took almost the last of the money Dr Ainslie had sent her, leaving her short, and she wondered if Vince's attack on her hadn't left her a little crazy, too.

Where in the world would she find another home? Seated in the corner of a Ladies Only compartment, she stared from the window as the train rattled its way south and refused to dwell on the past. A past that contained Vince and Captain Randle and the children . . .

In spite of her vow not to think backwards, the scene of the passing countryside blurred and she swallowed the lump in her throat. There were other women in the compartment and she did not want them staring and perhaps asking questions as to her welfare.

But the tears would not go away. It was as though something was telling her deep down that she was really alone now, with no one to turn to.

Joseph woke to lightning that forked across the dawn, cracking the gloomy skies asunder. Thunder rumbled over the sea and he turned over in his bunk, seeking the sleep from which he had just awakened. For in that sleep had been a dream of Gwenda. Would she still be angry with him for joining up like that? She had still been away visiting her aunt and uncle in Whitley Bay when he'd left home, so there had been no way to say goodbye to her.

Whitley Bay, he had thought then, must have more to offer than grim, grey old Ridley for she had shown great determination about going, laughing at him when he'd said, 'And what about us?'

'Us?' She'd raised dark eyebrows in a quizzical expression. 'What about us? I didn't realise we were a unit.'

Baffled by her teasing, he'd said, 'I thought you liked me.'

'I do. But that doesn't mean to say I've got to be with you and nobody else. Besides, if you're going away into the army or whatever, I'll have to continue to see my other friends, won't I? I can't suddenly become a nun, just because your conscience is bothering you about not being in uniform. I think you're crazy, anyway. You're not even due for call-up yet.'

Her words had pained him, he not realising that she was teasing, that she couldn't help it.

Joseph had travelled as far as Liverpool, falling in with a group of Irish lads who had an eye, like Joseph, to joining up. They did not much mind into which service they pledged themselves, just as long as there was a chance to fight. That first morning, exploring the city streets, busier and with more traffic than they had ever seen, they moved on to the docks.

There they found themselves stopping in front of a window in which posters pointed out the advantages of joining the Royal Navy.

'Better than joining the poor bloody Infantry,' observed one of the lads. 'Kinder on the feet,' remarked another and a third clinched it with the magic words, 'And free rum ration!'

The formalities were soon over and in a shorter time than he would have believed possible, Joseph was aboard one of His Majesty's ships on a distinctly choppy Atlantic. Their duty was to help guard the Merchant Navy ships bringing food to a beleaguered Britain. He enjoyed the company of the other men, the rough and tumble and the crude jokes about his age and being called Ginger.

Smugly thankful that he seemed immune to seasickness he took it all in his stride and dreamed of Gwenda. He filled out, losing the boyish hollows and the look of vulnerability. Always meaning to drop a line to Mam to let her know he was all right, somehow there was always something else to do.

Then came the night of the German submarine . . .

One moment he was asleep in his bunk, the next struggling in the icy sea. His flailing arms thrashed water. There was the thick taste of oil in his mouth. The waves were rainbow coloured with the spilt oil; a green and purple sheen floating on the tempestuous sea. Joseph could see patches where the oil was on fire, drifting towards him with every gust of wind. There were screams from men with savaged lungs and scorched skin. Continuous gusts of black smoke mingled with the flames.

He fought for consciousness, felt it slipping away while all around him he heard the helpless cries of his shipmates . . .

Remembering the stories told to him by men who had survived a sinking in the past, he dived and swam away from the flames. A strong swimmer, he held his breath until black spots appeared before his eyes and giddiness threatened to take over. When he surfaced, his eyes stung from the oil and seawater and he wondered just how long he could keep afloat before they were rescued. *If* they were rescued.

The casualties from sunken ships had been horrific and very few men in circumstances like this actually survived. The threat of the German submarine was ever present, waiting patiently with its cargo of torpedoes.

Everywhere he looked, it seemed to the boy, burning oil was waiting, grasping at him with greedy fingers. Try as he might he couldn't lift his hands from the burning surface of the water. It was impossible.

He held them aloft for as long as he could, groaning not so much from agony as disappointment. What sort of a future could he look forward to without being able to play the piano?

For much of the journey, Libby kept her eyes closed. She found the speeding countryside and the speculative gaze of her fellow passengers too prone to rush her into a state of nervous anxiety. Her mouth was dry, her throat burning with the threat of sickness.

Arriving in London, she felt completely overawed by the huge, high-domed Victorian station and conspicuous as she started violently when the steam engine bellowed out a sudden eruption of unspent energy. The sudden discharge of the passengers seemed just as volcanic. She felt bemused by it all and seemed to be hurling herself and her basket against a heaving tide of humanity. The vast place terrified her; the echoing roar of the engines, the shouts of the porters. Outside on the crowded street people were coming towards her, a wave that at any moment threatened to break over her, to take her, willy-nilly, wherever it was going.

'By the crin!' she thought, 'they'd trample you

under as soon as look at you.' Even so, it was exciting to be out there on the dark streets, stopping to gasp at this beautiful city, at the coloured lights and people queuing patiently outside the theatres.

She was surprised to see a name she recognised, a name in lights, over the entrance to one of the theatres. Josie St Clare! The girl James had spoken of that time at the concert – and then she was being urged on and the lights of the theatre were obscured in rain as a heavy shower began, causing everyone to hurry that much faster.

The crowds became a succession of weary grey figures that pushed past her, elbows and umbrellas used as weapons in the fray. Completely bewildered, beginning to feel a little frightened, at last she sought refuge in a dark alleyway that led off a busy square between tall buildings. The rain was coming down so hard it bounced knee-high off the pavement. Half-way down the narrow passageway she came upon the side entrance of a church, the door set deep into the thick stone walls. It gave some protection, if not much, and she huddled there, feeling suddenly too weak to stand. Her head began to spin, the street lights at the end of the alleyway wavered before her eyes. The sour taste of nausea rose in her throat and she was frightened she might be sick right there in the doorway.

She struggled to rise, to move on, knowing she had to find somewhere that would serve her with a meal, but her body refused to obey her commands.

She drew her knees up, tucking her skirt about her legs. Her skirt felt damp as she rested her cheek against her knees and thought of when she was a little girl, of Mam's constant anxiety that she shouldn't get wet. 'Get those damp things off,' she'd scold. 'Ought to know better, young Libby, that you ought.'

Whether it was her imagination or the chill dampness that seeped through to her very bones, suddenly she was experiencing that familiar tightness in her chest, the struggle for breath. She lifted her head, one hand going to her throat, tugging at the high collar of her coat in an effort to alleviate the choking feeling.

'Now then, what's all his? You can't sleep 'ere, my love. Not in this weather.' The elderly constable saw a pair of stricken eyes, a knitted beret pulled low over a white forehead. He wondered briefly if the girl was the worse for drink and bent to grasp her shoulders, giving her a shake. Drunken vagabonds were the last thing he needed on his beat!

Libby tried to explain. She required every ounce of will-power to draw the next breath and her voice came out a croak.

As he jerked her to her feet the thought that she might be ill and not drunk occurred to the constable. Without volition he drew her close, one hand patting her back as he would one of his grandchildren. Libby made no protest as he led her down the alleyway. Later, in the warmth and light of the police station, she felt marginally better. They gave her a cup of hot cocoa and told her to rest until she got her breath back. 'Is there anyone we can contact?' her rescuer enquired, looking at her with concern. Obviously a respectable young woman, he thought. Perhaps a servant girl changing positions, lost in her search for her new place of employment.

A name leaped into Libby's mind. A name that had flashed in the darkness over a London square. Hardly realising that she said it, she murmured, 'Josie St Clare.'

The constable repeated the name with some doubt. He had taken his wife to see the show only a few evenings ago. What could this girl be to the glamorous Josie? 'You work for her, do you?' he asked.

'No, I've never met her,' Libby had to admit. 'But, in the whole of London, hers is the only name I can think of.'

Apart, she told herself, from James Randle and to mention him was unthinkable. She imagined his embarrassment if she were to appear on his doorstep, wet and bedraggled as a stray kitten. Besides, she had no idea where he lived, only that it was in one of those secluded posh squares somewhere in the West End. Definitely, of the two, Josie was her best bet. If the actress could just let her stay for a little while, until she recovered her strength, she would promise she would be no trouble and leave as soon as she felt better. Miss St Clare might even know of a place where she could get a room, and, with a little bit of luck, a job . . . She would be prepared to do anything, make the tea, sweep the floor, sew, anything, so long as she could remain independent.

Chapter Nineteen

'I – I couldn't think of anything else,' said Libby, suddenly feeling very inadequate. 'But James – Captain Randle once mentioned you and when they asked me, at the police station, if I knew anyone in London, I found somehow I was giving them your name . . .'

'Jimmy Randle, eh?' Josie stared at the young girl with interest. Libby explained about the concert for the wounded men at the convalescent home and how James had spoken of her. Josie was amused, intrigued by the girl's revelations concerning James. The crafty young devil! she thought. 'E don't know what 'e's missed 'ere! The girl's in love with 'im, although she don't know it yet. And, her gaze lingering on the darkly shadowed eyes, the peaky look about the nose, I could bet my bottom dollar she's pregnant! Well, well! James, me boyo, you 'ave been a busy little man! Not wasted a minute of the time you've been 'ome! She thought of her own pregnancy, of how it had ended. She knew she had done the right thing, had never regretted it for one moment. This was no world to bring kids up in. She had thought it then and nothing had happened since to change her mind. Still, the girl looked all in, and if it was Jimmy's kid . . .

She asked the question aloud, disconcertingly
frank. Libby's eyes widened in astonishment, followed by a kind of horror. 'Bloody hell!' she
breathed, to Josie's amusement. 'Captain Randle was
always the perfect gentleman, never even tried to
kiss me – well,' thinking back to that dark landing,
'once he did. But it was only a goodbye kiss and to say
thank you . . .'

'What for? What was Jimmy thanking you for?'

Josie still looked amused and Libby began to
explain about the house at St Anne's Place, about the
Ainslies and the children, and once started she
couldn't seem to stop. She described how she had met
James, bumping him into him in the mist like that.

'He said I was like a little grey ghost . . .' For a
moment she was back on that lonely promenade, with
the sound of the sea in her ears and James' voice
coming to her through the gathering darkness.

'And then what 'appened?' prompted Josie, gently
teasing. 'Did 'e offer to see you 'ome safely?'

'Of course not! Why should he? He didn't know me
from Adam.'

Josie laughed then stood up, suddenly brisk. 'Meanwhile, you're stranded in London. I 'ave a spare
room. I don't mind you using it.'

'For tonight, at any road,' said Libby.

'For as long as you need. There's a comfortable bed
and you can take your time to get sorted out.'

'I don't want charity, Miss St Clare. You are different to what I expected and I don't know what I'd have
done without your kindness, but I can't just accept
help without giving something in return.'

'Stone the crows!' said Josie. 'Glad I ain't got that sort of pride! For now you'll stay in my flat safe and warm and we will worry about tomorrow when it comes. But on one condition! You call me Josie and cut out all that Miss St Clare crap. All right?'

'And you won't tell Captain Randle about me?' begged Libby. 'I couldn't bear his pity.'

'Not unless you want me to,' Josie assured her quietly.

Libby smiled and suddenly felt a load lifted from her shoulders. She liked Josie. Liked the vivacity of her and the merry blue eyes that continued to regard her with undisguised curiosity. Josie's voice was uneducated but not unpleasant to the ear. The room in which they sat, Josie's dressing room, to which she had been shown by a surprised doorman when she'd arrived, escorted by a police constable, was cluttered with stage costumes; brightly coloured feather boas draped the backs of chairs, sequins and satins and ruffled white petticoats. The air smelled of Phul Nana and the face powder that had been upset on the dressing table.

Josie, in Libby's opinion, was the most glamorous person she had ever met. Her hair was a darker shade than Libby's; more the colour of wine viewed through a crystal glass. It cascaded over her shoulders in an unruly tangle of waves and curls. It was her redeeming feature and drew her admirers' attention away from the plump cheeks and faint beginnings of a double chin, although Libby knew that the bright red lipstick that covered the singer's mouth would have caused Mam to frown and murmur,

'Hussy!' But her whole manner radiated kindness and at once Libby felt at ease in her presence.

With Libby's insistence that James not be told Josie was faced with a quandary. She decided that she would respect Libby's wishes and pray that Jimmy didn't think too badly of her if he should ever find out. He didn't visit her too often any more. Josie understood. He was busy with plans for his forthcoming marriage to some society rich bitch. When he did come it was as one old friend visiting another, and he would sit and drink tea and talk and laugh and go his way. Josie didn't resent this at all. She never had expected any more from Jimmy than what he was prepared to give. If he did find out about Libby, well, no one better than Josie St Clare for getting out of a scrape.

Much later that evening, after the show, she called a hansom and they drove through the dark streets to the flat in a quiet part of Bayswater. Throwing open the door with a grand gesture, Josie said, 'Here we are, then. Might not be much to some but to me it's Buckingham Palace.'

Libby gazed about her, wide-eyed. Part of the room was concealed by a large four-fold sceen arranged to form a kind of vestibule. The screen, in dark crimson, was unadorned on one side and decorated with a fire-breathing dragon on the other over which a profusion of picture postcards was tacked.

'From theatrical people I know,' Josie exclaimed, seeing Libby's interested glance. 'How about a cup of tea?'

'Yes, please, Josie. What an interesting room. I've never seen anything like it.'

Josie disappeared into an inner room, leaving Libby to gaze in awe at a parlour bright with colour and so crowded with curious objects it took her breath away. Clearly Josie St Clare was a person whose taste in furnishings was influenced not by current fashions but by her own fads and fancies. The two deep armchairs on either side of the fireplace were overstuffed crimson velvet. There were antimacassars embroidered in gold and silver thread protecting the backs of the chairs, and satin cushions, puffed and frilled in extravagant fashion, spilled over in a rainbow of colours.

Libby could think of nothing better than to be able to sink down into their soft comfiness, in front of the blazing fire which Josie soon got going. She had carried the tea tray in and set it on a walnut table to one side of the fireplace, refusing Libby's offer to help with lighting the fire.

'You look all in.' She sat back on her haunches before the fire and gazed up into Libby's face. 'Have your tea while I cook us something to eat.'

In spite of her long journey and early morning start, Libby discovered that her hunger had vanished, although she valiantly tried to swallow the scrambled eggs that Josie produced. Before the night was out she was burning up with a chill, distressing Josie by her struggle for breath. Her chest wheezed and the doctor Josie sent for listened through his stethoscope and proclaimed bed rest and warmth. He explained to Josie that the attack would pass, probably by the morning, but having perceived that the girl was pregnant he thought it advisable to keep her in bed until her chest was quite clear.

'Her husband at the front, I suppose?' he asked, guilelessly. He had noticed that the girl wore no ring.

Josie smiled and nodded and walked downstairs with him to the front door. 'I don't think you need worry,' he said, 'but if you feel the slightest concern send someone round for me.'

Josie thanked him and watched him walk away on the rain-shiny pavement. During the next few days, while Libby quickly recovered, Josie contemplated this new dilemma in her life. It was pleasant coming home from the theatre and finding the flat in such an agreeable state of tidiness instead of the mess she was used to. Her health restored, Libby had brought up the subject of finding a place of her own and a job, but the singer had waved her hands dismissively and frowned so fiercely that Libby laughed and said no more. With her rough, tough humour and love of life, Josie was just what the gentle, confused Libby needed.

'What's wrong with staying 'ere?' Josie demanded. 'And if it's a job you're after, what's wrong with keeping this place tidy and doin' a bit of shopping and cooking? And,' warming to her subject, 'how long do you think you'll be able to go on working when that begins to show?' Her gaze fell on Libby's body.

Libby knew she wasn't being unkind but realistic. With a protective gesture, Libby cradled her hands over her still flat stomach. Although the baby had been conceived in jealous anger and violence, already strong maternal feelings gripped her. She knew she would love it as though it had been placed there by the most loving act. Funny that! she thought. Must be something being pregnant does to you. I should be hating Vince. Already a sad-sweet memory of summer evenings on the promenade with Vince laughing beside her was taking the place of the sense of betrayal she had felt so short a time ago.

Josie recalled how once James had written about Libby and later corrected her when she said she supposed Libby was a 'fat old thing who wobbled when she walked'. She remembered him saying, in his drawling voice, 'Not at all. There is something about her that most girls of her class don't have . . .' and the look on his face as he'd said it.

One day the conversation got on to men and Josie said, 'Wouldn't you consider marrying him? Your boyfriend?'

'I'd hoped to, one time. For over a year I was in love with him.'

'But you're not now?'

Libby shook her head. 'I don't intend to marry – not now, not anytime.'

'But you need someone?' Josie replied, surprising herself. 'We all do, sooner or later.'

'I do not need any man!' exclaimed Libby defiantly. 'I am quite capable of taking care of myself.'

Realising that she was on a losing battle, Josie changed the subject.

The next day she produced a gold band for Libby to wear on her left hand. 'It'll be a kind of protection,' she told Libby. 'With the sort of people you can bump into in the theatre it might be safer.'

Feeling like an imposter, Libby slipped it on to her finger, for a fleeting moment wishing with all her heart it had been Vince's.

It was always lively and interesting backstage with the cast, with sparkling conversation, plenty of food and gossip. Libby's cheeks soon filled out and her face lost its pallor.

Keeping Josie's flat tidy didn't take up much of her time. She was quickly adopted by the rest of the cast and loved nothing better than to help with the costumes and shoes and fine silken stockings. She made endless cups of tea and cocoa and ran out to the pub on the corner for Guinness whenever Josie declared she was sick of tea. But the best part of her new life was the show. To Libby, the show was magical. When it was over and the curtain fell for the last time, she turned an enraptured face to Sidney, a friend of Josie's, breathing, 'Wasn't that wonderful? Oh, to be able to dance like that! I could die happily if I could only do half of what Josie did just now.'

Her enthusiasm amused him. Theatrical folk tried to be so blasé these days it left him with a feeling of such boredom he could scream. Josie had introduced Sidney to her with a whispered aside that Libby didn't fully understand. 'You'll be safe with Sidney. He doesn't like girls.'

But, thought Libby, for one who didn't like girls, Sidney had been kindness itself. He was the comic of the show, red-nosed and fatuous on stage, overly protective off. Libby found herself telling him all sorts of things about her past life, things she could never bring herself to talk about with Josie, even though Josie had been like a sister to her. Better than a sister, she thought, her nose wrinkling, thinking about Agnes.

One morning while Josie attended rehearsals, and she and Sidney were talking, Libby felt the strangest sensation. As though, momentarily, a butterfly had fluttered its wings inside her stomach. Seeing the look on her face, the way she suddenly stopped talking, the comic looked anxious and placed one hand over hers.

'All right, ducks?' he asked.

Libby nodded, the look of wonder still on her face. 'It was the oddest thing,' she told him. 'As though – as though . . .'

His fingers pressed hers. 'I think I know. It's your baby telling the world that he's here.'

His voice was so gentle it brought tears to Libby's eyes. 'He?'

Sidney shrugged. 'Well, he or she. Do you mind which?'

'Not really. As long as it's healthy.'

The sensation happened again and again, each time seeming to grow stronger. Libby wasn't alarmed. She would sit with her eyes closed, hands spread across her tummy, feeling the delicate tremor beneath them and marvel at the miracle of life.

She wrote to Father Brady, giving Josie's address, telling him she was fine so he wasn't to worry. If there was any news of Agnes or Joseph would he please let her know. She wrote to Mr Hobbins, reiterating how indebted she would always be for his help, sending her love to both him and Clara.

The days slipped by and the winter of 1916 arrived with snowstorms and icy winds.

Whenever women met, the advent of rationing was the main subject of conversation; they declared that at least it would be the fairest way for all, although some were not impressed. Folks with enough money never went short, anyway, was the general opinion of most housewives.

Poets were driven to new heights of literary powers. The words of Rupert Brooke brought tears to the eyes. 'Tipperary' and hits from Josie's show, which had all the promise of a record-breaking run, were whistled by delivery boys all over the country.

On the inside page of one of the papers was an announcement that Mr Paul Thomsson, the American millionaire, was returning to the United States after a successful business trip to Britain.

Chapter Twenty

As Libby's pregnancy became more evident Josie insisted that she consult the doctor she had summoned to her flat that night. The baby, Dr Lyle said, would be born in early May. The month of Our Lady, Libby thought. Of blue skies and apple blossom and, in spite of the terrible things that were happening on the other side of the Channel, the promise of new life.

Libby's thoughts returned less frequently to Vince and more to James Randle. She wondered how he was, whether he was still in England or had returned to the horror of combat. Once she mentioned her thoughts aloud and was strangely disturbed when Josie told her of James' impending marriage.

'Fenella Burroughs, 'e's marrying,' said Josie. 'Daughter of old Robert.' She smiled reminiscently. 'Knows him well, I do. 'Angs around the stage door often enough.'

'When – when is the wedding?' Libby hoped the question came out steadier than she felt it did. Josie gave her a quick look. 'Sorry, ducks, shouldn't 'ave blurted it out like that. But the gentry 'ave to marry their own kind, you know. Although I remember once, before the war it was, one of the chorus girls marrying old Lord Dochart. Got a castle in Scotland, she did, out o' that, as well as a title.'

Libby smiled. 'I see no reason why you couldn't do the same, Josie. All those officers clamouring for your attention every night.'

Josie shook her head. 'Bored stiff, I'd be. No, that life's not for yours truly. Got a career to think about, I 'ave.'

Idiot! she berated herself. Why can't you leave well alone! The girl obviously didn't know about the wedding. You can see how much it has upset her.

Then, one evening, Libby was in the dressing room, sewing a torn frill on one of Josie's petticoats, when there was a tap on the door. Before she could answer it was pushed open and she looked up to see James Randle standing in the opening.

He looked fit and well and astonished to see Libby sitting there, slim hands poised over the ruffled white garment bunched in her lap.

'Libby!' There was no doubt as to the genuineness of his delight. He came forward into the room, hands outstretched to clasp hers. 'My dear girl! I can't believe it! Where in the world did you spring from?'

She felt his hands take hers, drawing her to her feet and at the same moment the voluminous petticoat fell from her lap to reveal her pregnancy.

He stared at her hard and she watched a muscle tighten along the line of his jaw. Then he took one long, deep breath. In the awful silence she could hear her own heart beating. Her chest tightened as she held her breath. He was hurting her, the gold band of her bogus wedding ring cutting into her flesh. Still she had not spoken, had not even uttered his name. It was as though his sudden appearance had robbed her of speech.

Then colour rushed into her face, flushing her cheeks pink with shame as his eyes examined her.

There was a certain irony in his voice when he spoke. 'I see congratulations are in order!'

'I believe you, too, are to be congratulated.'

Looking up she saw how his expression changed. His mouth was still set in an almost contemptuous line but the first flush of anger had gone, a wary, thoughtful look taking its place. He thought of his own engagement and said, tersely, 'I guess you could say that.' Then: 'When is the baby due?'

'Next month,' she said. 'In May.' It had been early August when they had shared those few sun-kissed hours in the poppy field, when she had sobbed out her grief against his shoulder. The same night that he had watched from the end of the street as Vince pushed open her front door and vanished inside.

James wanted nothing more than to take her in his arms and promise he would never let her go, that he would protect her all her life, and chase away the past sadnesses. Filled with infinite tenderness, he knew this was the most powerful emotion of love he would ever feel in his life. But he had to turn away from her and remind himself of the life she had chosen and which did not include him. Time seemed to stand still as, for an endless moment, the two young people gazed into each other's eyes.

Then, making an abrupt gesture, James said, 'Are you happy, Libby?'

She nodded, not daring to trust her voice.

'And in good health?'

Again that silent inclination of the head.

He gave a searching glance around the cluttered room. 'I managed to obtain two tickets for tonight's performance and so was able to bring someone who I know has been dying to see it. As you must know, tickets are rarer than hen's teeth.'

The girl he is going to marry, thought Libby, watching his face. She had seen a picture of her in the newspaper; dark, fashionably bobbed hair, large dark eyes gazing from a piquant face. She had a look of pampered luxury and the dress she was wearing looked as though it would have kept Mam and the family in groceries for a month.

'Will you tell Josie I asked after her and extend my good wishes for the continued success of the show? And, Libby, take care. You know your happiness means a great deal to me.'

'You, too,' she said in a soft whisper. 'Be happy, James.'

He smiled, gave a mocking salute and was gone, closing the door on her pale little face.

Walking along the corridor from the dressing room, James frowned so darkly that people passing caught their breath and looked back over their shoulders, wondering what bothered the young officer to make him look like that.

So, he thought, that was the way of it! She was a married woman and soon, from all appearances, to be a mother, and he shouldn't be thinking the thoughts he was, but the encounter with Libby had affected him more than he would have believed possible. With her ridiculous, funny pride and her soft, vulnerable face, without knowing it she had wounded him quite beyond all recovery.

There was no denying that he loved her, had probably loved her from the moment he first saw her, there in the mist, both hands tugging at that silly green beret. That was a memory that shouldn't be encouraged to linger! He should be concerning himself with his forthcoming marriage; he hadn't seen much of Fenella lately but knew she had been seeing Paul Thomsson, being, as she said, a good ambassadress for her country and showing him the sights of the town.

It was no good him thinking that it could be any other way with Libby. Not now. Not after what he had just seen; although he longed to protect her, to care for her – that was not possible for had he not seen with his own eyes that she belonged to somebody else? And there was Fenella who wore his ring.

He must put all thoughts of Libby away from him, concentrate on his army career and the fact that this was his last night before being sent back to his regiment. The Army doctors had pronounced him fit enough for active service and he couldn't wait to shake the dust of London off his feet and get going. On reflection, the Front was the best place for him, cleansing his mind of all thoughts of Libby.

He made his way back to the seats where his mother was waiting. She gave one quick glance at his lowered brows and thought: Whoever this girl is that he's been to see, she doesn't seem to have given him much joy!

It was late and his mother had already gone to bed. James was enjoying a last drink with his father before saying goodnight when there was the sound of a motor car drawing up outside in the street. David Randle frowned. 'Bit late for a visitor,' he murmured. Going to the window he drew aside the heavy curtain to peer out.

He recognised the car parked outside as the American's, the man over whom Fenella had made such a fuss. Stepping from the front seat was Fenella, but it seemed the man seated behind the wheel had no intention of following her, for he lounged on the leather seat, a cigar puffing smoke into the damp night air. 'Damn funny!' muttered David. He moved from the window for James to take his place and at the same time a hollow knocking sounded on the front door.

'I'll get it.' James hurried through to the large hallway, not wanting any of the servants to be disturbed at such a late hour. As he opened the black varnished door with its ornate brass knocker, James heard Fenella say, in a conciliatory voice, 'It's only me, James.'

He peered behind her into the darkness to where the car waited. 'Isn't Paul coming in with you?'

Fenella had declined the second ticket to the show that evening, giving no reason that made sense and so James had taken Isobel. They didn't mind; they enjoyed each other's company.

Fenella shook her head at his question. 'No.' She hesitated, biting her lip before going on. 'James, we've got to talk.'

He smiled and stood back, with a sweep of his arm indicating the open door of the study where a bright fire still gleamed.

David Randle coughed and said from the darkness, 'I'm just off to bed. Leave you two young uns to talk. Goodnight.'

Fenella ignored James' gesture towards the study and stood twisting the long fringes of the heavy ivory silk shawl she wore over her gown of pale lavender.

'All right,' he said. 'What do you want to talk about?'

'About my promise to marry you, James. I want you to release me from that promise.'

James made a move towards her, but she held up one hand. 'Please, don't let's argue. I've thought carefully, very carefully, and I know it's the only thing I can do.' Her glance rested on him and there was no animosity, only a pleading for understanding. 'We have to accept the fact that our lives are moving on different paths, James. I've heard you talk about the Army, about your future career plans and I know deep down that's not for me. I want other things and although I'm very fond of you I realise that we would just make each other miserable if we went through with our marriage.' She smiled. 'Am I making any sense? Do you understand what I'm trying to say?'

James stood quietly listening, a thousand thoughts chasing around in his head. Instead of this great joy

329

that filled him, shouldn't he be feeling desolate, forsaken at the thought of losing this girl he had known for most of his young life?

She moved towards him and on impulse laid a hand against his cheek. 'I'm sorry if this comes as a shock, James, but really, you'll soon come to see that it's for the best.'

He caught her hand and pressed it against his lips, drawing a deep, steadying breath. 'What are your plans, now?'

His eyes went to the partly open front door, to the darkness beyond and reading his mind, she said, 'Paul has asked me to go to America with him. As a sort of – secretary.' Her lips quirked. 'Fine secretary I'd make, don't you think? Anyway, that's just for propriety's sake, to stop the tongues wagging, although Paul says they are much more liberally minded over there. Eventually, we plan to make it a more permanent relationship.' She smiled again, almost timidly, wondering at his silence, the way the muscles jumped at the side of his jaw.

He reached out and took her two hands in his. 'My dear, I wish you every happiness. Paul Thomsson is a fine man, he'll give you the sort of life you could never expect over here in poor old war-torn England, at least not for many years to come. In any case, I hadn't planned on staying here, once this lot is over.' Slowly his arms went about her and she felt his kiss rest briefly against the straight shining fringe that touched her thin eyebrows. 'Take care of yourself and have a safe journey.'

*   *   *

'Give the lady a coconut!' exclaimed Josie affectionately. 'Why on earth didn't you tell him the truth, that
Vince'd raped you and you were only wearing that
ring in a gesture to decorum?'

Libby looked stricken. 'Oh, Josie, how could I?
Whatever would he have thought about me?'

'You didn't ask for it. It wasn't your fault.'

'But it was! In a way. I deliberately left the front
door open for Vince to let himself in.'

Josie made an impatient gesture. 'I could get word
to him. To Jimmy . . .'

'No!' Libby's tone was emphatic. 'Leave well alone.
He was with that girl he is going to marry, said he
was lucky to get the tickets, that she'd been looking
forward to seeing the show. I was to tell you that he
asked after you and to wish you luck.'

The look Josie gave her spoke volumes. She would
dearly have loved to intervene in this young girl's life.
People in love were blind to the realities of things.
Libby was so beautiful, so fiery and loyal and certainly a lady in the way that Josie would never be. She
wondered about the girl James Randle was going to
marry, thinking of the picture she had seen in the
newspapers. From her looks she could tell Libby and
she were poles apart, yet a knowledge that had come
with hardship told her which woman James should
have preferred, had he the sense he was born with.

And there wasn't a thing she could do about it . . .

Chapter Twenty-One

Vince sat at the table, trying once again to finish the letter he had started the night before. The letter to Libby, begging her forgiveness, trying to explain why he had behaved the way he had. Vince was no scholar; he'd written few letters in his lifetime, had never felt the need to write to anyone. Trying to find the right words in an endeavour to get Libby to understand was proving a nightmare. What on earth had come over him, attacking Libby in the way he had?

Tortured by remorse he threw the pen down and with a groan dropped his head into his hands. The single weak bulb that hung from the ceiling cast shadows that wavered over the time-yellowed walls, barely hinting at the narrow bed, the hard-backed chair and wooden table that were the only furnishings. It had been all that Vince could afford; a dingy bedsit in a back street of Liverpool where the landlady took his money and didn't ask questions.

He had managed so far to evade the military police but he wondered how long his luck would hold. The future seemed bleak, he was haunted at times by thoughts of Libby and himself, snug and happy in their own little home . . .

He dragged his thoughts back to the letter. He *had* to finish it – he *had* to. The much-fingered envelope fell to the floor and picking it up he addressed it, forming the letters of Libby's address with exaggerated care. He folded the single piece of lined paper and slipped it into the envelope, wishing he could have improved on the few sentences it contained. They seemed so inadequate after what he'd done. Libby, with her capacity for sheer goodness, would surely understand . . .

Sounds of heavy footsteps on the landing outside his room caused him to look up; the door burst open with a resounding crash. There were shouts of: 'Got ya, ya bastard!' and the next moment Vince was fighting for his life. He was no match, however, for the two heavily built figures in the tight khaki uniforms and red-topped caps, although he managed to land a blow to the side of the head of one which had him sagging at the knees.

Between them they dragged him down the steep staircase and out to the waiting van. A small group of onlookers 'tut-tutted' in sympathy and the landlady watched without expression his stumbling gait.

As soon as the van was out of sight she hastened up to his room, sharp eyes peering into every corner, seeking out any valuables he might have left behind. There was a shabby overcoat hanging on a nail behind the door but little else, apart from the litter of screwed-up notepaper and a bottle of ink that had spilled from the table in the fight, leaving a stain that evoked a snort of disgust. Not that she expected to find anything. She knew a deserter when she saw one

and good-looking as the young man had been, with a
wink and a ready smile whenever he saw her, she
didn't hold with deserters. When she'd cleared the
table of its litter of paper she was surprised to find
an envelope underneath. She saw that it had been
stamped and sealed, ready for posting. She tossed
the envelope into the empty fireplace, then on the
point of leaving the room relented and plucked it from
the grate, dusting off the smudges of soot before
slipping it into the pocket of her pinny. It wouldn't do
any harm to post it, she thought. And the young man
had had a right cheeky smile . . .

Vince's letter had touched Libby. After the first hurried reading of it, she had tucked the grubby envelope into the back of a drawer and tried not to think
about it, but Vince's ill-formed words danced before
her eyes. Finally Josie took it from the drawer where
she had hidden it and tearing it across once and then
again, had said tightly, 'That's where that belongs.
And with 'im in it, too, burning in 'ell.'
   Although shocked, in spite of all that had happened, the way Vince had used her, how could Libby
hold a grudge against the father of her baby . . . ?

Libby was not one to pamper herself, so when the
ache low down in the small of her back suddenly
became too much to bear she allowed herself a few
minutes to lie down. She supposed she must have
fallen into a doze, because the next thing she knew
knives were stabbing into her side and she cried out
in fright. Waking up that morning with the backache

she had been persuaded by Josie to stay in the flat resting while Josie attended rehearsal.

Josie said that she would come straight home and that Libby was to take it easy. Now, drawing a deep, calming breath, Libby told herself it would pass. 'Must be something I've eaten,' she mused.

A sheen of perspiration filmed her forehead and upper lip as the stabbing pain came again and again and she twisted the corners of the pillow in damp fingers, biting back a cry. The mantel clock told her it was well into the afternoon. The cast must be having a difficult rehearsal or Josie would have been home long before this. Slight panic started to rise in her, the same kind of panic as when the Zeppelins came over, dropping their bombs over London.

She told herself not to be silly. Babies took an age to come and, in any case, it wasn't due for another two weeks so it must be something she ate . . .

A sudden, exceptionally vicious twisting of the knife in her side drew blood from her bottom lip as her teeth bit hard, and she suppressed a cry. The next she wasn't able to conquer. It overpowered her and she screamed the Lord's name, mingled with others; Mam's and Our Lady's and, unthinkingly, James', until the tide of agony receded, leaving her limp and breathless.

Then, thinking she must surely have fallen asleep and was dreaming, she heard a voice, calm, reassuring, cool hands on her brow, and knowing it was not a dream she gasped out, 'Sorry I'm being such a baby, but, oh, Josie, it hurts so much . . .'

'Hush, now, it'll be all right. I've sent a boy for the doctor.'

The voice was deeper than Josie's. Opening her eyes, she saw Sidney standing beside the bed, smiling down at her. He squeezed her hand gently. 'Just as well they decided to include that new song in the show, eh, my love, and sent me back for the sheet music.' He assumed one of his comic expressions, making her giggle in spite of everything. 'Sidney to the rescue once more!'

Although he spoke with a confidence that was supposed to reassure the frightened girl, inwardly he was shaking with fear. Suppose the baby arrived before the doctor? What would he do? What did he, a man of his persuasion, know of birthing babies?

To his intense relief, the doctor arrived, followed shortly afterwards by Josie, come to find out what was keeping the comic and worried about Libby.

The next few hours were to Libby a mingling of agonised torture, interspaced with a lethargy in which she wanted nothing but to sink into the bed and lie perfectly still, terrified of moving in case it brought back the pain.

She felt as though she were being torn in half, her body splitting asunder, and then her agony vanished like mist on a summer's morning as she heard her baby's first cry. She opened her eyes as Josie bent over her. 'A beautiful little girl,' she smiled. 'Perfect in every way.' She smoothed the hair, damp with perspiration, from Libby's forehead. 'Now you must sleep, dear. You've 'ad a 'ard time.'

The pattern of life ran very smoothly in the cosy flat in Bayswater. After the birth of her baby, christened Ellen but called affectionately Nellie by everyone, Libby bloomed like a rose, filled with energy and ecstatic in her joy. Life was so perfect that it left her no time to dwell on the dark happenings all about her.

Down-to-earth Josie, mixing with all kinds of people, lived no such illusion. There was always a goodly number of men in uniform in the audience, enjoying the show, whistling at the chorus girls. She heard first-hand of the endless mud, the misery that awaited them on their return from leave, the agonies of trench-foot and the gas.

She heard how the Germans sent the latter over in green and yellow clouds and how the respirators issued were only good for some gases, not all of them. When the wind wasn't right, they lobbed over gas-filled shells that burst in the trenches, their contents burning everything it touched.

She had held a young soldier one night in her arms as he cried, 'I hate it! I hate the thought of going back and I hate even more the people who tell you to pull yourself together and be a man. I want to go home to my family. I have a sweetheart – she lives next door, we were going to be married . . .'

She had watched him leave the dressing room with sadness in her eyes and wondered if he would ever marry his sweetheart. That night, unusual for Josie Higgins, she said a prayer for all such men who lived their lives under the terror of war.

Libby read the newspapers and thought of James. She had heard via Josie that he had returned to France and she wondered how his fiancée must feel, knowing the dangers, longing for his return so they could marry. She prayed every night that he would be safe.

It seemed that she could recall every word they had said to each other, every moment spent in his presence, his touch – the magic of those outings with the Ainslie children. But there was no going back to that enchanted time, that small island of contentment when she had walked beside him at the edge of the sea, the children running on ahead, shouting and capering like idiots in their freedom.

It was the following summer, in 1918 – with Nellie beginning to walk – when Josie came home from the theatre one evening, her cheeks glowing. She stood in the open doorway of the sitting room, smiling at Libby, excitement radiating from her.

'There's someone here to see you, Libby.'

'To see me?'

'Yes.' Her blue eyes sparkled with mischief. 'A young army officer.'

Libby rose from where she had been sitting beside the lamp, sewing a new dress for Nellie. The tiny bodice was covered with delicate intricate smocking and it had seemed as if Mam's fingers had guided her, showing her how to achieve the small, neat stitches.

At Josie's words she took a deep breath to steady the sudden pounding of her heart, which, foolishly, seemed at the same time to rise in her throat. Josie turned and beckoned to someone standing behind her at the top of the staircase, then with a wink at Libby, slipped quietly away to the kitchen muttering about making a cuppa.

A uniformed figure took her place.

'James!'

Slowly he came towards her, his eyes searching her face. He took both her hands in his, as he had the last time, pulling her towards him and holding her fingers pressed up against his chest.

'Why are you here?' she asked. 'I thought you were in France. It's not Joseph? You've not brought bad news of Joseph?'

'No. I've been sent home for training on those new tanks.' He stopped, scanning her face and figure. 'You look blooming. Josie tells me you have a daughter. If she is as lovely as her mother she'll be a real heartbreaker.'

Libby laughed and disengaged her hands, taking a step backwards. Suddenly she felt shy, and turned away from that searching gaze. 'I'm glad you came home safely,' she said. 'How long will you be here?'

'Long enough. I shall be busy, but I felt I just had to see the show one more time and all my friends. Josie told me all the news.'

Libby wanted to ask if she had also told him all about Vince, but felt perhaps it was too leading a question. Josie had promised not to say anything without her permission.

'And how are things with you?' she hazarded. 'How is your – wife?'

The dark brows rose in puzzlement. 'Wife?'

'Yes, the lady you married.'

'What makes you think I married?'

'It was in the papers – the newspapers said . . .'

'The newspapers are not always correct,' he said levelly, and the colour rose in her face; hot colour, her cheeks crimson, and with a little surge of anger that he should have let her babble on without stopping her.

'You mean you – didn't get married?'

'No more than you did, sweet maid of the mist.'

Now he *was* mocking her! She felt her anger spread, taking in Josie and her perfidious promise of silence as well as this self-assured man who came and went in her life like a debonair shadow. 'You know about Vince . . . ?'

'Don't talk about it. Water under the bridge.' His eyes were steady on her face, as if he asked a silent question.

She willed herself to look directly back into his eyes, aware of the melting sensation deep inside her, robbing her of speech and, mist-like, her anger vanished.

When he pulled her into his arms she made no move to pull away. It was like holding a child, he thought. A small, frightened child. Her cheek was petal soft, cool under his lips. Tilting her chin he looked into her eyes, surprised to see they were filled with tears. He was dismayed only for a moment. Then he lowered his face and kissed the corner of her mouth, where a tear drop had come to rest, tasting the saltiness of it on his lips. He said slowly and with effort, 'I've been a fool not to admit it before. I'm in love with you.' Immediately he felt a sense of relief. He kissed her again, this time full on the mouth.

When she could get her breath, she said softly, 'We've both been fools.'

He drew her closer towards him. She bowed her head away from his lips and he buried his face in her hair, sweet smelling and as fragrant as always. 'I love you,' he said, taking pleasure from speaking the words aloud, again and again. 'Love you, love you.'

His touch tantalised her. There was a need of him growing inside her like hunger. Yet it was not just a physical need. She felt caught in a beautiful web from which she had no desire to be free. She dared not think of the time when that web might be rent. The possibility did not exist. God couldn't be so cruel. Surely the lives of her mother and father and maybe her brother had been enough. He couldn't ask more of her . . .

She was responding to his kisses with a fervour that alarmed her. She felt his hands wander pleasurably over her body and suddenly Libby was afraid of her own feelings. For once, she was not in control and it scared her. For several long, unmeasured seconds her consciousness hung suspended on a single pivot of pleasure, then the automatic defence of her times, never so long defied, snapped into place.

'James!'

He recognised the plea in her voice and immediately released her, scooping her up and carrying her to the large chair beside the fireplace. Warm and safe on his lap, Libby allowed her head to come to rest on his shoulder, close enough to his mouth that could never seem to get enough of hers. She relaxed completely, murmuring wordless little feline sounds, interrupted by Josie's rattle on the door handle warning them of her arrival.

She attempted to slide from James' knee, feeling a

blush stain her cheeks. James held her possessively.

'Josie!' she warned breathlessly, and James gave a low laugh.

'Josie's seen it all before,' he said, and thought briefly of the time the singer had shared those same feelings with him. But no, not those same feelings, he thought. He had wanted her, had known where he stood with Josie. But that was all in the past. This was a new life, a new love. One that he had waited for so long and one which would never pass.

Josie made a light supper and they ate as they talked; of Nellie and the show and the difficulty of getting the right materials for the extravagant show costumes, carefully avoiding all mention of the war.

As they were finishing their meal, Sidney arrived and Josie managed to scrape up enough supper to please him.

'I was at a loose end,' the comic explained, his quiet gaze examining James as he lounged in the big chair, long legs extended in the glow of the firelight, 'and after being introduced once to Captain Randle at the theatre, thought I'd come over and renew his acquaintance.'

Libby remembered, on one of her walks with the children, James saying that a lot of people thought all they wanted to talk about when they came home on leave was their war experiences, but what they needed most was to have a mad, wonderful time, trying to forget them. And the first thing everyone always asked was: 'When are you going back?'

Suddenly, she heard Sidney uttering those words and James' reply, 'In about three weeks' time, after a course of retraining.'

'Then you'll want to get out on the town, have a bit of jollity,' said Sidney. 'Why don't you show Libby the sights of London?'

James caught Libby's eye across the room and a great bubble of excitement filled her throat as he gave a little nod, as though making up her mind for her.

'I don't know,' she began hesitantly. 'There's Nellie to think of – I've never left her before . . .'

'Poof!' Josie smiled kindly at her. 'There's me and Sidney 'ere. If we can't manage 'er I don't know who can.'

Libby knew the little girl seldom woke once she was asleep. Again she caught James' eye. 'Tomorrow, Libby,' his voice held a query, 'I'll come for you early and we'll spend the whole evening seeing London.'

'I'd love to,' she admitted, her eyes shining with pleasure. 'I've never really seen London yet.'

All London seemed to be infected with the same mad gaiety. Threadbare and going without the luxuries of life, still everyone seemed happy, making the best of things, taking a breather in this long, stagnating war. The news had been bad again but people smiled at the young man and his girl; he in his smart tailored uniform and peaked cap, she in a dress of pale pink with a loose, waist-length, jacket with inserts of delicate cream lace, and a beaded handbag with fine gilt chain, all borrowed from Josie. A hansom was summoned, the driver offering his arm to help Libby up the step, closing the cab door with a wide grin and a flourish.

They clip-clopped their way between tram cars, buses, bicycles, taxis and the occasional car with its gas bag of fuel. The rest of the evening was to Libby a blur of lights, dazzling her senses, of music and people talking and laughing, of clinking glasses and James' arms about her as she floated gracefully around a crowded floor. It seemed to her as though she were in a beautiful dream, that never before in her life had she experienced such perfect happiness and she pushed to the back of her mind a world in which she might never again know such joy.

The lights of the Embankment where they walked later gleamed on the river and the wide expanse of mud. 'Slack water,' said James. 'Nothing moving until the tide floods.'

He put his hand over hers as it lay on the stone wall, caressing it gently, his fingers cool. 'I have to report to HQ on Monday,' he said. 'That gives us barely two days. Not enough time to spread London at your feet, dear heart, as I had intended. But I will do my best.'

His hand clasped her fingers in his, carrying it to his mouth. She half-turned towards him, shaking her head as if to deny what she had heard. 'We mustn't allow this to become serious, James. I'm not the sort of girl your parents could accept as your wife. They will expect someone of breeding, someone of your own class . . .'

'Class!' She heard him draw a deep breath, his thoughts on Fenella and her perfidy and he said aloud, 'You have more breeding in your little finger than most of the so-called society girls I know. Besides, you admitted to loving me.' His arms went round her, drawing her close. 'You can't deny it, Libby, and I know you don't tell lies.'

What had this girl done to him? He did not understand the feelings she aroused and for the first time in his life he felt confused.

It was Libby's turn to draw her breath and turn away from his demanding lips, affecting a calmness that cost her dear. 'Let's walk back,' she suggested. 'It's a lovely moonlit night.'

James agreed, guessing the cause of her reluctance, but fully intending to overcome it the first chance he had. They were approaching the stately outline of Westminster when there was a sudden cacophony of whistles that had James slowing his step, pulling her back.

'Air raid,' he said, glancing about them for shelter. 'We'd better find somewhere to take cover.'

Suddenly the air vibrated to the shrill whine of falling bombs and they both flung themselves down, his arm across her back pressing her into the pavement. The earth seemed to lift and shake with the force of the explosions. After a moment James rose, dragging her with him. 'Come on, let's go!'

'Go?' Libby looked bewildered. 'Where?'

'Anywhere safe. Come on.'

The dark blocks of buildings loomed up in front of them. In one of them, James knew, was a small family hotel. 'We can wait here,' he said, 'at least, until the worst is over.'

They ducked into a doorway and Libby gazed around at the small lobby where they found themselves shivering. She knew it was partly fear, partly something else. 'It's very cold down here,' she murmured. 'Wouldn't they have a room?'

James grinned. 'My dear girl, what are you suggesting?'

Libby flushed, deciding to feign innocence. 'We could ask for a fire, James. I'm freezing.'

He gave her a long, steady look, then turned to speak to the wife of the proprietor.

In the bedroom, while James saw to the fire, which was already set with kindling, Libby waited in breathless anticipation. The flames going to his satisfaction, James stood up, and wiped his hands on a large handkerchief. He moved slowly to her, cupped her face in his hands and gently kissed her. Her knees went weak, the pit of her stomach swirled, her whole body tingled. And when he lifted her in his arms and carried her to the bed, she did not protest. His will and hers were one.

She wanted this man. And as he removed her clothes, his fingers clumsy in their impatience to press his bare skin to hers, that was all she could think about, how very much she wanted him. A fine, strong man, yet gentle, he was the only man she ever wanted to hold her in his arms, to caress, to savour. And as he made her move to his rhythm, he brought her to glorious ecstatic fulfilment.

'Have we any right to be so happy?' James murmured at one time, nuzzling her neck. 'Will we have to pay for it, somehow?'

'Don't say that, darling.' Libby shivered. She knew what he meant and again the shiver went through her. James raised himself on one elbow. 'Are you all right?'

'Yes. Yes. Someone must have walked over my grave.'

His arms closed around her and she relaxed against him.

'Libby!' The hand resting on her hip shook her gently and she stirred with a smile before opening her eyes.

James leaned over the bed and placed a soft kiss on her cheek. He was dressed and grinning down at her. 'You slept an hour, I hated to wake you but we ought to get back to Josie. That was quite a raid but I don't think it was anywhere close to here.'

She stretched lazily, gazing up at him under half-closed lids. The dark stubble on his chin made her senses stir and hastily she rose and began to slip on her clothing, feeling the blush rise on her cheeks as he sat on the edge of the bed, taking in her every movement.

'You're not sorry about this, Libby? Ought I to be on my knees, begging your forgiveness or am I to look forward to a lifetime of such nights?' He spoke teasingly, but she knew underneath he was deadly serious.

'What is there to forgive?' she asked, her eyes gleaming. 'I was as much to blame as you.'

She was in a jubilant mood, she had never felt happier in her life. Yet would it be tempting fate to go along with this feeling of blissful contentment? Could one still talk of a lifetime of anything? Who knew how long a lifetime this man would have once back in the horrors of Flanders?

In a teasing tone, to match his, she said, 'How long a lifetime did you have in mind?'

His hands circled her waist, pulled her to him to

stand between his legs. She was surprised and touched when his arms went around her and he laid his head on her breast.

He just held her like that for several moments. 'I thought about sixty years,' he murmured.

She wrapped her arms about his head to hold him closer, for she understood what he was telling her.

'You said before that you loved me, Libby. As much as that – that ...' He could not say it. Could not remind her of that darkly handsome man who had treated her so badly.

She gripped his head between her hands and forced him to look at her. 'You *can* say it, James. His name was Vince. I was devastated about what happened, before my little girl was born. But having her has made up for so much. I feel I can face the future, for her sake as well as my own.' She smiled. 'As for loving you, well, haven't I just proved it?'

He crushed her to him once again, then released her abruptly and whacked her behind. 'Get dressed, woman, or you'll be putting all sorts of ideas into my head.'

She laughed and moved away, out of his reach. She was not sure how she would react if James tried to make love to her again. On the one hand was the pleasure of it, on the other was the sinfulness of it. She did not want to decide between the two and she was grateful that James seemed to understand her feelings. She needed time to think about what had happened between them, to sort out the confusion that still filled her.

Chapter Twenty-Two

They found the scene outside worse than they had feared. As they neared that part of London where Josie lived, James could see several fires raging, one much nearer and larger than the rest. The flames reached hungrily for the sky. James cursed. 'God Almighty, that's too close for comfort!'

He set off down the street, dragging Libby in his wake. Even before he rounded the corner he could smell the acrid odour of burning paint and plaster.

'Holy Mother!' breathed Libby, momentarily brought to a standstill by the horror of it all, 'That's Josie's building.'

A crowd had gathered and a policeman was trying to keep them back. James went immediately to his aid. Luckily, the solid old Victorian building had held up long enough for most of the occupants to get out before it collapsed.

Most, but not all. Libby stared about her, frantically searching for sign of Josie or Sidney. With them would be Nellie. She told herself she mustn't have hysterics, that the little girl would be fine. She was with Josie, wasn't she? And Josie would never allow anything bad to happen to her.

There was a reverberating crash as huge rafters plummeted down and a thick cloud of dust billowed out, making Libby cough. There was a general murmur of concern and suddenly Libby could see Josie, who had also caught sight of her. They called each other's names and pushed their way through the crowd, Libby crying out questions that came out in a voice shrill with fear. 'Nellie! Is Nellie all right? Where is she?'

James appeared at her side and took her arm, pushing aside the crowd for her to pass. There was an impression of fire engines and ambulance bells clanging in her ears, of men shouting – but no sight of the little girl. Libby pressed crossed arms over her stomach and rocked back and forth. 'My baby, my baby!' she cried, her face twisted in anguish. 'Oh God, where's my baby –?'

Josie reached her and held tightly to her. 'Sidney took her down to the cellar when the raid started,' she said, gazing at James. 'I was following a few minutes later when the first bomb fell . . .'

'No, no!' cried Libby, pushing her away and struggling to make her way over to the rubble of walls and shattered glass. Broken pipes spewed water, soaking Libby's thin evening slippers. She didn't notice. Her one thought was to get to her child. Without a word, James joined her, realising the futility of it all but knowing he could do nothing less. Sympathetic voices urged her to go home, to leave the search to them. Libby didn't even hear. When at last she collapsed, James carried her in his arms to a cab Josie held waiting.

She struggled to jump out as the cab driver whipped up his horse. Only James' forceful grip held her
back. 'Damn you! Damn you!' she screamed. 'Let me
get to my baby.'

Her face was colourless, her eyes glazed and wild
as she turned to the man and girl sitting on either side
of her.

'Bastards!' she sobbed. Then she seemed to crumble again. 'I shouldn't have left her – I shouldn't have
left her.'

'Libby, darling, don't blame yourself,' James
began, his voice husky with smoke and tears. 'You
couldn't have done anything . . .'

She jerked towards him with flashing eyes. There
was relief in anger and Libby let it flow through her.
It made her guilt less tormenting. 'Keep away from
me, don't touch me.' Her voice rose in an anguished
lament. 'If I hadn't gone with you, if I hadn't stayed
with you in that place – Oh God . . .' And she put her
face in her hands in despair.

James knew of somewhere they could lodge, as it
would be a long time, if ever, before Josie's old
flat was habitable again. He saw to the financial
arrangements, making sure they would be secure for
as long as they needed. Then he kissed Josie on the
cheek and, his eyes bleak with pain, he picked up his
cap and left.

For Libby, during the nightmare weeks that followed,
the guilt was overwhelming. She couldn't rest,
couldn't sleep, always at the forefront of her mind

the feeling that if she hadn't been with James that night, Nellie would still be alive. That while she was engaged in those passionate moments with James poor Sidney and her little girl were . . .

She buried her face in her hands and sobbed. Useless Josie telling her she was wrong, that her own life could well have been forfeit as well as the child's.

'No more than I deserved,' raged Libby, in a fury that Josie would never have believed possible.

'Darling, darling!' Josie's voice was tight with pain. 'It was not your fault.'

Libby, submerged in her own mixture of grief and guilt, wouldn't listen, refusing to see James when he called, shutting herself in her room and staying there for days. She wanted forever to put that night with James from her mind, to pretend it had never happened. That while she trembled on the bed beneath him, shameless in her frenzy, abandoning herself to sensations never before experienced, Nellie was being buried in darkness and rubble, crying for her mummy . . .

The day before he returned to active service, James faced a worried Josie. 'She won't see you,' the singer reiterated. 'I'm sorry, Jimmy, but there it is. She fully believes that Nellie's death was her fault, that if she hadn't left her things would have been different . . .'

'But that's ridiculous,' James muttered through tight lips. 'The only difference would have been Libby losing her life, too.'

Josie, seeming on the verge of tears, repeated, 'She won't listen. Don't think I 'aven't tried. She seems to 'ave retreated to a place inside 'er 'ead where no one can get to 'er. She don't 'ear what I say 'alf the time, Jimmy, and every time someone mentions Sidney's name she bursts into tears. I think it's only now she's beginning to realise 'e's gone, too.'

'If only there was something I could do,' James said. He looked so utterly spent and dejected that Josie was filled with sudden tenderness. She had first met this man when he'd been so lost and vulnerable it touched her heart. She'd seen men like this, back from the poppy fields of Flanders, fumbling their way back into real life, eyes blank with the remembered horror of the war. She'd done all she could to comfort them. And, if it meant taking them to her bed, well, that, too, she would do if it helped. Better any time than any old doctor's pills, she'd laughed. James had recognised this and been grateful. Girls like Josie came into their own during a war. What would he have done without her?

The soldier in his rough khaki uniform made his way with difficulty through the narrow winding trenches. The message tucked into his buttoned top pocket was for Captain Randle and he intended to get it to him before the Jerries started lobbing the next round of shells. After that he'd have to take shelter and who knew how important the message might be. He liked Captain Randle and hoped it wasn't bad news. God knows they had enough to contend with without getting upsetting news from home. He lifted the piece of sacking that acted as a doorway and stepped into the roughly made dugout that operated as Battery

HQ. James looked up from his contemplation of the day's orders, returning the salute as the private snapped smartly to attention. 'A message, sir. Said it was important.'

'Thanks.' James felt a sickness rise in his stomach as his eyes scanned the written words. 'Private soldier, Vincent Remede, RAMC, in whom you professed an interest, presently under guard and awaiting court martial for desertion in the face of the enemy.' It was signed David Maddox, Captain, and at the bottom of the brief message was a scribbled postscript: 'Doesn't look good, James. Don't think I can help you here. The fellow was caught red-handed and put up such a fight one of the red-caps is still in hospital.'

The breath escaped from his chest in a long sigh as James crumpled the paper and thrust it into his pocket. He felt the soldier's eyes on him and turned away, knowing his face had lost all colour, leaving him pale and sickly looking.

'Are you all right, sir? Not bad news?' The man's solicitude caused the corner of his mouth to twitch. What could he answer to such a question? Bad news for Vince. Libby, he knew, would be shattered, in spite of everything. And, he wondered, in spite of everything, if she still loved the man.

They came for Vince at dawn. The uniformed escort, young men no older than himself, couldn't meet his eyes. They gave their orders in voices made harsh by their nervousness. They cursed the luck that caused them to be on duty at this particular time when it could so easily have been two other blokes. Vince was taken from his dark cell and marched into the early morning. In the east, the sky was coloured a deep pink, with ribbons of apricot and gold promising a fine day.

They offered him a last cigarette. He made it last as long as he could, drawing the smoke deep into his lungs. He fixed his eyes on the fading colours of the summer sky and thought of Libby.

Of Libby and himself. Of his first sight of her, there in the ice-cream parlour with Alice, so sweet and innocent looking, her hair gleaming in the rays of the sun caught in the wide window. Of her punching his arm and teasing him on their evenings in the shelter on the promenade. Of her small, pale face with the purple bruise slowly appearing where he had caught her on the chin with his fist, that last time in her bedroom . . .

He drew a last, long pull on his cigarette and then tossed it to the ground. Oh, how he'd wanted her! But not brutally, not the way it had ended. She had hurt him, and she had been stupid encouraging that officer and the old guy who'd walked her home, but he had never wished her any harm.

Lifting his head, he stared at the bright blue sky until it was blotted out by the blindfold they tied over his eyes and drawing one last breath of the summer-scented air, his last thoughts were of Libby . . .

Chapter Twenty-Three

For at least a week before it became a fact the announcement of peace was expected hourly. The events were reflected in the faces of the people as they hurried about their tasks. The Allied leaders and their staffs now knew that the war was over. Still the people were kept in the dark which, as one old East Londoner said, 'Was nothing new, anyway. We'd probably all be shaken if somebody actually *told* us something for a change.'

Newspapers were full of the German Armistice Delegation that left Berlin on 6 November and Field-Marshal Foch who left two days later. They said it would only be a matter of a few days before it was officially over. And still the politicians talked, arguing about the time and place, while guns still fired and men died on the fields of Flanders . . .

A bus conductress in her heavy uniform, the ticket machine strapped across her chest, murmured to Josie, 'Wouldn't you think they'd *know*? What's the good of 'em goin' on fighting? They bloomin' well know they're beat. I'd give in if I was them.'

Trr-rr-ing went the machine, clipping neat holes into the pink tuppenny ticket before she exchanged it for the heavy coppers. She grinned, saying, 'The next fight'll be over votes for women, you see if it ain't.'

Frustrating as it was, the snail's pace approach to peace enabled the war-weary British to adjust themselves to the fact of it and a spurt of energy seemed to flow through the land as they experienced in advance its pleasures and excitements. The rush to buy flags and bunting in readiness for the great day began in spite of the grey November weather. Plans for street parties were made in the East End. The large stores in the West End suddenly sprouted small forests of patriotic flags and banners. Large and small Union Jacks took pride of place beside flags of the Colonies.

For the whole of the Christmas period, continuing on until the spring, excitement was intense, touching even Libby who one evening standing by the window overlooking the street, watching the people strolling below, some breaking into a jig, turned to Josie and surprised her by saying, without preamble, 'Everyone's so happy. I think I'll go home.'

It had been five months since the tragic death of Nellie and although she would never get over it, the numbness of first sorrow had worn off. The opportunity, thought Josie, was there at last, and although she could not bring herself to admit that the thought of losing Libby chilled her, she said softly, 'That might be a good idea, ducks. See how you go on.'

Libby turned from the window, a smile on her lips. 'I've been feeling sorry for myself for long enough. Father Brady said in his last letter that Agnes was settling down at last. Now if we could just hear from

Joseph, everything would be all right.'

Josie thought of the letters Libby had allowed her to read, both from Father Brady and Mr Hobbins, of their kindness in keeping the small house on Mill Rise in Libby's name for as long as they could. Then, suddenly, with the house remaining empty for an untold number of months, Mr Hobbins, egged on by his sister, Clara, withdrew his arrangement, followed soon by Father Brady who was finding things financially difficult. It hadn't remained empty for long and a new family had moved in soon after.

Then Father Brady wrote that it was empty again and just after that Agnes arrived from London, alone and glad to be back where, she said, she really belonged.

Agnes had been working in a clothing factory in London, making uniforms, and had managed to keep herself and Mick until he decided he'd had enough of the war and went back to Ireland. Besides, the authorities were on the point of catching up with him and he didn't fancy going away to fight. He could do all his fighting in the local pub, thank you.

At first when they had gone south, Mick had had a job as a farmworker, something he was used to, and they lived in a small, damp and extremely cold cottage on a farm in Sussex, working for a bad-tempered man who seemed to expect miracles. Agnes had hated it. Hated the mud and the smell of cattle that Mick brought into the house every time he entered. Hated the loneliness, not being able to run out to the shops every time she wanted something. Most of all she hated not having somewhere to go at night. She was sick of Mick coming in and eating his supper then slumping into the old chair by the fire and falling asleep. Instead of the laughter and gossip of her friends, now all she heard was Mick's snores.

After a while she had rebelled and Mick, fed-up himself by now with the farmer's constant nagging, had agreed that London might be a better place after all. They had managed to rent a small place in a row of terraced houses in Hackney and although Mick seemed disinclined to look too hard for work, Agnes soon obtained a job sewing in a factory and for a while was quite happy. Until Mick heard from his cronies in the local pub that the authorities were getting hot on men evading the call-up and a number of his drinking cronies vanished overnight. It didn't take Mick long to follow them.

'She's changed, Libby,' Father Brady had written. 'She's much softer, seems more relaxed. I suspect her travels with that man she went off with, who never did get around to marrying her, I might add, showed her the way of things.'

Now Josie went to where Libby stood and put her arms about her, saying, gently, 'Poor little cow! Life's really had it in for you hasn't it? You go 'ome. You know you can always come back 'ere if it doesn't work out.'

The station at Ridley was just as she remembered it. She doubted that it would ever change. The only difference was the lack of uniformed figures rushing to catch trains for other destinations. Even then, there was still a few; men on their way home, kitbags on their shoulders, looking pleased that it was all behind them, the fighting and the worry.

To her surprise, Agnes met her, standing on the grimy platform scanning the passing carriages as they sped by. Whatever adversities Agnes had encountered in London, they seemed to have done her the world of good. As Father Brady had said, she seemed softer, less touchy and greeted Libby as she stepped down from the train with a hug and a kiss on the cheek.

After the first rush of greetings she bent to pick up Libby's suitcase and surprised her sister even more by saying warmly, 'It'll be nice having you home again. And, to make it even better, Libby, I've just had a letter from the Navy about Joseph . . .'

Hearing Libby's gasp, she smiled and said, 'Yes, and he's all right.' She went on to tell Libby about his ship being sunk and how she had had the sad task of writing to tell him about Mam and Dad. 'He didn't know, you see. It must have been terrible for him, on top of everything else . . .'

Joseph sat in the large canteen drinking a cup of tea from a thick white mug, while conversation punctuated with men's laughter washed over him, and thought how lucky he was to be alive. So many of his shipmates had been lost. The Irish boys he had joined up with were all missing, as were most of the other friends he'd made.

With a strangled sob he leaned his elbows on the rough table top and dropped his face into his hands. He was crying for all the lost hopes of young men who, tossed into that oil-polluted sea, would never see their homes again. What made him so special, that he could be saved when so many had perished?

He wondered if Gwenda would be waiting for him or if she had found someone new – young girls didn't like to wait too long in wartime. And then, drowning all else, came the thoughts of his parents' deaths, and his tears flowed anew.

He felt a hand on his shoulder, heard a voice saying: 'Come on, lad, it's all over now. You're safe and home again. A spot of medical treatment and then you'll be off to see your folks.'

Joseph lifted his head to gaze into the compassionate face of a man in a doctor's white coat. 'I don't need treatment,' he muttered, his voice stubborn. 'I just want to get home.'

'And you will, but after we've done something about those hands. You were lucky, they could have been a lot worse. As for your face, well ...' He frowned. 'It's going to be red and sore for a while but I don't think there'll be any lasting scars. You were fortunate to be picked up when you were. Much longer in the water and you'd have been joining Davy Jones in his locker.'

Joseph knew the doctor was only trying to cheer him up. But that didn't stop him from muttering, bleakly, 'Most of them did, anyway!'

He pushed back his chair and rose to his feet. It was time to begin the painful road to recovery, and eventually he went home.

*   *   *

Opening the door to a knock one night, Joseph's eyes widened when he saw the girl standing there. Dressed in a dark brown coat and hat, Gwenda gazed at him from under the low brim and smiled and immediately his melancholy vanished, to be replaced with a soaring of spirits so strong it made him want to shout aloud. Then he thought: She's come to tell me she's married! That she decided she wanted something different to what I could give her!

Even so, clearly she wasn't expecting to see him, for she blinked and then stared, as though wondering what he was doing here. Joseph said quietly, 'It's all right, Gwenda. It really is me. You're not seeing things.'

Still she stared at him, her eyes filling with tears, and the next moment she was clinging to him as if her very life depended on it. 'Joseph! Oh, Joseph, hold me. Tell me it was just a dream, that it really didn't happen,' she sobbed, 'and why didn't you write? I waited so long for a letter.'

'I didn't think you would want to hear from me,' he said, holding her tightly against him. 'But I'm all right now, battle-scarred and weary,' he grinned, trying to coax a smile from her tear-stained face, 'but all right.'

He let her cry herself out without saying more, there in the narrow dark hallway with just the light from the half-opened kitchen door high-lighting the gold in her hair.

There was no sound from the kitchen; his sisters obviously didn't want to intrude, although at one time Agnes would have been there, pointing a scornful

finger and making cutting remarks. After a moment
the kitchen door was quietly closed.

When the tears finally stopped Joseph held the girl
away from him and tenderly brushed the hair back
from her wet cheeks. 'Feel better now?'

'Not really.' She smiled weakly, gazing up into his
face. 'Just look at you! I let you out of my sight for five
minutes and see what happens.'

Unconsciously he raised a hand and touched the
still shiny and red burn marks on his face. 'I'm not
that bad!'

'Not outside a zoo, anyway.' Her laugh bubbled up
and he joined in, the first good laugh he'd had for
ages.

When they were silent, he said, softly, 'Why don't
we go in and have a cup of tea and a piece of cake?
Agnes has just finished baking a batch, enough to
last a month of Sundays.' His arms tightened for a
moment, taking her breath away. 'And then we can
talk.'

'What I'd like to do is go somewhere quiet with you,
where we could be alone. And then talk.'

It was said so simply, so honestly, that Joseph felt
the tears start in his eyes again. In his usual way of
joking about things he couldn't understand or which
alarmed him, he said lightly, 'You know the reputation us sailors have? Do you *really* want to be alone
with me, knowing that?'

'Oh, Joseph, stop being silly! Always acting the
fool, aren't you? I should have thought an experience
like you've just gone through would have made you
grow up. And pretty damn quick, too.'

It was Joseph's turn to blink. He'd never heard Gwenda use that tone of voice before. Before he could think of an answer, she went on, 'I shall understand if there are things you don't want to talk about, terrible things you want to forget. Oh, Joseph,' and her eyes glistened with fresh tears, 'there are also things I want to discuss. Things I just can't brush aside any longer.' She sniffed. 'I came to ask Agnes if she'd heard any more word of you, and now look at me!'

Joseph drew a deep breath and then looked over his shoulder at the kitchen door. All was quiet inside now and he imagined Agnes busy with the novel she had picked up from somewhere – Mam would have had a blue fit if she'd seen that type of literature in *her* kitchen!

He lifted his heavy Navy-issue top coat from its peg in the hall, and shrugged it on. 'We can't talk here. Let's go outside.'

In the street, the purple dusk had begun shrouding the ugly lines of the mill chimneys, softening the grim rows of windows, the soot-stained brick.

The young people stood as though uncertain what to do, Joseph's arm about Gwenda's waist, until Mrs Moran's door opened and her head poked out to ask if there was anything the matter. Muttering under his breath about her being a nosy old biddy, Joseph grabbed the girl's arm and led her across the street, to the small overgrown patch of derelict ground from where Vince had once spied on Libby.

The night was cold and the light dim from the faraway gas lamp, for Mill Rise boasted only two, too

far apart to illuminate but a few yards of cobble
stones. It didn't reach the fallen tree trunk where
they chose to sit.

'So you didn't find someone in Whitley Bay?' was
the first thing he said, his voice joking.

'Of course not. Were you hoping I would?' She
glanced at him from under her eyelashes. 'It can
always be arranged if that's what you want.'

Pulling her to him, he held her tightly, his laughter
sounding in the purple light. 'Just you try it, Gwenda
Naylor!' He kissed her soundly on the lips. 'How long
are you going to stay that? Gwenda Naylor! How
about changing it to Gray?' At her look of uncer-
tainty, he went on, 'Oh, not for a while, of course.
We're still a bit too young. But someday. As long as I
know it's going to happen.'

'Someday soon.' She nestled her head on his shoulder and smiled.

The morning lights drifted up to the heavens, warming away the pockets of grey mist lying in the dingy
streets and back alleyways of the small mining town.
Even though she was home, the dawn of the new day
did not bring a happy awakening to Libby. The deep
sorrow was still there; an aching heart that not even
the cheerful warmth of the spring sunshine would
assuage.

At the other end of England, Josie faced James
Randle in the sitting room of her flat. James would
never forget the look on her face when he told her he
had put in for a posting overseas with the army and
was sailing for India in a month's time.

'I shall be glad to get away,' he said. 'I've done quite a bit of soul-searching this past year and I see that my life does not present a pretty picture. If only I could change things, I would, but I know that's impossible, so the best thing for me is to get out from under everyone's feet and start a new life.'

Josie's reply taunted him. 'On your own?'

He flushed. 'Of course on my own.'

'And you think traipsing off to India will get Libby out of your system?'

He turned to her, his mouth a tight line, his face furious. 'If I stay away long enough it should do. Not one moment of that night with Libby do I regret. I understand the guilt she feels, of course I do. Don't you think I haven't felt it, too? What I can't understand is her continued coldness, her hatred.'

'You think she hates you?' Josie asked pointedly.

'What other explanation is there?' James' dark scowl made her want to smile. 'And if you're all ready to begin some sanctimonious twaddle about war nerves and shell shock, you can save your breath. I've had enough of that to last me a lifetime.'

'Jimmy!'

'I said don't.' He cut her off brusquely, his eyes dark and stormy. 'You think I like feeling this way? Feeling the guilt that twists my guts day and night, so that it never leaves me in peace?' Tension built up as he stared at her. 'It's like a demon, deep inside me, and if India will expunge it, then India it must be.'

She placed one hand gently on his sleeve. Look at yourself, Jimmy. You're ready to 'ave a go at me for pointing out what eats you. Why don't you go to 'er?

You obviously can't live without the girl, yet you make no effort to win 'er back.'

'Damn you, woman! Tell me how I am to win her back, as you call it, when she despises me? Tell me how to get near her when she hates me so?'

'Ah, Jimmy, these are only obstacles you make for yourself. You 'aven't even tried. Is it rejection you fear? To be rejected by Libby would be the end of your world, wouldn't it? Yet 'ow can you be sure until you at least *see* 'er, talk to 'er?'

When James remained silent, Josie pressed her advantage. ' 'Ow do you know that Libby isn't as desolate as you are? What if she's missing you, too? No, I will not 'old my tongue. Whatever 'appened is between you and Libby and you must make amends somehow. But 'ow can you do that until you see 'er? Go to 'er, go up to Ridley and tell 'er what is in your 'eart. If you love 'er, you'll find a way. Swallow your pride if you 'ave to, but speak from the 'eart. You 'ave nothing to lose and if you don't go, then all *is* lost.'

James thought back on his talk with Josie as his train rattled northwards. It had taken the singer's downright good sense to make him realise what a pig-headed fool he had been.

It was already late spring. Far too long had he wallowed in his misery and done nothing. Far too long had he been separated from Libby, churning with the anger of it. He should have sunk his pride and gone to her earlier. He should never have let her go to begin with . . .

He felt everything to be unreal, walking down that street again, to that same front door. He imagined the

inside as it had been, warm and cosy, and wondered
if it would still be the same. His knock was answered
by a young man and his heart sank, imagining for a
moment a competitor for Libby's affections. Unconsciously, his shoulders straightened, his chin jutted
and from somewhere behind the man – well, boy,
really, he looked so young – a voice called, 'Who is it,
Joseph? If they're collecting, tell 'em charity begins
at 'ome.'

The boy grinned, brows lifted inquiringly. 'Yes?'
he said and James chuckled, knowing this was the
brother Libby had been so worried about; home, safe
and sound.

Later, seated in Dad's old chair to one side of the
fire-place, James put down his empty cup and leaned
back, well-stocked with Agnes' baking. He was surprised although he tried not to show it. His impression of Agnes had been of a frivolous, flirty sort of
girl, one who cared only for her own enjoyment, but
she seemed quite homely. Although, he thought, from
the way she was looking at him now, from the corners
of her eyes, her mouth pursed with speculation, he
risked a guess that leopards do not so swiftly change
their spots.

'Libby's doing the church for Easter Sunday,'
explained Joseph. 'Why don't you take a walk that
way? It's not far.'

'Thanks, I will. If you'll just point me in the right
direction.'

In the churchyard he found Father Brady weeding
the rose bushes. The priest's face broke into a
delighted grin when James introduced himself. His

handclasp was warm. 'It's good to see you,' he murmured. 'Libby has mentioned you. I trust you are fully recovered from your wounds?'

James smiled. 'Yes, Father. Thank you, and I've heard about you. How is Libby?'

'Why don't you go in and see for yourself? She's in the church.'

James touched the peak of his cap in a salute and turned towards the arched doorway. Inside it was dim and very cool and he could see Libby leaning over a table laden with flowers. The light from a stained-glass window above her head shone down on her and the sight of her gave him a pleasure so intense it bordered on pain. Everything about her was so cleanly, fragrantly, sweetly young; her hair so glossy and abundant, her skin so perfect with those delicious freckles and the tinge of wild-rose across the cheeks.

She didn't know he was there until he spoke. She straightened so fast she hit her head on the corner of the windowsill. The rap on the head brought tears to her eyes. She blinked them away, hoping he hadn't noticed them or mistaken their cause. She'd known she would have to face him sooner or later; she had it all worked out in her mind – the casual smile, the cool, composed words of greeting. So much for plans. She did what she could to retrieve her dignity, trying to ignore the treacherous warmth that was spreading from his hand where he'd laid it on hers, up her arm and shoulder and into her body. She wore a brick red dress with a draped cream lace collar. Her hair was swept smoothly back from her forehead, slightly puffed at the sides and taken into a roll at the back of her head.

She had dreamed of him so many times, and now he was here. His eyes were positively ablaze with some inner emotion. Understandable, of course, after the way she had treated him. She wondered why he had even bothered to travel all this way to see her. Hadn't he better things to do? His quiet tones penetrated the fog of her vacillation. 'Aren't you going to ask me how I am?'

'Of course. I'm sorry. How are you?' She brushed a question mark of hair back from her cheek. 'What are you doing here?'

'Looking for you,' he said calmly. 'This time when Josie pointed out what a fool I had been I agreed with her. Shall I tell you what she said?'

'If you like.' Forcing a casualness she was far from feeling, she turned again to the flowers; white madonna lilies, pink carnations and delicate baby's breath. 'Josie's always so down-to-earth, I can imagine.'

He captured her hands, pulling her round to face him. 'Josie's got more sense in that head of hers than both of us put together. She spoke of obstacles and rejection and she was so right I felt my skin creep.' His voice softened and putting a hand under her chin he tilted her face so that she was forced to meet his gaze. 'Libby, Libby! Don't you think it's time we put a stop to all this heartache and thought of our own happiness? You can't go on for the rest of your life condemning yourself for your little girl's death.'

There, he'd said it! The words seemed to echo in

the little church. In her imagination they fell softly to the bare feet of the Virgin in her niche and the plaster face looked down with sorrowful eyes.

She drew herself away from his touch. 'You don't understand,' she said huskily. 'Every time I think about it, they die again. Nellie and Sidney, they keep dying, over and over, and the pain is engulfing. For moments here and there I forget – as I did when Joseph arrived home after a long spell in hospital for burns – I suppose he told you?' James nodded, not saying anything, and Libby went on, 'Then I suffocate with guilt at having abandoned them. I tell myself I should attempt to work out some sort of a future for myself because I'm still alive and they're not. It's what Agnes expects, and Joseph, too. Everyone becomes impatient with you, although they may not show it, if you grieve too long, or too visibly, if you don't pull yourself together as you're supposed to. You know you're embarrassing people with your ungovernable sense of loss, but what can you do . . . ?'

It was no use. He had pulled her to him and this time there was no escaping his hold. 'Look at me, Libby. Remember what we had, that we can have again, for as long as we live. Would you throw it all away for a guilt that –'

'Throw it all away?' The pain and anguish of the last months surged to the surface of Libby's mind. 'We never had anything to throw away. I left my baby and for that – for that . . .'

'For that you are punishing yourself so bitterly it will eat away your soul if you don't soon come to terms with it,' he said softly. 'Oh, my little love, I cherish every moment of that night, knowing if we hadn't spent it together you might well have been lost to me, too.'

'It would have been better,' she cried desperately, 'then I wouldn't have to suffer these nightmares.'

Tears coursed down her cheeks and she dashed them away with the back of her hand. A trembling seized her. Held close in his arms, she heard her own voice, muffled against his chest. 'How can we expect happiness, James, when we acted so badly . . . ?'

He dropped a kiss on her forehead, sensing her capitulation. 'We can make a fresh start,' he said, his face buried in her hair. He told her of his posting to India. 'We can begin again in a new life,' he whispered huskily, 'far away from the sorrow and pain of these last few years.'

'It's what I've wanted.' Her arms crept up around his neck to draw his face down to hers. 'I've wished and wished . . .'

He laid a finger across her lips, stopping the flow of words. 'We've got a lot of time to make up, Libby . . .'

His kiss submerged her in the wild sweet happiness she had thought she would never know again.

Unseen by the young lovers, a shadow darkened the church entrance and Father Brady stood, a smile on his lips. Then he turned and went back to his weeding. He had to concentrate on what he was doing, for thoughts jumbled around in his mind. There would be things to do, plans to make, a wedding to perform. And, from the look of the pair of them, it had better be soon . . .

PAMELA EVANS

LAMPLIGHT on the THAMES

The new London saga from the
author of *A Barrow in the Broadway*

*The fog swirled around the crowd at the graveside; Bob
Brown had been a popular man. But Bella's thoughts were
darker than the earth that was to cover the coffin – Frank
Bennett had killed her father as surely as if he had taken a
knife to him.*

Since the end of the war, when Bob Brown had taken
over the car workshop on Fulworth High Street in
London, Frank Bennett had been trying to get his hands
on it. An East Ender who had made good by his quick
wits and unscrupulous business methods, Frank was
determined to get the prime site – whatever the cost.

For as long as she could remember, Bella had been drawn
to the river, and to the ivy-covered house on the
promenade where she had first met Dezi Bennett. The
child and the young airman had become unlikely friends,
though both families had disapproved. Years later, their
love blossomed, and it seemed that nothing, not even the
feud between their fathers, could prevent their marriage.
Until Bob's tragic death and his dying request to Bella . . .

FICTION/SAGA   0 7472 3335 7   £3.99

A selection of bestsellers from Headline

FICTION		
BLOOD STOCK	John Francome & James MacGregor	£3.99 ☐
THE OLD SILENT	Martha Grimes	£4.50 ☐
ALL THAT GLITTERS	Katherine Stone	£4.50 ☐
A FAMILY MATTER	Nigel Rees	£4.50 ☐
EGYPT GREEN	Christopher Hyde	£4.50 ☐

NON-FICTION		
MY MOUNTBATTEN YEARS	William Evans	£4.50 ☐
WICKED LADY		
Salvador Dali's Muse	Tim McGirk	£4.99 ☐
THE FOOD OF SPAIN AND PORTUGAL	Elisabeth Lambert Ortiz	£5.99 ☐

SCIENCE FICTION AND FANTASY		
REVENGE OF THE FLUFFY BUNNIES Cineverse Cycle Book 3	Craig Shaw Gardner	£3.50 ☐
BROTHERS IN ARMS	Lois McMaster Bujold	£4.50 ☐
THE SEA SWORD	Adrienne Martine-Barnes	£3.50 ☐
NO HAVEN FOR THE GUILTY	Simon Green	£3.50 ☐
GREENBRIAR QUEEN	Sheila Gilluly	£4.50 ☐

All Headline books are available at your local bookshop or newsagent, or can be ordered direct from the publisher. Just tick the titles you want and fill in the form below. Prices and availability subject to change without notice.

Headline Book Publishing PLC, Cash Sales Department, PO Box 11, Falmouth, Cornwall, TR10 9EN, England.

Please enclose a cheque or postal order to the value of the cover price and allow the following for postage and packing:
UK: 80p for the first book and 20p for each additional book ordered up to a maximum charge of £2.00
BFPO: 80p for the first book and 20p for each additional book
OVERSEAS & EIRE: £1.50 for the first book, £1.00 for the second book and 30p for each subsequent book.

Name ....

Address ....

....

....